SECOND TERM

SECOND TERM

A Story of Spin, Sabotage and Seduction

SIMON WALTERS

First published in Great Britain 2000
Published by Politico's Publishing
8 Artillery Row
Westminster
London
SW1P 1RZ

Tel 020 7931 0090
Fax 020 7828 8111
Email publishing@politicos.co.uk
Website http://www.politicos.co.uk/publishing

First Published in Hardback 2000

A catalogue record of this book is available from the British Library.

ISBN 1 902301 68 4

Printed and bound in Great Britain by St. Edmundsbury Press.

For Karen

Special thanks to Stephen Garwood

Many thanks also to

Iain Dale, John Berry, Diana Roberts, Daisy Sampson,
Wendy Bailey, Les Wilson, Ian Stafford, Bonnie Rowe,
Amanda Platell, Mark Fox, Alan Simpson, A & K Walters,
Jeffrey Archer, R & M Gooch, Catherine Macleod,
Jill Turner, Harry Coen, Jonathan Lloyd, Barney Jones,
David Davis, Mark Adams, Jo Andrews, Martin Northrop,
Tina Stowell, Maddy Kaye, Jamie Ashfield, Rob Hayward,
Patrick O'Flynn, Susanna Jowett, Scott Clissold,
Joe Saumarez-Smith and Angela C Campbell

PROLOGUE

Charlie Redpath woke up at ten fifty five and felt sick.

Her eyes blinked open. Dazzling sunlight streamed in through an unfamiliar window. Panicking, she sat bolt upright, turned and was startled by the marble white body hanging half out of the other side of the bed. Then it came back. Not one nightmare, but two. This wasn't home. It belonged to the body that lay asleep in the bed they had shared. The person Charlie had made love to for the first time the night before. Made love to with passion, violence and reckless abandon. Far too reckless. A lust fuelled by longing, wanting and despair. As the feel of hands, arms, legs, lips, tongue, breath, hair, fingernails, cries and shouts flooded back, Charlie gently touched the body's smooth skin. There was no response.

The walls were lined with row after row of books, from the ceiling to the floor; hundreds strewn around and stacked everwhere. Bevan, Marx, Attlee, the Spanish Civil War, The Miners' Strike, The Great Depression; one or two novels, Kerouac, Orwell. On the desk was a computer with reams of paper tumbling out on to the threadbare carpet. And on the opposite wall, a banner showing a group of miners with the inscription 'National Union of Miners, North East Region'. Underneath it, on the mantelpiece, a shiny, ebony black lump of coal.

Still the soft white body didn't move.

Gathering up clothes scattered around the floor, Charlie wanted to be unconscious too. They could dream. But it was useless, their dreams were gone for ever.

They had been planning to get drunk for months; it was going to be the greatest night of their lives. The polls had said they were going to do it, the people on the doorsteps said they were going to do it, their leader said they were going to do it; and they believed him. But now in the sobering light of the morning after, rumours at the party HQ on the Tuesday, forty-eight hours before polling day came back. Rumours that their opponents were making a late surge, that voters were suffering a bout of nerves whipped up by the press in one last effort to put the frighteners on. Charlie put it down to a terror of optimism burned into the souls of the old hands by years of false hopes, an ingrained cautiousness among weary travellers who couldn't believe they were, at long last, about to reach the promised land.

Charlie shivered. The tremulous voice heard on the steps of the windswept office in south London twelve hours ago, just after midnight, swirled above. The office had been home to them all for the previous three weeks, where they had worked, sweated, worried, laughed, eaten, slept and thought about nothing but the election for nineteen hours a day, sometimes longer. Charlie had started the campaign as a junior aide and ended it by giving a daily briefing to the man whose voice seemed to bounce off the surrounding walls of the tiny flat like the howl of a wounded animal waiting to be put down.

'We fought this election positively and with dignity. We told the truth about the economy, the health service, about the condition of the education system, about the spread of poverty. We offered practical alternatives to failure and injustice and the erosion of the people's services. Now the Government will continue with the decline.

'I naturally feel a strong sense of disappointment, not for myself because I am very fortunate in my personal life. But I feel dismay, sorrow for so many people who do not share that personal satisfaction. They deserve better than they got last night. The whole country deserves better and we will work to ensure that the day will come when the country will get better in its spirit, in its soul, in its fortune.'

Any restraint the leader and his wife had shown on the balcony facing the world inside disintegrated the moment they were inside facing their friends, family and supporters. Tears were streaming down their faces. Most of the staff were crying too.

Not Charlie. Charlie was overwhelmed not by grief but by anger.

Anger that their opponents, no, not opponents, that their enemies had won again; anger at the incompetence of some of the party's so-called professional advisers; and anger at being on the losing side. Again. Charlie hated a lot of things, but most of all, hated losing.

An hour or so after the leader's speech, Charlie was paged by Gareth Greaves. They had known each other since meeting at an anti-poll tax rally. He had taken Charlie and a couple of friends on a tour of the Commons, and when he said he needed a research assistant, it was too good a chance to turn down. Charlie was out of work after spending a couple of years bumming round the Far East and Europe.

Gareth had only become an MP five years earlier, but they were already talking of him as the leader-after-next. His father was a miner on Tyneside; Charlie's dad Billy was a shipyard worker in Dawes' shipyard in the Upper Clyde docks. His father was chairman of the local party; Charlie's was a shop steward. There were some differences. His father was teetotal; Charlie's was an alcoholic.

Charlie remembered imagining how at this very moment, they would be marching into a Whitehall Ministry together to get their hands on the levers of power. Now their hands were up in surrender. Gareth would be MP for Wearside for another five years. Their only chance of getting inside a Whitehall Ministry would be if a minister deigned to allow them in to present a petition asking for a local school, hospital, factory or old people's home to be spared from yet another round of cuts.

'It's too awful Charlie, don't say anything. Look, I'm about to jump in my car ... I couldn't stand being around with all my locals wailing at me, it's bedlam. I'm going to drive straight down to the flat ... I'll be there by three am ... I'm going to need a drink when I get there, it won't be champagne ... sorry, that's not funny, meet me there ... please, please Charlie?'

It was an invitation she had been half expecting to happen for most of the three years she had worked for him.

Charlotte 'Charlie' Redpath had been voted the sexiest researcher in Westminster in a straw poll among the MPs and hacks who propped up the

Strangers Bar in the Commons. They queued up to get the best view of her in the skintight Levis and T-shirts she seemed to live in. Her glossy red lips were puckered into a half-cocky, half-defiant expression and her small chin opened out into high cheeks and a wide brow and her grey green eyes slanted downwards, catlike, towards her nose. The wavy Titian red hair that tumbled over her shoulders; the smattering of freckles; and the apricot glow of her taught, unlined skin came with the Celtic blood and temperament handed down by a Scottish Protestant father and an Irish Catholic mother. No one was sure about Charlie. One minute she was a good-time girl, the next she was fighting the revolution. Even when she flashed a seductive smile, you couldn't be sure she wasn't about to attack.

She liked Gareth, but had not been instantly attracted to him. Maybe it was the age gap; he was twelve years older than her. Maybe it was his shambolic style. He looked as though he hadn't changed his suit for a for a week and his wardrobe for a decade. He must have been the last thirty eight year old still wearing the striped college scarves that used to be seen on every campus.

To outsiders, his austere intellectualism, scruffy brown hair and dark brown eyes gave him a forbidding presence. He was tall and athletic enough to have been Northern Schools 400 metres champion two years in succession. If he stopped spending so much time with his boozy trade union pals he would have a better chance of getting into his old running shorts.

Charlie had never confronted it, but she was always attracted to the smarter, more polished men others expected her to despise; men like Stuart Donovan. She met him when she was sixteen when her school teamed up with the neighbouring boys private school to put on Romeo and Juliet. Charlie and Stuart had the lead roles. Donovan had jet black hair, was head boy, two years older than her, was charming, witty, had wealthy parents and the same effect on her off stage as he was scripted to have on it. She ignored warnings about his reputation.

She lost her virginity on the night of the dress rehearsal when he took her home in his Rover 2000 and made love to her on the back seat. When, three days later, heart thumping, she eagerly awaited him at the party after the last night show, he turned up with a pretty blonde, Rosemary Wilson, daughter of Graham Wilson, chairman of Edinburgh Rotary Club. Donovan bowled up to Charlie and said, 'Charlie; meet Rosemary, my girl-friend. Rosemary; this is Charlie. Her dad's the bloke your dad said was a Commie wrecker for bringing the shipyard out on strike; you know, "Red Billy" Redpath.'

The crowd of hangers-on who followed Donovan and his money every-where burst out laughing. Charlie snatched his pint of beer, tipped it over his head and turned on her heels.

Gareth was as unlike Donovan as a man could be.

He was her hero. She admired his idealism, his devotion to the party and its traditions and his refusal to give in to those who wanted it to dump its principles. He was destined for greatness. What was the point of power without principle? Gareth would never do that. And he was right.

But the election said they were both wrong.

When she had arrived at his flat behind Marsham Street, half a mile from the Commons just after three thirty am, he was already there. He opened the door and threw his arms around her. He had already finished one bottle of wine. It had been eleven years since she had touched a drop, but she needed one now.

Half way through their third bottle of Chilean red he had started telling her she looked like Jerry Hall; by the fourth she was Barbara Castle in her prime. Charlie leaned forward and grabbed his face with both hands and placed her mouth on his. She didn't know what to expect from him. He made love to her; at first uncontrolled and frantically, then slowly and ten-derly, kissing her from her toes all the way up to her lips and back down again, until they crumpled in each other's arms, soothed.

At least until the harsh morning light that had woken her. She looked in the mirror and held up a handful of her long tousled auburn hair; it had never been so tangled. She examined her mascara-smeared eyes and rum-maged in her bag for a brush. Damn it. She had left her sunglasses at her flat. If he woke up now he would think she was more like a ruined castle.

As she gazed at Gareth, gently dozing, he looked like a child. Intense yet innocent. Perhaps it was because he had never married, a fact that had led to gossip. She smiled again.

She tried to remember what he had said to her last night, what she had said to him. She thought he had told her that he loved her. She couldn't remember what she had said. Had she told him she loved him? She hoped not. How she hoped not. All those rules she had set herself after Donovan. Broken.

The words she could remember were not those Gareth had said last night, but the ones he had said a week before the election.

'We're nearly there Charlie, nearly there, we've got them, we really have. If we don't do it this time, we'll never do it; we might as well pack the whole thing in.' He was so enthused he knocked her cup of coffee over as he leant across the table to grip her wrists. 'You'd better not do that when you're sitting at the Cabinet table,' she had said, 'it's an antique, you know.' They had laughed. It wasn't funny now.

Charlie took one last look at Gareth's dark features and sighed. She dare not think how he would react when he awoke. She felt sorry for him, but she felt angry and let down too. It had all been so pointless, so utterly pointless. She could see it now. Gareth was never going to be leader. He was never going to be leader-after-next or the one after that. In any case, what was the point of anyone leading a party that was only led to defeat.

She walked across to the door and saw something glinting on the mantelpiece. A lump of ebony black coal. She picked it up, turned it around in her hand, kissed it and took one last look at Gareth's pale torso. She put the piece of coal in her bag and left.

Part One

CHAPTER ONE

Some years later ...

'Ladies and gentlemen, the Prime Minister.'

He was the youngest Prime Minister Britain had had for more than a century and looked even younger than his forty seven years. He rose to his feet in Downing Street's Green Drawing Room overlooking Horse Guards Parade. In one corner was the tiny 'knee hole desk' used by William Pitt. On the avocado walls, elegant protraits of Nelson and Wellington. Suspended from the ceiling in the middle of the room, an enormous Waterford crystal chandelier. And a magnificent Persian rug covering the parquet flooring.

It was a room fit for a leader. Today, it was full of people who had played their part in his rise from being an obscure Opposition MP just ten years ago, to the most popular tenant of Downing Street in peacetime. His friends, his family, his supporters who had stood by him and made him believe in himself, even when he doubted it in the dark days. The civil servants who were for ever telling him how much more authoritative he was than 'the last lot.' And his Ministers, who had been remarkably loyal to him from the very first day. Not that they had a great deal of choice. When the Prime Minister is so popular that his ratings disappear off the top of the pollsters' graphs and the rest of the Cabinet have a recognition factor of less than ten per cent, even the most ambitious politician is loyal to the man who appoints them. To his face, anyway.

How different it had all looked a few years ago when, bleary eyed, he woke up the morning after yet another defeat and considered chucking it in. Most of his colleagues had been too numb – or hungover – to speak.

But while they mourned the past, he seized the future.

It seemed only yesterday that he was described by the four million a day circulation The Globe, as 'hyper ambitious but yet to prove it is anything more than hype.' Eighteen months later he was leader of his party and five years after that he won the biggest election landslide for a century, something he was quick to remind the paper's owner, Warren McLintock, when he invited him to the first Downing Street reception after becoming Prime Minister, 'Not bad for a lot of hype, eh Warren?' He had been several times since.

But not tonight, this was a very private gathering.

The Prime Minister rose to address his audience. 'We are here today to celebrate the anniversaries of the two women in my life,' he started, pausing to smile. The guests reacted immediately to his cue to laugh.

'First of all, to my wife, on our twentieth wedding anniversary.' He turned to the woman standing beside him.

'Can you imagine what it is like having civil servants charge into your bedroom first thing in the morning, when you're both in your pyjamas, to tell you there's an important phone call which must be taken immediately? And then you find out it's the Leader of the Opposition in a flap about not being invited to the London Eye to watch the New Year firework show. I said, "I thought they said it was someone important".' Louder laughter.

'Then there's the times you go away for a quiet family holiday and find a press photographer hanging from a palm tree the moment you put your towel on the beach in the morning. After that we left it to the Germans and stayed on our balcony. And I kept my shirt on and did a few press-ups in case my belly' – he tapped his tummy self-mockingly, though he knew full well it was flatter than most men twenty years his junior – 'in case it appears on the front page of The Globe again. I don't mind it when they do it to me, I volunteered for this job and I'm not about to complain about the hassles that come with it … ' Then came the seamless switch in tone from folksy lightheartedness to furrowed brow sincerity. '... but it's nothing compared to the satisfaction I get – and you can all share it – of doing it as best we can, for this country.' A respectful murmur of 'hear hears.'

'But I do object when they do it to my family. I could not have survived the last three and a half years without this remarkable person,' he said turning to her. ' ... I really couldn't. I may not have a right to complain, but she does and I can assure you, she never has. I have no idea how much longer I'll be doing this job – it's the one thing I have no control over – and we all know what a momentous year we have ahead of us with a decision that will affect the future of our country for ever. But I couldn't do it for one more second, let alone years, without her love and support. So, my darling wife – happy anniversary!'

A man at the back standing in the middle of a circle of a predominantly male circle shouted 'hip, hip!' – and the audience responded with three hearty 'hoorays.'

The Prime Minister leant across to give his wife a kiss, turning his cheek to her side on as she stretched up towards him.

'And now let me turn to the other woman in my life.' He stopped to allow a broad smile spread across his face. The audience responded with a knowing chuckle. 'If the old adage about there being a good woman behind every good man – and perhaps I flatter myself – then in my case it is doubly true, because I have two. The "other woman" in my life – and it is her birthday tomorrow – hardly needs an introduction to you since popular legend has it that it is she and not me who runs this place!

'Indeed most of you probably dread being introduced to her because it's more than likely it means she's going to give you one of her famous tellings off! ... ' More laughter. ' ... though I think she has another way of putting it. What is it she says? Ah yes, "BS," the initials of which I gather stand for a certain malodorous substance produced from the rear end of a well known dairy animal. Don't worry, she does it to me too!'

The room erupted. 'I've lost count of the times I've been assailed by those two letters, "BS". In her defence all I can say is that if she is shouting at you, it's probably because I've just shouted at her – or more likely she's just shouted at me. Joking aside however, we all know how much we owe to her – her cajoling; her hard work; her spirit, her inspiration; her brilliance; the way she terrifies the Opposition' – cheers – 'and the press' – louder cheers, 'we especially love that. Her dedication to the party, to me and to everything we have always stood for, still stand for and will always stand for.'

The tall, elegant, woman his second set of remarks were addressed to stood at the opposite side of the room beside a bust of William Pitt, with her left hand on her hip and her right hand level with her face, holding a Marlboro Light cigarette, as desirable as she was intimidating. A few months ago she had featured in a cartoon on the front cover of The Spectator, when it emerged that the Prime Minister had ordered a scaled down version of the US President's Air Force One jet for his own foreign trips. The cartoon showed a picture of him in the cockpit with her emblazoned on the fuselage, all hips, lips, legs, bust and bottom, just like the girls on the American bombers in the war. It was one of only two pictures on her office wall. The other was of her mother.

The cartoon suited her; there was something of the Forties pin-up about her 'S' shaped figure. It had been good enough to get a job at the Playboy Club when she worked in Paris during a summer break at university. She did it for a 100 Franc bet with a girlfriend – and ended up earning another £200 when Fiesta magazine published the article and blurred photograph she sent them about how an American businessman offered her 20,000 dollars to sleep with her for one night. 'Fiesta' readers were not told whether she accepted the offer. Several newspapers had since spent vast sums trying to track down the businessman, to no avail.

She had changed since her Playboy Club days.

Her hair had been tamed into a sleek bob, and the inch-long red varnished fingernails were trimmed back. But she was proud to have preserved her twenty four inch waistline.

It had not been achieved without sacrifice, including missing breakfast every day for the last ten years. Not that she had a healthy lifestyle. She usually had a doughnut at eleven and left countless half-finished cups of black coffee and Diet Coke in her wake. The effect of her thirty cigarettes a day didn't worry her; she was far more concerned about constantly lying in her regular hour-long Friday night phone calls to her mother, Frances, about having given them up. A five mile run round Hampstead Heath every Sunday morning was her only excercise – and she hated that.

She was wearing a flame red Armani suit that was every bit as assertive as her confident smile. These days, she only wore Levis at home. The audience's response to the Prime Minister's sardonic but warm tribute suggested she was notoriously good at what she did and enjoyed both; being good at it and being notorious.

'Friends, let us wish happy birthday to my press secretary Charlie, Charlie Redpath,' said the Prime Minister.

The audience cheered wildly, with one or two wolf whistles. Only one man in the audience had slept with her. The others just fantasised about it.

The same man at the back who shouted 'hip, hip' for the Prime Minister's wife, remained silent this time, leaving it to someone else to lead the cheers, which were considerably more raucous than the ones they had offered a minute or so earlier.

Next to Charlie, the Prime Minister's wife Lucy appeared tiny and insignificant. Hundreds of appearances in public had failed to diminish her transparent discomfort at being in the public eye. It irritated her when the tabloids described her as a 'petite blonde' – until they merely called her 'blonde.' That irritated her even more. She had put on nearly two stones since the election, and, try as she did, she could not budge it. Her face still dazzled. Her flawless appleblossom skin, elfin face and tiny nose ensured she took a good 'head and shoulders' shot, but she had become wary of full length photographs that made her look pear shaped and matronly, not at all like the Peter Pan waif she had been at school. When Lucy saw her husband come out of the shower each morning, she couldn't help noticing how little his physique had changed since they married; and how much hers had. Her woman GP had told her it was the usual causes; childbirth and middle age. Middle age! At forty four. Lucy looked at Charlie. She would escape motherhood, but not the ageing process. Not the way she lived. Not if there was any justice.

Physically, socially, temperamentally and intellectually, the two women had as much in common as Glasgow and Guildford. Lucy came from Guildford. Lucy was forever in the papers and resented her image; Glaswegian Charlie was hardly ever in the papers, but gloried in hers.

As she gulped down the rest of her Coke and prepared to leave the party, Charlie leaned towards the Prime Minister and said, 'Don't forget – in your study at seven thirty tomorrow morning.'

'I'll be there.'

'See you,' said Charlie, before adding, 'bye Lucy.'

'Bye,' said Lucy, squinting her eyes and making a display of flapping the smoke from Charlie's cigarette away from her face. Lucy didn't smoke. Nor did Charlie when she was in public. Every time she left Number 10, the custodian in the hallway held out an ashtray so she could stub out her cigarette before emerging into the street; and when she returned, he was ready with an opened pack, so she could light up the moment she was inside.

Instead of heading straight for the door, Charlie walked towards the back of the room towards the man who had led the birthday cheers. She fixed her eyes on him, shutting out everyone else. He looked up sharply as she loomed on him.

'Fancy you leading the cheers for me, wonders will never cease,' Charlie scowled.

'You know me, loyal to the last,' the man replied with a thin smile.

'Pity you couldn't be bothered to clap,' she said, 'you're pathetic.'

She dug the stiletto heel of her left shoe deep into his right foot and turned towards the exit. The man's smile slipped as he grimaced with pain. But by then Charlie was on her way out.

She did not look back to see the thunderous look on the face of the Deputy Prime Minister, Gareth Greaves.

* * *

Jean Pierre, head waiter at The Berkeley Hotel, Knightsbridge, was preparing a tomato juice with four shots of Tabasco, half a spoon of horseradish and a stick of celery.

He knew which table the Chancellor of the Exchequer would want when he arrived for dinner at eight; the one in the far corner out of sight from most of the other tables. Ronnie Silverman had an arrangement with them: as long as he gave them two hours' notice they would keep it free for him. He was looking forward to his engagement at The Berkeley. It had already provoked the curiosity of his private office. They knew a minister's every movement, who he was seeing, where he was seeing them and why. Except for those engagements marked private. And this one was private.

Silverman was closer to the Prime Minister than any other Minister and had played a vital role in his rise to power, using contacts built up in his time as an official with the engineers union to push through the reforms that had helped get the party back into power. Nearly twenty years after the 'Winter of Discontent', voters were finally content that putting a cross on the ballot form next to a candidate representing his party did not mean that bodies and rubbish bags would be piled up in the streets within days of them taking office. Silverman could claim a large share of the credit for that contentment; and in turning the tables on their political opponents by reducing them to a cruel caricature as the party of fat cats, sleaze and incompetence. The caricature was just as untrue, but just as effective. Silverman had spent years copying and refining their tactics and could now beat them at their own game, where presentation and persuasion were indistinguishable from manipulation and distortion. He hoped it took them the same nineteen long years to recover from the smear as it had his own party.

Silverman was a chameleon: looked like one; moved like one; acted like one. Policies were like skins, to be cast off depending on the political climate. His speciality was vogue not vision. He tried so hard to ooze charm that his face had a veneer of shine, but it wasn't charm that oozed from his pores.

He had been a pretty boy who loved playing football with his father, a postman, but an attack of polio when he was five years old, owing to a mix up with his polio jab, had left him with a limp. Unable to kick a ball with friends on his council estate who laughed at him, he would spend hours in his backyard dressed in the kit of his favourite team, Arsenal, kicking a ball, too shy to join other boys in the park. An only child, he withdrew into a shell.

He was happier in his teens at Slough Grammar School, when his natural ability for all subjects gave him a new confidence. He came top in nearly everything. It made up for his self-consciousness about his limp, about his father, about his council house home. But the arrival of Giles Ashton changed all that. Silverman could only ever be second best to Ashton. No matter how hard he tried, Ashton beat him in every subject. Silverman developed an obsessive jealousy about the boy and the Ingersoll watch his merchant banker father gave him for his fifteenth birthday.

When he was in the sixth form, Silverman worked three nights a week at Slough greyhound stadium until he had enough money to buy one for himself. The watch had become a lucky charm and at the grand old age of forty five, he still wore it and would take it off and stroke it, particularly when he was irritated. He was tugging at the watch strap as he waited for his guest to arrive at The Berkeley. It was eight forty one pm and the appointment to meet the applicant for the vacant post of his political adviser was set for eight thirty pm.

Silverman liked meeting people at The Berkeley. It was about half way to Westminster from his Kensington flat. Knightsbridge had a special significance. His grandfather on his mother's side, a senior civil servant, who disowned her when she married his father, used to live there. Silverman recalled the day, when as a five year old, his parents made a rare Christmas trip to visit his grandfather when they heard he had been ill. They arrived at his imposing apartment block, his mother pressed the door buzzer at the entrance, announced who she was and why they had come, and a shaky voice at the other end crackled back: 'It's alright, I'm better now, it's rather inconvenient for you to call at the moment, could you phone in advance next time?' They returned to Slough and never went back.

Which is why Silverman took such a pleasure in dining at the Berkeley. He still couldn't afford to live in Knightsbridge. But he was getting closer. And he would get there. One day.

The Berkeley's decor was classic and formal: Silverman the architect of political fashion craved the respectability of social tradition and recognition. Like his grandfather, he was a snob.

More importantly, the Berkeley's La Tante Claire restaurant was discreet, well away from the Westminster dining circuit. More column inches were printed about Silverman than the rest of the Cabinet put together. He fretted every time they appeared, but fretted more when they didn't. It was another of his cravings since he first made the front page of three national newspapers as a young aspiring union assistant. His marriage to Chilean dissident Maria Gonzalez, which helped her obtain a British passport and escape persecution from General Pinochet in her home country where she had led a student riot, made headlines and gave him celebrity status among left wingers. It also helped quash unpleasant rumours about him among a few bigoted officials at the engineers union. The couple received a standing ovation at that year's party conference. Eleven months later they were divorced, but the marriage had been a success for both of them.

On the face of it there was no need for him to be secretive about his dinner with Joe Lomax. Not even the most assiduous lobby correspondent would have known Lomax from Adam. But Silverman loved to shroud his activities in secrecy; it was a way of life that sustained both the myth and the reality.

He had heard a lot about the young man from friends in Lancashire, where Silverman was an MP. Lomax had become chairman of a ward party at the age of twenty two and had a degree in Classics from Durham, where he was also disc jockey for the university radio station.

Silverman needed to fill the post quickly: he had a series of speeches to make in the next few months, and would have no time to do them himself with three pieces of Treasury legislation going through Commons standing committees. He knew Lomax could do it – a councillor friend had sent him a copy of a speech Lomax had written for him in an hour when he lost the one he had prepared himself. It was better than some Silverman had seen written by a whole team of speechwriters over a week for a Cabinet Minister at the annual conference. Some of the jokes were the type that were cut when ministers submitted their speeches in advance to Downing Street. Not because they were no good, but because they were so good, the PM wanted them for his own speech.

Silverman was beginning to wonder if Lomax was going to turn up when Jean Pierre walked towards him and introduced 'Monsieur Lomax' with the exaggerated flourish some regular clients, including this one, appreciated more than others.

The only clue to his appearance in his CV was his age, twenty five. But Silverman had obtained a far more detailed portrait of Lomax before the dinner date was fixed.

Five foot eight inches tall, fresh faced, blond hair with a long spiky fringe over his eyelids; slim, and a dapper dresser was how he had been described. Silverman could see with his own eyes that it was pleasingly accurate.

Lomax had the kind of delicate nose and lips a female model would envy, but any femininity in his bone structure was more than offset by a jaunty gait and cocky smile. He was wearing a pencil grey suit with a high collar over a black polo neck shirt. They shook hands. Silverman was impressed, very impressed; and Lomax hadn't opened his mouth. When he did, a slight scouse twang gave him an impudent air. It suited him. Lomax hadn't told Silverman he was actually the son of Anthony de Lyons-Lomax, former Lord Lieutenant of Westmorland, and had 'acquired' the scouse accent when he was expelled from his public school at sixteen, left home, switched to a sixth form college in Wigan and dropped the de Lyons – and the hyphen. But he needn't have worried. If he had told him, Silverman would have been even more impressed.

The interviewee knew a lot more about the interviewer. By the time the hors d'oeuvres arrived, Lomax had done more than enough to get through the interview, but this wasn't just an interview. Silverman didn't normally interview job applicants at The Berkeley. It was an audition.

He asked Lomax about that morning's *Financial Times* leader column. Before he had explained further, Lomax interrupted, 'You mean the one on waiting lists. I think what it was trying to say was that choosing between finding the extra cash to bring waiting lists down and putting up taxes to pay for them will show whether this Government is going to go into the next election as a really new party through and through; or whether its old instincts are beginning to reassert themselves. Or to put it another way, is the PM in charge or is Greaves moving in on him? That's how *the globe* would have put it, but their leaders are much better written.'

It was the kind of politics that interested Silverman: policies as they related to personalities. This boy is clever, he thought. He had summed up in three sentences what the FT said in thirty. Lifting another forkful of goujonette de sole to his mouth, he asked Lomax what his ambition was.

'To work for you for five years, get a safe seat, become an MP by the election after next and get into the Cabinet five years after that. By then I'll be thirty six, which means I'll have made it to the Cabinet five years before my hero did.'

'And who, pray, is that?' asked Silverman, straining to keep a straight face.

'You,' replied the young man, bursting into a juvenile giggle.

Silverman did a quick calculation and realised that yes, he had been forty one when he became Chancellor after the election four years ago. He laughed out loud, rare exercise for face muscles that were normally stretched no further than a lopsided smirk, 'My, you have done your homework.'

'I'm good with numbers as well as words, so I'll make sure the statistics back up your argument,' replied Lomax.

'And self esteem isn't a problem either, is it, Joe?' said Silverman, reining him in a bit. 'Don't overdo it.'

Lomax was everything he had been told; brainy, confident, and attractive; half boy and half man. It was almost too precocious, but Silverman was hooked. He struggled to contain his enthusiasm.

'Well, I think the job's yours, Joe. I'm afraid the pay is not great, political advisers get the same salary they were on before they joined the Government, so whatever your pay is now is what you'll get with me. Which probably isn't much. You won't be able to buy diamonds for your girl-friends, you know.'

'Diamonds are a girl's best friend, not a boy's,' quipped Lomax.

'Mmmm,' said Silverman, warily. 'At this point, all good employers ask their interviewees if there is anything they would like to ask them. Is there, Joe?'

'No, but since you mentioned girlfriends, there is something else I should clarify.'

'What is that, Joe?'

'I am gay, is that a problem for you?'

'No, Joe,' said Silverman, weighing his words, 'No, Joe, it's no problem at all.'

CHAPTER TWO

'Jesus, bloody BBC, how dare they!'

Charlie was alone in her Downing Street office. It was five to seven. She liked to be at her desk with a cup of coffee in time to hear BBC Radio 4's *Today* programme headlines on the radio. She rarely ate anything at her flat in Camden, North London. She had lived there for three years and had never once used the gas stove for anything more than heating a tin of tomato soup; the rest went in the micro.

Just as she feared, 'Today' had picked up on an item which appeared in the last edition of that morning's *Daily Telegraph*. She always had the first editions of the morning papers delivered to her home at 11.30 pm. If there was anything to worry about, she could deal with it there and then to stop it carrying through to the later editions in London, which had much more impact. There had been nothing in them to bother her last night; the only story of any interest appeared in the last edition of the Telegraph by political editor Drew Sharpe under the headline 'ELECTION COULD BE ON SAME DAY AS EURO POLL.' It claimed to be based on remarks made by the Prime Minister at the previous night's birthday party. The report read:

> *Speaking last night at a party for his wife, Lucy, and press secretary Charlotte Redpath, the Prime Minister is reported to have said Britain faced "momentous decisions" in the year ahead. Senior party sources drew attention to his use of the plural "decisions." The Government had been expected to call a general election this year, followed by a referendum on whether Britain should join the*

euro in the autumn or next spring.

But there has been growing speculation that they may stage both simultaneously. Support for the euro has gained with the resurgence of the single currency following its shaky start. Ministers argue that with a twenty five point lead over the Opposition, voters would be unlikely to vote for the government on one ballot form and NO to the euro on another.

One guest at the Number 10 party said, "No one at the party was left in any doubt as to what the PM meant. It was the clearest possible signal that there will be two votes on the same day".

In theory, the Government has another fifteen months to call an election. But the account of last night's party is in line with recent information from Ministers who say the PM is buoyed up by reports that his popularity rating has returned to its highest level for two years.

Charlie threw the paper down in disgust. The PM had said nothing of the sort last night. He had not talked of momentous decisions, in the plural, but of a momentous decision. She had specifically warned him not to give any clues about the timing of the election and, as usual, he had followed her instructions. As she calculated which of the guests might have leaked the deliberately distorted account and why, she was astonished to hear two of their backbenchers discussing the report on the 'Today' programme. 'The BBC don't even have the courtesy to phone me to check,' she railed. 'You'd think they'd had it confirmed by a Downing Street press release, not made up by some hack who wasn't even there.'

'There does seem to be a ring of truth about the report, doesn't there?' said the female presenter, crisply. How would you know Miss Home Counties? thought Charlie. It reminded her of the smug upper middle class girls at her convent school who laughed at her accent and second hand blazer when she first arrived. Her father found her crying in her room one day. 'Let them walk over you once girl and they'll walk over you as many times as they want,' he told her. The next time one of them laughed at her,

Charlie slapped her in the face. Her dad was right. They hadleft her alone after that.

She had all the direct phone lines of the TV and radio news teams and would harangue them if she heard or saw something that annoyed her. They didn't have to take any notice, but the steady supply of ministers made available for interviews suddenly dried up to those that didn't.

'It's seven twenty five,' said Miss Home Counties. Charlie punched the 'off' button to silence her, picked up her papers, mobile phone and cigarettes and strode out into the entrance hall and turned right into the 'long corridor' that ran from the front to the rear of Number 10. She passed the pre-Raphaelite painting of actress Ellen Terry. When the French Minister for Culture saw the picture during a visit, he told Charlie it reminded him of her, adding he had heard she had once worked at a bar in the Montmartre in Paris. For reasons best known to himself, he took her cursory nod as encouragement. At a reception that evening attended by the Archbishop of Canterbury, and with the minister's wife standing a few feet away, the oily Frenchman pinched Charlie's bottom. She turned round and told him in a very loud voice, 'Va-te faire enculer!' Fortunately, neither the Archbishop, nor most of the other guests knew the French for 'go and fuck yourself.' But the Frenchman did; and so did his wife. She had walked out and he followed her, beetroot red with rage and embarrassment.

Charlie turned into a small, unremarkable office adjoining the Cabinet room: the Prime Minister's study. Study wasn't really the right word for it. Not since the old mahogany desk had been removed and replaced with red and blue Habitat sofas and a pine desk at one side, a pine coffee table in the middle, trendy 'uplighters' to diffuse the light onto the ceiling and the obligatory picture of Nelson Mandela on the wall. Most of the Prime Minister's meetings were conducted with him sitting on one sofa and guests on the one opposite.

Charlie was standing at his desk, running her fingers along the gold lettering on his red ministerial briefcase when she heard a voice.

'THE RIGHT HONOURABLE DR STEVEN R CANE, PRIME MINISTER.'

Charlie swivelled round.

'I know what you're thinking Charlie, it still sounds funny to me,' said the man whose name was spelled out on the box.

Steven Cane's colouring was the first thing that struck you about him. At forty seven, he still had thick black hair – as shiny and even as an expensive clothes brush – and, unlike some politicians, he didn't dye it. Or his long dark eyelashes. He had inherited it all from his Italian mother, Carla, along with her luminous Canaletto sky blue eyes, slightly darkened lips and perfect teeth; rounded off by a tanned complexion it made him look a picture of health all year round. That was not all that set him apart from other MPs.

He had all the self-assuredness of someone who had gone to a direct grant school, Weston Boys in Bristol, after winning a scholarship, but none of the conceit that normally went with it. As one of the few day boys, some of the more conspicuous traits of public school boys were not inculcated into him. Nor was he a stranger to the rigours of life outside the comfort and stability of the English middle class.

He mixed with people from all backgrounds from a young age through his mother's lifelong involvement in voluntary work for everyone from the village Oxfam shop to running the local cub scouts. She had no English class consciousness or plummy accent to pass on to him. It all contrived to create a persona that was all things to all men – without any of them either appearing, or being, phoney. Playing basketball with the fifth formers as he opened a new gym at a comprehensive school in his constituency, he was the trendy gym teacher boy pupils referred to by his Christian name; and girl pupils fancied. Talking to the Queen without a trace of nervousness, he was the handsome, confident and clever son she never had.

Charlie had often seen Cane alongside Greaves and compared them. Cane's dark skin made Greaves' look even more milky white than it was, as though he had spent his life down a mine shaft – as indeed his father and grandfather had. Greaves had spent most of his formative years in a different kind of closed, airless world; that of libraries and political meetings. Cane looked as though he had spent most of his on a beach.

At forty seven, Cane was one year younger than Greaves and had the added responsibility of being Prime Minister, plus a wife, plus two children; and yet at times he looked ten years younger. Most of it came naturally; the rest from a self-discipline concealed by his easy-going air.

He played squash once a week with a doctor friend from medical school days and cycled three miles before breakfast every morning on the exercise machine he moved into the Downing Street flat two days after the election. He was the precise weight recommended for a male with a height of six foot one inch: thirteen stones exactly, only two pounds heavier than when he was a twenty year old student.

A few seconds after Cane arrived, the third member of the troika that ran the Government walked in.

'Hi Ronnie,' said Cane.

There was no written agenda; those were for the full Cabinet and Cabinet committees. This was no Cabinet meeting. For a start, the discussion would not be leaked to the press within an hour of it ending. Which is why it was where all the important Government decisions were taken – with the rest of the Cabinet kept out.

'Yes, I have seen the *Telegraph*, Charlie,' said Cane, anticipating the cause of the deeper than usual lines on her brow.

It didn't strike him as odd that he, the Prime Minister, should be more concerned about her reaction to a story in the press than she was about his. It didn't strike her either.

'We could have done without it; any ideas where it came from, Charlie? Ronnie?'

'A few ideas, but no evidence – yet,' she said, striking her lighter and studying the flame before holding it to her cigarette. She didn't mention any names to Cane. She never did. That was her backyard, and if anyone had fouled in it she would clear up the mess. She kept Cane away from that.

'Let's face it,' he said, 'they got the wrong sums but the right answer, didn't they? We knew something like this was going to happen.'

The three had decided a week ago that they must tackle speculation about the date of the euro vote and the election.

17

'Ronnie, you were going to look at the options and scenarios, let's have them,' said Cane.

'OK,' said Silverman, 'originally, we agreed we'd go for a May 3rd election this year followed by a vote on the euro maybe four months later around September. We're twenty five points ahead, so barring a disaster, winning the election still looks a certainty. And if we tell people to vote Yes to the euro a few months later, I can't see them doing the opposite. But,' he continued, after a pause, 'three things have changed. First, people are fed up with waiting for the euro vote and our focus groups say you're dithering.'

They all knew what happened to the last man in this building who was accused of that. That is why Silverman had said it.

Cane gave a weary grimace and raised his eyes for him to resume.

'Second, the Opposition is bound to change its leader if they're defeated – and there are one or two good candidates. That'd give them a big boost in the euro campaign. And third, there are signs of another EU budget crisis looming in the autumn. If Brussels grabs back another chunk of our rebate, getting people to vote Yes to the euro will be impossible. Greaves is pushing very hard for an early referendum. I know he's obsessed with getting us in, but he thinks that the recent fall in opposition to the euro after the rise in interest rates here gives us a window which we must take; and he's got a point.'

'Conclusion?' asked Cane.

'Do them both together – and soon,' said Silverman. 'If we hold the euro vote and the general election on May 3rd, local elections day, I'm convinced we'll win both.'

'Charlie?' said Cane.

'I agree.'

'Let me get the timings straight,' said Cane. 'We have to give five months notice of the euro vote to get all the legislation through, so that means announcing now if it's to be May 3rd.'

'Yes,' said Silverman.

'And we can plan an election on the same day without announcing it until a month beforehand, early April?'

'Yes,' said Silverman, 'the latest you can announce a May 3rd election is the first week in April, right at the start of the new tax year – perfect for a few Budget goodies.'

'As long as Greaves doesn't stick his oar in,' scoffed Charlie.

'Alright, alright,' said Cane, restraining her. 'So we announce the euro vote now and keep them guessing about the general election, for a while at least. Are we all agreed?'

He leaned forward in his seat in anticipation of Charlie and Silverman's reply, but before they could utter a word a flat, doleful voice interjected from the doorway.

'One coffee.' A tall, middle aged, rake thin black woman holding a tray was standing there with a face devoid of expression.

She walked up to Cane, plonked the cup and saucer on the table in front of him, didn't once look at Cane, completely ignored Silverman and Charlie and turned to leave.

'Er, d'you think we could have two more?' said Cane, as politely as she had been insolent.

'I was only told one,' she replied curtly, dangling the tray by her side.

'Well, would you mind if we had two more?'

'Whatever.'

She turned to leave again.

Cane cleared his throat. 'Ahem. And could we have some biscuits please?'

'First it's one coffee, then it's three, now it's biscuits an' all. Anytin' else?'

'No, that'll be all, thank you Dora.'

'You sure you ain' gonna go changin' again?'

'Quite sure, thank you, Dora.'

Dora Benjamin was one of the Downing Street messengers who spent much time fetching coffee for the PM, ministers and officials in the never ending round of meetings that went on in all parts of Number 10 from morn till night. When she wasn't busy, she would hang around the 'post room' just inside the black front door and next to Charlie's bow-windowed office overlooking Downing Street.

Dora's father had come to Britain from the West Indies in one of the first immigrant ships and her mother was four months pregnant with Dora when they docked at Southampton. Now in her fifties, she still had the tall gangly frame of a high jumper. There was nothing between her limbs, ankles and elbows.

No civil servant was less servile. A more insecure man would have slapped her down, but there was no pomp to Cane and Dora was a relief from the sycophants who bowed and scraped all day. There was no need to advertise for a jester to the court of King Steven: the job was taken.

'Yes, er, where was I?' said Cane, waiting until she had left before breaking into a grin. ' ... I think we were just about to make a historic decision, weren't we? The referendum, the election? May 3rd. Agreed?'

'Agreed' chorused Charlie and Silverman.

'OK Charlie, we'd better start planning the details,' said Cane. 'Who's going to tell Gareth?'

'Leave him to me,' Charlie butted in.

Silverman and Cane looked at each other. They weren't sure it was a good idea but neither spoke. They'd rather she confronted him than them.

Charlie looked in her briefcase and pulled out a pink file marked 'Election – Euro Plans – May 3rd.'

'I've already got a series of high profile media events lined up,' she said. 'We're going big on the family image, the others can't compete with you on it and they hate you rubbing their noses in it. Richard and Judy is already pencilled in, that's for you and Lucy together; *Woman's Own* want to do a family photo shoot; and Radio 2 have offered a slot with Jimmy Young. That'll cover the housewives. I thought I'd get you on Frank Skinner's new show; it's the nearest thing to serious viewing for half the male population. We'll do 'Today' – but only if they promise not to put Humphrys up against you. Ronnie and I have also been looking at a series of policy-led initiatives we can organise to maximise our support. It's only a start, Steven but ... '

' ... whoa , whoa, only a start? Sounds like the whole campaign to me!' said Cane.

'Steven,' she said, frowning, 'we've got to get on with this. I suggest the two of us sit down on Friday afternoon after your visit to Scotland and revise your programme in detail for the next four weeks before you go to Surrey. From now on, we have to imagine the election and the referendum campaigns are both under way.'

'Surrey?' asked Cane.

'Guildford, you're spending the weekend with your in-laws. I've lined up a camera team, it'll make great shots for a TV broadcast come the election.'

'Oh, of course, yes ... Friday afternoon, the family, good idea.'

Cane picked up his mug, 'Well it's only coffee, but let's drink to May 3rd. A second term.'

They echoed him: 'A second term.'

CHAPTER THREE

'Please stop fighting will you, you two; we're going to see grandma and granddad, so will you please tidy up these toys before we go,' said Lucy.

'Where's he got to this time?' she said, adding out of hearing to thirteen year old Sam and ten year old Jessica, 'he's late – even by his standards.'

She had been looking forward to the weekend at her parents for a long time. They had been ill with 'flu at Christmas and she and Cane had agreed to take the children there on the first weekend of the New Year.

'Come on Sam, Jessica, we must be ready for daddy.' Cane and Lucy had waited seven years before having Sam. She was twenty four when they married, three years his junior, and they agreed she should get established in her teaching career before they had a family. Jessica arrived three years later. Once or twice Cane had raised the possibility of having a third child. He had hated being an only child himself. But he could see Lucy wince every time he raised the subject.

'I've had enough.'

Lucy looked at her watch. It was seven fifteen. Cane was more than half an hour late. She couldn't shout down; his office was three floors, several flights of stairs and several corridors away from the flat, so she phoned a secretary.

'Is my husband back from his regional tour yet?' she asked.

'Yes, Mrs Cane, he got back half an hour ago. He's in Miss Redpath's office.'

'Half an hour ago?' Lucy exclaimed. 'I'll come down.'

When Lucy walked into Charlie's office he was crouched over a pile of papers with her at her desk under the bay window that looked out onto

Downing Street.

Lucy barged in. 'Steven! We were supposed to leave half an hour ago, you didn't even tell me you were back.'

'I'm sorry ... '

'You promised we'd get there on time. Mummy's cooking a roast. If we don't leave in ten minutes it'll be too late. The children are fighting, they're exhausted. Can't you ever think of us?'

'Lucy, I'm sorry, I'm so sorry,' said Cane. 'Darling, this is really important, ten minutes, I promise, we're nearly finished, I'll be with you.'

'There's always something else more important. For goodness sake, Steven. You promised to take them to the Big Wheel last week, but didn't turn up 'til it was too late. The poor things see it from our living room window every day and they still haven't been.'

'Darling, I promise, ten minutes.' Cane moved towards Lucy, but she turned and left.

Charlie said nothing. She never got involved in disputes between Cane and Lucy and had never uttered a word of criticism about Lucy to Cane or anyone. Lucy did her best to ignore Charlie at all times. It wasn't easy. Downing Street was Lucy's home, but Charlie was the woman of the house.

Charlie and Cane were just finishing twenty minutes later when they heard a car's engine revving up outside. He recognised the sound. He bolted out of Charlie's office, across the black and white tiled floor of the entrance hall and onto the steps of Number 10 as a dark green Range Rover pulled out from the parking bay opposite and sped off towards the wrought iron gates at the end of the street.

Cane shouted 'Lucy! Lucy!' and waved his arms frantically.

She could see him in her rear view mirror but didn't stop. Cane was worried: Lucy hated driving and in this frame of mind she could do something dangerous. She was going so fast, the police didn't have time to fully lower the anti-terrorist ramp half way along Downing Street. The front end of the Range Rover leapt up and crashed down before careering on to the gates. Cane could make out the tear-stained little face of Jessica looking at him from the back window, with her palms pawing at the glass. He couldn't hear her crying out, 'daddy! daddy!' But he could see her mouthing the words.

Cane thought of chasing after them. He ran towards the gates 100 yards away, but it was no good. He was fit enough to sprint the whole distance but he would never get there in time; the gates were already parting to let the car through; and what would the tourists pressed against the railings make of it?

He stood, exasperated and humiliated, with his face thrust up to the heavens. 'I don't believe it, I just don't believe it.' As he looked down he was suddenly aware of a giant telephoto lens pointing directly at him from only 20 feet away across the street.

'Oh hell! Not that as well!'

He rushed back in to Number 10, where Charlie was standing in the lobby.

'There's a bloody photographer. Stop him, for Christ's sake, please.'

'Steven, it's not fair, I can't get involved.'

There was no mention of sorting out the Prime Minister's marital spats in her job description.

'Please Charlie, please. I can't do it,' he implored.

She looked long and hard at him, willing him not to make her do it. She shunned the limelight. She was not going to make the same mistake as Cane's first press secretary who became a public figure in his own right before the party won power and described the party's foreign affairs spokesman as 'off his rocker' in an off the record aside to newsmen after an on the record press conference. A Sky News TV crew hovering in the background picked up the remark and broadcast it – live. The press secretary was sacked.

Charlie preferred the discipline of the fiercest press secretary of them all, Harold Wilson's Joe Haines, who 'fined' staff a bottle of wine for the office party every time they were referred to in the press.

If it was a choice between famous poison and effective poison, Charlie knew which she preferred. But this time she had no choice. She stubbed her cigarette out on the black and white tiled floor, thrust her documents into Cane's stomach, ran out and saw the silhouette of an overweight man wearing a combat jacket, pockets bulging and heavy objects dangling from his neck and bouncing off his large bottom, waddling in the same direction as the Range Rover. She instantly recognised the shambling figure.

'Blackie!' she bawled as she threw down her cigarette and ran after him. 'Blackie Cole, come here!'

She didn't give a damn about the tourists, she was going to catch him. 'Stop him!' she screamed at the policemen on duty at the gates, who had only just clanked them shut behind Lucy's screeching car. Hearing the kerfuffle, and fearing a terrorist incident, they drew their guns and ran towards Cole.

He was gasping when Charlie reached him. She steeled herself.

'Put your guns down boys, it's Mr Les Cole of *The Globe*, a gentleman of the press,' she said. 'Leave him to me.' The police didn't understand what was going on, but they knew better than to question her.

'Just what the hell d'you think you're doing, Blackie?'

Cole, bent over double and gasping for air, spluttered, 'I'll tell ... you ... what ... I'm ... doing ... I've ... just ... done ... the ... splash picture ... and I'm right ... on ... edition time.'

He had run only forty yards but sweat was dripping from his brow.

He'd had a lean spell since Diana's death. He had spent ten years following her all over the world. They had become friends. She would look for his tubby frame and bespectacled, weathered face among the sea of lenses and as soon as she heard the Cockney 'darlin' on the end, would flash the broadest smile in his direction. Cole was not like the rest of the paparazzi – 'the flash and brash brigade' – as he called them. He was in his fifties, a warm avuncular figure, not a vulture.

He had never got over her death; he had lost a friend, an idol – and a career. He was put back on the picture desk rota. Taking photographs of the Deputy PM and Chief Whip at Number 12 for a feature article, which is why he was there tonight, was no match for Diana at the Taj Mahal, Diana in Hollywood – or Diana anywhere. Diana wasn't the only one who had a soft spot for Blackie. Charlie had got to know him when he accompanied the PM's team on a series of foreign trips and he was one of the few photographers she liked. But she couldn't go back to Number 10 unless she had that film. And Cole couldn't go back to his office without it.

'Don't get sarky with me Blackie, you know that taking photos of the PM's children without permission is totally against the Press Complaint Commission's code of conduct.'

'Yeah, but we're not going to print any pictures of the kids,' said Cole, gradually recovering, 'and you know it; just Cane and his missus.'

'Bullshit. Hand over the film. Now!'

Cole was not easily angered. 'Oh it's the heavy treatment, is it? I'm not one of your lobby correspondent poodles you can bully around you know. There's no law against taking pictures of the Prime Minister in a flap – unless you've brought one in in the last few days.'

'You had no right to be there in the first place.'

'Yes I did, I was invited here to take some profile shots of the DPM, he's going to a reception at Number 12, here's my press pass.' He waved it in her face. 'See! But he was late – as usual. It's not my fault if Cane and his missus have a bust up in front of my nose is it?'

'Listen to me Blackie, if you think you're going to get those pictures in *The Globe*, you're as stupid as every other monkey who ever held a camera. I wonder what a certain Mr Warren McLintock would say. He's your proprietor – in case you'd forgotten – the same Warren McLintock who two weeks ago publicly declared it was time for *The Globe* to clean up its act; the same Warren McLintock who is coming to have tea with the PM next Tuesday.'

'Don't threaten me Redpath, I was taking pictures of Prime Ministers when your mother was wiping your arse. Call me old fashioned, but I'm going to walk out of these gates, go back to my office and give this film to the editor. Cos he's the one that puts them in the paper, not you darlin'. And I don't give a tuppenny toss what McLintock thinks. Got it, darlin'?'

'Can I quote you on that?'

'Anytime, why don't you just make it up? You usually do?'

She was losing.

'Let them walk over you once and they'll walk over you as many times as they want.'

She couldn't hit Blackie, and threatening him with the wrath of his employer had failed. She tried to look as cool and composed as possible.

'Do as you please Blackie, but don't forget about all those lovely foreign trips the PM has got coming up,' she said.

'So? What about them?'

'So, I've got all the press applications in my desk, including yours. I know how you love them since Lady Di left you deskbound - especially the expenses. Remember how you bragged about putting the £500 you blew when you got drunk in Ankara on a topless lapdancer as "entertaining Ugandan ambassador". Very droll. The boys gave me a souvenir shot of you groping her. Mrs Cole has probably got one on the mantelpiece, or then again, maybe she hasn't?'

Cole's bedraggled frame sagged visibly.

'You swine, Redpath, you low-down swine,' he said slowly and venomously. 'You know, for one moment when you started this job I thought your hard nut act was just that, all put on, and that underneath it you were genuine. But it's not an act at all, is it? It's all there is. You and Cane were a breath of fresh air when you took over, but I'll tell you for nothin' – there's a bad smell from this place these days.'

'Then keep your nose out. You're not the only one who has a job to do. Don't lecture me. You've got one aim and one aim only: to get the scummiest pictures you can to sell your scummy newspaper. You can't even imagine how much I despise you. The film; give it!' she snapped.

He flipped open the back of one of the two Nikon F5s he carried with him constantly – each had a different lens – and handed over the film.

'And the film from the other one.'

Blackie flipped that open too and handed it over.

'You really are a nasty bit of work, aren't you, Redpath? Good fucking riddance to you.' He turned round to go.

'Oh no you don't Blackie. I wasn't born yesterday.'

He stopped, but didn't face her.

'Let's have the one you palmed, the one I saw you shove in your left pocket as you ran off. Come on.'

Cole looked at the policemen. He fumbled in his pocket and threw the last yellow and black roll at her feet and spat on the ground where it landed.

She stooped to pick them up, turned and walked away without looking at him.

When she reached Number 10, Cane was waiting anxiously inside the door.

'Don't worry, I got what you wanted,' she said brusquely, handing them to him.

'Thank God, well done,' said Cane, who looked embarrassed. 'Charlie ... I ... '

'You don't have to say anything. It's my job, isn't it?'

She took her documents from him, picked up her bag and walked straight past.

* * *

Relations between Charlie and Greaves had been fraught since the day he woke up to come to terms with losing an election – and Charlie, nine years earlier.

He had no idea where Charlie had gone that night; or why. He couldn't even remember what had happened. The last thing he recalled was waiting for her at his flat. He knew they had got drunk, but he hadn't got a clue what had happened in bed. Had he made a fool of himself? Had he forced himself on her? Was that why she had left without a word? There was no answer when he rang her flat after finally waking up at lunchtime to find himself alone. He rang everyone he knew, everyone she knew, but no one had seen her. Three days later he rang her home in Glasgow. Her mother told him, 'I'm sorry, she's out, we don't know when she'll be coming in.'

She gave the same reply each of the dozen times Greaves made the same call over the next three weeks. Her brothers told him in no uncertain terms to leave her alone. He assumed she would come back. That, like him, she needed time to recover from defeat. She may not love him, but she loved politics, she'd soon be back.

But she wasn't.

A month later she wrote to him saying she was resigning as his assistant. She had been in touch with an old university friend who had told her a US Senator wanted a speech writer with special knowledge of the UK and Europe. She was fed up with Britain. She wanted to get out and had taken the job.

It wasn't the whole story. She hadn't told her mother the whole story – and that was rare. Greaves felt the way he did when they lost the election – only worse.

They didn't meet again until two in the morning, five years almost to the day, hours after the result of another May election.

This time it was the enemy who were drowning their sorrows. Cane was the new Prime Minister and would be arriving any moment at London's Festival Hall where Charlie, Greaves and thousands of other jubilant supporters were waiting to hail his sensational triumph.

Greaves didn't recognise her immediately; the shoulder pads, the make up, the shorter hair style. The blue-jeaned student rebel who had worked for him was transformed into a stunning, polished professional. But the lippiness had not been tamed by Washington's salons. 'You're still as scruffy as a rag, Gareth Greaves, and your hair's still too long.'

In the time it took him to register who had delivered the sentence, Greaves' bitterness at the way they had parted evaporated. His feelings for her surged back.

'I don't believe it! Charlie, you're back, my God! You look so ... so different, so great. I knew you'd get bored with those Yanks ... that's not politics, its showbiz! Hey, never mind my hair, where's yours all gone, those flaming tresses?'

She remembered him burying his head in her hair when they made love in his flat and saying he wanted to cut a lock of it in the morning to keep with him. He never saw her in the morning.

'Went out of fashion years ago, trust you not to know,' she said quickly.

He threw his arms around her before adding, 'Charlie, are you coming back to us?'

'Er, yes, didn't you get my letter?'

'No, God, I haven't opened my mail for a month – I haven't been home for a month! Charlie, I just can't believe it.' He laughed hysterically, joyously.

Shit, thought Charlie. Shit, shit, shit!

'It's brilliant, brilliant,' said Greaves. 'Oh, this is too much! More drink,' he shouted to the barman.

'Diet Coke for me,' said Charlie.

'Still suffering from that hangover?' Greaves examined her face for any reaction to his reference to the last time they had been together. He didn't detect one.

He seized a glass of champagne and offered her one. She declined.

'Careful Gareth, Deputy Prime Ministers aren't supposed to get drunk, you know,' said Charlie.

Greaves beamed. 'I know, the job's not official, but it will be in an hour or two.'

He was desperate to ask her if she would come back to work for him, though not as desperate as she was to explain why she had returned. But before either could make themselves heard, they were separated in the crush when Cane and Lucy entered the hall. By the time they were back together a few minutes later, Lucy appeared in their midst, swept towards them like a piece of flotsam on a political tidal wave.

'Gareth, Charlie! We've done it, we've done it!' she shouted above the din.

'And isn't it marvellous news about Charlie, Gareth?'

'That she's back, yeah it's great, just great!' said Greaves.

'No, I mean that she's coming to work for Steven at Number 10.'

'Sorry?' said Greaves.

'Charlie! She's going to be Steven's press secretary.'

Greaves' expression of glee melted.

'Is that right. Charlie?'

She nodded, but shuddered inside. How she wished he had got her letter, that she had told him first. But it was too late.

Now, fours year after that night at the Festival Hall, and nine years after they had slept together, as she looked at Greaves in his study in the Cabinet Office, how she still wished she had told him first. He could forgive her for the way she left, but not for the way she returned.

Charlie walked to his study straight after her confrontation with Blackie Cole. The front door of the Cabinet Office, half way down Whitehall, was some 400 yards from the front door of Number 10 at the far end of Downing Street. But because the buildings were at right angles to each other, they were joined at the rear. Charlie marched down Number 10's long corridor, turned right at the end, past the PM's study, right again, up a short stairway, turned left then right and came to a door. On the other side was another room. She swiped her security pass through a black meter on the wall, waited to hear a faint click, pushed the door and stepped over the threshold.

She was in the Cabinet Office. The Prime Minister's office and that of the deputy Prime Minister were at one at the same time, joined and divided.

She walked through the galleried chamber that was alongside the remains of Henry VIII's tennis court from the original Palace of Whitehall, summoned the lift at the far end, pressed number three, stared at the tacky brown lining as the lift juddered up two floors, walked through a pale blue waiting room and approached another door.

This one was half open. She could see the long shadows cast across Horse Guards Parade and the outline of the Admiralty Buildings through the arched window on the far side of the room. And as the back of her right hand was poised, ready to tap on the door, she could hear the manic clatter of a computer keyboard coming from the left, behind the door.

It had taken her less than two minutes to get there after giving Cole's films to Cane. She might as well get all her confrontations over in one go.

As she appeared in his room, and peered round to her left, where Greaves was sitting, he looked up, surprised.

'Mind if I come in?'

'Er, no,' he said continuing his writing. 'I was just finishing some work, before going to the reception at Number 12.'

'You missed your photo call.'

He looked at his watch.

'So I did, I never noticed the time. It wasn't important. Is that all?'

His desk was placed in the corner of the vast room looking diagonally towards the stem bronze chandelier in the centre and beyond to Horse Guards Parade. On the right of his desk was an opened copy of *Country Life*, with a picture of a girl with long chestnut hair riding a horse. He saw her looking at the magazine and looked at her, but said nothing.

'Didn't know you'd joined the horsey set,' she said casually. 'Thought *Tribune* was more your thing.'

Greaves closed the magazine, silently. Small talk was not his strong point, even when he was trying. And he wasn't trying.

'What is it that you want to discuss, Charlie? I take it it's the euro vote now we – or should I say now you've – announced the date?' he said in a matter of fact tone.

'We need to sort out some details, but it's not why I am here.'

'Really?' said Greaves. He leaned right back in his seat, with his hands clasped behind his head, relishing the prospect of a confrontation.

'I understand you are canvassing for support to raise the issue of a wealth tax at the Cabinet in the next few weeks – to meet hospital under-funding,' said Charlie.

'Who told you that?'

'That's not exactly a denial, Gareth.'

'It's not exactly a confirmation either, Charlie.'

'We can't play games.'

'I never have with you, Charlie, you don't play by the rules.'

'We cannot break our promise not to put income tax up.'

'But we can break our promise on hospital waiting lists?'

'You know what happened to us when we made a mistake on taxes in the past, don't you?'

'A lot of mistakes were made in the past – and they weren't all to do with policies.'

Charlie's split second delay was enough for Greaves to know he had hit home. But she pressed on, 'There's no way we can go into these elections putting up taxes.'

'Who said anything about two elections? I only know about one. Or did I miss one of your announcements? I do occasionally.'

'The general election has not been decided,' she said, lying to cover up her slip.

She moved on, hoping he wouldn't detect her momentary self doubt. 'Gareth, you wanted the euro vote to be held as soon as possible; you have been telling the PM to do it early for more than a year. Now he has done exactly what you wanted.'

'I'm glad he agrees with me.'

'But he does not agree with you on tax, Gareth; you must, you really must realise that.'

'That sounds remarkably close to an ultimatum to me, Charlie.'

She didn't answer. There was no point.

'It's a funny old world isn't it, Charlie? The day I met you, I had to pull you off a poll tax barricade to stop you being thrown into a Black Maria. We've all changed, Charlie, but no one's changed as much as you. You're on the other side of the barricade these days, aren't you?'

CHAPTER FOUR

Injit Joshi and his wife Yasmin expected to queue when they took eleven year old Aniel and his sister Maya, seven, for a ride on the London Eye.

'Look, here come some clowns. Thank goodness, that'll amuse them for a while,' said Mr Joshi. The two children joined a small circle on the Thames towpath around the clown who was juggling coloured balls. He asked for two volunteers to play a game. Aniel's hand shot up first and the clown asked him and his sister to come to the front.

'We need a grown up to complete our act,' said the clown.

He spotted a young couple walking past and grabbed the woman by the arm. The woman, who was wearing a green anorak and checked trousers, didn't have much choice. Her partner shrugged his shoulders and after putting down a bag with a brightly coloured Mickey Mouse motif, was brought into the middle of the circle.

'And you, madam, what is your name?' the clown asked the young woman. 'Er ... Eileen,' she replied.

'Everybody shout "Eileen!" at the tops of their voices so she doesn't forget who she is.'

'Eileen!' bawled fifty little sets of lungs. Eileen looked awkward.

The clown got Aniel to hand Maya a magic wand, told her to blow on it three times, say 'abracadabra' and hold one end while giving the other to Eileen. She gave it a tug; there was a bang followed by a puff of smoke and out came the biggest bra you ever saw. The captive audience laughed out loud and applauded. The clown told Aniel and Maya to take a bow and went to get Eileen to take a bow, but she was moving away. Aniel heard her partner call out something to her and Eileen walked off to join him at a nearby burger stall.

'Hey, you haven't got your prize,' the clown shouted to Eileen, but she didn't seem to hear.

'Well I think Maya should have it,' said the clown.

It was a model of the Big Wheel.

* * *

'Five seconds, Richie. Judy? Everyone? Ready!'

'Today on This Morning With Richard and Judy,' said Richard, teeth gleaming, 'we are privileged today to bring you the first television interview with Prime Minister Steven Cane since he announced that the vote on whether Britain should replace sterling with the euro will take place on May 3rd.'

'And before you rush to turn off your set,' said Judy, 'it won't all be about euros and elections, he has brought his wife Lucy with him. She has agreed to give a rare glimpse of what life is really like behind the Number 10 curtains.'

'I want to ask the Prime Minister that first,' said Richard. 'What is it really like to live in that famous house?'

'Well, Richard, people find it hard to believe, but our home life is very much like everyone else's. We try to have breakfast together, the kids want to leave their Weetabix and race off and watch TV before going to school. It's an everyday scene of domestic morning mayhem.'

'And did you dream as a schoolboy that you would be Prime Minister one day?'

'Good gracious no, I was more interested in riding my bike or playing football with my mates.'

Charlie smiled to herself. Bikes and footie sounded more like her childhood than the one Cane spent at prep school in Bristol.

Judy chipped in, 'And Lucy, in the morning, does he help the children with last minute homework and polish their shoes?'

'Well, he has been known to once or twice,' she said, smiling and looking at Cane.

Charlie had briefed them both on how to handle the show, from their clothes to their answers. It was one of the few occasions Lucy and Charlie had direct contact with each other. Lucy didn't enjoy doing interviews; she did not enjoy being told by Charlie how to conduct herself; and she enjoyed even less seeing her tell Cane what he could and couldn't do or say.

'Don't be fooled by Richard's smile, he's as good as Paxman only you won't feel the knife go in,' Charlie said. 'He won't go for you Lucy, he'll throw the tough ones at Steven, but be on your guard. Most of your questions will come from Judy, what the kids have for breakfast, juggling two jobs, what you cook for Steven, you know the sort of thing. Remember to wear that pink outfit. I know it's not your favourite, but it does look good on telly.' Lucy bit her lip. When she did her first interview with Richard and Judy after the election, she had worn her favourite checked green suit which made her look overweight and mumsy. The *Daily Mail* ran a two page feature headed: 'HAS LUCY LOST THE FASHION PLOT?' The next time she went on TV, Charlie told her to wear pink, which Lucy hated, but it got a rave review in the Mail. Charlie sent her the cutting.

'Now,' said Richard, 'for what I call the dad's litmus test, what about the last school run?' But he didn't specifically address the question to Cane or Lucy. Instead he looked Cane in the eye, then Lucy.

'A week ago, wasn't it?' said Cane.

Which would have been fine had she not already started to answer, 'A month or so I think.' They all burst out laughing, but Cane realised exactly what Richard had done and glanced automatically at Charlie in the wings.

'I think we should ask Richard when he last did the school run,' joked Cane.

'This morning!' said Richard, triumphantly. 'Am I telling the truth, darling?'

'Is he?' asked Cane.

'I'm afraid he is, Prime Minister,' said Judy, 'don't you just hate him?'

Charlie fidgeted. They're not far off taking the mick; they'd better not go much further.

'We'd better do some serious talking too, Prime Minister,' said Richard, who realised he had ruffled the Prime Ministerial plumage and quickly moved on. 'You've announced the referendum on the euro is going to take place on May 3rd, but many people think you're going to call a general election on that date too. Is that true?'

Careful, careful, Charlie mouthed silently. This is how Richard oh-so-casually lures unsuspecting politicians into his trap

'Well, I'm concentrating on the euro vote at the moment,' said Cane, switching to autopilot. 'I think people will be glad to have that issue out of the way since we've been talking about it so long. I have no plans to call an election at present, but when I do have, you'll be the first to know, Richard. I think our opponents are more worried than anybody because they know they'll lose.'

Perfect, thought Charlie. Light hearted and firm.

Judy took up the questioning: 'Isn't it difficult living in Number 10, Lucy, when there's all those Sir Humphrey characters marching up and down the corridors demanding meetings on world crises and every subject under the sun when you're trying to get the kids bathed?'

'You soon learn to ignore them,' she said. 'At least he hasn't got any excuse to be late home from work – not that it stops him sometimes.'

Was that a little dig for last Friday, wondered Charlie?

'It must make it difficult to have a row, with all those people about,' said Richard.

Charlie marched over to the producer. 'You'd better tell your darling Richie to cut it out; he's talking to the Prime Minister, not some bloody soap star.'

The producer muttered something into the wire-like microphone that curled in front of his face. Richard looked up.

* * *

'Mum, it's fabulous. Look we're miles higher than Big Ben, much higher!' said Aniel, as their glass pod reached the very top of the wheel.

The Joshis had had a day to remember. But the day they would remember was just about to begin.

* * *

'What I want to know, Prime Minister,' said Judy, 'is why you think you have been so successful. We know what the pundits say, but what do you put it down to? I mean, you are a zillion miles ahead in the opinion polls, you were voted the sexiest man in Britain by *New Woman* magazine last month, strikes and unemployment are lower than they have ever been since goodness knows when, you have got the Olympics coming our way and you are now beginning to persuade people that they might actually prefer to do their shopping in euros instead of pounds, shillings and pence. How on earth do you do it all?'

That's more like it, thought Charlie, but she stayed at the producer's elbow just in case.

'Well, I don't think it is so much down to me,' said Cane. 'It's down to getting the right policies, having the right team to put them into action, having the right sort of back-up and, dare I say it, it's about having a bit of luck. I'm the first to admit I've been lucky. Lucky to be party leader, lucky to be Prime Minister,' he said, and, holding his hand out to Lucy, 'lucky to be married to Lucy.'

Richard was about to ask Cane whether luck was the most important quality a Prime Minister needed, when he was stopped mid sentence by a message over his earpiece. 'Cut the question, Richie, we are going to the newsroom in five, OK?'

'News has just come in of an explosion at the Big Wheel,' said the newsreader. 'As yet, there are no reports of casualties. The entire area has been sealed off by police. The Press Association news agency received a warning from a man who was said to have given a recognised call sign used by the so called "Continuity IRA". We will bring you fresh information as soon as it is available. And now back to Richard and Judy.'

The newsflash had barely begun when Charlie's pager went off. She had had to switch off her mobile phone in the TV studio. 'London Eye, bomb! Ring office.' There wasn't time. By the time the newsreader had mentioned an explosion at the Wheel, Cane's own alarm system had gone off. Charlie saw him look at her, and then at Lucy. He was live on TV, it looked like the Wheel had been blown up by the IRA or their friends – and he had seconds to decide his response. What was he supposed to say? He looked at Charlie. She drew her right forefinger across her throat, like a knife. It meant shut up and get out, now.

'That is appalling news, Prime Minister,' said Richard. 'It is unfair to ask you to comment when so little is known, but may I ask you your reaction?'

'It is truly dreadful,' said Cane, composing himself. 'You're right, I think it would be quite wrong for me to comment on it before hearing more information. In the circumstances, I am sure you will understand if I say Lucy and I must get back to Downing Street immediately.'

'Of course Prime Minister – and good luck,' said Richard.

* * *

Cane walked to the microphone a few feet in front of the Number 10 door.

The dull bronze tie Charlie had selected for him for daytime time TV had been replaced by a dark purple one. The light blue shirt by a white one. She tied the knot for him as they stood behind the door, the last thing he did before facing the cameras.

The arc of reporters, film crews, broadcasters, photographers, some at the back perched on ladders so they could get a view; others crouched down behind the rope keeping them a few feet away from Cane, was twice the number that usually attended Downing Street press conferences. The US networks, CNN and CBS were there too – and they only turned up for something big.

'This morning a bomb exploded on the Millennium Wheel,' said Cane, gravely. 'You can see the terrible damage it has caused.' He raised his arm and pointed towards the mangled remains of the monstrous machine that could be seen across the river directly from Number 10's front door, with one section cut out, like a piece of metallic cake. Five pods, including the one containing the bomb and two each side had been blown to smithereens like light bulbs.

'A telephone warning that a device had been planted at the Wheel was received by the Press Association twenty minutes before it went off. The police immediately ordered that the Wheel be evacuated,' he continued. 'Approximately 300 people were on the Wheel and another 500 were in the vicinity on the ground. Owing to a magnificent operation by the emergency services, every single person was clear when the device exploded. At present, no fatalities have been reported. However, several people were injured by debris and are being treated in St Thomas's hospital. A republican splinter group have said they were responsible for the explosion. I have a message for them. We did not come this far down the road to peace in Northern Ireland to give in the moment a handful of terrorists try and destroy it. The peace process will go on. It will not be stopped by one bomb; or by a thousand bombs. When this morning's explosion occurred, the Wheel was full of families ... families like my own ... young children with their mothers and fathers enjoying a special holiday treat.'

'Brilliant,' muttered Charlie to herself, fifteen feet away. 'Brilliant.'

'Pardon ma'am?' said a police constable standing a foot away.

'Oh nothing, nothing,' she replied.

' ... It is for the sake of those children, future generations, that we will not give up the struggle to find peace. The people of this country have never surrendered to threats, violence, war, invasion and I am not going to surrender to terrorism. Not ever.' He paused. 'Thank you.'

Cane turned on his heels and went back inside.

* * *

The young girl came to at twenty past five that evening. Her face was barely visible. The bandages covered everything but her eyes, which were closed. She tried to open her eyes, but couldn't. They were stuck together. She tried again.

'Injit! She's waking! Nurse! She's waking!' The girl's mother saw her child's eyes flicker; after a few seconds they opened; the left followed by the right. 'Nurse, quickly, fetch Injit.'

The Joshis were the last passengers to get off the Wheel, four minutes before the bomb went off. They were running towards Westminster bridge when they were showered with glass and metal, bits of which were still embedded in Maya.

Mr Joshi noticed activity at the end of the corridor. Some doctors were addressing a youngish couple in the middle of a group which was moving towards Maya's room like a swarm of bees. There was a man in front of them walking backwards, holding an enormous camera on his shoulder.

'Keep back please, keep back!' said a strident female voice.

Charlie didn't want the cameraman too close, tripping over patients. But she didn't want him too far away either. She had got one of her staff to call ITN and tell them to get straight to St Thomas's hospital so that they could film Cane and Lucy visiting victims of the Wheel bomb. They had to be quick if he was to be first there. The Mayor of London was due to arrive at six and Charlie was damned if she was going to let him steal yet another of her photo stunts. Thirty people had been injured, including nine children. Maya's injuries were among the worst. The Prime Minister's entourage arrived at her room and Cane and Lucy were ushered in by a woman doctor, followed by the ITN man, who was ushered in by Charlie in spite of her telling the hospital the cameras would not be allowed inside the rooms of bomb victims.

'This is Maya, Prime Minister,' said the doctor. 'She is a very brave little girl.' Cane turned to Mr and Mrs Joshi. 'How is she?'

Charlie leaned back, allowing the boom mike to reach over her shoulder to the crowded bedside.

'She's doing OK, thank you Prime Minister,' said Mrs Joshi. 'The doctors have been marvellous.'

'Who could do a terrible thing like this, Prime Minister?' said Mrs Joshi.

'I don't know, Mrs Joshi, but we will catch them, Mrs Joshi, you have my word. For Maya's sake, we will catch them.'

Charlie looked at her watch: it was 4.55 pm. Brilliant. Just in time to get the pictures on the ITN 6.30 news.

CHAPTER FIVE

February 5th

Dear Colleague,

       As you know, the referendum on the euro is to take place on May 3rd. The three-month period in the run-up to the referendum is going to be extremely busy for the Government. Every department will be affected by the debate over the euro. It is essential that we co-ordinate the responses to be made to inquiries by the media. The Prime Minister has made it clear that he regards a clear vote in favour of joining the euro as essential to the future of this country.

       To ensure that the public have all the information they need to come to the right decision, I would like you to draw up a list of all the key areas in your department which you think will be affected by the euro campaign. I would like each Director of Communications to provide suggestions as to how we can persuade the public that membership of the euro will have positive effects and how best to counter the negative and extremist arguments of the Opposition. It is time we ALL took the gloves off. Please send me your suggestions in the next fourteen days.

       Charlotte Redpath.

Patrick Armitage had seen thousands of confidential memos since he left St Catharine's College, Cambridge, in 1959 to go straight to Whitehall, where he had spent the intervening four decades. But he had rarely seen one like the one Charlie had sent to the heads of communications at each government department. And he wasn't going to let it pass.

'Thank you so much for coming to see me, Miss Redpath,' said the Cabinet Secretary. 'Can I get you a cup of coffee?'

'No thanks.'

Armitage's office represented everything Charlie hated about him. It was probably eight times as big as the fourth floor flat she, her mother and father and four brothers had lived in. And as high as the entire block. The dull oak panelled walls gave it a heavy, gloomy atmosphere that suited its tenant. Above the fireplace a portrait of Napoleon glowered down.

Armitage liked and respected Cane. Charlie represented everything he disliked and disrespected about Cane's administration. One Permanent Secretary had joked that the three represented the three main social groups in the country: Armitage the urbane, Cane the suburban and Charlie the urban.

Charlie was well aware of his feelings. Even his body language implied contempt. Whenever she addressed a meeting he was attending, she would notice him raise one of his eyebrows the merest fraction. It was enough. He moved slowly, as if every muscle movement was planned with the same care and calculation as his sentences. At first she had tried to work with him, but not after reading a press report which claimed the civil service thought she was not up to the job. Charlie set about finding out where it came from. One of her spies in the Press Gallery was only too pleased to do her dirty work for her. The culprit turned out to be one of Armitage's junior officials who had been spotted at lunch with a political correspondent at 'Christopher's' restaurant off The Strand. The fool. Hadn't anyone told him it was known as the lobby canteen?

After that the cultural and social gap between them became an unbridgeable chasm. Armitage was all reflection; she was all reflex. He stuck his chin upwards and forwards to sip his Earl Grey tea from a china cup, elbow and little finger extended horizontally; her chin almost touched her desk when she drank her black coffee before tossing another polystyrene cup into the bin. He rolled his Parker fountain pen in his long spindly hands; she flicked cigarette ash into an ashtray with her red, nail-varnished, nicotine-stained forefinger. Only his eyes moved as he sat motionless in his seat; Charlie's eyes were the only part of her that remained fixed – on him. He digested everything silently; she spewed out instructions like machine-gun fire and blew smoke rings upwards.

A halo had rarely looked so out of place.

'You wanted to talk to me about the memo to heads of communications?' said Charlie.

'Yes.'

'Is there a problem?'

Charlie knew when she wrote it that it might cause a fuss; and she fully expected the fuss to be made by Armitage. She was counting on it.

'Some of the heads of communications have expressed serious concern about some of its implications.'

'What implications?' she said, tersely.

Armitage knew what the implications were. Charlie knew what they were. Armitage knew Charlie knew what they were. And she knew he knew that she knew. The day she entered Number 10 with Cane, Armitage's colleagues thought Cane had made a big mistake giving Charlie such an important job. They knew she had worked for a US Senator, but that was no training for Whitehall.

'If I may say so ... ' Armitage said languidly.

'Say what you like,' Charlie butted in.

' ... the difficulty with your memo, as I interpret it, is that it ignores the fact that it is the duty of civil servants to explain and inform the public about the actions and activities of the government of the day to the best of their ability and ... '

Charlie finished the sentence for him, ' ... and it's important they do that with the euro so people know what they're voting for.'

'That is where the difficulty arises,' said Armitage, measuring his words. He never ran one into another. Charlie could have filled the gap between each of his syllables with a sentence.

'Oh? Why?'

Armitage ignored her facetious tone.

'Because, Miss Redpath ... '

'Yes, let's be formal, Mister Armitage.'

' ... because Miss Redpath,' he replied, finally taking up the gauntlet she had thrown down, 'this memo goes somewhat further than asking civil servants to explain and inform. If carried out, it would mean them taking sides in a political debate. They would have to be partial in favour of the governing party and against the Opposition. That is a political matter and not one for civil servants to get involved in. And as for ... '

' ... as for what?'

'Miss Redpath, as for your reference to gloves coming off, that really is not the kind of instruction that can be given to a civil servant.'

They both knew that by asking heads of communications to draw up ideas for promoting the euro, Charlie was, in effect, asking them to get involved in the referendum campaign.

'Civil servants have to keep a certain distance Miss Redpath, or they would be in breach of their contract.'

'Come off it,' she fired back. 'That's an absurd interpretation of the rules. What happened in Thatcher's day? She declared war on half the country – and I don't remember hearing civil servants complaining about the lack of impartiality. They took their gloves off for her, didn't they? What did they do when the press asked them about the miners' strike? Reply that they couldn't get involved because the Prime Minister was waging class war? No, they told them the miners were a threat to democracy and had to be smashed to a pulp. What did they do when she made three million unemployed and closed down half the industries in the country? They said it was all needed to beat inflation. Where was the distance in that? You tell me, after all, you were around at the time.'

Armitage had read thrillers where people were held with a broken bottle against their neck in a back street of Glasgow. Now he knew what it felt like. Disputes between civil servants of his rank were usually conducted by hints, intonation and raised eyebrows, not verbal assault and battery.

'Miss Redpath, that is not my recollection of what happened ... '

'Well, that's what it looked like from the NUM picket line in the South Yorkshire pits when the Government sent the police in – I was there! I saw them hit miners' wives and I saw government spokesmen justify it in the papers the next day. Those spokesmen were your impartial civil servants, Mister Armitage, probably working to your instructions. You didn't seem to have any difficulties with that, did you?'

'Miss Redpath, we are not talking about the past, we are talking about the present. I have to tell you that several senior officials in the service have told me that they are uneasy about complying with your instructions and they ... '

'None of them's raised it with me.'

'They regarded it as more appropriate for me to raise it with you.'

'Which ones?'

'I do not think it would be helpful to discuss names. Miss Redpath, you should not underestimate the strength of feeling on this.'

'Are you telling me they are threatening to resign?'

'Some do feel very strongly about it.'

'I take it that's yes. Well if you think I'm alarmed by the prospect, you're mistaken.'

Charlie had already sacked a dozen officials inherited from the previous regime for leaking against the Government. She was staggered by the level of laziness and incompetence in some parts of the civil service. She had a drawer full of applications to replace them, disaffected BBC journalists who wanted to be press officers, and a whole host of other bright young things who were flocking to the party now it was in power again.

'You see Mr Armitage,' she said, 'I have concluded there are two types of civil servants: the ones at the bottom who find it hard to adjust to us and the ones at the top who want to sabotage us.'

'Miss Redpath, may I remind you that you came to this job from a party post and that traditionally ... '

'Yes, and may I remind you Mr Armitage that tradition isn't everything. Like the tradition that put you where you are and the tradition that seems to make you think you can tell me exactly what I can and can't do. I'm sure you remember that two days after the election the Prime Minister got an Order in Council – whatever that is – to enable me to give orders to people like you. If you don't like it, then you had better take it up with the Prime Minister, or the Queen; I think she signed the form.'

'I don't think it is going to be helpful to either of us to continue this conversation, Miss Redpath.'

'On the contrary, I think it's been very helpful, Mr Armitage.'

* * *

It was the knock at the door that Councillor Tony Quinlan had been dreading.

'Mr Quinlan?' said a burly man in a sheepskin jacket.

'Yeh.'

'You 'aven't been returnin' Mr 'Arris' calls or letters, he sent me to remind you, like.'

'Sod off, mate.'

Tony closed the door, but the man knocked again. Harder. So hard that Tony's trilby fell off its peg on the inside of the front door.

'Mr 'Arris would appreciate an answer, Mr Quinlan. No use 'idin'.'

The banging got louder, but Tony ignored it.

'Have it your way, Quinlan. I'm goin' back home now, but you can't keep me out for ever. I'll be back,' the man shouted through the letter box. 'And sooner than you think!'

Tony hadn't shaved for three days and had been wearing the same clothes for four. It wasn't like him. He usually took a pride in his appearance; it was one of the things that first attracted his wife Sheila to him when they met at a Saturday Night Fever disco. His friends nicknamed him 'Hancock'; he never went out without his trilby though his hangdog expression belied his genial warmth and dry wit. They had run a fish and chip shop on the Knowsley Estate two miles from their home. It was the latest in a long line of shops. None had been very successful, which was hardly surprising since Tony spent more time at Mersey City Hall, where he had been a councillor for nearly thirty years, than he did behind the counter.

It hadn't all been in vain. No one had done more than he to stop Militant Tendency wrecking the party and the city he loved. And he had made quite a name for himself pioneering computerised voting at council meetings.

But he'd paid a price. Trade at the chippie had been on the wane when a local minicab firm came up for sale.

'You'll finally be able to get the smell of batter out of your hair, pet,' said Tony.

The price was £35,000. His bank manager refused to make him a loan, but Harris Finance Limited, who advertised in the local newsagent's, agreed to put up the money. Tony paid cash after rumours that several other people were interested in buying it. But the man who sold it to him didn't mention that the biggest account, ferrying officials from the health authority to different NHS meetings, ran out in three weeks and that they had signed up with a rival cab firm. Without it, the business was virtually worthless. The Quinlans spent weeks trying to find him, but he had done a moonlight flit.

They faced ruin.

'You know what this means for the mayor's job, don't you, pet?' Tony said to his wife. 'I can't do it because I'm ... ' He couldn't bring himself to say it.

'Why can't you do it? You're still a good councillor. You'd be a great mayor and I'll be a crackin' mayoress; they all say you've done brilliantly by getting the computer thing under way. We can get through this.'

'You don't understand, love. We can't because ... because I'm as close as a gnat's dick to bankruptcy and bankrupts are banned from public life. If I tried to hide it and became mayor, I'd be jailed.'

That was assuming he didn't get beaten senseless by the man in the sheepskin jacket and his cronies first, he thought to himself. 'I've no choice, I'll have to resign. I'm finished.'

Sheila heard a knock at the door. She pulled back the sitting room curtain to see who it was.

'Eh, luv, there's a man in a sheepskin coat at the door. He's got two other men with him. Are they mates of yours?'

'Oh, Christ.'

CHAPTER SIX

Cane was happy with his morning's work in Newlyn, Cornwall. The whole country had been in a state of shock for a fortnight over the London Eye bomb. It was a miracle there were no fatalities. The Metropolitan Police Commissioner told Cane that scores, possibly hundreds, would have been killed had the Wheel not been evacuated so quickly. The fact that the bomb had not been properly detonated also helped. The worst injuries were broken bones and cuts, like those suffered by Maya Joshi, now back home and making a good recovery.

While the media were full of stories of people injured by the bomb, Charlie's mind was on Cane and how he would recover. Ending terrorism was supposed to have been one of his great successes. Two days after the explosion, when they met to devise a strategy for dealing with its aftermath, he was still in a state of shock. She had to jolt him out of it.

'You've got to look at how Thatcher dealt with this sort of thing. Look at all the disasters that happened in her time; Lockerbie, the Herald of Free Enterprise, the Falklands War, Hillsborough, Enniskillen and countless IRA atrocities. Did her personal standing suffer? Not a jot. It improved. She milked them for all they were worth and showed if you handle them well, you can turn them into an advantage.'

Charlie knew how much Cane admired Thatcher; he knew how much she hated her. Nowhere was Thatcher hated more than the streets of Glasgow. Someone who had had a comfortable middle-class upbringing in Bristol and been to a private school could not possibly feel the same way. Cane didn't hate Thatcher's politics; he didn't hate anything. He cared enough about other people's suffering to be passionately committed to relieving it, but he hadn't suffered enough personally to want to hate anything. Certainly not Margaret Thatcher. Far from hating her leadership, he wanted to emulate it. It was one area where he had brought Charlie round to his view, even if it appealed to her for a different reason. 'It's a deal,' she had said. 'We'll use her methods to do to them what they did to us.'

Ten days after the bomb, the Queen went to St Thomas's to visit the Wheel manager, who had been acclaimed as a hero for the way he had organised the evacuation. He was in hospital with a broken back and the Queen told him she had awarded him the George Cross. In fact, the Palace resisted the idea, arguing it would have to be considered in the normal way, which would take months. The suggestion was made by Cane, on Charlie's advice.

The Globe ran a full page editorial under the headline, 'HAIL CITIZEN CANE', praising the way he had reacted to the tragedy, ensuring that the Wheel manager was decorated immediately, unlike 'HER ROYAL SLOWNESS.' It was perhaps not surprising that *The Globe* should salute Cane's conduct. It was the least they could do after Charlie leaked the story to them.

Cane also announced a £5 million grant, to be paid for from the proceeds of the sale of the Millennium Dome, for the Wheel to be rebuilt. *The Globe* newspaper put up a £1 million reward for any information leading to the terrorists' arrest. A poll conducted three weeks after the bomb showed Cane's ratings had increased. 'It has set us up perfectly,' Charlie told him. 'I told you it would; what you've got to do now is use it.'

The two to one majority against joining the euro had turned into a narrow lead for the Yes camp and Charlie and Cane were convinced the trend would continue. Not that it was Charlie's habit merely to observe trends: she preferred to set them.

Cane's biggest problem was the charge made by anti-EU critics that joining the euro made him the 'poodle of Brussels' – which is why he had been to Newlyn, home of the Cornish fishing fleet, that morning. As his helicopter took off from Penzance to get him back to London in time for Prime Minister's questions at three o'clock, he reflected how nervous he had been at the prospect of meeting Cornish fishermen. They had staged a series of demos in protest at EU plans to increase the quotas of Spanish trawlers who competed with British vessels for fish off the English and French coast. When Cane sent his Fisheries Minister to meet them two weeks earlier, they had dumped three tons of rotting tuna fish over the minister's Rover.

Three weeks earlier, they would have been able to sell the fish, but the EU had cut their quota. They had carried on catching their old quota. The way they delivered it to the Fisheries Minister led to thirteen arrests. One of them was Neville Penhaligon, unofficial leader of Cornish fishermen.

Penhaligon spent a night in jail before being freed by local magistrates and was carried shoulder high through the streets of Newlyn before his mates threw him into the harbour in defiant celebration.

But three weeks after the rotting fish episode, Cane scented a more pleasant smell when he stood on a lobster pot in the car park of the Fisherman's Arms by the quay in Newlyn: the whiff of victory. He announced two new ships were to be added immediately to the Royal Navy Fisheries Protection Fleet patrolling the Cornish coast to keep the Spanish at bay. Penhaligon and his men had been calling for extra Naval protection for nearly a year.

'They have my full authority to take whatever action is necessary to protect our waters, our boats and our fish stocks from this modern armada,' he declared in front of the 1,100 people crammed into the car park.

'And if you don't believe me, look out to sea and you will see two grey pinpricks on the horizon. They are HMS Gallant and HMS Perseus, the two new ships.'

Cane pointed. The crowd of fishermen followed the direction of his arm and gasped in astonishment, then cheered when the warships came into view, their arrival timed to perfection. Charlie's hours of preparation – and threats – to the notoriously incompetent MoD officials – had paid off.

'Sink the Spanish bastards!' shouted Penhaligon. He'd have carried Cane through the streets of Newlyn on his own two ox-like shoulders if he'd had the chance.

But Cane was off. He and Charlie spent the flight to RAF Northolt in North London, and the thirty minute drive in his Jaguar to Westminster on the M40, discussing what might come up in Prime Minister's questions.

Government backbenchers among the MPs who had come in the first seven or eight places in the weekly backbenchers' ballot had been briefed by the whips to raise the crackdown on Spanish trawlers, new figures showing an upturn in the economy or a poll showing that, for the first time, a majority of voters wanted to join the euro. When they landed at Northolt, they phoned Silverman.

'We've got a problem on the Big Wheel bomb,' Silverman told Charlie, as she walked across the runway, a few feet away from Cane.

'What is it?' she asked.

'You'd better prepare Steven for a shock.'

'What is it?'

'The police think one of the bombers was Fallon.'

'Fallon?' said Charlie. 'Mary Fallon?'

'Yes, Mary Fallon.'

'It's running on the news. Bathurst will go for the jugular.'

* * *

Being leader of Her Majesty's Opposition at the lowest point in the party's history was not an easy task. Taking on a governing party at the strongest point in its history didn't make it any easier. The fact that the Government was led by one of the most charismatic British leaders in modern times made the job still harder. And even Madeleine Bathurst's most steadfast friends and admirers would not claim she was charismatic. Her parents had no way of knowing she would marry a man called Bathurst and end up in the public eye as a leading right-wing politician. Otherwise they would not have chosen a Christian name, which, together with her surname, could be shortened to 'Mad Bat' – as it was by *The Globe* the first time she did something controversial. And calling for women prisoners to be sterilised to prevent them having more children was controversial.

At 51, Bathurst was four years older than Cane, but she looked more like a dotty aunt. She was nearly twelve inches shorter and her waistline six inches thicker. Side by side on formal occasions like the State Opening of Parliament or at the Cenotaph, they looked like the Odd Couple; and there was no doubt who was the odd one. She looked a lot less eccentric along-side her husband; but sixty eight year old, rake thin, wispy-haired zoologist, Professor Arnold Bathurst wasn't exactly Mr Normal. Asked why they had no children, she once replied, 'He's more interested in chasing elephants round the jungle than chasing me round the bedroom!'

She had 'bottom' – in every sense of the word – and her feisty Commons performances meant Cane had to be on his toes in their week-ly confrontations across the despatch box.

Bathurst was relishing today's contest.

Scotland Yard had issued a picture of the woman they suspected was involved in the Wheel attack: Mary Fallon. They named her after inter-viewing all 832 visitors and staff at the Wheel on the day of the explosion. More than a dozen said they saw a young couple acting suspiciously on the towpath. But it was two children who provided the breakthrough. When the police arrived at the home of the Joshis two weeks after the bomb, it was only a day after they had brought Maya home. Her face was still bandaged and bruised, but she was improving by the day and the doctors were confident the scars on her face would heal in a year or so. When the police told the Joshis that a man, whose name was unknown, and a woman thought to be called Mary Fallon, had been seen near a burger van, Mr Joshi said to Maya and her brother Aniel, 'The woman who did the trick with you and the clown, she was with a man, they went over to the burger stall!'

They explained to the police how the woman had got roped into per-forming a trick. But Aniel said, 'No, dad, her name wasn't Eileen, it was Mary, that's what her boyfriend called her.'

'What d'you mean?' said the policemen.

'When she left us, the man who was with her said "come on Mary, we've got to go," or something; he definitely called her Mary. I thought it was funny because she told the clown her name was Eileen.'

'You beauty,' said the policeman. 'It's her, it's Mary Fallon, she must have lied about her first name and then her accomplice blurted it out when he called her away.'

He showed the family pictures of Fallon.

'That's her, that's her,' said Aniel, pointing to a picture of a woman with a thin face and short black hair. 'Yes,' said Maya, 'she's got the same green coat on.'

'Bloody Mary' had acquired her nickname from her role in the bomb blast that had killed fifteen people in the City of London ten years earlier. She was jailed for life but had got out.

It was how she had got out that provided Madeleine Bathurst with her big chance. And it was the way she had got out that prevented Cane eating the light lunch of ham sandwiches and tea he normally had before question time. Charlie fired every conceivable question at him and he fired back every conceivable answer. Not today. She had prepared all the questions and went through them with him, but he sat in silence. He looked ill. When Dora came in to collect their untouched meals, even she realised it was no time for caustic remarks. She picked them up and left. Charlie wanted to hold Cane's hand. She would have gladly faced the howling mob awaiting him herself. But she could do neither.

'Mrs Bathurst!' boomed Madam Speaker.

The Leader of the Opposition pulled herself up to the despatch box. Cane gulped hard.

'Is the Prime Minister proud of the fact,' said Bathurst, 'that he personally negotiated the agreement which led to the early release from prison three months ago of convicted terrorist Mary Fallon ... ?' Bathurst's MPs shouted 'oh, oh, oh!' in mock surprise, to highlight the damning revelation – even though it had been all over the lunchtime news. ' ... the same woman who is suspected of having blown up the London Eye?'

'Shame, shame, shame!' chanted Opposition MPs, like hyenas seizing on a carcass.

'Order!' bellowed Madam Speaker.

Cane replied, 'The police have named a number of people they want to interview in connection with this atrocity. I suggest we let them carry out their difficult task rather than try to find scapegoats for an evil crime.'

'It's your fault, your fault!'

Madam Speaker intervened again. 'I will not have this House reduced to a bear garden. Stop this disgraceful noise!'

Bathurst returned to the attack. 'Does the Prime Minister recall our exchange on November 11 last year, when, and I quote from Column 487 of Hansard, I said to him, "If the Right Honourable Gentleman carries on releasing dangerous terrorists on to the streets in an attempt to persuade the IRA to hand over more of its weapons, he will find that one day, one of these released terrorists will use some of the arsenal they have held on to, to carry out another terrorist attack?" Shall I spell it in simple terms for the Right Honourable Gentleman? He was warned this would happen – warned – warned by me. And it has. Now he should take responsibility for it!'

Every MP facing him seemed to be on their feet shouting abuse at Cane. They had waited a long time to see him humbled like this; they were going to make the most of it.

He steadied himself. 'Perhaps I should point out to the Leader of the Opposition that since the agreement we signed with all the major parties in Northern Ireland three years ago, this Government has made considerable progress on the path to peace. Perhaps she would like to pay tribute to that progress before leaping to condemn one small aspect of it.'

'Pathetic, pathetic, pathetic,' chanted the Opposition.

Madam Speaker screeched: 'If this appalling behaviour doesn't stop immediately I will suspend the sitting until you have all got control of yourselves!'

Bathurst moved in for the kill. 'The day after the bomb, the Right Honourable Gentleman was filmed visiting one of the victims, a young girl, Miss Maya Joshi, in hospital and said, "For Maya's sake, we will catch them." Well, I ask him now: Doesn't he think that for Maya's sake he shouldn't have released them?!'

She sat down to a deafening roar of approval from the benches behind her. 'Hear, hear, at-a-girl Maddie!' They waved their order papers in the air. At long last they had Cane on the ropes. Bathurst had drawn blood.

'TRAITOR CANE!' The cry could be heard even above all the sound and fury of 400 other MPs shouting at each other. Which was hardly surprising. Sir Quentin Poynter had the loudest views, the loudest ties and the loudest mouth in Parliament, especially after lunch, and displayed all three whenever the opportunity presented itself.

If he hadn't wanted his regular extreme observations to be heard by Madam Speaker, he wouldn't have sat three rows from the front or shouted at several hundred decibels. He normally got away with a telling off – but not this time. Calling another Honourable member a 'cad' or 'pipsqueak' was against the rules. 'Traitor' was off the Richter scale of permitted abuse. Madam Speaker ordered him to apologise.

Poynter straightened his shoulders and stood as ramrod straight as the Guards officer he used to be.

'With the greatest of respect to you Madam Speaker, I'm afraid I cannot apologise. The Prime Minister is a dangerous young whippersnapper who is playing with dark forces of which he has little or no knowledge. I most certainly do not apologise!'

With that, he let out a huge belch.

'Out, out, out!' shouted Cane's MPs. 'He's drunk, he's drunk!'

Madam Speaker had no choice. The Serjeant at Arms, ceremonial sword dangling at his side, escorted him, holding his elbow as much to stop him falling over as to guide him out of the chamber and out of the black carriage gates facing Parliament Square where Poynter was surrounded by a throng of newsmen.

Back in the chamber, it was a full minute before Madam Speaker regained control. Poynter's expulsion had only served to make his supporters even more angry. All Cane could see were their twisted contorted fat red faces, slavering lips, snarling teeth, shouting, scowling and screaming at him. It was bedlam – yet Cane couldn't hear a word. All he could see was a grotesque mime show.

When Madame Speaker called him to speak, he remained in his seat, hypnotised.

Again she called him, 'The Prime Minister!'

'Wake up Cane!'

If he'd had been a boxer, Madam Speaker would have stopped the fight.

She would need to if Charlie was his trainer, because she would never throw in the towel. Charlie cursed that, from her vantage point at the side gallery, slightly behind and to the right of The Speaker's chair, where officials had a ringside seat for question time, it was impossible to make eye contact with Cane.

'For God's sake Steven, get up, get up, get up!' she said, rising to her feet before a colleague dragged her down again.

He rose slowly and stood at the despatch box, staring in front of him. Charlie wasn't sure if he was waiting for the racket to subside. He couldn't have lost his nerve? It was impossible, surely. Forty five seconds passed; he stood, sat down, stood up again as Madam Speaker demanded quiet. Eventually, the hordes exhausted themselves.

Cane rose again and spoke quietly; he was almost inaudible. 'Perhaps the Right Honourable Lady might like to remember this,' he said, 'that in nineteen years under the last administration, thousands – yes thousands of people were killed in year after year after year of IRA outrages. Do I need to list them: Enniskillen, Brighton, Mountbatten, Warren Point, Warrington, Airey Neave, Canary Wharf, Ian Gow, Omagh. I could go on for an hour.' He leant forward, gradually turning up the volume. 'The last government tried to end the violence but it failed. Why did it fail? It failed because it lacked the guts, lacked the judgement and lacked the skill in making the decisions that this government has made.' Now Cane's supporters were on their feet shouting him on. 'Does the Right Honourable Lady know how many thousands of people died as a result of her government's failure? Yes, thousands. Does she want their names, because I can give them to her if she would like! We could come back here tomorrow and I could read out every single one!'

Cane was often accused of faking his emotions, playing to the gallery. But this was different.

He increased the pace and jabbed his finger in a sweeping movement along the front row of the Opposition. 'There they are, the people who failed the unemployed, failed the homeless, failed the health service, failed the young, failed the old and the failed the victims of terrorism!' Charlie had never heard him shout so loud. 'In the three and a half years we've have been in office, Northern Ireland – and the rest of Britain – has enjoyed the benefits of a virtual cessation in violence. For the most part, the killing has stopped; yes, there have been exceptions, yes, the London Eye bomb could have been much worse, but we will carry on doing what we have done successfully, and what the Right Honourable Lady's government failed miserably to achieve – to bring a lasting peace – and we will, I tell her again we will!' His backbenchers leapt to their feet, but Cane hadn't finished yet. He held up his arm regally – and they obediently subsided.

'To those who shout shame, I say to them the only shame is on them for trying to make political capital out of terrorism. And to the Right Honourable Lady, I say shame on you! I wish you well in the gutter of politics where you so clearly belong!'

With that, he sat down to tumultuous cheers from his MPs and was engulfed by colleagues thumping him on the back in congratulation at one of the most remarkable performances the Commons had witnessed in years.

Cane had set an elephant trap as big as any set by Professor Arnold Bathurst in the jungle; and his wife had fallen right into it. Cane had fooled her. He had fooled them all – including Charlie.

She had to restrain herself from leaping up and punching the air in triumph. Instead she sat with her hands in front of her mouth, in astonishment, in wonder and in awe.

She knew he was a consumate political performer, but she never dreamed he had the fire and passion to stir emotions. Including hers.

CHAPTER SEVEN

'I don't drink, but don't let me stop you,' *The Globe*'s owner, Warren McLintock, told his guest in the private dining room in The Savoy.

'Ribena is the strongest drink I've had in fifteen years,' replied Charlie.

'You're not another one of these ex-winos, are you? There's only two types of journalists: winos and ex-winos. Correction – there's two more these days: druggies and ex-druggies.'

'I wasn't, but my dad was.'

'He's dead?'

'Yes, drink killed him on January 23rd, 1986. I haven't touched it since.'

Billy Redpath's alcoholism was not unrelated to his politics. He had led a series of strikes at his yard and when he broke his back falling from a gantry, the owners refused to pay compensation, claiming he had been drinking. Billy denied the allegations and accused the owner, a Scottish hereditary peer, Lord Archie MacLeish, of using it to get revenge on him for his union activities.

When the family were left penniless, the drinking charge became self fulfilling. Billy was confined to a wheelchair, unable to work, ashamed of reducing his wife Mary and five children to living on handouts, and became an embittered alcoholic.

Charlie was twelve when the accident happened and had just won a place at St Anne's' Convent, Glasgow. She escaped her father's drunken rages by locking herself in her bedroom to do her homework while her four younger brothers went in the opposite direction. They were in and out of trouble as often as they were in and out of school. The succession of top of the form reports brought home by their big sister and held up to them as a shining example by her proud mother, didn't help. The oldest three turned away from school when they realised they could not match her.

Robbie was divorced and separated from his ex-wife and three children; Ewan worked in Germany as a brickie, and Gerry, a brilliant schoolboy footballer, never recovered after being taken on by Celtic, only to be dumped after one game in the reserves.

Billy junior, 24, was the youngest and just as clever as Charlie. He was her favourite; and she his.

As a young teenager he had been inspired by his sister's political views and she encouraged him to study so that he could follow her to university. When she first worked for Greaves she would return home once a month and check on his schoolwork and discuss politics and how to bring down the Government. But when she was in America and he was coming up to his GCSEs, his schoolwork declined dramatically. Without her to spur him on he lost his way and fell into the same bad company as his brothers. He left school without even sitting his exams, just like they had. By the time she returned to join Cane, it was much too late. Billy despised her political transformation and joined the Socialist Workers Party, partly to spite her.

And like Billy senior, Billy junior drank whisky.

Charlie couldn't look at it without recalling the day she came home from school to find her father slumped in his wheelchair in front of the television with a glass in one hand and a three-quarters empty bottle in the other. Billy Redpath did not appreciate being called a 'lousy drunk' by his teenage daughter. He hurled the bottle at her. It bounced off her brow as she tried to duck.

The scar just below her hairline was visible when she brushed her fringe back. The others were invisible. It didn't stop her drinking her fellow students under the common-room table for two and a half of her three years at Oxford. She revelled in the fiery, hardbitten, hard drinking left-wing reputation she soon acquired; and cultivated it. Her chances of passing her finals were being poured down the drain.

Just after noon, one Sunday in January, she was woken to be told by her mother that her father had died from liver failure. Charlie tried to hide it, but her mother knew she was still in bed, with a hangover.

It was just as well she couldn't see her room. It hadn't been cleaned for months and piles of washing were on the floor. The dustbin was overflowing with empty beer cans and wine bottles.

'Don't lie to me Charlotte, I can tell. Don't do it Charlotte, please, not you, it was different for him, he had nothing. You've got everything. I couldn't take it if you threw it all away. You think your father hated you, but he didn't. He loved you. I sometimes think he loved you more than he ever loved me. He couldn't show it. It wasn't his fault, it was just him – him and MacLeish. The shipyard destroyed him just as if they'd shot him. You were too young to understand, Charlotte. But don't go the same way as him. Please. Please. For his sake. For my sake.'

For the next six months Billy Redpath's daughter locked herself in her digs with her books, just as she had in her bedroom when she was a schoolgirl. This time she wasn't escaping from his drinking, but her own. The effect was the same. She passed her exams; a first class degree in politics, philosophy and economics.

It wasn't completely true that she hadn't touched alcohol since that night. There was one occasion, but she wasn't going to give McLintock the pleasure of hearing her tell him that *The Globe* had driven her to it; and driven her out of the country by destroying her party and handing victory on a front page platter to her enemies.

'How's the soaraway Globe?' she said cheerily.

'Great. We've just gone two million ahead of The Mirror – if I chucked the politics out of the paper and put more girls in we'd get another million!'

'Why don't you?'

'Because politics is more important to me than sex, but sex is more important to the readers.'

Anyone who read *The Globe* – and the vast majority of those who didn't – might think its owner was a lout. But while McLintock's readers were watching Coronation Street, he was more likely to be at the Opera watching his second wife, Canadian soprano Lydia, perform.

Nor did he look like a tabloid media mogul. He was no crimson-cheeked fat cat, but a lean, hungry white wolf. His cheeks curved so far inwards they could meet in the middle if he sucked in hard. His eyelids drooped down forming a tent shape over his brown eyes and his dark blue lips looked cold enough to turn water to ice. He expected people to come to the point quickly and, uncharacteristically, Charlie hadn't – so far.

'Is that why you've devoted so much space to your campaign to tell people to vote No to the euro?' she asked.

'Let's not beat about the bush,' said McLintock. 'The EU stinks, the euro stinks, Brussels stinks. *The Globe*'s readers think that and by a happy coincidence, I think that. Cane can talk all he likes about changing the EU and making it more like America. It's all crap and you know it. The French, the Germans, the Italians, the Spanish; they're all socialists. Once we get dragged into a European state they'll strangle me. Why? Because they hate mavericks. Oh, they like their big corporate multi-nationals, but one-offs like me? They'd love to screw me. I'm surprised Cane can't see it. One thing's for sure about Cane. He ain't no socialist. He could be running any party. That's why I backed him at the last election! But you knew all that. So why the lunch today? You're paying – and looking at this menu here it'd probably cost the taxpayer £100 if we asked for a ham sandwich. *The Globe*'s had politicians sacked for wasting less than that. The bottom line please Miss Redpath.'

It wasn't often that Charlie dealt with someone more direct than she was.

'Don't you think your campaign on the euro is slightly over the top?'

'Ah? Is that it?' McLintock cut in. 'You want me to drop it. I thought as much. If that's all you wanted, save your money, the answer's no.' His jaw snapped shut like a Venus flytrap.

McLintock pushed his knife and fork together and wiped his mouth with his napkin, making as if to leave. Charlie put her hand on his arm. 'I'm not asking you to do anything, Warren.'

He sat down again.

'But I'm puzzled,' she said. 'There's only four weeks to go to the referendum and the polls show a Yes vote is likely. Aren't you going to look daft if you back the wrong side? I thought you backed winners.'

'If you were sure of that, you wouldn't be here. *The Globe*'s got a few more surprises left Miss Redpath. It ain't over till it's over.'

It was true that the polls were showing a small lead for the Yes campaign. When the Government first signalled it planned to join the single currency, the idea was massively unpopular. But despite an uncertain start by the euro, people gradually came to think of it as inevitable that the UK would join. Fear of being left out grew; and the anti-camp were not helped by the fact that some of their leading supporters were geriatric or eccentric – or both.

But it wasn't in the bag and 'a few more surprises' from *The Globe* could do to Cane's party what it had done in the not so distant past – defeat it.

'We have a duty to tell people the truth,' said McLintock. 'Look at the so-called quality press and look at the BBC – they're so biased they might as well change their name to the Brussels Broadcasting Corporation and read out the Nine O'Clock News in French.'

Charlie was glad he had raised the BBC; it was McLintock's hobby horse as well as hers. *The Globe* had printed a blistering attack on Cane for not opposing the appointment of well known pro-EU fanatic, millionaire entrepreneur Tim Price as its new Director General.

'Price is only pumping out this euro propaganda on the Beeb because he thinks it'll save it from privatisation,' he said. 'I don't know why they bother, Cane hasn't got the balls to do it; he'd be frightened of what his friends would say the next time he goes to dinner in Islington.'

'You're wrong Warren.'

'About what?'

'About changing the BBC.'

McLintock put down his glass of sparkling mineral water.

'What changes might they be?' he asked, taking the bait.

'Well, we'd never change the licence fee or interfere with BBC TV, but there's a case for getting rid of Radios One and Two; it's hard to see what they contribute to the BBC's public service duties.'

McLintock pushed away his half-eaten, blue sirloin steak. A different appetite had been whetted.

Charlie added, 'And I seem to recall you were keen to move from satellite TV into national radio, but couldn't find the airwaves because of the BBC's dominance.'

'Radio One and Radio Two, eh? Interesting – but limited.'

'But the BBC World Service isn't limited is it, Warren?' said Charlie, tossing her ace across the table like a poker player. 'No limit to its audience and no limit to its prestige, either?'

His eyes glistened as she stressed the word prestige. The BBC World Service? At a stroke, it would give him a worldwide radio station to go with his worldwide TV station – and crucially, one with an unrivalled reputation, something no amount of McLintock's wheeler dealering could buy.

And it would achieve something else he wanted even more desperately: the humiliation of Price.

'Of course, if we did make them sell it, whoever bought it would have to give certain guarantees ... ' said Charlie, ' ... and it'd be a little way down the road.'

'But if I support you on the euro you might ... in the future?'

Charlie tilted her head as McLintock scrutinised her for a response.

'Like how far in the future?'

'We won't be doing anything for at least six months ... after the referendum.'

'Quarantine eh? Clever, Miss Redpath, very clever indeed.'

* * *

Lomax had joined Soho House within a month of arriving in London. It was one of the new London clubs set up in the early Nineties for the new generation of professionals who regarded the traditional gentleman's clubs as rest homes for old – and young – fogies.

It was at Soho House that a political adviser to another minister told him that the Chancellor was looking for an assistant. Now he was earning £55,550 a year, and had an expense account, he was able to dine at Soho House as often as he liked. Political advisers were paid whatever they had been earning in their previous posts, so his salary should have been £35,550, his pay before joining Silverman. But he had added on £20,000 when he was asked what he had been earning – and Silverman either failed to check it or turned a blind eye. Lomax often went to the club for a drink before going home to the flat he shared in Brixton.

He was there today for lunch with an old college friend, Marcus Williams, an accountant with a City firm. Williams was twenty five, the same age as Lomax and had moved to London straight from Durham. With Williams' help, Lomax got to know all the Soho House regulars and was invited to parties most weekends. At Durham, the pair were known for pranks such as stealing the vice principal's Austin Healey and driving it to London and back without him noticing. They caught out a Cabinet Minister when Williams phoned his home, pretended to be an angry constituent, recorded the minister's four letter reply and played it on Lomax's show on the university radio station. It made the front pages of three national papers.

And Williams would bet on anything – as long as the odds were rigged.

When he and Lomax organised the rag week, they recruited five attractive female student helpers. Lomax bet Williams £250 he wouldn't sleep with all of them before the week was out. Lomax won the bet: Williams slept with four but the fifth was one of Lomax's gay friends in drag. When Williams took him to bed and the male revealed himself, Lomax rushed in, caught it all on video and showed the film in the students' union bar.

'What's it like working for a real live Cabinet Minister, Joe?' said Williams, as they ordered more champagne.

'Brilliant, brilliant,' said Lomax, 'the great thing is that Ronnie ... '

'It's Ronnie already is it, not Mr Silverman sir? What do you call the Prime Minister? Stevie baby?'

'Fuck off.'

Lomax explained that the job entailed organising Silverman's diary, helping with speeches, dealing with lobby journalists, talking to all the other special advisers to make sure they were all 'on message'.

'Are he and Cane as close as they're made out to be?'

Lomax knew before taking the job that Cane and Silverman were close. But he was shocked when he discovered just how close. They spoke three, maybe four times on the phone every day. The previous week when Cane had been in Cornwall meeting the fishermen and gave a television interview at lunchtime, Lomax was watching in Silverman's office while waiting for Silverman to return from the Permanent Secretary's office. Silverman's phone was lying on the desk. When it rang, Lomax picked it up and found himself talking to the Prime Minister.

'The interview had only ended twenty seconds earlier and Cane phoned him up straightaway wanting to know how well he'd done,' said Lomax. 'It happens all the time; the three of them, Cane, Ronnie and Charlie Redpath, the PM's press secretary, they're never off the phone to each other. The three of them are running the country, largely via Cellnet, from what I can see.'

'Do they really have documents with TOP SECRET in red ink, you know, printed in blotchy capital letters at an angle?'

'Yes, but that's only for the big stuff, like spies and wars. There's a whole series of gradings for them. I've seen several ones marked "confidential".'

'What sort of stuff do they have in them?'

'Most of it's pretty obscure, really. We get some interesting bits from the DTI, takeovers, commercially sensitive stuff, you know, which firm is going to win the contract for a sprockets and grommets order and get an export credit guarantee.'

'Really?'

'Yeah, there was one I saw yesterday, something to do with the decision on whether to help a defence firm with a huge defence order from the Middle East.'

'Remember the name?'

'Not sure, Johnson and something.'

'Johnson and what?'

' ... and Griffiths, I think, Johnson and Griffiths Aviation, no ... Avionics.'

'When's that due to be announced?'

'Soon, I think.' Lomax put his bubbly down. 'Now don't go getting any clever ideas Marc,' said Lomax forcefully. 'I don't want to blot my copy-book. If I impress Ronnie, he's got the clout to get me a seat, not this election, but maybe the next one.'

'You reckon?'

'I don't see why not. Listen, I've met some of the dickheads who got in last time and some of the deadbeats who have been there for donkey's years; and I tell you, I know I'm good enough. But I'll have to work my balls off for Ronnie ... '

' ... shouldn't be a problem for you, Joe.'

'Fuck off Marc. Seriously, I wouldn't want to cross him.' Lomax shook his head. 'You should have seen the bollocking he gave one of the junior ministers the other day – right in front of me!'

'Probably gets his kicks that way. Which one?'

'No way.'

'My, we have gone straight, haven't we?'

'Yes, we have.'

'Not too straight, though, I trust. They call Silverman "Ronnie rent boy" here. Has he made a pass at you yet?'

'Fuck off.' Lomax looked at the clock. 'Christ! I'm five minutes late already! I said I'd be there at nine.'

'Where?'

'I said I'd meet Ronnie to go over a speech he's doing tomorrow.'

Lomax knocked back the dregs of his champagne, picked up his document holder, and dashed towards the stairs.

Luckily he had spent an hour over lunch reading the forty page briefing on 'Europe and UK – economic trends' provided by the Treasury's research office. Lomax could remember it almost word for word. It was the same memory as had enabled him to get three grade 'A' A levels at his comprehensive in spite of being suspended for a month for leading a sixth form strike after the headmaster sacked a teacher who had come out as homosexual in the school magazine edited by Lomax.

The torrential downpour meant it was ten minutes before he hailed a cab outside Soho House. By the time he reached his destination he was forty five minutes late – and drenched. He ran to the front door of the three storey terraced Victorian house in Alfreton Street, Kensington and pressed the buzzer.

The door opened.

'Hi, I'm sorry, really sorry I'm late,' gabbled Lomax, 'I've got no excuse, I was with an old college mate ... '

'Goodness gracious, Joe,' said Silverman languidly, 'did you swim down the Thames to get here? Aren't we paying you enough to buy a raincoat?' Silverman had a flat over Downing Street, but rarely used it. His Kensington home provided more privacy.

It was the first time Joe had been there. Silverman was so formal, conservative even, that it was hard to imagine him in anything other than a charcoal suit, white shirt, briefcase in hand or sat behind a desk. It was odd to see him in an informal setting. He was wearing stonewash blue jeans with a red velour open-neck shirt and a beautiful grey cardigan with a coloured Peruvian pattern along the edges where the buttons were left undone; a gift from his ex-wife Maria. There were no other signs of their marriage in the house.

He had brown leather moccasins on his feet, but no socks. He looked more like a wealthy gay businessman in downtown San Francisco than a Cabinet Minister.

'Where've you been?' asked Silverman. 'Soho House, by any chance?'

'Er, yes, I suddenly realised the time. Christ I am sorry Ronnie.'

'For goodness sake, relax Joe, you're not working for a Victorian mill owner you know.'

'No, but I said I'd be here at nine and I wasn't.'

'Joe, if you want to torture yourself, please do it in the privacy of your own home, not here; I have more important things to worry about than your overdeveloped sense of remorse.'

Silverman took a step back and cast his eyes up and down Joe's dripping frame. 'Let's have a look at you.' His jacket, trousers and shoes and socks were soaked.

'We can't have a Cabinet Minister being briefed by a drowned rat; I'd be breaking health and safety regulations.' He marched off to his bedroom and came back with a sweatshirt and tracksuit bottoms, handed them to Lomax and pointed him to the bathroom.

'There's a clean towel in there for you, the yellow one.'

When Lomax returned, dressed in Silverman's clothes, the Chancellor surveyed him closely, lingering over his V-neck sweater with no shirt underneath; and handed him one of two large whiskies poured out on the cocktail cabinet. 'That'll keep the pneumonia at bay. Now let's get cracking.'

Silverman had called him to his house to help prepare a speech to a pro-euro rally at Wembley arena the following day.

'Let's sit on the settee, Joe, and show me these figures you were going to dig out for me. As long as you have got those right, I'll ignore the fact the fact that you look like a beatnik rather than a Cabinet Minister's adviser.'

The two went through the speech, with Lomax inserting the relevant figures to illustrate the points Silverman wanted to make. Fifty five minutes, and two more whiskys later, they had finished. Silverman turned to Lomax and said, 'Do you know Joe, you really are a remarkable young man?'

'Am I?'

'I used to have to give that sort of briefing to union leaders when I was your age and do you know it took me three times as long and I didn't do it half as well as you just have.'

'It's amazing how hard you try when you think you might lose your job for being late,' said Lomax.

'No Joe,' said Silverman, putting his left hand on the young man's shoulder, on the grey sweatshirt he had given him. He halted, excited by the sight of Lomax wearing his clothes. Clothes that had touched his skin, now touching the boy's skin.

'No Joe, you do it that well every time. Every speech I have done since you joined me has got good reviews. I hope we're going to be together for a long time.'

'So do I,' said Lomax, putting his left hand on top of Silverman's hand on his shoulder. Lomax moved fractionally closer. Through the sweater, he could feel Silverman's fingers gently begin to squeeze him, moving along to the nape of his neck.

Lomax extended his hand gradually along Silverman's arm, tilted his face and kissed him on the lips.

Silverman did not resist and leaned back, pulling Lomax on top of him.

The Chancellor of the Exchequer's government limousine arrived to pick him up to take him to Wembley at nine am the following morning. Silverman got in alone.

Lomax had left half an hour earlier.

CHAPTER EIGHT

'Smile a lot, stand up first, clap first and say absolutely nothing,' Lucy said to the tall woman with long chestnut hair sitting next to her.

If beauty and blandness were the qualities needed to be a successful political wife, Sandy Laidlaw fitted the bill.

Lucy thought how much better equipped Sandy was for the role than she was. At thirty one, she had the slim long-legged figure that was flattered by the camera from every angle. And Sandy knew which angles suited her best; it was the first thing she learned when she was a model before launching a public relations agency with a girlfriend who had good contacts in the party.

They spotted the market for advising companies who had ignored the party for twenty years, but were desperate to forge links with it now it was ready and willing to do business with them – and was in power. Business had thought of the party's women members as boiler-suited Greenham Common peace wimmin. Elegant Sandy was at finishing school when cruise missiles were being trundled into Greenham Common.

'I beg your pardon,' she said.

'I met Denis Thatcher at a dinner at the Palace a couple of years ago,' said Lucy, 'and that was his advice to me on how to behave in public as spouse of a Prime Minister!'

The two women were sitting on the platform at a pro-euro rally at Wembley Arena called by Cane to boost support for the Yes To The Euro campaign.

'How are you and Gareth getting on?' asked Lucy.

'Fine, really fine, he's a lovely man.'

'I didn't know you were going out until yesterday when Steven said you'd be here. It's amazing you've kept it so secret. Didn't anybody know?'

'They still don't, not a soul. We've been going out together for several months, only ... well you know what he's like ... he told me to keep quiet about it. He suddenly said to me last night, why didn't I 'come out' – so to speak – today.'

'I hope you know what you're letting yourself in for.'

The two women became aware of activity at the side of the stage. Cane was about to appear. The audience stood up and cheered, waving 'YES' flags as he walked centre stage, with loud music reverberating around the arena.

Lucy remembered the last time she and Cane were at the Arena; it was for a Bruce Springsteen concert, the year before Sam was born. The two of them had gone with friends and danced in the aisles to 'Born In The USA' and 'Dancing In The Dark'. After that they all went out for a curry and then on to Ronnie Scott's in London and she and Cane had tumbled into bed at three o'clock in the morning. She was convinced that was the night that Sam was conceived. They used to joke about it when they went out for a curry or a Chinese. When had they last done that? When had they last done anything together?

'It's not easy you know,' said Lucy, 'being in love with a politician.'

'A life of being squeezed between the euro and the GDP,' laughed Sandy.

'Now, there's another useful tip,' said Lucy conspiratorially, leaning towards Sandy and pointing at a woman standing at the side of the stage. 'If I want to know where Steven is, it's usually quicker to work out where she is.'

'Do you know her well?' asked Sandy, following Lucy's eyes to Charlie.

'We get on,' said Lucy, before adding, 'after a fashion. You know she worked for Gareth before joining Steven, don't you?'

'No I didn't. Gareth didn't mention it.'

'Oh,' said Lucy embarrassed, ' ... it was years ago.'

'I've read a lot about her. What's she like?'

'I've never been able to make her out really. She gets on much better with men than with women, but she doesn't seem to have any boyfriends. Apparently there was a bloke in America, but I don't know what happened to him.'

'She's supposed to be very clever and very ... ' said Sandy, searching for the right word.

'Hard?' said Lucy.

'Well ... '

'Don't feel shy. I've heard a lot worse. Steven says she had a tough family life, they still cause her problems, apparently. All I can say is it must have been very tough indeed. You should see her temper. There's a lot of anger in her.'

She hated Charlie's smoking, the trail of cigarette butts and overflowing ashtrays and, more than anything, hated the smell of smoke in Steven's hair and clothes when he finally came to bed with her.

Standing at the side of the platform, Charlie could feel the two pairs of eyes on her and took a long drag on her Marlboro.

'That's her up there,' said Silverman, alongside her.

'I've seen her. I think it's rather more important that I read this, don't you?' she snapped.

Silverman had wondered how Charlie would react to the first public appearance of Greaves' new girlfriend. Charlie was checking a copy of one of the speeches due to be made at the rally. Cane was first up. There was no need to check his: Charlie had written it.

It was the following speech that she was scanning. It had been written by and would be delivered by Greaves. He was the only minister who refused to send his speeches to her office in advance. She had tried and failed to persuade Cane to force him to do so, but he had refused.

She was trying to concentrate on the speech but each time she looked at it, the words were obscured by another image in her mind. It was of a girl on a horse, her hair flowing behind her as she jumped over a fence. That was it. It was the magazine open on Greaves' desk. The girl was Sandy.

Charlie struggled to concentrate on the words in front of her. She read each sentence twice, but she couldn't see anything in it to cause any controversy.

Despite their row in his office over loyalty, he had done exactly as she had asked in the run-up to euro vote. It would have been suicidal to do otherwise. He had been responsible for urging Cane to hold the euro vote as soon as possible and if he caused a Cabinet split over tax in the run-up to the referendum, the whole campaign could collapse; and it would be his fault. He wasn't going to fall for that one.

'Nothing in there to worry about,' Charlie said to Silverman.

Cane won a standing ovation for his speech and then invited the audience to give another ovation to 'the best Deputy Prime Minister in history.'

'Ladies and gentlemen, friends ... ' Greaves began.

'Seems only yesterday he was calling everyone comrade,' Charlie muttered to Silverman.

'It is with great honour,' said Greaves, 'that I open this rally which we hope will prove beyond any shadow of doubt that on May 3rd this country is going to vote for the euro and a bright future for Britain ... '

Lucy leaned across to Sandy. 'I'm so pleased Gareth agreed to launch the rally. It means so much to Steven to have his support.'

'Gareth was thrilled that Steven agreed to bring the vote forward,' said Sandy.

' ... it is not just a vote for Britain, it is vote for tomorrow not yesterday, there's no future for this nation sulking and whingeing on the fringes ... '

'He's a fine one to talk about sulking and whingeing...' grunted Charlie.

' ... a vote for the euro is also a vote for leadership, the leadership of this party.' The audience took his cue to give Cane a standing ovation.

'Notice he can't actually bring himself to say "the leadership of this man Steven Cane".'

'Careful Charlie, there's a lot of long-range mikes around here,' said Silverman.

' ... anyone who is still in any doubt as to which way they should vote on May 3rd has to do only one thing: look at us,' said Greaves, 'and to look at the leader of the Opposition, Mrs Madeleine Bathurst. You'd be MAD to vote NO!' The crowd cheered.

'See, he did it again,' said Charlie.

Sandy leapt to her feet.

'Look at the silly cow! Give her a pair of pom poms,' sneered Charlie.

'We'd better get used to Ms Laidlaw,' said Silverman, 'and don't be surprised if he's got her lined up to be Mrs Greaves.'

'I doubt it,' said Charlie.

'What makes you say that?'

'I doubt it, that's all, I just doubt it.'

'You know how ambitious he is – and if he wants to walk into Number
10 when Cane walks out of it, he'll have to walk down the aisle first,' said
Silverman.

Charlie didn't see his smirk, or the way his eyes strained sideways
towards her without moving his head.

'Gareth Greaves will never do either of those things,' she replied, staring at Sandy, who was still cheering and applauding.

'Oh?' said Silverman.

'I don't know her, but I know him.'

* * *

'It went so well darling, and Gareth's speech was marvellous,' Lucy said to
Cane on their return from the rally, as they closed behind them the mag-
nolia door of their flat, marked 'PRIVATE' in black lettering on a silver
plate.

It should offer a reasonable degree of privacy, situated as it was, on the
top floor of the most heavily guarded residence in the land. In fact there
was a never ending stream of visitors, officials, aides, secretaries and others,
some of whom pressed the buzzer to the side of the door, some of whom
didn't bother and marched straight in. To Lucy, it felt about as private as
Trafalgar Square.

'Thanks, darling. Even the press'll have a job turning that into a split,' said Cane.

They walked up the half dozen steps and through a set of double doors into a towering galleried lobby that took up two tiers of the building. Visitors were always amazed by the size of the 'flat' hidden at the top of Downing Street. They passed the baby grand they constantly tried – and usually failed – to persuade the children to practise on, beneath the gold chandelier and up the sweeping staircase, along the corridor and into the kitchen.

Lucy hated the peeling cork-tiled floor and tatty pine units. She had wanted a completely new fitted kitchen and new carpet to replace the threadbare ones throughout the flat, but had been over-ruled after someone, she never found out who, leaked the request within weeks of them moving in, provoking hostile 'Who Does Madam Cane Think She Is?' headlines in the papers. Though small and scruffy, the kitchen had one great virtue. Few people realised that, when they faced the door of Number 10, the PM's flat extended left not just over the door of Number 11, but over the Chief Whip's office at Number 12 too. The Canes' kitchen was in fact side on to Number 10, some forty feet away, giving both it and the lounge below spectacular views of the entire length of Downing Street including the Big Wheel perched behind the Ministry of Defence. Jessica had called it the 'giant's bicycle' and made fairy stories up about it cycling round the world. But that was before it was blown up. Seeing the twisted white spokes, still under repair after the bomb, every single day from their home was a chilling reminder of how vulnerable they were.

Cane draped his jacket over one of the chairs around the pine table.

'I must say, the turnout was fantastic,' he said as she put the kettle on. 'Did you see how many young people were there? Compare that with the weirdos who turned up for the NO bash in Birmingham last week. Ours'll look so much better on TV.'

'Well done, darling,' said Lucy. 'I'm so glad. I think Sandy enjoyed her first outing.'

'Yes, I'm glad,' said Cane disinterestedly. 'She seems nice enough.'

It was as far as any of their conversations on politics went these days.

Before she met Cane, Lucy's only contact with politics had been through the Young Conservatives. Her father Sir Norman Hawthorne, a big man with bushy eyebrows and an owl-like face, was a leading mason. Uckfield Ladies College, where Lucy boarded from the age of eleven to eighteen, had produced quite a few socialites in its 175 year history, but few socialists. Girls were sent there not to be socialists.

Lucy got eight O-levels and was expected to do well enough in her Art, History and English 'A' levels to get to university. But it all went wrong in her last year. Her parents blamed it on missing three weeks of the last term after an attack of nerves. Her C in Art, grade E in History and failure in English meant she could not take up the place she had been offered at Kent to study English. She decided to teach special needs children and scraped into teachers training college, after Sir Norman had a word with the chairman of the local education authority.

It was through a dance organised by her father at St Bernard's hospital, Hackney, where he was a surgeon, that she met a young doctor fresh out of medical school.

'Come and meet one of my pupils,' said Sir Norman. 'He's just your type; tall, dark and handsome and doesn't drink himself silly every night.'

The young doctor was twenty five, she was twenty two. They danced, had dinner a week later, were engaged in eighteen months and, two years later, at St Peter's church Guildford, she said, 'I, Lucy Anne Hawthorne take Steven Romano Cane to be my lawful wedded husband.'

All sixteen children from Lucy's class at Amberton Special School in Bromley, Kent, attended the wedding. Cane adored her; she was bright, pretty and devoted to her schoolwork. She adored Cane; he was clever, witty and didn't share the arrogant streak she despised in so many of the other young medics had father had introduced her to. They were always bragging about their exploits with birds and bars, and were obsessed with testosterone and Testarossas. Most showed little interest in healing the sick. They were more interested in getting drunk and being sick.

Not that Cane was dull. He picked her up one Friday afternoon, told her to get her passport and whisked her off to New York for the weekend to see Elton John at Madison Square Garden. But he was less wild and more wholesome than some of the self-centred medics Lucy had met. He wasn't one of those junior doctors who talked about the patients as though they were members of some kind of underclass.

She looked forward to the same lifestyle her mother had enjoyed; a four-bedroomed detached house in the Home Counties with a paddock, two children at prep school and holidays in the Dordogne.

Which is probably what she would have had, had it not been for what happened one Sunday lunch with her parents. They had gone to celebrate Lucy's father's sixtieth birthday. Cane knew of Sir Norman's political contacts and after three glasses of Sir Norman's favourite Barolo red wine, mentioned rumours at St Bernard's that it might be affected by a new round of cuts. Sir Norman said, 'I can't say too much Steven, but I think there's probably something in them.'

Cane became agitated and pressed his father-in-law.

'Look, Steven,' said Sir Norman, 'dear old Bernard's is ancient and creaking and spread over umpteen sites. It makes sense to rationalise services and to use more modern facilities at other hospitals in the area.'

'Rationalise?' said Cane. 'Isn't that politicians' speak for cutting costs?' The dispute rapidly became heated as Cane accused Sir Norman of 'putting his party before his patients.' Sir Norman exploded when Cane brought up his friendship with Health Secretary Sir Henry Bowler and referred to 'knights of the shires sticking together.' Sir Norman told Cane to leave and Lucy cried most of the journey home to their semi in Blackheath.

The following day, Cane wrote to his father-in-law apologising, but explained he passionately believed the hospital must stay open to continue serving local people, some of the poorest in the country. It was not his first flirtation with politics. Cane's mother Carla, a nurse, took part in the CND Aldermaston marches in the 1960s. Her father had been a prominent Italian communist who came to Britain to flee Mussolini.

It was his mother's love of her homeland that made her give her son the middle name of Romano – her grandfather's name – and it was her love of

Europe that she passed on to Cane that inspired him to win the debating prize as a fifth former at Weston Boys. The motion was, 'This House believes Britain's future lies in Europe.' Cane argued for the motion – and won over a sceptical audience. It was good experience for his later life.

At Oxford, he considered politics as a career, but there were too many extremists, and there was nothing extreme about Cane. He was pelted with eggs at a students union meeting when he said that although he abhorred Enoch Powell's views, he defended his right to address students at the college.

So he channelled his energies into his studies and playing football. The nearest he got to politics was to help set up a rape advice centre for women students. His father, Douglas, a successful barrister, wanted him to join his law practice. It had been Cane's ambition too, but he abandoned it the day his father left his mother for a young female barrister colleague when Cane was seventeen. Instead, he followed his mother into medicine. He figured it was more rewarding than politics; but there was another reason: it would make his mother happy. She had worked in the NHS for thirty three years and believed in it passionately,

And that would have been that, had it not been for the plan to close St Bernard's. Cane had formed a close attachment to the hospital and the East End in the two years he had trained there. He was shocked by the health and living conditions. They didn't live like that in the part of the world he was brought up in.

The plan to close St Bernard's was the spark that re-ignited the fuse. Cane was surprised by how outraged he felt, as was Lucy. It was a side of him she had never seen. First her husband and father had fallen out over the dinner table; now Cane was writing letters to all and sundry about the closure and was invited by the chairman of the local party to join an action group to save the hospital. When Health Secretary Bowler came to a public meeting in Hackney to defend the cuts, Cane took him on from the floor and tore him to shreds.

It led to a repeat performance on BBC 2's *Newsnight* when Cane humiliated him a second time; this time in front of millions of viewers. The

Weston Boys School fifth form debating champion had lost none of his touch; and the gutsy student who took on Oxford's lefties none of his nerve. This time the lefties – and the entire East End of London – were cheering him on.

He rediscovered he was a natural performer; and that he enjoyed performing. The young party chairman who invited Cane to join the action group was not so overjoyed. Cane had not set out to do so, but had effectively taken over the leadership of the campaign by sheer style and personality. Four weeks later, the Government was forced to back down, prompting the headline in the *London Evening Standard,* 'CANE MUTINY SAVES BERNIE'S.'

He was now a local celebrity and when, shortly before the 1983 election, the retiring West Ham MP stood down, Cane was flabbergasted – and flattered – to receive a last minute request to apply. It was another blow for the chairman. He had spent five years nursing the seat for himself, knowing the sitting MP was about to retire; and his selection had appeared a formality. But Cane's victory for St Bernard's swung it. He was picked to be Parliamentary candidate for West Ham at the forthcoming general election by 121 votes to 95.

The devastated chairman never fully recovered; and never forgave him.

He wasn't the only one who was shocked by Cane's meteoric success. As a teenage member of the Young Conservatives, Lucy used to imagine what it would be like to married to an MP. But the imaginary MP had a seat in cosy, picturesque Sussex, not too far from her old school and Mummy and Daddy, not the crime-ridden, poverty-stricken heart of London's East End.

She wasn't sure which part of his constituency frightened her more: the white part which still idolised the Kray brothers; or the Asian part that seemed more like Calcutta to her. Lucy liked watching *EastEnders*, but living in it was a different matter.

She reluctantly agreed to let Cane become an MP on condition that they carried on living in Blackheath, and that if he was still a backbencher in five years, with no prospect of earning a decent living from politics, he would go back to medicine.

'Don't worry, I'm sure I'll have a stethoscope round my neck again in five years,' he said to her cheerily.

He had lost count of the times she had reminded him of the remark since he became Prime Minister.

By most people's standards, the Prime Minister's salary of £154,187 was a decent living – though only a fraction of the indecent fortunes Cane's contemporaries at medical college were now earning from a three day week in Harley Street. Hard though Lucy had found it to adjust to life as the Prime Minister's wife, she had no regrets about marrying him. She was proud of him; his decency; his sincerity; his compassion; his hard work. They were qualities he brought not just to his role as Prime Minister, but to his role as father and a husband too. And they were qualities that had enabled them to repair relations with her parents.

'You've taken your party so far to the right that even an old Fascist like me can vote for you,' Sir Norman joked to his son-in-law.

It didn't mean Lucy found it easy; she found it as unnatural to be the Prime Minister's wife as Cane found it natural to be Prime Minister. Her shyness made it hard for her to adjust to her public role as 'First Lady' – and bringing up two young children in the glare of publicity was a night-mare. Jessica had sparked a mass police search across the entire south of England when she failed to turn up at the school gates to be collected by the chauffeur. It was feared she had been seized by terrorists. Cane was called back from a summit in Geneva; Lucy was hysterical. Three hours later Jessica was dropped off at the rear entrance of Downing Street by a coach. She had decided to go and watch a friend play in a school hockey match and had forgotten to tell anyone, including the headteacher.

Cane did his best to help her cope, but even now, as she congratulated him on his success at the euro rally, he suspected something was troubling her.

He cupped his hand under her chin as she returned to the bedroom from the bathroom.

'There's nothing wrong is there? I know this is a hectic period and we've hardly seen each other and it's not going to get any easier for a while. You seem to have been ... well, down for a month or so. I noticed it when you came back from seeing Aunt Mimi.'

'No, I'm fine. I was a bit upset when I saw Mimi, she's got one or two problems but there's nothing wrong with me. I suppose it just all seems too much sometimes, this goldfish bowl life. That's why I drove off the other day. I'm really sorry, I just snapped, I shouldn't have done it.'

'It's alright, I understand, it's forgotten.'

'I'm so cross with myself for doing it in front of Charlie.'

'Don't worry about that. She won't tell anyone.'

'That's not what I mean, I don't like her getting involved ... getting involved in our marriage.'

'Charlie saved us that night.'

'What do you mean?'

'There was a press photographer outside. He got pictures of you, the kids, me on the steps in a state, the lot. They would have been in the papers, but she ran after him and got the pictures.'

'She did it for your sake not mine.'

'That's unfair.'

'You're right, oh I'm so sorry.' She threw her arms round him.

'Lucy, calm down, calm down, everything is alright.'

They cuddled together in bed and Cane stroked his wife's forehead until her eyes closed.

She was calm, but he didn't believe everything was alright.

CHAPTER NINE

The wild behaviour at the Fisherman's Arms started just after midday when first reports of the clash between HMS Gallant and the Spanish trawler, 'Rosita', came through. Word soon got round the quay and they gathered at the pub to find out what had happened. Early reports said HMS Gallant had drawn alongside Rosita in a freak storm 120 miles off Lands End after the Spanish ship was suspected of trying to cut the nets of a British trawler from Falmouth. Rosita became entangled with the Gallant leaving the 'Rosita' badly damaged and listing to one side.

'Yeeeees!' roared Neville Penhaligon. 'We've got one of the bastards, we've taught one of 'em a lesson, now let's teach 'em all a lesson!' he shouted above the din. More than a hundred men echoed his war cry. They listened eagerly to the news on the TV above the bar.

'A Spanish trawler has sunk off the Cornish coast after colliding with the Royal Navy Fisheries Protection vessel, HMS Gallant. A full scale emergency operation has been launched to try and rescue the twenty five crew members. Seven have been picked up by HMS Gallant, but eighteen others are missing. Royal Navy helicopters have joined the search which is being hampered by 125 mph winds which have got significantly worse in the last hour, creating waves of up to sixty feet high. The sinking follows a series of clashes between the Navy and Spanish trawlers in recent weeks. Prime Minister Steven Cane sent more ships to patrol the area last month after the Spanish were accused of breaching EU rules on fishing limits.'

The word 'sunk' echoed round the bar of the Fisherman's Arms like the dull thud of a hull hitting the sea bed.

But Penhaligon wasn't thinking about Rosita. He was thinking about the

Penlee lifeboat that he knew would have been sent out to help in the rescue. He knew it would be in trouble with sixty foot waves and 125 mph winds.

In the hour that followed the two o'clock bulletin, Penhaligon didn't say a word. He sat on his bar stool, waiting for the next hourly bulletin.

'It is feared that twenty Spanish fishermen have died after their trawler was in collision with a Royal Navy Fisheries Protection boat. And in the last fifteen minutes it's been reported that the Penlee lifeboat, which was sent to help in the rescue operation, has capsized with the loss of the coxswain and one crew member.'

Penhaligon knew the coxswain. His name was Ben Penhaligon, his younger brother.

'Sink the Spanish bastards!'

Penhaligon remembered how he had shaken Cane's hand and told him, 'Do anything you can to stop them Mr Cane, sir, they're slowly killing us.' Now the killing was for real. And his brother had been killed.

* * *

Within ninety minutes of the tragedy, the Spanish ambassador had demanded to see Cane.

Within two hours, a mob had gathered outside the British embassy in Madrid and were throwing bricks. Within three, Charlie called Silverman, and Cane cancelled all his diary engagements.

'The Spanish are going berserk,' he said. 'What in hell's name are we going to say?'

'Let's get the facts first,' said Charlie. 'According to the Navy, Rosita was clearly in breach of the EU's fishing ruling.'

'It didn't give them the right to sink it, though, did it?' said Cane.

'We must stay calm,' said Silverman. 'The first thing to do is to announce an inquiry into how the sinking occurred. It could be that the Spanish provoked it. And you can't be blamed for a Navy blunder, if that's what it was.'

'Of course I'll be blamed!' said Cane. 'I sent the ships there, didn't I? If I hadn't done it wouldn't have been sunk! The lifeboat wouldn't have been sunk!'

'You - and the Queen - must send personal messages of sympathy to the people of Spain and to the families of the dead fishermen,' said Charlie. 'I'll write something out for the Queen to say; it'll save time. There's nothing else we can do at the moment. We'll have to see how it plays tomorrow. I'll get on to the press and make sure they know how the Spanish have been risking something like this for years.'

The situation escalated rapidly. The Spanish Prime Minister reopened the row over Gibraltar, ordering Spanish troops to surround it. And he threatened to invade unless Cane agreed to talks on a phased withdrawal and the eventual handover of the tiny colony.

At seven pm, the Spanish ambassador to London, Senor Pedro Migueras, walked solemnly into Cane's study. Wearing a black suit and black tie, he stood erect, exuding wounded Latin pride, breathing contempt for Cane from every inch of his tubby, five feet three inches frame as he looked down his flared nostrils.

Cane made a grovelling apology and told him he had ordered a full independent investigation. He offered to let the Spanish Government take part in the inquiry so that it was seen to be even handed, but said the Spanish had no right to use the incident to make threats against Gibraltar.

'Prime Minister,' Ambassador Migueras replied, 'thees was no accident. Twenty Spanish men and two Englishmen 'ave been killed as a result of a reckless attempt by you to show that you can defy the European Union. This 'ad nothing to do with fishing policy; it was a piece of electioneering to 'elp you with the referendum. The 'ole world knows that - and certainly the people of Spain know it. These men drowned because you wanted to win a few more votes. Your Navy sank Rosita just as if they 'ad fired an Exocet at 'er - it was an act of aggression and that is why we 'ave responded as we 'ave. Spain will meet British force with Spanish force. Britannia no longer rules the waves, Prime Minister, and very soon you will no longer rule Gibraltar. Good day senor!'

Migueras wasn't the only one who was ranting. *The Globe* urged Cane to 'do a Falklands' and send a task force to defend Gibraltar, and Madrid's popular press matched them by urging the Spanish Government to march into Gibraltar. But public opinion in Britain was more divided than it had been during the Falklands. The Guardian said the UK should have returned the colony to Spain years ago and published a fiercely critical editorial headlined, 'CANE: BETWEEN A ROCK AND A HARD PLACE.'

He ruled out sending a task force. It was impossible; tantamount to declaring war on another EU nation. Matters were taken out of his hands when the EU exercised its new powers over Europe's foreign policy, calling an emergency summit in Brussels where the sixteen leaders agreed to send the newly formed European Defence Force, made up of soldiers from every EU nation, to keep the peace in Gibraltar. No British or Spanish troops would be part of the force to ensure it remained neutral. At the same time, an EU team would be set up to recommend how it should be run in the future and would investigate a possible joint sovereignty deal. They had astutely copied the one Cane had recently proposed to Argentina for the Falklands, so he could hardly protest.

With the Gibraltar crisis contained, for the time being at least, he flew back from Brussels to London on Tuesday, knowing he had forty eight hours to solve one of equal magnitude.

He was due to give a press conference in Downing Street to announce that the general election was to be held in four weeks on May 3rd, the same day as the euro referendum.

It was the last day on which the necessary four weeks notice of an election could be given. Speculation had been rife in the press that Cane might pull the trigger for an election, which is exactly what he, Charlie and Silverman had been planning all along. The decision he and Charlie had to take when they met alone in his study was whether to go ahead with it as planned – or call it off. Cane argued anything could happen in Gibraltar, it would be a tremendous risk. It was impossible to delay the euro referendum, the date had been set by law. But what was the point of risking the general election when there was still time to postpone, without anyone knowing they had planned to hold it?

Charlie told him recent findings from focus groups showed voters blamed him for the sinking of the trawler and the Gibraltar crisis that ensued, and it was likely to lead to a No vote in the euro referendum, and could, just possibly, risk the general election.

Bathurst was behind by five points, the closest she had ever been, though private polls showed that if she was replaced by either Simon Darius or Mike Turnbull, two formidable former Cabinet Ministers who had lost their seats at the last election, the Opposition would be neck and neck with the Government. Holding both on the same day was too dangerous, she argued. If Cane lost both he'd regret it for ever; there was a year to go before the election had to be held. Why not wait? If he lost the euro vote, at least he would still be in power; it would be hard but he could recover; he wouldn't have lost everything.

'Since we haven't actually made any public commitment to hold the general election on May 3rd, there's no real loss of face,' she said.

Cane was not looking at Charlie, he was leaning forward, hands on his knees, head down.

'You OK, Steven?'

'Yes,' he said perfunctorily.

He looked shattered. She thought of putting a consoling arm round his shoulder, but decided against.

'It's different for you, you're not the one blamed for killing twenty two men. Did you see the picture yesterday of Neville Penhaligon at his brother's funeral in Mousehole?'

For once, she spoke softly, reassuringly: 'Steven, this is no time for self doubt. Look at what you have achieved, you've had success after success. So what if it's got rough lately. Didn't you say it would and didn't you say that'd be when we found out if we were up to it? Didn't we? You can't let a couple of setbacks put you off. That's what marks the great leaders from the ordinary ones.'

Her tone changed from sympathy to defiance as she moved closer. 'If you lose your nerve now, everything you have done will have been a complete waste of time. Is that what you really want? Is it? There are thousands of Neville Penhaligons out there who need you; a fat lot of good you're going to do him and his like if you chuck it in. You'd kiss goodbye to it all because of one setback? I tell you this Steven Cane, I won't let you!'

Her face was inches from Cane's when she heard a voice at the door.

'What in heaven's name is going on down here?'

It was Lucy. 'I could hear the shouting from upstairs – so could the children. What is happening? Steven?'

'We've had a difficult time, love,' spluttered Cane, as Charlie backed off quickly. 'Things are getting a bit overwrought.'

'So I see,' said Lucy, looking at Charlie in disgust.

Lucy swung round and left.

* * *

'Two bottles of the best champagne, please! And none of that house crap, either.'

'You won the lottery or something, Marc?' said Lomax.

'Kind of.'

'What?'

'You won it for me, actually, Joe.'

'What are you talking about?'

'Your little tip about that defence contract.'

'What tip?'

'You know, the defence company you said was about to get a Middle East contract?'

'What about it?'

'I had a little flutter on their shares.'

'You what!?'

'I bought some of their shares and I must say Joe, you are very well informed. Made a couple of grand.'

'Shit, Marc!'

'How do you want your share? In cash or bubbly? Talking of which here it is. Soho House' best. Cheers Maxie, happy days.'

'Bloody hell, Marc, I don't believe you did that.'

'Correction Joe, we did it.'

'Did you really make £2,000?'

'Yep, here it is.' Williams reached into his inside jacket pocket and brought out a wad of £50 notes. 'You can do a lot on a night out in London with forty of these. You gonna help me?'

'Put it away for Christ's sake.'

'Don't act so bloody innocent, Joe Lomax. Look me in the eye and tell me you didn't deliberately give me that tip.'

'I didn't.'

'You could have fooled me. You mean you slipped the name in, Johnson and Griffiths Avionics, by accident? Come off it. And don't tell me you aren't trying to work out what the next scam might be, either. How long have I known you?'

'It's fucking dangerous, Marc.'

'Don't be ridiculous. Millions of people do it every day; buy and sell shares. The only ones who make any money are those who are better informed than the others.'

'It's called insider dealing and it's illegal.'

'It's illegal if you do it, not if I do though, is it?' Williams leant across; 'Joe, listen to me, we have got the chance to make serious money here. We would be mad not to take it. You have got access to information which is worth a fortune, you may never be in the same position, use it for goodness sake. We have known each other for years, we trust each other, it's perfect. There won't even be any victims, it's the victimless crime.'

'I'm nervous about using stuff from the department. It could be traced back to me you know ... '

'Yeah, but there must be lots of stuff that can't be.'

'So?'

'So, Maxie baby, if I – sorry if we ... ' He waved a wad of £50 notes in

Lomax's face.

'Put it away.'

But Williams waved it closer. 'Look at it Maxie, feel it. If we can make this kind of dough from "confidential" stuff, imagine what we can make from the "top secret" stuff. Eh? Just imagine.'

Lomax looked around to check no one was listening and leaned towards his friend.

'Now shut up and let me finish, Marc. There is a way of making money that doesn't involve government information. It's safer; it doesn't involve Silverman. We'd have to raise a few grand to make it work, but we could earn a lot, and I mean, a lot.'

'What's a lot?'

'£100,000, maybe more,' said Lomax.

'That's the old Maxie, count me in,' said Williams. 'I fucking love you.' He grabbed Lomax's glass and filled it with Moét until it spilled onto the floor.

CHAPTER TEN

'Feeling lucky, Charlie?'

She recognised the accent: minor public school mixed with estuary English. McLintock's voice might grate, but it had been music to her ears in the last few weeks. If Cane lost tomorrow's euro referendum, he would not be able to blame *The Globe.*

'I never leave things to luck, Warren.'

'No, you leave it to me,' he cackled. Charlie did not join his laughter. She had to swallow hard doing business with McLintock. She had grown up hating his paper and its right-wing ravings in the Eighties. She once joined a demo in London where huge stacks of *The Globe* and pictures of its owner were burned outside its printing plant in protest at its bloodthirsty, xenophobic coverage of the Falklands War. Yet here she was talking to the same man whose face was on the poster, toasting what they hoped would be a famous victory together.

'It was damn hard to hold our new pro-euro line after you went and sank that Spanish trawler,' said McLintock. 'If it hadn't all come out that the Spaniards had crammed Rosita with militant fishermen who had said they were out to provoke a fight with the Navy, Cane would have been scuppered himself. Funny how World In Action got all those secret messages sent by Spanish intelligence saying their fishing unions were looking for a dust-up with the Brits. Don't suppose MI5 gave them a helping hand, did they? Soon as I saw that I thought to myself: Special agent Redpath's fingerprints all over it. Am I right, Charlie? The Navy sink a Spanish fishing boat, kill twenty Spaniards plus two British lifeboatmen and the Spaniards end up getting the blame? Nice work.'

Charlie denied it. McLintock laughed. She was not about to pick an argument with him. He was returning her call.

They had spoken regularly in the six weeks since *The Globe*'s extraordinary decision to declare its support for the euro. He had been to Downing Street several times, though not once through the front door. It would hardly do for people to think *The Globe* was in Cane's pocket, or vice versa.

He usually entered unnoticed through the Cabinet Office. The dunderheads of Her Majesty's press whose lenses were permanently focused on the shiny black bomb proof door never watched that. It was for visitors who would rather not be photographed brandishing the world's most famous lion's head knocker, and preferred a more discreet way to get to the heart of the lion's den.

Either that, or they were dropped off near the statue of Montgomery by the L-shaped road at the back which led to a door at the basement of 12 Downing Street, and then walked through to Number 10. McLintock had sat in the rose garden having tea with Cane as they planned the pro-euro campaign, feet away from the spot where the IRA mortar bomb that nearly killed the Cabinet had landed. Some of Cane's MPs would sooner have tea with the men who fired the mortar.

The day after McLintock and Cane had sipped tea in the garden, *The Globe* kicked off its campaign with a five page special 'NIGHTMARE OUTSIDE EUROLAND' with a picture of a dole queue stretching from Land's End to John O'Groats. As the campaign went on, it gradually turned up the volume.

McLintock was particularly proud of 'ONLY NUTTERS SAY NO'. It featured a rogues gallery of the oddest opponents of the euro that *The Globe* could find. There was no shortage. One former right-wing minister featured, Nigel Cobbett, was suing the paper, though since he was on record as having said that if Britain voted Yes, Cane might as well stand on the roof of Number 10, do a 'Heil Hitler' salute, sing the German national anthem and shoot his children, it was hard to see him getting much sympathy from a court.

'Warren, you guys have been great, we'd never have got this far without you,' said Charlie.

'You've only got one more day Charlie, one last shot. Got any ideas for the front page?'

He already had one of his own made up and ready to go on the computer in his office: 'IF BRITAIN SAYS NO TODAY, WILL THE LAST PERSON TO LEAVE THE COUNTRY PLEASE TURN THE LIGHTS OUT.'

Not exactly original, but it was tried and tested.

'Actually, Warren, I have got something you might be interested in.'

He was listening.

'I have in front of me an article which says that if Britain votes No, then every Japanese firm in the country is likely to leave Britain, taking with them hundreds of thousands of jobs because they could not afford to run the risk of losing their access to European Union markets.'

'Charlie, I'm willing to help, but I can't go running every flimsy scare story you come up with on my front page. We have our credibility to think of. Don't tell me – it came from Spanish intelligence!'

'No, Warren.'

'Well, which crackpot has written it for you?'

'I don't think this person would appreciate you calling him a crackpot, Warren.'

'I can call anyone a crackpot Charlie, including Steven Cane, if it takes my fancy.'

'This "crackpot", Warren, is better known as Noburo Sokato, Prime Minister of Japan.'

'Charlie, look at the calender, this is May 2nd not April 1st.'

'I'm serious Warren, I've got it right in front of me.'

'I love it, tell me more, tell me more.'

The Japanese Government had told Cane months ago of their concern of facing tariffs on goods made by their firms in Britain if the UK stayed out of the single currency. It would make their British-based car, television, computer and other hightech factories less competitive with similar factories inside euroland. They had already laid off thousands. If Britain stayed out of the euro they would be off for good to Germany, Spain or Italy. Cane told them to say so publicly, but the Japanese wanted to keep out of the referendum campaign.

'They thought people would gradually come round to supporting the euro,' said Charlie, 'but now they can see there's a real danger of a No vote, they're worried, really worried. Their ambassador met the PM a week or so ago and asked if there was anything he could do to help. We said the only thing that might make a difference would be if the Japanese Prime Minister made a statement setting out his views.'

'And?'

'And, Warren, I got it last night and they've agreed to let us handle its publication. I thought you might be interested.'

'What does it say?'

'That Japanese firms would move to Europe if the people of Britain were foolish enough not to adopt the euro.'

'Are you quoting from it?'

'Verbatim.'

'Really?'

'Really.'

'Then I think you could say I am interested, very interested indeed.'

He couldn't believe it.

'Charlie, you sure 'bout this?'

'Do I ever joke?'

'No, you don't. OK, Charlie, I'm clearing the whole paper. Front page: JAP JOBS SHOCK. Underneath: Half A Million Jobs Down The Swannee If Britain Votes NO. Inside: A giant map of Britain with big black marks showing how many jobs will be lost in each area. Headline: NO TO THE EURO AND YES TO THE DOLE. I love it, I love it, I love it! What did you say his name was?'

'Noburo Sokato.'

'NOBBY THE NIP NOBBLES THE EURO. No, not enough gravitas.'

'I've got it, I've got it: SOKATO SOCKS IT TO 'EM. When can I see it?'

'It's on a bike on the way to your office as we speak, Warren. If this doesn't have an impact, nothing will.'

'Charlie, by the time I'm finished with it, it'll have more impact than Hiroshima.'

* * *

As the presses of *The Globe* started to roll, McLintock switched on the TV in his windowless office to check the Nine O'Clock TV News. He chuckled as he thought how the BBC, whom he hated with every fibre of his being, were totally unaware that the last dramatic twist in the euro referendum campaign was about to unfold – and unfold in *The Globe*, which the BBC hated with every fibre of its corporate being.

'Good evening,' began Michael Buerk.

'On the eve of the referendum on the euro a poll for the BBC has showed that the Yes camp has drawn level with opponents of the single currency for the first time since the Gibraltar crisis. Supporters of the single currency were marginally ahead until last month's crisis over the sinking of the Spanish trawler 'Rosita' which inflamed anti-European opinion. Supporters of the euro claim they have regained the initiative since the highly controversial claim – disputed by Spain – that militant Spanish fishermen deliberately provoked the incident which had been blamed on Britain.

'The result of tomorrow's vote will have enormous implications not just for the future of Britain, but also for the future of the Government. The Yes campaign has been led by Prime Minister Steven Cane and his critics say that if he loses, it'll be a major vote of no confidence in his administration. The Government must call a general election some time in the next twelve months and Opposition leader Madeleine Bathurst, who's leading the campaign for a No vote, is expected to call for Mr Cane's resignation if the result goes against him.'

McLintock rolled up the cuff of his white shirt and laughed. 'Wait to see *The Globe* tomorrow, you're a day behind with the news as usual Auntie!'

He hit number two on his phone memory bank.

'You're evens according to the BBC – and tomorrow's story about the Japs should clinch it for you Charlie. We're sending a million extra copies to all the areas with Jap firms: South Wales, Merseyside, the North East. You're home and dry. We're not even in the euro and I'm already making money out of it!'

'We'll see Warren,' said Charlie. 'I'm glad you called, there's someone here who would like to have a word with you.'

'Hi, Warren.'

'That's either Rory Bremner or Steven Cane. How do I know which?'

'I'm the straight man,' said Cane.

'You're going to win, Prime Minister.'

'We'll see; it's too close to call, but I wanted to say thanks for everything you've done. Your campaign has been fantastic; win or lose I wanted you to know that.'

McLintock thought of replying, 'Well, don't forget our little deal Mr Prime Minister: Radio One and the World Service on a plate in six months, thank you very much; or I'll drop you in it as fast as I pulled you out of it.'

But after all, he was talking on a phone. And the man he was talking to was the Prime Minister. He restricted himself to, 'No problem, Steven. I only ever back winners; didn't I tell you that once before?'

'You did, Warren.'

'And did I let you down?'

'You didn't, Warren.'

'And I won't let you down this time either. I keep my bargains, Steven.'

McLintock knew Charlie would be listening in.

He wondered just how much Charlie told Cane. He assumed he knew of all the deals Charlie did on his behalf, including the BBC deal. But he couldn't be certain. He had had several conversations with her where Cane had not been present and where she had appeared to make decisions. He had had others where Cane had been present and Charlie had corrected him; he'd heard her swear at him once. Did she have Cane's authority in advance, or did she get it afterwards? Did she get it at all?

Warren McLintock would never give such power to one of his editors.

* * *

Dora had just brought in Charlie's second cup of black coffee when the *Today* programme seven o'clock news came on.

She was eager to know how the BBC would report *The Globe*'s front page, which was lying on her desk on top of all the other morning papers. Its front page was just as McLintock had said it would be: **JAP JOBS SHOCK**. He'd been as good as his word; it ran to nine pages inside.

The pips that lead up to the news rang out.

'This is the BBC *Today* programme seven o'clock news. On the eve of today's historic referendum on the euro, there has been a dramatic last minute twist in the campaign. The Japanese Prime Minister Noburo Sokato has said that Britain would be foolish not to join the single European currency and that if it didn't, Japanese companies based in Britain would move to other European countries, putting hundreds of thousands of jobs at risk. He said it would be the only way to avoid the risk of new European Union tariffs which it's thought may be imposed on United Kingdom companies by Brussels. In an article written by Mr Sokato in today's edition of *The Globe*, he says a No vote would be very damaging for Japanese firms in this country and that they must act to protect their own national interests. His surprise intervention could affect the outcome in areas where large numbers of jobs depend on Japanese employers.'

For once, just for once, the *Today* programme has reported it straight, thought Charlie. The Japanese PM's remarks were on the front pages of every newspaper. She made sure they got the story in time for the second editions. It suited both her and McLintock: *The Globe* got the credit for breaking the story and Charlie got the widest possible coverage before the polling stations opened.

Just as she had hoped, the story sparked a frenzy in areas like the North East and South Wales where tens of thousands of workers were employed by Japanese car firms, computer firms, TV firms and other high tech industries.

It dominated the television coverage. While some accused the Japanese of trying to frighten British voters into voting Yes, more were alarmed at the prospect of losing their jobs.

Several news organisations tried to contact the Japanese Prime Minister in person. But the time lag meant it was already late evening in Japan; they would have to wait until tomorrow to interview him – after the polls had closed.

The early morning TV news showed workers at a Japanese car factory in Derby.

'I don't think the Japanese should meddle in our affairs,' said a middle-aged man in blue overalls leaving a plant in Swansea, 'but they are great employers; and where else am I going to get a job round here?'

'If I waited to get a job with a British car firm, I'd be redundant for ever,' said another.

It wasn't often that Charlie sat around and did nothing. It was why she couldn't stand polling days. The complete lack of control was anathema to her. There was no point in briefing the press; no point in holding meetings with Cane or Silverman, or with civil servants. The Government had shut up shop. Cane had gone to his constituency with Lucy where they would be filmed voting.

Charlie passed the time phoning officials to check how voting was going. She was pleased when Silverman rang to tell her the turnout was higher than expected in areas which had large numbers of Japanese firms.

She was less pleased when Patrick Armitage phoned, asking to see her immediately. Since their falling out over her memo to directors of communications, the coolness between them had become arctic. Charlie tried to avoid him, knowing he was due to retire next year and that she would have a big say in his replacement. She had already discussed with Cane the possibility of recruiting someone from the private sector and dreamed of the day when she could call Armitage in and tell him his successor was to be a brash, ex-comprehensive school, thirty-something millionaire head of a dot.com company. It would her be final insult to Armitage and everything he represented.

He had also kept out of her way, in spite of growing pressure from colleagues to make a stand against her and her methods.

Armitage was not one of *The Globe*'s regular readers. If there was something important in it, one of his officials would send him the cutting. The Cabinet Secretary would dangle it from his fingers as though it was a piece of lavatory paper. He preferred not to have pictures of topless girls from Basildon called Tracey and the confessions of soap opera stars lying on the mahogany desk that had been in his office since Queen Victoria's reign. His wife Elizabeth preferred not to have them lying round their home in Epsom; she had never even seen a copy of *The Globe*, let alone read one. The article by Prime Minister Sokato caught his eye immediately. His assistant had brought it to him the moment he arrived in his office at eight thirty am.

Armitage knew Sokato believed Britain should join the euro, but was surprised that such a cultured man should have put pen to paper for *The Globe*.

'What's the problem, Patrick?' she said as she strode in to his office.

Charlie's tone had become increasingly offhand since their falling out, and now bordered on the abusive.

'The FCO have drawn my attention to this article by Prime Minister Sokato in *The Globe*.'

'What about it?'

'I understand you were involved?'

'Sokato told us when he came over that he was very keen for Britain to join the euro; you ought to remember, you were there when he said it.'

'That's not what I meant. I meant I understand you were instrumental in getting him to write the article.'

'Yes. Is there something wrong in enabling him to express his view?'

'The FCO are surprised that you didn't inform them; it would normally be done through them.'

'There wasn't time for all that. The vote's today – in case you hadn't noticed. There wouldn't be much point in running the piece tomorrow, would there? Though I'm sure the Opposition wouldn't mind.'

He ignored the dig. 'The FCO have expressed concern.'

'What concern?'

'Concern that the article that appeared is not the same as the one that was submitted to your office – I gather you were acting as ... an intermediary.' His words dripped with condescension.

'Look, *The Globe* asked me to help them contact the Japanese Prime Minister. It was very late in Japan and believe it or not *The Globe* didn't have his home number and I got on to the embassy in London and asked them to help out. They were only too pleased to assist.'

'You should have asked me.'

'Pardon?'

'For Mr Sokato's home phone number, I have it.'

'You what?'

'I have his phone number and I have just been speaking to him.'

'I don't know what you are talking about.'

'He's a friend.'

Armitage had struck up a friendship with Sokato during the Japanese Prime Minister's visit to London the previous year. Sokato was fascinated when he discovered the Cabinet Secretary collected Japanese silk prints and had promised to send him a book on the subject from his private library in Tokyo.

'I have been speaking to Mr Sokato about his article. And Miss Redpath, when I read it out to him he was a little taken aback. He said the wording had been changed.'

'The Japanese asked me to handle it and make any minor alterations needed to make it fit *The Globe*'s style,' said Charlie. 'There aren't any tabloids in Japan, I believe.'

Armitage produced two sheets of typed A4 paper, holding them up like exhibits in a court case.

'I have a copy of the article the embassy sent to you and there are several alterations to the one that appeared in *The Globe*.'

'I see we have launched a one-man inquiry, Mr Armitage. What a pity you don't always display such resourcefulness in your work for this administration, but then perhaps your heart isn't in it.'

'Miss Redpath, the original article by Mr Sokato states that Britain should consider saying Yes to the euro and that some Japanese firms might consider moving to Europe if it didn't. The version that appeared in *The Globe* says Britain would be foolish to say No and that all Japanese companies would definitely move to Europe. There is a big difference in emphasis, Miss Redpath ... '

'You're being pedantic. Have the Japanese complained?'

'No, not as far as I am aware.'

'Then why the hell should you?'

'Because it is my job to ensure the affairs of government are conducted properly. May I ask if any of this is connected to the recent discussion between the DPM and the Honda car company's application for a £200 million government grant for a new factory in Birmingham – and your memo to him last week urging him to see it is approved quickly?'

'What are you suggesting, Mr Armitage?'

'I'm not suggesting anything, Miss Redpath. other than that I am not as naive as you appear to think I am.'

'All I did was to put in plain English what the Japanese Prime Minister said. It's no use the Japanese complaining, they wrote to me asking to check the article and clear up any necessary points. That's all I did.'

'The Japanese Prime Minister is an honourable man, Miss Redpath, I am not certain this article does justice to his honour.'

'How dare you speak to me of honour! The only reason you cling on here is in the hope that you might finally pick up an honour – so Mrs Armitage can be Lady Elizabeth – it's your last chance next time, isn't it

Mister Armitage?'

'If that was some kind of a threat, Miss Redpath, you're wasting your time. I would rather leave this place with my own honour intact and able to look my wife in the eye than be honoured for complying with your methods. It's a matter of ethics, Miss Redpath, not something I imagine, keeps you awake at night. You know, when I started in the civil service a woman like you would never have been allowed to join, let alone given high office. No wonder it has lost all its respect.'

'Is that so, Mr Armitage?'

'Yes it most certainly is,' he said, inwardly thrilled that he had finally released the loathing that had been bottled up inside him for so long. 'And now, Miss Redpath, I'd be very grateful if you would kindly leave my office.'

'Oh but I hadn't quite finished, Mr Armitage.'

'What?'

'I said, I haven't finished.'

She narrowed her eyes. 'Would you say it was a matter of ethics when you took your secretary to a weekend conference at Gleneagles Hotel in Scotland last year, Mr Armitage? Would you say it was a matter of ethics that the trip was made at the expense of taxpayers, Mr Armitage? Have you looked Mrs Armitage in the eye and told her that, Mr Armitage?'

The Cabinet Secretary looked as though he had turned to stone.

Gotcha, thought Charlie, bloody well gotcha. That'd teach him to leak against her. By God it would.

CHAPTER ELEVEN

There was a tear in Sheila Quinlan's eye as she took her husband's trilby from the front door peg, gave it to him and said goodbye. They had managed to raise some of the money they needed to pay their creditors, but they still owed Harris Finance £21,678.77p

Sheila knew her husband would have to declare himself bankrupt. He would never be mayor. She would never be Lady Mayoress. Instead of being whisked round the town in a black limousine and envied by all their friends, they would be walking, pitied by their friends, sniggered at by the rest. Bastards.

She couldn't understand why Tony had put off the inevitable for so long. 'The sooner we face it, the sooner we're out of it,' she had told him time and again. But Tony appeared to live in the vain hope that something would turn up. But he asked his wife to give him one last wish: he had agreed to organise the euro referendum and wanted it to be his swansong in a career in local government that spanned three decades.

Mersey was one of six constituencies in a government trial using computers to count votes. The council had been given £200,000 to show there was a quicker, more reliable and cheaper way of counting votes than the ancient ritual of stacking up bits of paper in piles. Tony was certain he could deliver the fastest result ever. It would be his place in history.

He was proud to have been among the first to buy a PC in the Eighties – even if it was off the back of a lorry – and after leading the campaign to persuade the council to take part in computerised voting in committees, was chosen to help make sure it was a success on referendum night. He was determined to be there.

'This is me' moment, pet,' he told his wife. 'After that, I'll never set foot in the building again, but I'm goin' out on a high, and I'll show 'em I'm good at running the town hall – even if I'm no bloody good at running anythin' else.'

The big cities were always first to declare because the polling stations were all within a few miles of the counting centre, unlike far-flung outposts, like Highlands West in Scotland, where they didn't bother to start counting until the following day.

Tony didn't actually bother to vote in the referendum. If he had, he would have voted Yes, if only to save the Merseyside jobs he was convinced would be lost by staying out of the euro.

But Councillor Quinlan was not thinking about politics today.

* * *

Charlie and Silverman sat in Cane's office in Number 10, when Dora walked in with a tray of sandwiches.

'I shouldn' be doin' this, my shif' finish already Mr Cane.'

'We're very grateful, Dora, thank you,' said Cane. It was five to ten and the three were waiting eagerly for the bulletin when they would get the first indication of the result of the euro poll. Cane would know whether he had a political future – or a short, dismal past. He had hardly slept for four days. Whether Dora had worked after her finishing time was not the most important thing to him.

'I don' know why you's all gettin' so excited 'bout this euro.'

'It's very important that we win it, Dora,' said Cane, struggling to remain civil.

'Europe ain't done nothing for me, except stop me buying bananas from my cousins back home. Dey broke 'cos of Europe. I tol' you Mr Cane, de people gonna vote no, like I done 'fore I comin' to work.'

With that, the waitress closed the door. She wasn't interested in the Prime Minister's reply. Silverman shook his head in disapproval, but

Cane laughed.

'You should've heard what she said to Clinton.' Cane imitated her West Indian drawl. '"Don' you go trying your tricks on me Mr Clinton, I's read all about you's in the papers and I'm tellin' you dis, maa husband is a big man – an' I mean beeeg, ya hear? So you keep your hands in your pockets, ya hear me?" Clinton fell apart.'

Cane wondered whether she did it to ease the tension. If so, he was grateful. There had been few moments as tense as this.

'The turnout's been high, particularly in areas with Japanese business-es,' said Silverman, filling time as they awaited the ten o'clock chimes.

Before Charlie could reply, a voice from BBC's euro election studio could be heard.

'And now we are going to Downing Street, where our political editor Andrew Marr has details of the exit poll.'

'Well, the results are absolutely fascinating. They show that the No camp have a lead of less than one half of one per cent. Let me repeat that, the No camp are ahead are by less than one half of one per cent. Now this is our poll carried out at polling stations of people who have actually voted. These polls are normally accurate to within half a per cent so it means that while it would seem that the No camp are ahead by the tiniest of margins, it's not enough, repeat, not enough to say that they're going to win. To use a cliche, it really is too close to call.'

'Is there any evidence of regional variations to the voting, Andrew?'

'This is where the poll's particularly interesting. There are some signs that the Yes vote has been bigger than expected in areas affected by today's controversy over reported remarks by the Japanese Prime Minister that Japanese firms would move to the Continent to avoid EU trade tariffs if the United Kingdom voted to keep sterling.'

'What will the Prime Minister do if the vote goes against him? He's staked a lot on a Yes vote, hasn't he?'

'He most certainly has. Even as we speak,' and Marr turned round and pointed at Number 10 behind him, 'the Prime Minister is closeted with his closest advisers; that probably includes his press secretary Charlotte

Redpath and the Chancellor, Ronnie Silverman; they'll be discussing what he should do if he loses. They know that if they lose, they face serious difficulties. There'll be a crisis in our relations with Europe, they'll be saddled with a policy they don't believe in and of course, they must hold a general election by this time next year at the latest. There's no escaping the fact that a No vote will be disastrous for the Prime Minister, whatever spin they try to put on it.'

Less than thirty feet away, behind the black brick Georgian facade of 10 Downing Street, the man Marr was referring to, paced the room in his shirtsleeves as he listened to the analysis. Cane bit his lip. He could not disagree with a word Marr had said.

Silverman stretched his Ingersoll strap to breaking point. Charlie's thumb was raw where she had been rubbing it slowly and hard against the strike of her lighter.

* * *

Everything was going to plan on Tony Quinlan's last day.

The race was on to declare at ten past ten and beat the five other constituencies taking part in the computerised experiment.

'You're going to be hard pushed to follow this in the general election next year, Tony,' the mayor said to him. Tony smiled. He observed the other officials busying themselves, making sure all the computers were functioning properly.

Tony's mobile phone was one of the first casualties when his cab firm went bust. But he knew he had an important phone call to make. Shortly before ten pm, he slipped into a side room where he knew there was a land line.

Cane was still pacing the room, one eye on the TV, with Charlie and Silverman when the newsreader said,

'We're expecting the first results in the euro referendum in the next ten minutes; the first is expected to be from Mersey or Sunderland, two constituencies which are taking part in a computerised counting experiment.'

Behind him was a split screen showing Mersey City Hall and Sunderland City Hall.

'I think we can now go to Mersey ... yes we're going there now where the mayor is ready with the first result in the European referendum.'

The television was silent for twenty seconds as the mayor came to the microphone. Cane was sitting down, leaning forward in his seat waiting for the figures.

'The total number of votes cast in the referendum on the euro in Mersey was 37,505,' said the mayor. 'The number of votes in favour of the euro was 16,310; the number of votes against the euro was 21,195.'

In less than two seconds the result and margin in favour was flashed onto the screen. 'Mersey votes No to euro.'

'It's a slightly higher No vote than we expected,' said Silverman.

'What does it mean nationally?' said a frantic Cane. 'Is it enough, is it enough?'

He received the answer three seconds later from the television.

'According to our analysis, if the Merseyside trend is repeated nationally it will mean a majority for the No campaign of just 60,000 votes out of some thirty million,' said the newsreader.

'I don't ruddy believe it, for fuck's sake ... we're finished.'

Charlie often swore, usually at journalists; and occasionally at diplomats and ministers. But it wasn't Charlie who was cursing at the TV set; it was Cane, who rarely swore, let alone used the f-word.

'I don't believe it's happening, I thought we'd done enough, what the fuck do we do now?' he said banging his palm against his brow.

'We're going to wait for the final result before we lose our heads,' said Charlie.

'It is highly unlikely the final result will be known until the last region declares – and that won't be till midday tomorrow,' said Silverman. 'That gives us time to plan our response – whichever way it goes – and it looks like we're going to need it.'

'Anybody spoken to Greaves?' said Cane.

The other two looked at him. They knew what he was thinking. It had been Greaves' idea to push for an early referendum. He had made all manner of powerful arguments as to why the 'go early' option – as Greaves always called it – gave them the best chance of success. Charlie had warned him the only 'go early' option Greaves wanted was for Cane to go as Prime Minister as early as possible, so he could take over, she told him. Cane had always dismissed the conspiracy theory, but from his expression tonight, it looked as though he might be about to change his mind.

'No, he went back North last night for the Wearside result,' said Charlie.

'I wonder if he feels the way we do,' mused Cane. He very rarely said anything disparaging about Greaves. But the pressure was getting to him.

Charlie seized on it.

'He'll have his funeral face on for the cameras; and a smile as wide as the Tyne Bridge when they're gone.'

The three spent the next four hours monitoring the results as they came in. By the time Cane finally went upstairs at three thirty, the television computers had revised their prediction of the final result. The forecast was now down a fraction to a 20,000 vote defeat. Still not enough to save him.

He climbed into bed next to Lucy, trying not to disturb her. She had called down to say goodnight at midnight knowing the result was on a knife edge and knowing what was at stake for her husband. She woke when he entered the bedroom, but pretended to be asleep. She could tell from the silent way he climbed into bed alongside her and clung to her that nothing had changed.

CHAPTER TWELVE

When the Queen Elizabeth II Conference Centre in Westminster was chosen as the headquarters of the count for the euro referendum, no one imagined it would be centre stage when the final result was announced at tea time on Friday more than nineteen hours after the polling stations had closed. That was expected to emerge long before the last 60,000 or so votes from Highlands West were counted. But only one thing was clear about the referendum: the result was going to remain unclear until the end.

Charlie and Silverman were with Cane in his study at five past six and had resumed the positions they had occupied less than nine hours earlier. Cane, pacing up and down the same stretch of the maroon carpet, stared down at the fleur de lys pattern and up at the television perched in the corner of his room as the experts' view changed by the minute. Charlie sent a press officer out to get more cigarettes and Silverman was busy trying to contact Lomax to see if he knew what was happening in the Highlands West vote. He had sent him to party HQ the previous night to monitor the result and relay information back to him in Downing Street. Lomax had seemed fine, high spirited almost, when Silverman spoke to him at midnight. So much so that Silverman rebuked him for being over optimistic. But he hadn't called since.

Silverman's mobile rang. 'Joe, at last, where in heaven's name have you been? I've been trying to get you all morning.'

'Sorry, Ronnie ... I went to Soho House last night ... '

'I know that, I spoke to you there, where have you been today?'

'I'm sorry, what time is it?'

'Eleven thirty five.'

'God, sorry ... how's the vote going?'

'You don't even know that?!' exploded Silverman. 'For crying out loud, Joe, what have you been doing? You're paid to help me – not to go out and get drunk when I need you. What's the matter with you?'

'Ronnie, I'm sorry, really sorry, I'll get straight down ... '

'You'd better,' said Silverman, pressing the red button on his Nokia to cut him off.

Lomax picked up the remote control to the television, pressed number one and saw the BBC's Peter Snow with his hand on the swingometer. One side of a giant circle was coloured dark blue with little gold stars; the other a mass of horizontal, vertical and diagonal red, white and blue stripes. Snow was holding the arrow at the end of the swingometer exactly where the number six would be on a clock. 'It's the closest finish to any poll I can remember,' he said, lurching from one side to the other like a demented scarecrow. 'With just one constituency to declare, there are only 40,894 votes in it.'

'Christ almighty,' said Lomax, flicking the set off again. He thought of all the champagne he and Williams had ordered at Soho House the previous night. He tried to remember who else had seen him. It was all a blur.

Very little drink was consumed by the current occupants of Downing Street. Not like the days when Churchill had Chablis with breakfast, champagne with lunch and brandy with supper, or when Denis kept his tumbler of Gordon's topped up. Cane had the occasional spritzer. He didn't like beer; the only time he drank it was when he went to his local party club at West Ham to meet the faithful. Cane had never heard anyone order a spritzer at the bar; and he wasn't going to be the first. But there was plenty of Dom Perignon in Number 10's cellar, and if he won tonight, he planned to use it.

Highlands West was due any moment. The No camp were still ahead by a few thousand, but there was still hope. Scottish pundits had forecast a vote of slightly more than two to one in favour of the euro, just enough to clinch it for the Yes camp. As Cane stood in front of the sofa where, six months ago, he had pleaded with a delegation from the Scottish Nationalist

Party not to go for full independence from Westminster, he was glued to the live coverage of the count at Westminster, willing the Scots to have voted against sterling, against the Queen, against England, against Westminster, against the Union Flag, against anything – as long as it made them vote for the euro – and for him.

'Here it comes, Steven,' said Silverman, breathlessly. Like an eagle spotting a rabbit in the undergrowth, he had seen movement to the side of the platform at the conference centre before Cane or Charlie, or even the TV reporter at the scene had done so. The official from the Electoral Reform Society, who had overseen the vote, walked to the microphone.

Charlie sat forward, her right elbow on her knee, her right hand to her mouth inhaling deeply from a cigarette. Cane was upright, leaning forward with his hands on his hips, legs apart.

'I will firstly announce the result of the vote in Highlands West,' said the official. 'And after that I will announce the final tally of votes nationally.'

'Please, let's get it over with,' moaned Cane, looking up at the cherubs on the ornate ceiling of his study and wishing he could fly away as easily.

'The votes cast in Highlands West are as follows: in favour of the euro 64,324; against the euro 33,208.'

'It's two to one!' blurted out Cane. 'What's the result, what's the fucking result?'

Before Cane had finished the sentence, or the official had begun to announce it, the TV computer did the calculation for them. It appeared on the screen in letters and numbers.

YES votes: 15,762,741 votes.

NO votes: 15,772,519 votes.

A second later, as Cane frantically scanned the jumble of figures trying to work out which was bigger, three giant words were flashed on the screen.

BRITAIN VOTES NO.

The words flashed on and off every second, hitting Cane between the eyes like a sledgehammer. He stood blinking at the screen in disbelief.

BRITAIN VOTES NO BY 9,778 VOTES.

He had never experienced a feeling like it. It was too much to take in.

He felt overwhelmed, it was like drowning. He had tried to prepare for it, but now it had happened, he wasn't prepared at all. It was such an awful thought, that even when he had only imagined what it might feel like; how he might react if he lost; what he should do; what he should say; he had only been going through the motions. His mind had refused to let him think the unthinkable. During the day, at least. At night, when he woke up feverish, it was a different matter.

He was wide awake now – and sweating. It had happened. When the figures came on a screen for a second time, ten seconds later, Cane stared at them, praying there had been a mistake.

There hadn't.

He heard the Sky News anchor man declare, 'In the most sensational climax to the referendum on the euro, Britain has voted by 9,778 votes, a majority of nought point nought, nought, nought three per cent in favour of keeping sterling and rejecting the euro. The result is a disaster and personal humiliation for Prime Minister Steven Cane who had led the Yes campaign. It is a spectacular success for Opposition leader Madeleine Bathurst who the led No campaign. It is not clear how Mr Cane will respond to the biggest crisis he has faced since coming to office. We are going straight to the Queen Elizabeth II Conference Centre where the No campaigners have started wild celebrations.'

The moment the result was announced anti-euro supporters in the crowd started singing 'Rule Britannia'. It looked like the Last Night of the Proms.

For sixty seconds after **BRITAIN VOTES NO** was flashed on the screen, Cane was unable to speak. He slumped on to the sofa, head in his hands, saying 'no, no, no, no,' over and over again. All he could see, feel, think and hear were those two letters N-O. All his hopes and dreams of being a Prime Minister who would leave a lasting mark on Britain had been destroyed. He would be remembered as the Prime Minister who asked people to back his vision of the future and the people had replied N-O. Now there was no future for him, no way back, no hope and worst of all – no second term.

He would be lucky to see out his first.

Twenty minutes after the result, the light on the Downing Street 'Switch' reserved for personal calls for the Prime Minister flashed. It was Lucy, calling from her school. She had heard the result in between lessons and wanted to comfort Cane. 'Switch' put her through to Cane's office. They had been told that he would take no calls in his study. An official knocked on the door, put his head round and said, 'I'm sorry Prime Minister, it's Mrs Cane on the line.' Cane looked at Charlie.

'We said no calls!' she snapped at the official.

'Tell her I'll call her later,' added Cane hastily. 'Explain I'm about to make a statement on TV.'

He was due to address the nation. In the event of victory Charlie would have called a press conference on the steps of Number 10. But the moment there was a danger of defeat she cancelled it. The last thing she wanted was someone shouting at him, 'Are you going to resign, Prime Minister?' A TV statement was less risky.

Cane pulled the knot on his tie a fraction tighter and waited for the studio producer's cue.

'Today, the people of Britain have voted not to join the single European currency. The majority of those wishing to keep sterling was very very small, just 9,778 voters out of the thirty two million who voted. But in a democracy, a majority of one is sufficient. I encouraged you to vote Yes to the euro because I believed it was the right decision for our country. But from the outset of this debate, from when I was first elected Prime Minister, I said we would not join the euro without holding a referendum so that the people could decide. I kept my promise. The people have decided and I will carry out the wishes of the people. I have asked the Deputy Prime Minister to launch an inquiry to establish how our trading relations with Europe and the rest of the world will be affected by today's vote. There is one other matter I should like to address.

'My political opponents have already said that because the referendum has gone against me, I should resign as Prime Minister. I wish to make it plain that I have no intention of doing so. At some stage in the next twelve months there will be a general election in this country. That is the appropriate opportunity to decide whether you wish my government to remain in office.

In the meantime, I appeal to the supporters of both sides in the campaign to bury their differences and work together from now on. Thank you.'

Cane and Charlie agreed before his TV statement that he must see Greaves straight afterwards. It was Charlie who told Cane to announce that Greaves was to carry out an investigation into the implications of the referendum result. And it was Charlie who told him to do it without telling the Deputy Prime Minister.

And it was Charlie who told him to take the attack to the enemy. Normally, Cane would have summoned his deputy to come to him. But that would remove the element of surprise. Charlie didn't want Greaves to know what was about to hit him.

They walked in silence via the rear entrance to the Cabinet Office, past the remains of Henry VIII's tennis court in the original Whitehall Palace and the brick Tudor corridor where Elizabeth I had walked with her courtiers.

As they faced each other in the tiny lift, bodies almost pressed against each other, Charlie placed a reassuring hand on Cane's chest. She felt her palm rise as he took a deep breath.

'Don't bottle it, Steven, just don't bottle it.'

She wanted him to see Greaves immediately, before his anger over the vote subsided. In all the years she had known the two, she had never seen Cane confront Greaves. She often asked herself why. There was no doubt who was the superior politician. Cane was streets ahead in all the areas that mattered: charisma, charm, popularity, image, family. Greaves may be the better orator and have greater intellectual depth. Fifty years ago they were the qualities that made you party leader and Prime Minister, but not today.

She wondered whether Cane's reluctance to tackle Greaves was guilt. After all, Cane wouldn't have got into Parliament, never mind Downing Street, had it not been for the invitation from the former West Ham party chairman, the young aspiring politician who met him on a march to save St Bernard's hospital and asked him to take part in a public meeting where Health Secretary Sir Henry Bowler would be present. The doctor became an overnight sensation.

He was selected as Parliamentary candidate for the seat on the eve of an election, thwarting the carefully laid plans of the ambitious chairman, who had spent years nurturing it for himself.

The chairman's name was Gareth Greaves.

Greaves had wanted to be a politician from his sixteenth birthday when his father George took him to the House of Commons to watch Harold Wilson in debate with Edward Heath. Unlike Cane, Greaves had never stopped wanting to be a politician. To be Prime Minister. Everything he did was with that one aim in mind.

Greaves left his grammar school for a place at the London School of Economics, where he was president of the students union. He rented digs in Hackney, because he wanted to live among real working-class people, and stayed there when he became an economics professor at the LSE. The veteran MP for West Ham, Ernie James, took Greaves to his local party and told them, 'Comrades, the next MP for West Ham is going to become the leader of our party.' By 1980, Greaves had become chairman in West Ham and James privately promised him he would retire so he could have his seat at the next election.

He kept his promise and Greaves would have inherited the seat had it not been for his invitation to a junior doctor to join him on the hospital demo.

Ernie James's prediction came true; his successor at West Ham did go on to become party leader. But his name was not Greaves, but Cane.

It took Greaves another four years to get into the Commons, as MP for his native Wearside. But by then Cane was on the Opposition front bench. Greaves rose quickly, desperate to make up for lost time, to catch up with Cane. He was gaining too. But when the leadership became vacant, he hadn't gained quite enough. He considered standing for it, but the odds were stacked against him. He could not have lived with being beaten. Not

117

by him. Not again.

And the one person who might conceivably help Greaves win it, his brilliant young Scottish assistant, had gone to America, disillusioned with politics and disillusioned with him. Until she returned five years later – to walk into Number 10 as press secretary to the man who won.

Greaves' burning ambition would remain unfulfilled, all because the young doctor he plucked from a hospital demo became the Prime Minister he, Gareth Greaves wanted to be. And Charlie, who Greaves had plucked from a poll tax demo and who had turned into the most brilliant spin doctor of the age, had helped him do it. There was no cure for bitterness and envy on that scale.

Cane did his best to ease the pain by making Greaves his Deputy Prime Minister and giving him wide ranging powers across the entire Cabinet. But he knew it would never fully satisfy him. He liked Greaves, respected him, needed him, felt sorry for him. But Cane was no fool: he had to guard against him.

And who better to do that than the lionness standing alongside Cane as he swept in to Greaves' office.

Outside in the spring sun, the bellowed orders of the Lifeguards preparing for the Trooping the Colour ceremony next month could be heard through Greaves' open window.

'Steven!' said Greaves. A second later, he saw Charlie. His look changed from surprise to alarm.

'You were brilliant on the TV, Steven,' he said, leaping from his seat and walking round his desk to pat him on the back.

'You did absolutely the right thing, the result was terrible, but you made it clear you are carrying on, it's not the end by any means. When the dust has settled and people look at you and look at the alternative, they are going to beg you to stay.'

Charlie smirked at his reference to 'the alternative'.

'It's a great idea too,' said Greaves, 'that I should look into the implications of what it all means for the economy; it'll give us breathing space.'

Cut the bullshit, thought Charlie.

The two men walked across the blue carpet to the window, Greaves' hand still on Cane's back.

Come on, Steven, come on, thought Charlie.

Cane was standing at the tall arched window in the centre of the room, his hands resting on the white cast iron Victorian radiator, watching the soldiers march up and down, obeying the barked instructions of their officer.

He gripped the radiator hard, then pushed himself off and turned to face Greaves.

'Gareth, we have to have this conversation and it is best we have it now and then move on.'

Thank God.

'What conversation?'

Phoney, thought Charlie.

'Gareth, we are going to face some difficult times in the next few days and weeks. There are going to be problems from our opponents and from some inside the party. You will recall, no doubt, that you were the most outspoken voice in Cabinet in favour of holding the referendum now, rather than later, and I was persuaded. Well, with hindsight, we know we would have done it differently ... '

Yes, yes.

'Steven I don't ... '

'Let me finish Gareth. I am not blaming you or anybody for what has happened. As Prime Minister,' he looked up at Greaves, paused and repeated the words. He saw Greaves' jaw lock.

'As Prime Minister ... ' he repeated,

That's right, she thought, remind him who's Prime Minister.

' ... I take full responsibility for it. But I will say this. In the weeks ahead I hope I can rely on you to ensure that some of your over-enthusiastic supporters do not muddy the waters and put round stories of differences between us. We know what has happened in the past and we can do without it now.'

'Steven, I can assure you I have never ... '

'Gareth!' Cane interrupted him. It was the first time Charlie had ever seen him raise his voice to Greaves. Cane regained his composure. 'Gareth, no ifs, no buts, just-do-as-I-ask.'

'Of course I will,' said Greaves, with a thunderous look that belied his emotionless tone.

'Is that all, Prime Minister?'

'Yes.'

Cane walked past Greaves, with Charlie behind him. She slammed the door shut.

They retraced their steps to the lift.

Once inside, Cane cupped his hands over his face and rubbed his eyes in relief. He was glad it was over.

'Well done Steven, that was brilliant,' said Greaves' former Scottish assistant, gripping the Prime Minister's shoulders.

She had a feeling of dèjá vu; the same sensation she had experienced when he destroyed Bathurst in the Commons. The same glow. Only this time it was stronger, much stronger.

* * *

The veins on the side of Silverman's temple stood out. The look in his unforgiving brown eyes, cold and murderous.

He was furious with the result of the euro vote, but even more furious with Lomax. After finally making contact with him at midday, he had gone missing again. His mobile phone was either flat or switched off. There was pandemonium; dozens of TV and radio interviews and press briefings to be done, and he was nowhere to be seen. Silverman had to rely on a clueless temporary press officer who was filling in for the head of information he had sacked three weeks earlier.

When he finally got home at ten pm, he was still in a rage. He should have known better than to indulge and flatter such a conceited young boy. When would he learn the dangers of sleeping with someone he employed? He had even chosen him with that in mind. He would sack any official who was one hundredth as self indulgent, as irresponsible. The boy had become so arrogant he thought he could go missing, or go drinking more like, when Silverman needed him most, when the entire Government was on the brink of disintegration. He was angry with himself. But he was even angrier with Lomax. He would kill him when he got hold of him.

He turned the key in the front door of his house, put the light on and walked along the hallway. He needed a whisky and as he reached the end of the hall, he could see the half-open glass door of the drinks cabinet reflecting the faint silver-blue moonlight. Silverman didn't remember leaving the door open. The rest of the sitting room was inky black. He went to stride across as his right foot ploughed into a large object on the floor.

He tumbled over and had no time to break his fall. His face hit the wooden floor around the rug with an agonising crash. It was like being hit in the face with a rock. He scrambled to get to his feet, instinctively putting his right hand to his nose, which was in agony. As he got up his left hand brushed across a piece of flesh. He felt the features of a face. Silverman stumbled over to the light, shouting, 'Leave me, leave me, there's nothing of value,' as his hand slid up and down the wall, frantically searching for the switch.

As it finally clicked on, he half-cowered behind the door in case the intruder had a gun. The intruder was lying sprawled on the floor; motionless.

A body lay stretched out on an Indian carpet Silverman was given during a trade mission to the Far East. Beside, was the whisky bottle Silverman had been searching for. It was empty. Nearby was a broken tumbler. Silverman could see blood on the glass and more blood on the cuff of the man's checked shirt. It looked familiar. And so did the leather jacket.

He grabbed the man's shoulders and shook him. There was no response.

'No, no, no, you're not dead, you're not dead, you can't be,' Silverman wailed.

'Open your eyes, for God's sake open your eyes!' he shouted. 'Please!'

He cradled his head, hoping for signs of life, urging his eyes to open.

121

Still there was no response. Silverman seized the wrist that wasn't cut, ripped back the cuff, but couldn't feel a pulse.

'Please Joe, talk to me, talk to me, say something.'

Lomax groaned. He struggled to open his eyelids, his head lolling about. 'Ronnie, I'm ...'

'Thank God, oh thank God, you're alive!'

Silverman embraced Lomax, kissing him, hugging him and crying with relief. He remained with his arms clamped around Lomax's body, his head buried in Silverman's heaving chest, for ten seconds before he pulled back.

'Joe, thank God, thank God. What is it Joe, what's happened?'

'Ronnie, I'm ... I'm ... I'm sorry ... '

'What do you mean?'

'It was my fault ... '

'What? Joe? What?'

'What is it, Joe, what's happened?' he pleaded again.

Lomax jerked his head on one side like a rag doll and passed out.

Part two

CHAPTER THIRTEEN

'What do we want?' shouted a man holding a loudhailer. 'Cane out!' thundered the reply from thousands of voices. 'When do we want it?' he asked. 'NOW!' they bawled.

Anti-euro supporters gathered in Trafalgar Square to celebrate as soon as the referendum result was announced. It started as a giant street party, but by the late evening, a group of hardline supporters marched down Whitehall, led by ex-British National Party activists. They had been kept out of the referendum campaign by the No camp for good reasons. But there was no denying them now.

'What do we want?'

'Cane out!'

'When do we want it?'

'Now!'

The man the mob's hate was directed at sat on his lounge sofa watching television pictures of the snarling crowd.

He walked across the lime patterned carpet, past the shelves groaning with books and children's videos and opened the window. Now he could hear the snarling, chanting mob in stereo; in one ear from the crowd at the end of the road; and in the other, a split second later, from the speaker on his television ten feet away. He leaned out and looked directly down the street. He could see the crowd hemmed against the gates with his own eyes. All this hatred directed against him. Hadn't they got enough? Hadn't they hurt him enough? They had won the vote. What more did they want? Did they have to taunt him and threaten him? He had had eight hours sleep in three days. He took a deep breath to revive himself but inhaled a wave of sound and fury that drifted towards him.

He felt dizzy as the competing strains of 'Cane Out, Cane Out, Cane Out!' from television, crowd, television, crowd ricocheted round his head. He stared towards the crowd but could only see the backs of three rows of policemen standing, arms locked, behind the gates in case they swarmed over. There was nothing in the 100 yards between them, nothing except the black tarmac of the cul de sac.

He thought he saw something at the far end. Two matchstick figures; a blur that appeared, then disappeared into the afternoon haze. Slowly, it formed into the outline of two people walking towards him; a man and a woman. As they got closer the man looked to be in his early thirties. He was smiling, holding hands with the woman. She must be in her twenties; blonde, dazzlingly pretty. She kept looking up at him. They were zig-zag-ging down the street, crossing from one side to the other, stopping a few seconds here and there. There was another crowd, this one was closer and lined the street. People were smiling, waving flags, crying, reaching out to touch or kiss them. Who were they? What were they doing here? They weren't alone. There were two tiny figures either side of them; two little children. A girl with blonde pony tails; a boy, darker, wearing a football shirt and spotless white trainers. The man's outline became clearer. He had a tall slim frame, an open oval face full of optimism; a smile bursting to please, eyes brimming with the hope and enthusiasm of hope. The woman clasped his hand and each was holding hands with one of the children, who clung to them for safety. As the four of them reached the front door beneath him, they disappeared out of view, hidden by the window sill he was leaning on.

'Daddy! daddy! daddy! What are those horrible people doing?'

Cane hit his head on the window frame, jolted out of his dream by Jessica's screams as she ran up behind him.

She had got rid of the pony tails eighteen months ago, when the rest of her schoolfriends had. Sam ran in behind her; the football shirt was the same colour, but the sponsor's name was different. He had been through countless more pairs of trainers since the spotless new white ones he wore the first day the family walked up Downing Street together.

'Don't worry, don't worry,' said Cane, quickly pulling the window shut and embracing them. 'They're silly people shouting silly things. Don't listen to them.'

The children had heard the noise from their bedrooms even though they were on the other side of Downing Street, away from the street.

They had just got home from school. They were driven there each day for security reasons. The drivers normally dropped them off at the front door, but that meant going through the gates. Today they had been warned as they left to collect them, that they'd better bring them back via the L-shaped road at the rear next to Horse Guards Parade. It was as well they did.

'Steven, are you alright?' It was the woman with the dazzling smile; a little less dazzling than it was on that memorable day four years ago, but still a sight that lifted Cane.

'Steven, you look ill,' said Lucy.

'I'm fine,' he shrugged, trying to recover, patting the children, 'I was just ... '

'You were just what?' she said.

'Remembering ... '

'Remembering what?'

'The day we ... '

'The day we arrived here, yes, I've remembered it a good many times too.' There was nostalgia, no sentiment in her voice; only regret.

'I think what those people are doing is outrageous,' she said indignantly. 'They disgust me, you don't deserve this, we don't deserve it, I don't deserve it. It's awful. It makes me wish I'd never set foot in this building.'

Cane looked at his wife with raised eyebrows, and from her to his children. What had he done to them?

Jessica, blonde like her mother, had had a difficult time since she moved from primary school to one of London's top comprehensives in September. Lucy and Cane, who had both gone to private schools, argued long and hard over which secondary schools to send the children to. Lucy wanted them to go to a private school, and for a moment Cane was tempted to agree. He knew there would be political uproar from some of his supporters. But did they really matter any more? They could afford it – and Lucy's parents were so horrified at the prospect of their grandchildren going to a comprehensive that they offered pay half the fees. And wouldn't it be the clearest possible signal to the middle classes Cane was so keen to keep aboard that the party had changed for ever, that it had turned its back on old-style dogmatic socialism?

He was tempted – so he discussed it with Charlie. Her reply was simple: send them to a private school and she would resign. She told him it would be an insult to the millions of working-class supporters who had accepted him as one of them. But they would only tolerate so much. The violence of her response shocked Cane. It reminded him of the difference between them. The gap between North and South, between Glasgow and Bristol, and the chasm between Glasgow and Guildford.

In the end Cane agreed a compromise. Sam sat – and passed – an informal test to get into The Academy, a grammar school in all but name on the outskirts of South London. And Jessica, who was less able, would go to the best Church of England comprehensive school in London, St John's in Westminster. The headteacher was not allowed to select pupils by ability, but he was able to ask their parents about their church-going record. By a strange coincidence, most of them were white middle-class professionals just like the Canes. But Convent girl Charlie could hardly object to that.

Even that was not without difficulties. Jessica had been subjected to playground abuse, and one incident, where she hit another girl who had been swearing at her, was only kept out of the papers after Charlie intervened. She was no longer a child, refused to eat anything unless it had large dollops of Branston Pickle on it and would spend hours in her room.

Sam was more than a handful for Lucy. And Cane wasn't there to help her when she needed him. Sam was already taller than Lucy, far more outgoing than Jessica and basked in his celebrity status; far too much in his parents' view. Every time his pictures appeared in the papers he received sackloads of love letters from teenage girl admirers. He was naturally clever, so much so that he was always top of the class even though Lucy could never get him to do his homework. 'Don't worry mum, I can wing it,' he would say. Not only that, but he was popular with girls and was good at all sports. Just like his father. The main problem was prising him away from his TV video games. And he was always up to something. One weekend when Lucy and the children stayed at her parents' house and left Sam alone one afternoon while they went for a walk, he spent three hours ringing a phone sex chat line a school pal had told him about. What the pal didn't tell him was that the number was in Brazil. And Lucy's mum was not pleased when she noticed her monthly bill had shot up by £175. After her mother falsely accused Sir Norman, Sam finally owned up and was given a good hiding by his father, the only time he had ever hit one of his children, and confined to his room for three weekends.

Not that discipline worked with Sam. A French au pair drafted in to help, left abruptly after she smacked Sam and woke up the next morning to find a bag of marbles outside her bedroom door. She didn't see them until after she had tripped over them; she spent three days at St Thomas's with a broken leg and went back to Brittany and never returned.

There had been lighter moments. Such as when Jessica had been allowed to sing with the Spice Girls at a secret recording session.

And farcical ones. Such as when Sam had been told to clear up the sitting room in the flat as a puinishment for teasing his sister – again – and accidentally threw out with the rubbish the only copy of a secret NATO policy document Cane was supposed to gen up on over the weekend. At least, Cane assumed it was an accident. It was just as well no one saw the Prime Minister rummaging through the Downing Street dustbins one Sunday afternoon. Luckily, he found it.

And almost catastrophic ones. Such as when Sam and Jessica made breakfast in bed for Cane and Lucy in the flat on Lucy's birthday, and put a huge slice of bread in the toaster which jammed and set fire to the kitchen. Cane was leaping about naked, dousing it down with a fire extinguisher when the sirens screamed up Downing Street and a ladder with a man in a yellow helmet perched on top appeared at the kitchen window, smashed it and stuck his hose through.

'Well, I always told you all it wouldn't all be fun and games, free Cup Final tickets and shaking hands with pop stars, didn't I kids?' said Cane, snapping out of his reverie and trying to put a brave face on it.

He was the one who had put them through all this. They were under siege in a building that was supposed to be their home; his wife was turning into a nervous wreck; his daughter was clinging to his side for fear of the howling mob outside; his son couldn't join his mates in the park for a Sunday morning soccer game without a policeman hiding in the trees in case he was kidnapped. And what for? They could be living happily in a detached house in the Home Counties in the country like millions of other ordinary middle-class families did – and just as Lucy had always wanted.

Cane could never reveal his own doubts. They relied on him to pull them through, to tell them it was worth it. It was a question he had never asked himself until now. Did he regret becoming Prime Minister? The truth was he had been amazed by his own success, his rise from hospital doctor to MP, to party leader to Prime Minister. It had all happened in a blur. He had been just as amazed at how much he enjoyed it. The thrill of winning, the thrill of fame. And the thrill of trying to put right all the things his mother had told him were wrong since he was a boy. But what had his family got out of it? Did they enjoy it? Lucy was still in a state of shock at being catapulted into the public eye. And what about the kids? They had even less say in the matter. At first it was a novelty. Then came the playground jokes. 'S'pose you think you're special just cos your dad's Prime Minister, do you?' How would it affect them later? Would they for ever be known as the son and daughter of a Prime Minister, a minor celebrity status that had made the relatives of several famous politicians tragic figures with wasted lives, laughing stocks.

'I said there'd be times like this, didn't I, the first time we walked down that street?' said Cane, trying to cheer them all up. He looked at Lucy, but she wasn't looking at him. She was looking through the same window where moments ago he had seen that young innocent family full of hopes and dreams – and happiness. He wondered if she could see them too; and whether she was thinking the same as he was.

Whatever happened to that family?

* * *

The patient realised where he was as soon as he woke up. And it wasn't a hospital.

He recognised the cream duvet, the maroon walls and the enormous Damien Hirst painting of two intersecting triangles, one orange, the other lemon, opposite the end of the bed over a black Victorian fireplace. He recognised the photographs on the wall; friends and godchildren. He knew he was alive; and he knew he was in trouble.

Lomax was alone in bed, but he could hear a radio or television on in another room. His right wrist felt tight, he lifted it and saw the bandage. He remembered; the whisky, the tumbler; the blood. After that – nothing. He could recall what had happened before; he didn't want to but he would have to. He had to think fast, but he had less time than he thought. 'Joe, are you awake?' Silverman's head appeared round the door.

Even if he had wanted to hide what had happened, he couldn't now.

'I don't know what has been going on my dear Joe, but you had better explain it to me – fast,' said Silverman, half intimate, half intimidating.

'I don't know whether you know what's been going on in the world...but there's a Government crisis out there and I've had to spend the last twelve hours saving your life and deserting the Prime Minister in his hour of need.' Then more gently, 'I'll get you a cup of tea and then you can tell me - everything.'

When he returned, Silverman said, 'You do know what happened, Joe, don't you ... in the referendum?'

'Yes, I know.'

'Then what has happened to you?'

'It was the result.'

'What do you mean?'

'The result ... that's why I did it.'

'Joe, you're not making any sense, what are you talking about? I come home to my flat, fall over what I thought was a dead body, find out it's you, think you're dead, find your wrists slashed! I have to save your bloody life, I risk my bloody job, I've probably broken the law by not taking you to hospital, the Government's about to bloody collapse and you talk gibberish to me!'

Lomax lifted his arm up to shield himself from Silverman's onslaught. 'Joe, I'm sorry, you really must explain it to me, properly. For God's sake.'

Lomax closed his eyes and breathed in – hard.

'I don't know how I'm going to explain this, Ronnie, and I don't know what you're going to say. But when I've finished, you'll understand why ... why I did what I did here last night ... and you'll wish you had never saved me.'

Lomax was half right. By the time he had finished his story, Silverman did understand why he had tried to kill himself. He was glad he had saved him, but if he'd known what he was going to do in advance, he would have killed him with his own bare hands.

'The result, Ronnie ... ' Lomax struggled to find the courage to spit it out.

'What about it, Joe? What is all this? Have you gone mad? Is it drugs?'

'Ronnie, the No vote ... it's wrong.'

'Don't be stupid!' Silverman got up from the bedside to walk away, convinced Lomax had lost his mind. 'I haven't got time for this nonsense, Joe, I'm going ... '

'You can't!' Lomax screamed.

Silverman rushed back to his bedside, terrified the neighbours might hear. 'Calm down, calm down.'

'Ronnie, the vote in Liverpool was fixed ... '

'What?'

'Hear me out. I know because ... because I was ... '

'You were what?'

'I was involved.'

Silverman fell silent. Until this point he hadn't believed him, he thought Lomax was hallucinating. But he could tell from his voice, he meant it. 'You'd better start talking, Joe.'

'I had a bet on the result in Liverpool ... with a friend.'

'What friend?'

'An old college friend.'

'What's his name?'

'Marcus Williams. He works in the city.'

Silverman shuddered; he imagined he was hearing the opening lines of the most frightening horror story he had ever read. Even worse, he sensed he was going to discover he was in it.

'Marc and I thought we'd have a bet on the result in Mersey. We knew pretty well what the result was going to be because someone gave me the figures of the party's canvass returns. It was close but the Noes were clearly in the lead, so we had a bet on it, quite a few bets on it, actually.'

'You shouldn't have, but I don't understand. Mersey did vote No, so what's it got to do with anything?'

'Well, to make sure we got good odds on a No vote, we leaked them bogus figures from the canvass returns and told them ... we told them the result was going to be Yes in Mersey. It meant we got great odds on voting for a No result.'

'You fiddled the odds using confidential party information.'

' ... yes.'

'You bloody idiot.'

Lomax looked at Silverman. He knew from the boy's look that it got worse from here. A lot worse. 'And ... ?'

'Well, because of the row about Japanese jobs, there was a last minute swing in Mersey, like there was in lots of places, against voting No. As the vote was going on through the day, it became obvious the Mersey result was going to be Yes, not No.'

'How the hell could you have known?'

'Because someone told us.'

'What do you mean "someone told you"?'

'A bloke called Tony Quinlan.'

'Who the hell is Tony Quinlan?'

'He's an old mate of mine, one of our councillors in Mersey, he's a brilliant guy, he was fantastic at getting rid of Militant, you've no idea what this party owes to blokes like him, a really decent ... '

'What did he do?' shouted Silverman.

'Tony was in charge of the computer experiment counting the total number of votes.'

Lomax shut his eyes, sighed, swallowed – and continued, 'Tony's in big trouble, his business went bust, it wasn't ... it wasn't his fault, he's gonna go bankrupt and be kicked off ... '

'Get to the point, Joe!'

'There's nothing Marc doesn't know about gambling. He has accounts everywhere in all sorts of names and places. He's got one in Malaysia!'

'Never mind fucking Malaysia, get on with it!'

'Tony had been put in charge of all the computer gear – Mersey was one of the ones given government money to see if they speeded up counts. Marc did computer studies at college and there. Tony showed him the programme and Marc found a loophole in it. We never expected to do it because we were certain we had the result right, but we knew if we were wrong we could ... '

' ... fiddle it.'

'Yes.'

The referendum had become a kind of political Grand National, with the bookmakers eager to cash in by offering all manner of bets. Lomax explained how, he, Williams and Quinlan had staked dozens of different bets on Mersey voting No. They stood to win £100,000. Or lose almost as much if the result was Yes.

Silverman sat on the end of the bed, pulling his watch strap to breaking point. 'But why, Joe, why, why did you do it?'

132

'Tony was desperate. He needed the money. He could pay his debts and stay on the council,' gabbled Lomax, ' ... he's mayor next year ... '

'And you?'

'What?'

'Don't pretend you weren't making money out of it, you and this ... this Williams.'

'I wanted to buy a flat nearer to you Ronnie.'

He hadn't got the nerve to tell him the truth; that Williams was planning to use it to set up his own lobby firm. He already had one good government contact.

'Go on,' said Silverman, 'tell me the rest.'

'Wel,l when Tony realised the result was going to be Yes, he ... '

'He what?'

'He moved some votes.'

'Moved?'

'Yes, he moved 5,000 votes from the Yes total to the No total and of course it changed the whole fucking national result.'

'How?'

'By hacking into the computer. He and Marc had worked it all out in advance in case anything went wrong. Apparently as long as the total number of votes was not altered, no one would notice. And of course, Tony knew all the important passwords. He was in charge of the whole thing.'

Lomax lurched forward to clasp Silverman for comfort. But Silverman slowly pulled his arms off him, sat back and locked his fingers behind his neck. He remained silent for a minute. He had never placed a bet with a bookie in his life, but in those seconds, Silverman's brain worked as fast as any computer to calculate every permutation of the implications of what had happened, what it meant for him; for Cane; for Lomax – and what each should do.

'Joe, I'm going to ask you some questions. I want straight and honest – and I mean honest – answers to all of them. Is that understood?'

'Yes, Ronnie.'

'Have you involved me in any way in this ... this bet?'

'No, Ronnie, I swear, I haven't.'

'Sure?'

'I'm sure, I swear it Ronnie.'

'Have you picked up the money?'

'No, Marc was going to do it. He put the bets on in a variety of different accounts. He was going to collect it tomorrow and give me mine and Tony's share. He'll be wondering where I am and Tony'll be wondering why I haven't been in contact.'

'Right, Joe, I am going to tell you what you are going to do and you are going to follow my instructions to the last letter, is that clear?'

'Yes.'

'You are going to tell your friend Councillor Quinlan to own up to a mistake in the count ... '

'Mistake? You must be ... '

'Shut up, Joe! And do as I say! Do you hear?' Silverman screamed.

Lomax recoiled. Silverman's face was white, hard and frightening.

'You are going to tell Quinlan someone spotted him acting suspiciously and he'd better own up to a mistake before he is accused of corruption. Tell him to say it happened because he was in such a rush to get the result declared first, the computers were playing up, it was a new system, someone else hacked into it, that he didn't realise his error until he got home. I don't give a damn what his excuse is but he'd better well do it!' Silverman bawled, grabbing Lomax by the shoulders.

He relaxed his grip and continued. 'They did old-style ballot paper votes as well in Mersey, didn't they? As a back-up for the experiment?'

'Yes.'

'Right. They can get all the votes out and recount them in the old-fashioned way – and if what you say is right, the result will be reversed. The bookmakers can't open until first thing tomorrow morning and if the recount is announced before then, Williams won't get the money.'

'What if Tony says no? He's desperate for the ... '

'I don't give a fucking tuppenny piece about Councillor Quinlan and his fucking debts! You will make anonymous phone calls to the police, the town hall and the local papers saying a mistake was made. I'll get someone to tip off the Yes campaigners in Liverpool. Quinlan'll lose his nerve, he'll have to own up.'

'But what if he blabs?'

'Tell him he'll go to jail for election fraud – he's got no choice. The same applies to your smart-arsed little crook from the bookies. Tell him someone has rumbled the scam in Liverpool and that if he picks up his winnings he'll go to jail too.'

'Christ, it won't be easy.'

'Just do it! Ever been inside Strangeways, Joe?' said Silverman, reverting to his calm, controlled, normal self.

'No.'

'Well, I have, several times. It's where all the head cases from my constituency are sent. And I can tell you, some pretty unpleasant things are done to young men like you, Joe.'

* * *

'We can't tell him any of this.'

Charlie and Silverman had spent two hours in her office discussing what to do about Lomax and the referendum.

They worked well together, ever since that first doomed election campaign. It was Greaves who recommended Charlie to Silverman, a fast-rising figure at party headquarters earned from his reputation as a union fixer. Silverman spotted a kindred spirit when she fooled a BBC political reporter into believing that new figures he had been given by the Government showing hospital waiting lists had gone down were a fraud. It led the Nine O'Clock TV News. In fact the figures were genuine. But by the time the Health Minister had established that, it was three days later and the damage was done.

Within ten days Silverman had promoted Charlie to the task of briefing the party leader on that day's press coverage.

Silverman was surprised to find she had left Greaves and gone to America after the election defeat, but thought little more of it. However, when, three years later, he went to a US political conference in Los Angeles, Charlie was the talk of the town. She had transformed an obscure Senator into a much talked of 'president in the making'.

Silverman took her out to dinner and asked her if she would work for Cane. She declined. She loved America and Americans loved Charlie; none more than her married US Senator boss.

But Silverman was not one to give up. A month before Cane won power, he spotted a paragraph in the Wall Street Journal. 'British spin doctor Charlie Redpath is giving up the possibility of working in the White House to return to live in Britain after her elderly mother Frances had a heart attack.'

Charlie returned home to help nurse her mother back to health. Racked with guilt, she knew she could never go so far from home again.

The second time Silverman offered her the job, she accepted and agreed to start straight after the election. There was one condition: she would work for Prime Minister Cane, but not Leader of Her Majesty's Opposition Cane.

Her animal instinct complemented Silverman's analytical one. Both had political talents best used behind closed doors. Both realised that Cane was the key to both of them realising their own ambitions. They were equally devoted to and dependent on him. The dependency was two way.

Charlie had never been attracted by the public side of public life. She was too intolerant to do the necessary glad-handing with petty local party functionaries to be selected for a seat, too outspoken to go round kissing babies and opening fetes to get elected and too impatient to wait the ten years or more it could take to get from backbench to frontbench.

Silverman was living testimony to the difficulties of moving from the political shadows into the daylight. Off screen, when he was pulling the strings as a union and party official, he looked like a genius. The moment he moved into the Cabinet limelight, he looked more sinister than minister. The unfairness of it all gnawed away inside him, yet no one was more responsible than he was for turning British politics from the battle of ideas into the battle of images.

The master image maker could conjure one up for almost anyone – except himself. Charlie had learned a lot in America, and Silverman was more than willing and capable of filling in any gaps in her knowledge about British politics.

It was part of their strategy to keep Cane one step removed from the 'crafts' they specialised in. If Cane was to retain his image, it was essential to protect him from the indecent business of making someone seem decent.

'I've told Lomax to tell this individual Quinlan to say there was a foul up with the new computer system or admit he made a mistake and blame pressure to get a quick result,' Silverman said to Charlie. 'Neither he nor Williams, the one who placed the bet, can risk admitting the truth; they'd go to jail. I've told Lomax to tell them that too.'

'You know the risk we're taking just having this discussion, don't you?'

She knew it was a defining moment in her life. Until this point, everything she had done was, well, legitimate. They had played hard, but by the rules. This was different. But what else could they do? There was no other way of saving Cane. And saving Cane was not just important to her, it was important to the whole country. It was like a war. You couldn't always abide by the Geneva Convention.

Silverman looked up at her. He knew what she was thinking.

Cane's brave words in public meant nothing. He could never be the same again. Major never recovered after Black Wednesday and nor would Cane after his Fatal Fridal, as the tabloids had called the dramatic referendum result announcement at the QEII Centre. The glow, the invincibility, the magic, the confidence, were gone; shattered and wouldn't come back.

'It's just as risky if we do nothing,' said Silverman. 'There is a good chance it will all come out; Lomax will go to jail and I'll be destroyed.'

'OK, Ronnie, OK,' said Charlie, grimly.

There was no going back now.

CHAPTER FOURTEEN

Cane was annoyed that Charlie's mind seemed elsewhere on the Saturday afternoon after Fatal Friday. He needed her help in planning their next step after the No vote. There was no time to lose. But Charlie was waiting for a phone call. She had gone to join Cane at Chequers, the Prime Minister's official country residence in Buckinghamshire, where his family spent most weekends, straight after her meeting with Silverman.

'Charlie you're not concentrating, for goodness sake; we've got to confront it, it's no use wishing it would go away,' he snapped.

'Sorry.'

She kept thinking. Perhaps Quinlan had refused to co-operate. It was hours since she and Silverman had decided on their plan of action. Why hadn't he called?

'Charlie, come on, come on will you?' Cane lost his temper. 'I'm the one who's got to face this, I'm the one who's the biggest joke in the world, you can walk away any time you like, but look at you, you're just sitting there!'

'I'm sorry.' She jumped up from her armchair and walked over to where he was sitting, a few feet opposite her in jeans and a light blue denim shirt. She wanted to embrace him, but she couldn't. She had never done so. He sat looking between his knees in despair. Charlie was weighing up whether to reach a hand out to him when her mobile phone rang. She pressed the green receiver button and slammed it to her ear. She stood in silence, listening, her eyes darting from one side to the other. Cane wondered who it could be.

'YES, YES, YES, YEE-ES!' she shouted, clenching her fist.

'What on earth is it?' said Cane.

Charlie interrupted the voice at the other end. 'Ronnie, hold on, Steven's with me now, I've got to tell him. Don't go. Steven you're not going to believe this.'

'What are you on about?'

She reached out, held his hand and spoke calmly. 'Steven, there was a mistake in the referendum.'

'What do you mean a mistake? Have you gone stark staring mad?'

'Steven, my dear Steven, listen to me carefully. Some votes were not counted properly.'

'What? What votes? Where?'

'In Mersey. Remember they were using computers and were the first to declare? Apparently there was a computer error. They ... they got the votes wrong.'

'Are you serious?'

'Oh yes, I'm deadly serious. Deadly.'

'How many votes?'

'It looks like 5,000.'

'5,000? But that won't change it, will it? We lost by 5,000 and they're probably evenly split, it won't make a difference.'

'It could, Steven.'

'How?'

'Because, Steven,' Charlie knelt down. She felt like a gaoler about to tell a condemned man he was free to go, and she wanted to savour the moment.

'Charlie, tell me, please!'

'Because my dearest Steven, they think – they're not sure yet – but they think that all 5,000 were wrongly switched from one block to the other.'

Cane went rigid.

'And? ... ' His eyes were bursting.

'And yes, it looks as though they were wrongly switched from Yes to No.'

'I don't believe it! I don't believe it!' He jumped up and hugged Charlie before putting her down as quickly and holding her with arms outstretched.

'So if they're all Yes votes, we've ... '

'Yes Steven, if they're all Yes votes we've – not we've, you've – you've won.'

He hugged her again and jumped up and down, still hugging her. He still couldn't take it in. 'Charlie, are you sure? Has it been announced? Put the TV on, quick.'

'Calm down, Ronnie's waiting on the phone, he's got the details.'

Cane grabbed it from her. 'Ronnie, hi, I can't believe all this. Tell me it's true, please!'

Silverman told him he only had sketchy details, but he had heard from the Home Office, which was in charge of election law, that an official in Mersey had told the returning officer a mistake had been made and had ordered a recount immediately. The mayor of Mersey was going to make an announcement at a press conference any moment.

'Here it is, it's on TV now!' shouted Cane.

'It 'as been drawn to our attention by an official,' said the mayor, 'that some of the votes may've been counted incorrectly owing to a technical fault. The Electoral Commission which was supervising the process 'as decided under the special rules agreed for the computer experiment, that in the event of any error the votes should be recounted this afternoon in the old way, avoiding the need for a full inquiry before the result can be altered. I 'ave instructed officials to retrieve the ballot papers from storage.'

'He didn't say they were Yes votes. How do you know, Charlie?' stumbled Cane. 'Are you sure?'

'It's what the Home Office told Ronnie. We don't know any more than that.'

Charlie wanted Cane to return to Number 10 immediately. He would need to seize the initiative as soon as the revised Mersey result came through in the afternoon and there were no facilities for holding a press conference in Chequers. Cane agreed but suddenly remembered he had promised to take the children and Lucy to the new Disney film in the afternoon and then to McDonald's. They hadn't been out as a family for weeks and he had given Lucy his word that as soon as the referendum was over, the first Saturday afternoon would be devoted to a family jaunt. The children had been looking forward to it for weeks.

'I can't go to Number 10, I've promised Lucy I'll take the kids to the cinema.'

'But this afternoon is probably going to be the most momentous day since you became Prime Minister. It's a chance for you to get out there and repair all the damage that has been done to you in the last 48 hours. It's perfect timing for the Sunday papers. You give a live press conference at four on the steps of Number 10 and you'll be cover to cover on every single paper tomorrow. You'll be back where you were three days ago – in charge!'

'I can't,' said Cane, 'I've promised.'

'Ste-phen,' Charlie implored, lowering her voice, 'Lucy will understand. She'll be the first to be thrilled if the vote is reversed; it hurt her as much as you.'

'I know what she'll say; she'll say me giving a press conference isn't absolutely necessary and won't make a jot of difference to the result.'

How could he be so selfish? She had taken the biggest risk in her life, an insane risk, all to save him and his career. And he wouldn't even give up a trip to the cinema for her?

'Let's face it,' said Charlie, holding up her arms in exasperation, 'you've given a lot of press conferences that weren't absolutely necessary but some of them have made an absolutely bloody crucial difference to your standing, haven't they? It's what you're so brilliant at. Don't you see? You can take the kids to the flicks tomorrow, they'll still be open.'

Cane and Charlie didn't often argue. But when they did, they did so as equals. Modern Prime Ministers had long ceased being the first among equals in their Cabinets, but this was the first to be joint equal first with a press secretary. Silverman and Greaves were equal third. The rest equalled nothing.

But where his family was concerned, Cane remained more than equal to Charlie. 'No, I really can't. I've said I'll take them and I'm going to.

We'll do it in a press release and I'll go on TV tomorrow.'

'Well, if that's what you want, I'd better get back to Downing Street straight away,' she said abruptly. 'Ronnie's going to be there so he can help. I don't think he's watching cartoons this afternoon.'

'I've made my decision and it's final,' he said, raising his voice. 'Work's not the only place where I'm under pressure you know, Charlie.'

'Nor me, but what would you know about that, Prime Minister?'

* * *

'The result of the recount of votes cast in the European referendum in Mersey is as follows,' said the mayor. 'Total votes cast: 37,505.'

'It's the same!' said Charlie, watching with Silverman from her Downing Street study.

'Votes in favour of the euro, 21,310.'

'Its up, it's up!' shouted Charlie.

'Wait, just wait, it's not enough,' said Silverman.

'Votes against the euro, 16,195.'

'It's down Ronnie, it's down! What's the total? Please!' Charlie screamed in agony, waiting to hear if it was enough. She was tearing at her hair.

Before the camera had switched to the national returning officer at the Queen Elizabeth II Centre in Westminster, who was about to give the new final result, it was there on the screen.

Total UK Yes votes: 15,770,289. Total UK No votes: 15,770,067. Majority in favour of euro: 222.

NEW EURO RESULT – BRITAIN VOTES YES.

'I don't believe it, I don't believe it!' said Ronnie, hugging Charlie and lifting her into the air.

'Bloody hell, Ronnie, if only they knew, if only they knew!' she said as they danced around the room in an embrace.

'But they don't, and we had better make sure that they never find out,' he said as she released him from her grip.

'Wait!' shouted Charlie.

'What is it?'

'Steven! He won't know! He's gone to the bloody cinema with the kids. We've got to tell him!'

'Page him, he always leaves his bleeper on.'

'Yeah, I arranged it with him. No, wait!' said Charlie. 'I've got a better idea.'

* * *

'Prime Minister? Prime Minister? Mrs Cane? Look this way please, look this way please!'

As Cane, Lucy and the children emerged blinking from the UCI Cinema in High Wycombe, they were confronted not so much by the mass media as mass hysteria. 'Steven, what's going on, what are they doing here?' said Lucy, as a microphone was shoved in front of Steven and a cable caught round Sam's leg, tripping him up.

'Mind the children!' shouted Lucy. 'This is intolerable, it's a family day out, what are you all doing here?'

But her words were drowned by the barrage of questions. 'Prime Minister, what's your reaction to the new euro vote, I take it you've been told?' said the reporter holding the mike as he was squeezed between two burly photographers.

Cane was thrown. He didn't know what the result was. Why hadn't Charlie told him? Who the dickens had told the press he was at the cinema?

He tried to keep calm and prayed Charlie's inside information was right. If it wasn't, he was about to look the biggest fool in history.

'Er, I don't actually know the result, as you see I've been to the cinema with my family.'

He could feel his pulse racing.

'It's Yes, Mr Cane!' said the reporter, now barely visible in the melee. 'You've won by 222 votes; there was a computer mistake in Mersey.'

'Are you kidding? I don't believe you.'

'It's true, Prime Minister, that's why we're all here.'

Cane was open mouthed.

'I ... I ... er ... ' He burst out laughing.

'You mean you don't know, sir?' said the stupefied reporter, who realised he had just written himself into history.

'Er, no ... er, you've stumped me, you really have. I don't know what to say, I really don't. It's ... it's fantastic; incredible; unbelievable!' He turned to Lucy and embraced her, then embraced the children. His arms were round all of them.

'I'm completely gobsmacked. I'm sorry ... ' Cane pulled a handkerchief from his pocket and wiped his eye.

'Are you really saying, you didn't know about the result, Prime Minister?' said the reporter.

'Yes, I know it sounds daft, but we were going to the cinema, I couldn't see the point of calling it off ... it's like those penalty shoot outs, I can't bear to watch them. What did you say the majority was?'

'222.'

'Wow! You sure? There's no more recounts?' he burst out laughing.

'It's final.'

'Well, I am absolutely delighted,' he said. The emotional family scene captured on film, Cane the statesman was back in control. 'I know it is only a tiny margin, but just as we accepted the result when it went against us by a very small majority, I hope all sides will accept this result. As I said after the first result, in a democracy, a majority of one is sufficient – and 222 will do nicely thank you.'

'Do you have anything to say to the anti-euro campaigners who demonstrated outside Downing Street last night, Prime Minister?'

'No, other than, let us put the past behind us and get on with the future.'

'What are your plans now Prime Minister?'

'Well, we were going to go to McDonalds, but I'm not sure there's enough Big Macs to feed you lot!'

'Fantastic, absobloodylutely fantastic! Charlie, that was the greatest stroke of genius I have ever seen!' said Silverman, shaking his head in wonder at the live TV pictures.

'He was good, wasn't he?' said Charlie, dabbing her eyes.

Silverman had never seen Charlie cry. He had never seen Cane cry until a minute ago on the television.

'I'm not talking about Cane, don't sit there like Little Miss Innocent, I'm talking about you Charlie Redpath.'

She knew he was. You could tell from the red lipstick grin that stretched from one ear to the other.

'You didn't tell him, did you?' said Silverman. 'When you said you'd paged him with the result when you went to the loo, you were lying, weren't you?'

Her body was beginning to convulse with silent laughter.

'You kept him in the bloody dark and you told the press where he was. You wanted them to find him with the kids having an everyday Saturday afternoon when his whole world could have been falling apart. Genius, pure bloody genius.'

'Playing bowls didn't do Francis Drake much harm, did it?' she said. 'In centuries to come, kids will learn how Steven Cane watched Donald Duck as the anti-European armada was sunk in the River Mersey!'

'And then went off to have a Big Mac!' Silverman finished the sentence for her.

The two of them laughed and laughed till tears streamed down both their faces. They were laughing so loudly that Charlie only just heard her mobile phone ring. It was Cane, calling from the mobile in the limousine that was waiting to pick up the family outside the cinema.

'I'll kill you for this.'

'Nah, you won't, Steven,'

'You set me up, didn't you?'

'Yep. Any complaints?'

'Yes, I nearly died of shock.'

'You looked OK to me.'

'Did it look OK on the telly?'

'Brilliant, just brilliant, you were brilliant, Steven.'

'I can't get over the result, 222 votes, it's incredible.'

'Steven, that line about "222 will do nicely" – beautiful.'

'You know what it all means, Charlie, don't you?'

'What?'

'We're back in business, aren't we?'

'You bet. And that's not all it means.'

'What do you mean?'

'It means we start planning the election. Second term here we bloody well come.'

The Sunday papers were spread over the dining table in the White Parlour at Chequers the morning after when Lucy joined Cane for breakfast. While she had a lie in, he had been up early to read them all and had gone for a walk along the gravel Victory Drive lined with beech trees planted by Winston Churchill.

Cane had come through his Dunkirk.

* * *

'222 WILL DO,' screamed the News of The World. And below, 'Super Cool Cane Hails Yes Vote Sensation. He takes wife and kids to Disney film, hears shock result and says, "Where's our Big Macs?" '

The papers were strewn across the table as the waitress served Lucy and Cane their breakfast at Chequers. Scrambled egg for her; bacon and eggs for him.

The Sunday Mirror version was, 'YES! DAD'S MY BOY!' While the Sunday Times offered, 'STRAIGHT OUT OF THE MOVIES – IT'S YES'. The UCI Cinema in High Wycombe became world famous as pictures of the family on the steps of the cinema appeared on the front page of every paper in Britain and scores of others all over the world.

Lucy glanced at the headlines one by one.

'Steven?' she said. 'How did the papers know we were at the cinema? Who told them?'

'They were all demanding to know where I was.'

'Yes, but they're not supposed to know when we're out with the children, are they?'

'No, not normally.'

'So who told them?'

'The Number 10 Press Office, I suppose.'

'You mean Charlie, Charlie told them, didn't she? It wasn't an accident, it was a publicity stunt.'

'Does it really matter? We all look fine in the paper.'

'Yes we do, don't we, that's what matters, isn't it?' she said, pushing her barely touched breakfast away.

Cane was engrossed in reading the papers.

'Steven?'

'Yes,' he said, without looking up.

'Steven, now it's over, tell me the truth; if the result had remained No would you have been able to survive?'

'Truthfully?'

'Of course.'

'Well,' said Cane, putting the paper down, 'the truth is I was going to talk about it with you tonight. I was planning to tell Charlie and Ronnie on Monday that I wanted to stand down, but obviously I wanted to speak to you first. Does that surprise you?'

'Yes and No,' she said, 'forgive the pun.'

'But there's no need now. We got away with it. It has changed everything, we really can win that second term now.'

Lucy smiled, and nodded in agreement, but with resignation, not enthusiasm. The second term she wanted was a second term of a normal life, like the one they had before Dr Steven Cane became Prime Minister Cane.

'I couldn't have carried out a No decision, Lucy,' said Cane, 'I couldn't live a lie, could I?'

Lucy looked down and sipped her tea, and heard a knock at the door.

'Sorry to disturb you, sir, madam, there's an urgent phone call for Mrs Cane.' It was one of the Chequers' staff.

'Who is it?' said Lucy.

'It's your Aunt Mimi, maam.'

'Can you tell her Lucy'll call her back in half an hour?' said Cane. 'We're in the middle of breakfast.'

'No, no, I'll take it now, Steven, I must.'

He went back to reading a feature in the Mail on Sunday titled, 'The Perfect Family Man Who Kept Britain In The Euro Family.'

CHAPTER FIFTEEN

Tony Quinlan had never been to the Crown and Cushion pub in Knutsford. It was thirty miles from Knowsley and on the edge of one of a string of new executive homes that had been built in the Cheshire country-side in recent years. This was where Mersey ended and the rest of the world began. Tony didn't know anyone from Knutsford. He'd been there several years ago to a house-warming party held by a neighbour who'd won the Football Pools. Tony always lost. That was life. His life.

Lomax was nervous about meeting him. He had made an excuse to meet at the Crown and Cushion in Knutsford because he thought there was less chance of Quinlan causing a scene – or bringing some mates with him.

Lomax had spent more than two weeks avoiding his calls. If Quinlan was in a nervous state before their aborted attempt to make £100,000 from the euro referendum, he was close to suicidal now. He had done as Lomax told him and said he was convinced there had been a computer error and that he hadn't realised the mistake until the morning after the count. Lomax warned he had no choice – and not to try any tricks – because if the truth came out that they had tried to fix the vote, they would both go to jail.

But it meant Quinlan had lost his last chance of paying off Harris Finance and their heavies. He had promised he would pay them in full a week after the referendum. When he failed to do so, he was stopped one night while walking home from his mother-in-law's house on the neigh-bouring estate. The next thing he knew he was in hospital with his arm in a sling and his head bandaged.

He didn't see his attacker but Quinlan smelled him when he was hit over the head and spun round, his face sliding down his assailant's coat before he hit the pavement.

He smelled of sheepskin.

When Quinlan got out of hospital a day later and arrived home, a letter from the town hall was waiting for him. It was from the leader of his own ruling group. They were formally asking him to stand down as next year's mayor and retire from the council as a result of his mistake in the referendum. They had protected him from being exposed as the man who cocked it up, partly out of loyalty but also because they knew there was some truth in his claim that the count had been rushed. But they considered it 'best for all concerned' if he stood down and, if he agreed, they would issue a press release saying it was for 'personal reasons'. Good mates. Bastards.

They didn't know it, but they were doing Quinlan a favour. He knew he would have to resign because of his debts. His only hope now was to protect his wife Sheila from the ruin that was about to engulf them. To do that he had to get some money, somehow, from someone. That someone had to be the man sitting opposite him in the Crown and Cushion snug bar. There was no one else.

'What happened to you?' said Lomax, looking at Quinlan's bandages.

'A slight altercation with a business contact.'

'I know you've got terrible problems, but I can't help you, I can't.'

'Joe, you 'ave to help me or I am dead.'

'I've been through this with you. We couldn't collect the bet even if we'd wanted to. As soon as the recount was ordered, if we'd cashed it, the bookies would have been on to us, then the police.'

'Joe, you're not 'earing me,' said Quinlan, clenching his jaw and leaning over to within an inch of Lomax's face. He could see each piece of black and grey stubble on Quinlan's unshaved chin. The brim of his trilby was nudging against Lomax's forehead.

'Tony, I haven't got any money. What do you want to me to say?'

'Say you'll find it Joe, otherwise I'm fucked. Look at your fancy clothes, you've got money alright, or you know where to find it.' Quinlan spat. He got hold of Lomax's sweater and spoke slowly, looking directly at him. 'And your mate Silverman, he's got money, hasn't he?'

Lomax's eyes flashed from Quinlan to the landlord, who had noticed the dispute. Quinlan backed off.

'You're the one who coughed up to the police that the vote was wrong, aren't you, you little bastard,' he said. He had dropped his voice, but he was only just starting to increase the pressure. 'You did it because the result went the wrong way an you suddenly realised our little scam had fucked your precious little Government. I bet that fuckin' Silverman told you to do it, didn't he, didn't he? I'm right, aren't I? If you hadn't blown the whistle, and forced me to own up, we could've 'ad the dough and no one would have known. But we couldn't, could we, because you panicked and told Silverman what you'd done.'

Quinlan had figured the whole thing out.

'Well, Mr Lomax, you had better go and tell your friend Mr Silverman to produce some money fast – or I'll start talking.'

'You can't, you'll go to jail.'

'Only if Silverman reports me to the police. But he's not going to do that, is he, little Joe, because if he does, he won't be able to screw the arse off his little scouse faggot any more, will he?'

Lomax was too petrified to answer.

'Now you just listen to me. All I want is the thirty grand that you promised. I effin' well earned it and you took it away to please your Mr effin' Silverman. Well you can get it back from him. Do that and you'll never 'ear from me again. You're lucky I'm not askin' for more, 'cos I effin' well could, and you well know it. All I want is enough to clear me debts so I can look Sheila in the eye again. I don't care less what 'appens to me, but I'm gonna see her alright, if it's the last thing I do in my life. Do that, and you'll never 'ear from me again. Don't and I'll take the whole fuckin' lot of you down with me.'

* * *

The warning was still reverberating in Lomax's head when he stood on

Silverman's doorstep forty eight hours later.

'Come in, Joe.'

Silverman took Lomax's jacket and hung it up on the Victorian wooden coathanger in his hallway. Lomax had every reason to look nervous. Quinlan wasn't the only one making threats.

Williams had phoned Lomax the previous morning.

'I've been thinking Joe,' he had said, 'I don't see why I should be out of pocket by £33,000 just so you could get this poxy Government off the hook.'

'What are you saying Marc?' said Lomax.

'I'm saying, why shouldn't I be compensated for my loss?'

'Compensated?!' exclaimed Lomax.

'Why not?'

'And who is going to pay this compensation?'

'I'm sure Ronnie can get hold of some cash from some of his rich friends, don't you agree?'

'I can't believe you are doing this Marc. We've been mates for nearly ten years. You realise what this is don't you? Blackmail.'

'Bollocks, Joe. Listen, you do it properly and there's no reason why you shouldn't get a share of it. How long d'you think Silverman's going to stay besotted with you? Most of his other boyfriends got the push after six months. You're only screwing him because you think he can help you become an MP – if you believe that you're mad. You'd better use him while you can – it's all he's doing with you.'

'But Ronnie knew nothing about the bet. I only told him afterwards. If he wanted to turn us over to the law he could do it tomorrow!'

'He certainly likes turning you over!' Williams guffawed. 'Listen, you've got him where you want him, we both have. Tell him I've demanded £60,000 to keep quiet – and we can split it. It's perfect. It's like a game of poker: I'm gambling on the fact that your darling Ronnie is a darned sight more worried about getting dragged into a scandal which would cost him his job, than he is about whether a nonentity like me goes to prison. And remember, Joe, when did you ever see me beaten at cards?'

Silverman had spotted Lomax's edginess the second he walked in.

'Sit down and listen to me, Joe. I think I may be able to solve your problem.'

Lomax noticed how Silverman always referred to the matter as his, Lomax's problem, as a reminder, not that he needed one, that he was on his own; Silverman was merely helping him and would disown him if anything went wrong.

'I believe I may be able to obtain the resources you require to sort yourself out,' said Silverman, revolving his Ingersoll. 'It goes without saying, that I'm not going to tell you where I got the money from and that you're not going to tell anyone where you got the money from. I take it that is understood.'

The hypnotic aura around Silverman that had sent a tingle down Lomax's spine the first night they sat in this room was still there, only this time it made him shiver.

He nodded meekly. Silverman could see the fear in Lomax's eyes. The blood-stained white tassels on the Indian rug beneath his feet were a reminder of how fragile, how volatile Lomax was.

'Joe, Joe, I know I must seem hard,' said Silverman, bending down to sit beside him. 'I'm trying to help you, I really am. You'll never know the lengths I've gone to sort this out for you. D'you think I would have done it for anyone else? You'd have ended up in jail.' He stroked Lomax's hand.

'Joe, don't worry, I will look after you, we're going to be alright, both of us, I promise. One day we won't be sitting on a sofa together, you'll be behind me on the green benches of the House of Commons, think of that Joe.'

Silverman put his hand under Lomax's chin and lifted it towards his face.

He kissed him on the lips, placed Lomax's hand around his back, pulled back, swept his fringe off his forehead and said, 'Joe Lomax, I love you.'

Lomax put his arms around Silverman's neck and pulled him on top of him and plunged his tongue into the Chancellor's mouth.

He could taste the sharp tang of Tabasco.

* * *

Charlie had never been inside a Rosebury's supermarket. The first Rosebury's general provisions store opened in the week of Queen Victoria's death in 1901.

Some of the shelves looked as though they were still carrying the same stock. All that changed when it was bought by Tom Innes, who had invited Charlie to lunch at his office in Smithfield. There was nothing Victorian about Innes.

He shaved his head bald ten years ago when he started thinning on top. The features that stood out most on his sculpted tanned head were a diamond stud in his right ear lobe, a stubby silver beard and a libidinous grin. His usually wore a white suit and a tight white T-shirt that was intended to show – and succeeded – in showing he was still as lithe as when he trekked round South America a quarter of a century ago on a diet of a line of cocaine, one meal and several beers a day.

He instructed his managers not to employ ugly check-out girls where possible. The fact that third wife Liv Johansen was a Dutch former super-model, did not stop him flirting with other women. Most didn't resist and when they did Innes saw it as a challenge. He had spent his whole life setting himself challenges and overcoming them. He hadn't overcome Charlie yet. But when he saw the plunging neckline of the tight black jacket she was wearing for their lunch, with no blouse underneath, he resolved to try again.

After getting a degree in English at Essex University in its rebellious heyday, Innes spent two years backpacking round the world. When he returned he wrote a guide book for students, 'Laidbackpacking', on the cheapest hotels from Jaipur to Jakarta and how to avoid bandit country. He was speaking from experience – Peru's Sendero Luminoso terrorists threatened to kill him when got lost taking a short cut across the Andes to Machu Picchu. Another section called 'laid-backpacking' listed the best pick-up joints in each city and was condemned by rent-a-quote MPs; which was exactly Innes's intention when he phoned up a newspaper and gave the story to a journalist in return for a free holiday if it made the front page.

It did – and made the book a smash hit and inspired him to set up a holiday company by the same name offering cheap flights, tours and overland safaris to a new generation ready to try Bangladesh instead of Benidorm. In five years he was a multi-millionaire and had revolutionised the travel industry; in ten he stunned everyone by selling up for £95 million and buying a little known northern chain of grocery stores, Rosebury's.

Innes could see the recession coming, and realised the holiday industry would be hit hard. He figured supermarkets would be the last to be hit by the slump; people would go without two weeks holiday in Thailand long before they went without two weeks shopping. From his travels, he could see British supermarkets were in a dire state. Where were the efficient check-out staff of German stores? Where were the hundreds of wines of French ones, the dozens of breads of Italian ones? Where were the smiling check-out staff of US stores? Did people really want no more than processed cheese and ovenbake chips? Innes had proved people would buy exotic holidays; common sense told him they would buy ready-to-cook versions of the exotic food they had sampled there. They didn't have to go half way round the world to get them, just drive to the out-of-town Rosebury's mega-hyperstores Innes was building as fast as he could.

The supermarket moguls mocked him when he bought Rosebury's, but within two years they were mimicking him. Rundown Rosebury's became a runaway success. Meanwhile Laidbackpacking ran into trouble and collapsed.

Having pioneered New Holidays and New Supermarkets, it was only a matter of time before the pioneers of a new political movement turned to him.

It was after Innes spoke at a CBI conference, accusing the Government of failing a generation by wasting North Sea oil revenue instead of investing it in training for unemployed young people, that he got the call.

Silverman was a junior frontbencher recruiting businessmen to give their support – and cash – to the party. Innes had seen the 1980s business slump coming, and he saw the slump of a fast tiring Government coming too.

His decision to buy into Steven Cane was as shrewd as his decision to buy into Rosebury's. He became one of the first donors to Cane's blind trust, set up when he became party leader to pay for office costs, foreign trips, research and campaigns. After he became Prime Minister, Innes gave £5 million to create a 'Cadets of Industry Training College' where bright young entrepreneurs could win scholarships to boost their business skills.

Now Lord Innes, known in the popular press as Lord Laidback, he won more acclaim when he volunteered to head a new body to turn part of the old Millennium Dome site into an Olympic stadium.

But Innes was not playing games when he sat down to lunch with Charlie, not yet anyway. He was alarmed by reports that the Government was about to introduce new curbs on out-of-town shopping centres in response to growing complaints that they were destroying traditional town centres. He wanted to build twenty new superstores to extend his empire to the remaining parts of southern England it had missed so far.

'I do feel that these proposals have been badly thought out, Charlie. My new shops would create more than 8,500 jobs in provincial areas where unemployment is much higher than the national average.'

'I appreciate that, Tom, but first of all you've got to realise I cannot get involved directly in this; the Chancellor has set up a study into the whole subject, as you know.'

'Yes,' smiled Innes, 'the Chancellor. How is Ronnie? I was so sorry he couldn't make lunch with me today, but I am delighted you could come instead.'

'We can't ignore the strength of feeling,' said Charlie, ignoring his leer. Innes was too shrewd not to realise why Silverman had pulled out at the last minute, to be replaced by Charlie. Horses for courses.

'There's been well attended protest marches through each town centre and surveys have shown a three to one majority against more superstores and in favour of keeping more local shops,' she continued.

'I thought this government wanted to keep prices down?' said Innes. 'The goods in our shops are up to thirty per cent cheaper than those in town centres. If you want US-style bargain basement prices for designer clothes, trainers, coffee, baby buggies, you are going have to allow US-style stores. Our customers are working-class people trying to make ends meet. Aren't they your supporters?'

'We have to take account of all groups now, Tom. Consensuality, that's our motto.'

'I heard you preferred sensuality.'

She rolled her eyes, but not too dismissively. Innes was more than a flirt; he was lecherous. But he was also very clever. He acted the buffoon but was highly intelligent, the opposite of most politicians Charlie had dealt with.

'I don't see what's consensual about protecting the NIMBY brigade in their Volvos who can afford to pay through the nose for their food in an old-style market town and to hell with those who need to scrimp and save,' said Innes.

'That's an oversimplification. Tom, I know you've been a loyal and generous supporter over the years – your £100,000 donation to the blind trust before the last election was so appreciated by Steven – and goodness knows, with an election coming up we desperately need more support like that. The last thing we want to do is to make an enemy of you but this isn't the States – I spent more on TV ads for one Senator when I worked there than we have for Steven's entire general election campaign budget. But if we're going to win debates like this we have to be out there arguing and campaigning – and it all costs money.'

'I think I see where you're coming from. Ronnie said you were looking for more donations in the next few weeks to build up your election war chest. There's a good chance I can do the same as last time,' he said looking into her eyes.

'That'd be brilliant Tom,' said Charlie, putting down her knife and fork to rest her hand on his. 'And remember, the White Paper on out-of-town stores isn't completed yet. Ronnie agrees it is vital to take account of the job implications on the rural economy as well as the environmental impact. He thinks a review might be the best way forward, as long as it gets a positive response from all sides, otherwise we'd be back to square one.'

'Perhaps I could look at ways of making the stores more environmentally sensitive, extra landscaping, maybe using some of the space to create mini outdoor parks for families,' said Innes. 'Why not get Cane's brood to come and try one out in the election campaign? I'm sure I could knock one up!'

'You're on, Innes!' said Charlie.

'It's a deal, Redpath.'

'I can assure you your £100,000 will be put to good use.'

'I'm sure it will, Charlie, I'm sure it will.'

This time it was Innes's hand that reached towards her. But it wasn't on the table, it was under it. Charlie was not his anorexic wife Liv, who was more bone than flesh. She was more flesh than bone. And he wanted to devour every ounce. His wife may have been devoid of any bulge, but Lord Laidback's was clearly visible.

'What's in your diary this afternoon?' he asked.

'Very little,' said Charlie.

'Why don't we discuss this further in my studio?'

'Why not, m'Lud?'

His hand slid further along her skirt.

CHAPTER SIXTEEN

It was no surprise the nurses had invited Greaves to address their protest rally at the Albert Hall in September.

Buoyed up by their success in winning a big pay rise shortly after the last election, they were out to use their muscle to force the Government to increase hospital spending. A severe winter the previous year had seen a record number of deaths from hypothermia, partly because it followed the longest ever sequence of mild winters.

The Health Secretary Fred Hodgson had rashly called the outcry it provoked an 'outbreak of hysteria not hypothermia.' He had been forced to make a grovelling apology.

If Hodgson was the nurses' villain, Greaves was their hero ever since Treasury sources leaked the fact that he had tried and failed to persuade Cane to introduce a wealth tax on high earners to raise an extra £400 million for hospitals. Greaves knew the dangers of agreeing to speak at the meeting. He would have only had to cough at the wrong moment for it to set off another rash of 'Cane Mutiny' headlines.

Luckily, he was due to attend a United Nations conference in Singapore the day before the nurses rally, and to make sure he wasn't back in time, hastily added a visit to nearby Indonesia to see how IMF support had helped them rebuild their economy. Shortly after replying to the nurses, he was with Charlie at a meeting called to discuss plans for the party conference. 'Oh Charlie, I've had to tell the nurses I can't make their rally, don't suppose you know anyone else who might want to go?' he said with a sarcastic grin. Calling Charlie's bluff was a dangerous game. She went straight to Cane.

'Greaves has turned down an invite to address the nurses conference; he's in the Far East.'

'Thank goodness for that,' said Cane.

'It means we'll have to send someone else.'

'Who? The poor sod'll get torn to pieces.'

'Why don't you do it?'

'Me? Do you want to see me lynched? They hate me.'

'Think about it. It's not so mad. Yes, the blessed angels always get public opinion on their side, but it depends how you tackle it. If you ask people should the NHS have more money, they say yes. If you ask them would they support a wealth tax to pay for it, they'd probably say yes. But there's an election coming up. If we break our promise not to put taxes up, it will destroy our campaign before we've even started. The Mail will say we're going back to our bad old ways – and they'd be right. Go to the nurses, Steven, take them on. Show them you're not frightened of them. You used to be a doctor; talk to them in language they understand to get your argument over to the wider audience outside.

'Mmmm ... '

'And you can pull a rabbit out of a hat and say you've found another few hundred million quid for the NHS. Daa-daa!' said Charlie, mimicking a conjurer taking a bow.

'Another few hundred million? And where is that going to be magicked from, may I ask, Chancellor Redpath?'

'Ronnie won't mind, but you'd better not tell the DPM. If he'd known there was money for the nurses you could be damned sure he'd have cancelled his UN meeting and made the speech himself so he could take the credit.'

'We'd better be careful not to upset him.'

'Just tell Hodgson to find it. What does it matter where it comes from? I don't know ... reserves, contingencies, rearrange the books, put something else off for a year or two, get rid of a few bureaucrats – that always goes down well. If you tell Hodgson to do it, he'll do it. He knows he was lucky not to be sacked for his "hysteria not hypothermia" gaffe – if you said jump, he'd hurdle the bloody Albert Hall. And don't worry about Gareth. By the time he gets back, it will all be done and I can't see how he can complain. It's what he wanted isn't it?'

Charlie had gone to a lot of trouble to make sure the nurses didn't boo Cane when he stood up to address the rally. She had spoken to one of the Royal College of Nursing union officials, Linda Murphy, who was on the list of Parliamentary candidates and desperately keen to become one of Cane's MPs. Charlie told her that if she and one or two friends would like to applaud when he stood up, it would be greatly appreciated. She would appreciate it even more if they were wearing their uniforms and were spread in little groups around the hall.

'Colleagues,' said the chairman, 'please welcome the Prime Minister the Right Honourable Doctor ... ' heavily emphasising the doctor, ' ... Dr Steven Cane.'

A handful of scruffy militants booed. Then on the other side of the hall, right on cue, nurse Murphy and her uniformed friends leapt up and down, cheering and applauding, one or two flashing a glimpse of stocking. It didn't take a genius to work out who the flashguns were aimed at.

That should take care of the pictures, let's just hope the story works out OK, thought Charlie.

Cane's speech went exactly as she had planned. The enthusiastic response from nurse Murphy and her friends drowned out the militants' demo – and paved the way for his 'spontaneous' ice breaker.

'The last time I heard a nurse applaud was when I managed to get a splinter out of a drunk's backside,' he said, when the noise had subsided.

Even the troublemakers found it hard not to laugh at such an opening line from a Prime Minister. Nearly every previous speaker had droned on about comrades and composite such and such, or this or that reference back. Cane didn't care for comrades and composites and preferred to refer to himself.

'He ended up with me at my old hospital, St Bernard's, after being found in a rubbish skip with a six inch splinter in his rear. He'd been so frisky with the nurses that they refused to treat him – and I was muggins.

I'd only started training there the previous week. Anyway, when I got the splinter out, the drunk screamed and the nurses started clapping!'

By the time he approached the £400 million grant for extra beds, Dr Cane had removed another splinter – a political one. But Charlie was in a panic. Off stage, she had seen something. She would have only been slightly less alarmed to see a man with a gun. She had heard Greaves' trip to Indonesia had been cut short because of riots in Jakarta. But she never dreamed he'd come to the nurses rally. Yet there he was. What the hell was he up to?

He was standing behind the platform with one of the union officials, out of sight of the press. Charlie, who was also in the area barred to the media, behind a pillar, could see him nodding his head disdainfully as Cane spoke.

As she watched, she gasped out loud. Cane was about to get to the bit where he announced the extra £400 million. Greaves didn't know about it.

'And I am glad to be able to announce today,' said Cane, 'that we have found an extra £400 million to provide additional beds for the coming winter.'

Linda Murphy and her stockinged cheerleaders reacted as vociferously as Charlie hoped, leaping to their feet.

And Greaves reacted as violently she had feared.

As the applause died down, she saw him do a double take. She could lip-read him say to the union crony with him, 'Did he say £400 million? Did he say £400 million?'

As Greaves looked around, he saw Charlie, looking at him. He marched over pointing his finger at her. 'How dare you announce major spending plans without telling me? You ask me to be loyal then wait till I am out of the country so you can pull off some cynical stunt to con the nurses. Where's this money coming from, I demand to know. You're always saying there's no spare money for giveaways, but when he gets up to make a difficult speech, you can throw in £400 million, just like that. It's a bit pricey isn't it? £400 million a speech. You'd better keep his speaking commitments down or he'll bust the reserves.'

'For Christ's sake keep your voice down, Gareth,' hissed Charlie, raising her arms to quieten him. 'You'll cause a bloody commotion.'

He jabbed his right forefinger so close to her face she could see the dirt in his jagged fingernail. 'Don't lecture me, Redpath! You'll be sorry you did this!'

Charlie looked around to make sure no pressmen had got into the restricted zone. They hadn't. Thank God they were all still trying to get a shot of the nurses' suspender belts. All except one, that is.

Blackie Cole's orders when he was sent to the rally, were simple: get a strong shot of the PM for *The Globe*'s nurses' campaign. And get it back early. The paper was running a centre-page spread which would have to be prepared by four pm at the latest. Blackie got the picture he wanted the moment Cane stood up: the PM framed by a row of pretty nurses holding up placards. All he needed to do was to find somewhere quiet to 'ping' it down a phone line via his Apple Mac so that it got to the office on time. He found the spot he wanted at the back of the stage, sat down and started to wire up. As the pictures started to transmit, he heard a kerfuffle behind the partition separating him from the area behind the platform. He knew that voice. Blackie scurried along the wall looking for a gap. There wasn't one. But at the end of the partition he found a door that opened out on to where the argument was going on. He looked around to make sure no one had seen him, eased the door open with his foot and watched through the view finder.

He held his finger over the button and pressed. That was one in the bag. Now for something a little more risky. He waited for the right moment.

It came when Charlie jabbed her finger right in Greaves' face.

Blackie let the motor drive go and shot the entire roll of 36 frames in a twelve-second burst. The whole violent sequence was captured on film. Every blow and counter blow, every grimace, every snarl.

* * *

'Look, Kelly, your friend Ursula has come to see you.'

Kelly's face shone as brightly as the sun emerging from behind a black cloud as Ursula Jennings kissed and embraced her. Kelly threw her arms round Mrs Jennings and hugged her even tighter.

'And how is Kelly today?' said Mrs Jennings when the two sat next to each other.

'Having a really good day, thank you.'

'And what was lunch today?'

'Toad in the hole, potatoes, carrots followed by spotted dick and custard, yum, yum.'

'Lucky girl, and did Kelly eat it all up?'

'Yes, every single spoonful.'

'Good girl.'

'And had seconds!'

If you judged her by her clear, blossom pink face and curly blonde hair you might say Kelly was eighteen; if you judged her by her laugh you might put it at eleven; if you judged her by her clothes, you'd think she was thirty; if you judged her by her conversation you wouldn't have a clue. Kelly could understand quite a lot, though no one knew how much. That is why Mrs Jennings liked to speak to her, but it's also why she usually did so in the third person. Kelly had never uttered a single word in her entire life. The questions were always answered for her by the third person with them, Kelly's carer at Oakwood House; Roz.

It was one of the few places Kelly was not stared at. There were lots of people like her at Oakwood House in Norfolk. She was confined to a wheelchair, leaning forward from a bent spine, arms moving spasmodically, head permanently on one side and prone to lash out without warning. Homes for the severely mentally and physically handicapped were there to look after such people – when no one else could, or in some cases, would.

No one else included Kelly's parents.

They abandoned her when she was twelve months old after finding it impossible to cope with her severe disabilities. For the first few years, they kept regular contact with her, but after the couple divorced, contact became less and less frequent until now, her mother, who had remarried and had two more children, visited her once a year on her birthday; her father hadn't seen her for ten years.

If Kelly was not a curiosity at Oakwood, Mrs Jennings was. Few other visitors – and certainly none of the staff – came wearing a beige angora sweater, tweed trousers and drove a Morris Minor Convertible that looked as though it had come straight from the showroom. But few of them were as well spoken, well dressed, or well intentioned as Ursula Jennings. Which is not to say much, since there were few visitors at all. And that said it all.

'She's been doing really well, Mrs Jennings, honestly, we're really pleased,' said Roz, a care assistant in her late twenties. 'Haven't you mate?' Roz playfully tickled Kelly's chin. 'We've been working hard on her interaction skills with her peers and she's getting on really well; we're really pleased with her.' Roz turned to Kelly and spoke louder, closer to her face, 'We're really pleased with you Kelly, aren't we, me and Pete? Yes, 'course we are.' Pete was another of Kelly's carers. He didn't say much.

Mrs Jennings had been visiting Kelly for years and had grown very fond of her. She usually went on the last Friday of every month and took her for a walk round the grounds of the old stately home, had tea with her and read to her before driving home to Peterborough, where she ran a guest house with her husband.

Mrs Jennings wasn't sure what to make of Roz. She had been Kelly's fourth carer in five years; the staff never stayed long, but Mrs Jennings didn't hold that against them. She found it hard to look after Kelly for an afternoon; she could imagine how hard it was to do it full time. You couldn't fault her qualifications; she had two degrees, one in psychology and another in sociology. Mrs Jennings was impressed by her encyclopaedic knowledge of every type of handicap and the constant round of staff meetings, reviews, statements and action plans all designed to help Kelly's development.

Each time Mrs Jennings came, Kelly's carer (this time Roz, though it seemed to be someone different every time) would pull out a vast folder of notes covered in ticks marking the tasks she had and hadn't performed; and another containing the next set of targets.

They seemed to have every aspect covered, though their obsession with mumbo jumbo welfare words like 'interface, interaction and interpersonal' irritated Mrs Jennings. She felt she needed an interpreter. Why couldn't they use ordinary words like 'meet, play and mix'? She had long since given up trying to understand what it all meant. She was no expert. She didn't have any qualifications, just lots of love and affection and she wanted to give some to Kelly, that was all. It was the least the child deserved.

It was easy to imagine Roz as a student; she still looked like one. She looked untidy enough next to most people. Next to neat Mrs Jennings she looked like a tramp. She made her think of a lesbian drug addict daughter of a film star she'd read about in the Daily Mail. She chided herself for being so judgmental, but couldn't help it.

Roz had on the sort of baggy grey trousers you saw in Oxfam shops – on the menswear hangers – a tatty green jumper over a stained white T-shirt and always wore sandals. Why did so many social workers wear sandals, even in winter? Mrs Jennings could picture her selling the Big Issue in the market square in Peterborough, or hitching a lift to Glastonbury. Mrs Jennings didn't buy the Big Issue. She occasionally picked up hitch hikers, but she was choosy about who sat in the red passenger seat of her white open top Morris Minor; and she wouldn't have chosen Roz. Or Pete.

Nor would Kelly.

* * *

'Drew? It's Charlie, you wanted lunch, I'm free today ... it'll have to be quick ... where? Sheekey's? ... See you there at one.'

Charlie rarely answered the countless invitations she received from lobby journalists to go out to lunch. She was too busy and many of them were time wasters who took ministers, officials, MPs – or if they were really desperate, a fellow journalist – out to lunch to pour drink down their throat in the hope that they would let slip some piece of valuable information or gossip which they could blow up out of all proportion so they could justify their vast expenses bills. In any case, Charlie's figure mattered far more to her than her appetite. A bacon sandwich and black coffee collected by Dora from Churchill's, the cafe almost directly opposite Downing Street on the other side of Whitehall, in her office suited her fine.

She met the lobby journalists at eleven every morning in a dingy conference room in a basement by the tiny patch of grass between Number 10 and the Cabinet Office. The journalists reached it by walking down a dank, dark set of stone steps off Downing Street. It was like the entrance to a dungeon.

Until recently press secretaries met the lobby a second time each day, this time as their 'guest' in a turret hidden at the top of a spiral staircase at the Commons. But Charlie had scrapped the 'four o'clock' – as it was known. Meeting the lobby once a day was more than enough. And the ten minute walk each way from Downing Street, up Whitehall, across the traffic lights by Churchill's statue in Parliament Square, and not to mention the walking up a spiral staircase in a tight skirt, was all very inconvenient. The two meetings could take up to three hours out of her day. Now it was down to one – and she occasionally delegated that to a junior. She could have more effect over the way politics was reported by one discreet phone call in the privacy of her office, than by a thousand hours of lobby briefings.

Lobby briefings had the mystique of a masonic lodge. In truth they were generally bland affairs. Several journalists used them as an excuse to engage in verbal gymnastics with Charlie, but most of it was self-indulgent showboating. They rarely got the better of her.

Whenever they pushed their luck, which was often, or were getting near the truth, which was virtually never, her usual answer was, 'BS' – shorthand for bullshit. It had got to the stage that she would dismiss all ill informed, irrelevant or inconvenient questions – and there were far more of the first two than the last – by replying, simply, 'BS. Next?' Or 'total BS' if she wanted to use emphasis and 'total and utter BS' as a last resort.

Either that or by ridiculing the questioner. 'Alexander, I know you think you're clever but everyone else thinks you're a prat,' or 'Duncan, you've obviously made up the headline, so you'll just have to make up the story too,' or 'Bill, have you had the lobotomy yet?'

The hacks would ramble on for half an hour or more. They got nothing out of her – and it looked like open government. And she could never let her guard down. The frustrated politicians, the drunks and the idle didn't bother her. She could ignore them or manipulate them. But some were good, very good. And one or two were downright dangerous.

If they were on to a big story they would be mad to raise it at a lobby meeting: their rivals would be straight on to it. Like her, they preferred to do it over the phone or over a plate of skate wing, which was what Charlie had ordered when she met Drew Sharpe of the Telegraph at Sheekey's restaurant in St Martin's Court, an alleyway off St Martin's Lane.

When Charlie accepted lunch invitations it was for one of three reasons: it was someone important, she wanted to leak something or she wanted to discover something from the journalist. Sharpe was one of the few reporters Charlie got to know while working for Greaves before she went America. He had good contacts on both sides of the House and was particularly close to some of the MPs in Greaves' circle. He knew damn all about the intricacies of economic policy, one of the disadvantages of leaving school at sixteen. But he could spot a story from a mile off, one of the advantages of starting as a runner for a local freelance after the local college rejected his application to join a three year media studies course, explaining that with only one 'O' level – in religious education – he was not bright enough to be a journalist. By the time the students who got on the course were finishing their third year and looking for jobs with local freesheets, Sharpe was doing shifts in Fleet Street.

He was discreet, a rare commodity in the lobby. And good looking; an even rarer one. He had dark hair with a few wisps of grey, a tall, wiry frame, was witty, thirty five years old, had never married and was currently going out with a twenty one year old graduate trainee on The Telegraph. His previous girlfriend was a ballet dancer. She was twenty two. Charlie knew three MPs who had slept with him. All had been impressed.

His charm seemed to have the same bewitching effect on Cabinet ministers. He usually got what he wanted and had tried to get Charlie into bed once, only narrowly failing. Today, he was content to get her into a restaurant. He had asked her out to lunch several times since *The Globe* published the photograph of Charlie and Greaves rowing backstage at the nurses rally.

It sparked fresh speculation about relations between Greaves and Cane. Charlie was surprised when she saw the picture by-line, Brian Cole. Had he forgotten the threat she had made when he tried to defy her before? Far from it. Blackie had thought about nothing else. He couldn't believe a fellow photographer would give her a picture of him fondling a lap dancer in a Turkish nightclub. So he investigated and discovered they hadn't given the film to anyone – they had thrown it into the Bosphorus. Charlie had lied. And Blackie laid low, biding his time.

It wasn't the only conversation Blackie had had with his colleagues. The day after his picture scoop at the nurses rally, Sharpe, who had travelled half the world with Blackie, phoned him up to congratulate him, and to ask him if he had heard any of the words exchanged by Greaves and Charlie.

'Nah, they were too far away Drew, sorry lad.'

'It's great to put one over on this lot, isn't it?'

'Specially Redpath, she's evil.'

'Evil? Bit strong, Blackie.'

'Not if you'd seen what I'd seen, lad.'

'What d'you mean?'

'Look Drew, there's a far bigger row goin' on than the one between Cane and Greaves. I've seen it with my own eyes.'

'Who?'

'Cane and someone else.'

'What? You mean Cane and Charlie?'

'No.'

'Cane and Silverman?'

'No.'

'I don't understand, there's nobody else.'

'Think Drew, close to him.'

'There's only Lucy ... you're kidding, Blackie?'

'I'm not Drew. I've seen it, lad. Don't rat on me, Drew, or I'll kill you.'

As Sharpe picked at his dozen Colchester Native oysters and sipped at a glass of the £36 bottle of Robert Mondavi Napa Valley Chardonnay 1996 he intended to consume on his own, he wasn't sure which issue to raise first, Greaves versus Cane or Cane versus Cane. But he wasn't the only one after some information. Charlie had only accepted the invite because she wanted to pump Sharpe for information about Greaves' camp. She needed to know how far he might push his tax campaign in the run-up to the election. Sharpe probably knew, and, if she offered something in exchange, she might get it out of him.

'How's your friend the Deputy Prime Minister?' asked Sharpe. 'Or should I have said how's your enemy the Deputy Prime Minister?'

'Fine thanks, Drew,' said Charlie, returning his facetious grin.

'Been posing for any nice family album shots with him lately? Bet you haven't got the one in *The Globe* on your desk.'

'That was a storm in a tea cup, it wasn't the way it looked.'

'What is it that cameras never do?'

'They do lie when they're pointed by Blackie effing Cole,' she said, putting down a forkful of poached salmon to jab her finger at him.

'Yeah, yeah, yeah. Charlie, the point is: when is Cane going to do something about it? You can't just ignore Greaves, he's starting to take the mick.'

'How?'

'Well, where do you think all these stories about him not trusting Cane are coming from?'

'Your imagination, I should think.'

'Uh, uh,' said Sharpe, shaking his head.

The conversation was going exactly where Charlie wanted it to go. She had to know if Greaves was up to something; if he was, she was ready to take drastic action to stop it wrecking the election campaign. She could not afford a repeat of the nurses rally fiasco. But Sharpe knew what he was doing. He had hung out his bait, now he wanted to hook her. If he could get her to confirm Cane planned to take action to rein in Greaves, he would have a story on his hands, a real one.

'So what's Cane going to do. Just sit there and take it like Major used to when he started to go down the pan?' said Sharpe.

'The Prime Minister is totally relaxed and has full confidence in his deputy,' said Charlie, playing a straight bat.

The last thing she wanted was for Sharpe to go away and write 'Cane reins in Greaves.' Relations were tense enough as they were; another explosive story about the rift in a paper not known for invention, would lead to all-out war. By the time Charlie's large Espresso and Sharpe's filter coffee arrived, they were both still hungry for information.

'How's the PM's wife these days? We don't see as much of her as we used to, do we?' said Sharpe.

It was not what she had expected him to say, but she was happy to let him continue.

'Why do you ask?' she said.

'Oh, you hear things,' said Sharpe, lighting a cigarette for himself and leaning across to light her Marlboro.

'Lucy's fine ... just fine.'

'What plans you got for her in the election? Family photo calls, modern mum juggling work with kids, the usual sort of thing I suppose.'

'Yes, why do you ask?'

'Someone said she was getting cheesed off with it all; you know, Cane never home, her coping on her own, never really been happy in the limelight, the odd tiff between them.'

The last five words of the sentence were lobbed across the table as gently as a bath sponge – with all the potential of a sprung hand grenade.

'I don't know what you're talking about.'

'Well, you pick up the odd rumour about Lucy getting fed up with people making fun of her weight, her dress – and taking it out on Cane.'

'Really ... ' said Charlie, disinterestedly, shrugging her shoulders.

Sharpe's ears pricked up. It wasn't like Charlie to stumble. He'd fully expected her to say 'BS, Drew. Next.' But she hadn't. Was she trying to tell him something? He could hardly write a story saying Cane's marriage was in trouble on the basis of Charlie saying 'really ... ' and shrugging her shoulders when he had given her the chance to deny it. Yet he'd known journalists boast about writing front page stories when a previous Number 10 press secretary had done no more than raise one of his bushy eyebrows.

'It's like the rumours you hear that Greaves is planning a few more tricks to undermine Cane, isn't it, Drew? We'd love to know but can't find out – you probably know more than we do.'

Sharpe knew Charlie well enough to spot the symptoms a mile off. She was trying to do a deal.

'They're planning that alright. Greaves's going to make a big speech about poverty next month. Apparently there'll be lots of coded language in it. I'm writing about it next Monday, so keep it under your hat.'

'Really?'

'We were talking about Lucy ... '

'Yes, oh the stories about her being depressed over her image? They're somewhat exaggerated I'd say.'

Somewhat exaggerated? Now it was getting interesting.

'She's bound to be upset over the unfair criticism she gets from people like you over her clothes and weight. It's had her in tears once or twice and I don't blame her.'

There was no mistaking it this time.

'Of course Steven doesn't like it when his wife is criticised,' Charlie continued. 'He's been marvellous in thinking up ways she can cheer herself up and pep up her image in time for the election. New wardrobe, the lot. The last thing he wants is for her to feel down. You wait and see, you won't be disappointed, you're in for a treat when you see her in the campaign. Now it's been lovely having lunch with you, Drew,' said Charlie, picking up her handbag, 'but I have got important business to see to.'

You've just done the business and you know it, thought Sharpe. He'd never heard anyone shout 'eureka!' or 'hold the front page!' in Sheekey's.

But he yearned to do both.

CHAPTER SEVENTEEN

'Please stop crying,' Cane pleaded, as he sat opposite Lucy at the dinner table.

'I can't take any more of this,' she sobbed. 'I don't know how people can be so horrible. Who told the Telegraph that I've been crying at the criticism? Who told them!?'

'I don't know, darling; you've got to ignore it, it's trivial rubbish.'

'Look at it! They have deliberately chosen the worst possible picture of me. I look horrible! And look at what it says, "PM's PLAN TO PEP UP LUCY." Who told them all this? Who told them, "Mr Cane naturally worries when his wife is feeling down." ? Feeling down? Who told them? Who told them?' she groaned, throwing the paper at him. 'They make me sound like some kind of manic depressive. And that awful bit about you worrying about my image. Whatever I wear they tear it to pieces. It's not my fault I've put on weight, I can't help it, I've tried. Oh Steven, I can't go on like this.'

Cane had racked his brain to work out where it could have come from. Charlie had immediately offered to launch an inquiry, but Cane told her not to bother: it was pointless. Countless ministers, officials and friends knew Lucy was irritated by attacks on her dowdy image and that he was worried about it. The story was exaggerated. There had been some sniping at Lucy, but it was no worse than that endured by every previous Prime Minister's spouse.

Cane was far more concerned at the aspects of Lucy's behaviour the paper had not reported. She had been increasingly short tempered with him in recent months. Her tantrum the night she drove off from Number 10 without him was not an isolated incident. He knew she didn't find the role of 'First Lady' easy but he felt she could make more of an effort to support him. Whatever the pressure on her, it was far greater on him: he was running the country, she only had to run a family. When he had said as much to her one night, she got so angry with him one of the Downing Street staff heard the noise and, fearing a break in, sounded the security alarm. Three policemen came charging into the flat to find her on the stairs in tears.

Cane hoped one good thing would come out of the Telegraph story: she would agree to Charlie's plan for her to attend the top women's 'personal shopper' and diet consultant in Britain. Lucy had been resisting it for months. Cane had told Charlie she should talk to Lucy in person and try to talk her round. Charlie refused, saying that kind of direct approach would not work.

But she found another one that did.

The Yolanda Hussey studios was not the sort of place Lucy would have chosen to spend an afternoon in London. And Charlie Redpath was not the sort of person she would have chosen to spend an afternoon with anywhere. Lucy had reluctantly agreed to go to get some advice on what clothes she should wear for the election campaign. She wasn't really interested in fashion.

She had spent much of her childhood at home outdoors, riding horses and the rest of the time at boarding school, where there was little chance to wear the latest styles. It didn't bother her: she was happier in green wellies than high heels and didn't like pop music, so had no desire to look like Olivia Newton John in *Grease*, as many of her friends did. The only designer dress Lucy had bought was her wedding dress. She bought her clothes from the same place as her mother had always bought them: Thorntons department store, Guildford, est.1913.

That was part of the problem. She was beginning to look like her mother. Lucy's idea of being classic was a Jaeger jacket; her idea of flair was an Aquascutum scarf; her idea of smart casual was Marks and Sparks and her idea of trendy was Laura Ashley. She liked to wear jeans but always bought stretch pairs, on the basis that she planned to lose weight but could still squeeze into them if she didn't. After a year, they never stretched far enough.

At first she ignored the catty comments such as the woman columnist who said she had 'Princess Anne's flair and Fergie's bum.'

What angered her most was that virtually all the criticism was made by other women; the same women who complained about sexism, yet judged other women not by their ability but by appearance, clothes, hairstyle, make-up. But the article in the Telegraph was the last straw. She couldn't face the prospect of spending the best part of three weeks on the election trail with Steven and be subjected to the same treatment day in day out. So she yielded and agreed to visit the Hussey studio. Yolanda had done wonders for him, Cane told her, showing him how to choose the right tie, right suit, right hair – even the right shoes – for the right setting. So there was no need for her to be embarrassed about going. Lucy agreed, on the basis that she would give it a try – once. Her appointment was at half past eleven. She was hoping to use one of the new outfits for the first part of the pre-election programme Charlie had arranged for Cane and Lucy together, a visit to Amberton special needs school in Surrey, where Lucy worked as a part time teacher. The first surprise was when she arrived to find Yolanda was not alone.

'Hello Lucy, I thought I'd come and give Yolanda a run down of the places you're likely to be visiting in the election campaign so she can find the right outfit for each one,' said Charlie.

Lucy did not feel at all comfortable at the prospect of having her fashion faults ironed out in front of Charlie. But she could hardly tell her to get out. Charlie would not have bought a pair of socks from Thorntons of Guildford. She was wearing a cherry red jacket and dress, the combination she kept for Downing Street receptions, important press conferences and the last visit by the US President.

Even Lucy could tell it cost a fortune. Charlie had had her hair done and was wearing red high heel shoes and red nail varnish on her fingers and toes. She looked Amazonian compared to Liliputian Lucy. Lucy saw Charlie eye her up and down, and saw her smiling. It was a few seconds before Lucy realised why. She was wearing the same pink outfit Charlie had persuaded her to wear on the Richard and Judy show. She could have kicked herself.

'Well, I must say Lucy, pink suits you,' said Yolanda. Charlie's smile spread wider.

To Lucy, Yolanda had stepped straight out of Dynasty. She was Joan Collins with added lipgloss. If you think I'm leaving here looking like that, you've got another think coming, thought Lucy.

'Now that's what I call glamorous, Yolanda,' said Charlie. 'I love your purple blouse, I've seen them at Harvey Nick's.'

Oh dear, thought Lucy.

'Don't worry, Lucy,' said Yolanda, reading her thoughts. 'I'm not going to make you look like this. We're going to make you look like the smartest Prime Minister's wife in the world, not a frustrated middle-aged ex-model like me!'

At least she had a sense of humour.

Lucy spent the next ninety minutes under a blinding spotlight in her bra and pants stepping in and out of more than thirty different outfits mostly from designer labels she had never heard of: 'Marella'; 'Gerard Darel'; 'Pennyblack'.

It wasn't the glare of the spotlight that made her feel exposed. It was being so exposed to Charlie's glare: cellulite, caesarian scar and all.

'Right. That's the clothes taken care of, now for lifestyle advice,' said Yolanda.

'Lifestyle?' echoed Lucy.

'Yes, diet, hair, make-up, a personal shopper, that sort of thing.'

'Pardon?'

'It was all fixed up ... '

Lucy looked at Charlie.

'I thought Steven had explained,' said Charlie. 'I told him to tell you Yolanda would take care of everything.'

Yes, and you did it in such a vague way, you cunning little madam, thought Lucy, that he wouldn't know what you meant, and I wouldn't find out until I got here.

'I've got a whole programme drawn up here, Mrs Cane, based on what Charlie told me about your election programme,' said Yolanda.

Lucy had been bounced. First she had been told why her clothes were all wrong, now she was to be told why the body underneath them was all wrong too.

'I'd say that for a mother of two you have done remarkably well,' said Yolanda.

'You mean I look older than women who haven't got children,' replied Lucy, looking at Charlie.

'Let's sort out our priorities,' said Yolanda. 'Your face is beautiful; slender, big eyes, lovely lips and a pure skin. Gorgeous. Now,' she said taking a breath, 'the problem areas. I'd say you suffered from a slow metabolic rate and high water retention.'

'Ha, you mean I'm overweight!' said Lucy. 'I already have a sensible diet. I can assure I don't raid the fridge at midnight, Yolanda, the hips are genetic,' she said slapping them. 'I got them from mummy, bless her. We've got enough herbal remedies and gels in our bathroom to open a Downing Street branch of The Body Shop. Good gracious, I was taking mud baths until I realised, for every ten minutes in the bath you spent thirty cleaning the scum marks off. It got so dirty we had to buy a new bath because the children refused to get in it! Look, Yolanda, I could try all sorts of quack cures and diets – or maybe just take up smoking – but I'm not one of those women who put their waistline before their health.'

Charlie had just struck up another Marlboro, her third since arriving at the studio. She waited until Lucy had finished her sentence, put it to her lips slowly and inhaled.

Yolanda filled the silence. 'Our programmes are specifically designed with healthy living ... '

'It's very good of you to offer to help out. I'll take the beige trouser suit and wear it at the school this afternoon. But don't expect me to turn into a stick insect, or start looking like a supermodel. It's a bit hard when you're rushing to get to school in time. Goodness! I'm late! I've got to meet Steven at school in an hour, I'd better be off. Someone's picking me up aren't they, Charlie?'

'They'll be outside.'

'Oh dear, I forgot. Who do I pay for the clothes?'

'It's taken care of,' said Charlie.

'There's no charge Mrs Cane, it is our privilege,' said Yolanda.

'No, I expect you to send a bill. Don't think I'm being rude, but this will be the last time I wear this beige suit if you don't.'

Lucy arrived at Amberton school shortly before Cane got there. The visit had been arranged by Charlie to coincide with a schools initiative planned by Cane. He had been accused of ignoring less able pupils after launching a series of moves to provide extra help for talented youngsters. Now he wanted to redress the balance. He had intended to call a press conference but changed his mind after he and Charlie had been discussing new ways of improving Lucy's image.

Why not coincide the announcement in the Commons by the Education Secretary with a visit by Cane and Lucy to her school? It would provide an ideal opportunity for Cane to launch the initiative and an ideal opportunity to draw attention to Lucy's caring nature. Or to give it another name: a photo opportunity. Lucy first taught there twenty years ago after leaving college. She had a gap of six years when the children were born, and had been there part time since Jessica started primary school.

There were all sorts of children at Amberton. They all had special needs and their needs were all different. They were all there through no fault of their own. Some had Downs Syndrome, some were autistic, some had spina bifida, some had conditions that had still to be diagnosed. And some were there entirely through the fault of their parents. They were completely normal at birth but had been abused, neglected, abandoned or simply ignored by their abnormal parents. Some were sent to school with the same set of clothes and underwear for a week at a time. They had only one special need – some decent parents.

'He-llo Mrs-s Ca-ane!' the children in Lucy's Class Six shouted in metronomic unison when she walked in with Cane at her side. He so admired her. Few people from her privileged background chose such a difficult profession. It was one of the reasons she reminded him of his darling mother.

People were entitled to accuse him of being like any other politician, driven by ambition and vanity; but no one could accuse Prime Minister Cane of being cut off from the cruel realities of life, not when his wife had dedicated herself to helping the most pitiable victims of its cruelty. Lucy showed Cane the children's exercise books and he leant down with her to pose for pictures. The photographers asked them to sit with Suzi, an eight year old who was doubly handicapped.

The press seized on her because she looked pretty – and pretty normal. They couldn't understand when she ignored their instructions. It was because she was severely autistic. The autism was her first handicap; looking normal was the second. After visiting the other classrooms, Cane made a brief speech on his new initiative.

'We have made big strides in providing new opportunities for children in our schools. But there is no greater need than to improve facilities for children with special needs. I know through my wife's work here at Amberton how much can be achieved with the right facilities. But we do not have enough schools like Amberton. There are too many people with special needs, children and adults too, who are in dilapidated and outdated institutions, where their horizons are limited.

'We owe it to these people to give them the chance to get as much out of life as the rest of us can. A century ago, people with special needs were shunned, locked up and much worse. We've come a long way since then but I am today announcing a major new programme to make it possible for more children with special needs to lead a full life. We will provide an extra £250 million, to be shared by every special needs school, to provide additional teaching staff. It will mean more teaching, more caring, and, I sincerely hope, more special needs children whose needs are met and more special needs teachers. Now they really are special!'

Cane beamed at Lucy next to him, clasped her hand and kissed her.

He didn't feel her quake.

CHAPTER EIGHTEEN

No one was ever in Flat 3, Parkside Terrace, Pimlico at the weekends. Not many people were in the other fifteen flats in the small apartment block either. So it was not the hardest place to break into. Especially for a professional.

He had done his homework and watched the building for three weeks before making a move. He noticed that the occupant left most week days at eight thirty am and returned between six and midnight and sometimes not until the following evening. Occasionally, there would be a guest for dinner, usually the same person. The pattern at weekends was more consistent. On each of the three weekends the intruder had been watching, the flat was empty from Friday morning until Sunday night at tennish.

He had waited until two am to make his move, late enough for the place to be empty, but not so late that he couldn't be a late party goer returning home. The electronic device at the entrance to the flat was easily fooled by the all-purpose plip control the intruder had brought with him. He had already checked to make sure there wasn't an all-night warden. He glided silently up two flights of stairs in his black air cushion heeled trainers, then slid one of eight spider keys on his ring into the lock. The plain white wooden door opened. It was as easy as that. Few people were as expert as him, but he hadn't used his real expertise yet. He glanced around. The one-bedroom flat was so tidy, it was hard to believe it was lived in.

The torch light shone on gleaming white kitchen work surfaces. A well stocked wooden herb tray was at the back alongside a box of cappucino coffee sachets. A small pine dining table stood in the middle, and directly above it – a lampshade within arm reach. Perfect. He moved to the sittingroom. A large selection of glossy magazines: Cosmopolitan, Homes and Gardens, Girl About Town, The Look, Country Life, Horse and Hound and The New Statesman were on the coffee table. The navy blue Ikea sofa was directly beneath the window overlooking a quadrangle. He stood on a chair and fiddled behind the curtain rail. On to the bedroom. A print of the Mermaid Inn at Rye in Sussex was on the wall and a silver-framed photo of a beaming thirty-somethingish couple on the bedside cabinet. He studied the man in the picture and raised an eyebrow.

He put his hand under the cabinet and left.

* * *

The red and green concoction weaved its way around tables of busily engaged diners, perched high on a silver tray like a multi-coloured saucer swaying at the top of a juggler's pole. The man at the corner table grabbed the stick of celery and started stirring the drink without diverting his gaze from the Parliamentary reports page of the Financial Times.

Silverman was chewing at the tomato-stained remains of the celery stick, when he heard a distinguished voice.

'Ronnie, it's so very good to see you.'

He lowered the salmon pink sheets of his newspaper and saw the bright and radiant face of Simon Darius. Silverman had known him since they started and left Fitzwilliam College, Cambridge, on the same day.

It didn't matter whether Darius was wearing a plain navy suit, with a blue checked shirt and midnight blue tie with red teardrop pattern, as he was today; a scruffy track suit, as he used to when Silverman would call in at his college flat; or green corduroy trousers and an Arran sweater riddled with holes, as he did when they went punting on the Cam together. It didn't matter how he dressed; he always looked stylish. It didn't matter how Silverman dressed; he never looked stylish. Darius was constantly sweeping his fringe off his eyebrows, only for it to fall back again. Silverman counted it once while Darius was explaining to him why Keynesianism was doomed to fail; it took forty three seconds.

Elegance and style were not words normally applied to Silverman or his home town of Slough. But they were compulsory a mile down the road where Darius spent his formative years. The yearly cost of sending Darius to Eton College was little more than a few days' interest on the fortune owned by his stockbroker father and American heiress mother. It was a year's salary to Silverman's school caretaker father, Len, which is why Silverman thanked his lucky stars that his home town was one of the few that had escaped the purge of grammar schools by his political predecessors in the Sixties.

Slough Grammar school's playing fields bordered Eton's and when they first met at Fitzwilliam and Silverman told Darius he had attended Slough Grammar, Darius thought he was teasing. Private Eye referred to Eton College as Slough Grammar, a joke intended to highlight the social and cultural gulf between them. It was personified by Darius and Silverman. While Darius honed his gifts and grace at Eton, Silverman did it by grit and graft in Slough.

'How's the book, Simon?' said Silverman, ordering a Kir Royale for Darius. It was his first memory of meeting Darius at Cambridge. He had invited him to his flat and offered him a Kir Royale. Silverman didn't know what it was. Darius told him he drank a glass every single night.

'I'm just coming up to the difficult bit.'

'What's that? How you're going to sweep back into power next year?'

'No – why we lost it.'

'Oh, that's easy, I'll write it for you.'

'I may well take you up on that.'

Silverman and Darius had spent much of their college years talking about power. Marxist Silverman had argued passionately against the way the IMF pulled the plug on British governments in the Seventies and had led a sit-in on the college campus.

The week before they left Cambridge, they went for dinner at their favourite French bistro in the city. Silverman already had a job lined up with the engineers union, one of the fast tracks to becoming an MP. Darius was off to spend a year with the research department at the Institute of Directors, another fast track to becoming an MP.

Over two large Armagnacs, they shook hands on a bet – whichever one reached the Cabinet first would pay for another meal at the restaurant. Fourteen and a half years later, when they were both thirty five years old, they were back. When the bill arrived, the waiter gave it to the Secretary of State for Transport, the Right Honourable Simon Darius, the newest and youngest member of the Cabinet. Silverman, whose party had lost again, accepted the free meal with good grace.

But Darius's career in office was short lived. He refused to support his party's softer stance on Europe. And three years after that, he lost his Commons seat in the election. His fall had been as sudden and dramatic as his rise.

But the events that swept Darius out had swept Silverman in. Slough had finally overtaken Eton.

Silverman had spent years working out where his own party had gone wrong in the Eighties when he had been an observer. Now Darius was going through the same cathartic process about his party – and himself – in the Nineties in a book called 'Why We Deserved To Lose'.

'How far have you got with the book?'

'I'm up to the moment I realised we'd had it.'

'When was that?'

'It was when I knocked on the door of an elderly lady in an affluent area where we normally had ninety per cent support. She said, "Mr Darius, I've voted for your party all my life but you don't stand for anything any more, other than keeping the other lot out." I couldn't answer her; I stood on the doorstep in silence. She said, "well young man, what have you got to say?" You know I just looked at her and said, "Madam, I agree with you." I just couldn't pretend any more. I felt better for having said it, as though it had to come out. Funniest of all was her reply. You'd have thought she'd have been moved to hear a politician tell the truth for once. Not a bit of it. She said "in that case young man, you deserve to lose" – and slammed the door. It's where I got the title for the book. I panicked afterwards and thought, heavens, what if she phones the press and tells them what I said. Luckily she didn't.'

'You always did live dangerously. But you're right. And we're going to keep your lot out for just as long as you kept us out, I warn you. Got a seat lined up for next time yet?' said Silverman. 'You'd better hurry.'

'Is that a clue to the election date?'

'No.'

'I'm just about to choose one. I need to make sure I get it right – after last time.' Darius winced in painful memory of the moment the returning officer uttered the words, 'Darius, Simon Lindsay, 19,442 votes; Briggs, Julian Graham, 20,130 votes; I therefore declare Julian Graham Briggs has been elected as Member of Parliament for North Suffolk.' Briggs was as shocked to win the seat as Darius was to lose it.

'How's Batty Bathurst doing?' asked Darius.

'Much better than any of us expected, frankly,' said Silverman. 'It's perfect for us. With you and Turnbull nicely out of the way.'

'Yes, how clever of Cane to make Turnbull a European Commissioner – and how foolish of Turnbull to accept.'

'Wasn't it, just? As I was saying, with you and Turnbull out of the way, and Bathurst there at least until the election, we can't believe our luck. Our only problem would be if there was a by-election before the election and you or Turnbull got in. Bathurst'd be out and you or he'd take over. Now that would be interesting. Thankfully, it hasn't happened and there's not long to go now. We know you'll be back after the election, but we'll have won again by then.'

'You may, you may ... '

'Yes I know, events, events.'

'What about you? Where'll you go after the election, move to Foreign Secretary? Greaves isn't going to be around for ever, it's bound to end some time between him and Cane. If that happens people may start to talk of you as Cane's successor, not Greaves. Thought about that, Ronnie?'

'No.'

It was untrue. Since the beginning of time politicians and monarchs had been gay and got away with it by pretending not to be. A decade or so from now, the stigma would be gone and no longer would people like Silverman have to pretend. An openly gay Prime Minister would be no more shocking than a woman Prime Minister, or one who had played in a pop group. There had been huge strides: people accepted openly gay Cabinet Ministers. But a gay Prime Minister now? One who walked along Downing Street on victory day hand in hand with his male partner? No. Not yet.

It was Silverman's fate to be in public life, trapped between the age when hypocrisy and secrecy gave homosexuals effective equality; and the fast approaching age of honesty and openness when they would have real equality. Silverman could neither lie, because, despite his brief marriage, it was an open secret that he was gay, nor be honest, because he still wanted to be Prime Minister. He wanted to despise those who went through sham marriages, but how could he? He had done it himself.

He wasn't aided by those who perpetuated the myth that a politician with a pretty wife and two point four beautiful children was better than one with none. Such as the person who choreographed the Canes playing happy families at a picnic in the garden at Chequers the week after he won power when the press were invited in to take photographs.

The choreographer's name was Silverman.

'How's Olivia?' he asked Darius sharply, stretching his watch strap.

'Oh ... Olivia's fine thanks,' said Darius.

'Still with the bank?'

'Yes.'

'In London?'

'No ... she's running the Sydney office.'

'Ah, I see.'

Silverman was there when Darius married merchant banker Olivia Scott-Sanderson three years after they left Cambridge. It was a white wedding in St Paul's Cathedral, followed by a reception at Cliveden stately home at Taplow, overlooking the Thames, where John Profumo had had an affair with Christine Keeler.

He saw Darius kiss Olivia before they left for their honeymoon in

Morocco. He had only seen him kiss one person before. That person was Silverman himself.

And on that occasion Darius had done it a lot more convincingly.

* * *

'Come on sweetie, just one more kiss,' the voice in the dark said softly. The beautiful girl lay in bed, woken by the hand moving under the sheets. The girl did not stir. She did not resist. She lay there. She could feel a body move into bed beside her. The body and the sound of the body were familiar to her. She heard a whisper.

'Ssssh sweetie, it's only me, I've come for a cuddle. Move over sweetie, let me cuddle up with you. There, there's a good girl, that's it. Gently now sweetie.'

The body slid into the single bed, easing the girl across to allow enough room for them both to lie together. The body slowly climbed on top of the girl, whispering all the time, 'Gently does it now sweetie, let's be gentle, real gentle.' The girl knew who it was and lay there. She knew what would follow.

'Please, please sweetie, do as I say, please.'

Then the girl heard a second, deeper, voice. 'Come on, what's going on there?'

'She's more tense than usual, that's all,' said the body, 'she'll be alright.'

But she wasn't alright. She was starting to panic and suddenly screamed, 'Aaaaagh!' and thrashed around violently.

'For fuck's sake, stop her quick!' said the body, forcing a hand across the girl's mouth. 'What the fuck is she doing? Help me for fuck's sake, she doesn't normally make this sort of fuss.'

'I thought you said there'd be no problem, you idiot,' said the deeper voice. 'What are we going to do if someone hears it?'

'Don't worry, I've taken care of that, I'm not stupid, am I?'

'You wanna give her a good hiding, that'd teach her.'

186

'Shut up will you, do as I say.'

The body looked at the girl, her eyes blinking over the hand that was still lying across her mouth.

'Now you will be good, won't you?' The girl did not say anything.

They could tell by looking at her frightened face that she understood.

'We have a little agreement, don't we sweetie, it's our little secret, isn't it? Eh now?

'Come on Roz, let's get out before someone comes,' said the deeper voice.

'Kelly, calm down, calm down, sweetie. Let's go, Pete.'

* * *

'How d'you like your meat balls? Spicy or plain?'

'Any way you serve it up.'

Cane was proud of his Italian cooking talents. His mother had taught him.

Until the children were born, when Lucy was working full time, he would often cook when they had dinner parties at their house in Blackheath. But once the children were born and Lucy gave up work, she took over most of the domestic chores. And once he became Prime Minister, he had hardly made a sandwich, let alone a meal.

He had never once cooked a proper meal for Lucy in the flat. He was about to cook one now. But not for Lucy. She had taken the children to her parents straight after school. Cane had been to Wales for talks with the Welsh First Minister, back to Number 10 for a meeting with Charlie and Silverman about the election and had agreed to join Lucy at Guildford in the morning. At 8.30 pm, Silverman left for dinner. Charlie was still going through Cane's election programme when he sighed and said, 'I'm starving.'

'Me too.'

'Where you eating tonight?'

'Nowhere. Why? Home, I suppose.'

'I fancy knocking up some grub in the flat; how about it? I can't stand cooking for one; why don't you join me? Bring your documents; we can finish them up there.'

Charlie was taken by surprise. 'If you want to, you sure?'

'Of course I'm sure,' said Cane brightly, clapping his hands and getting up. 'I'm bloody starving, come on. Cooking makes me relax, but not if I'm eating on my own.'

'OK.'

She followed him up the narrow flight of stairs to the flat. It was more like a large hotel suite than a home. Cane rummaged in the fridge. 'Here we are, lovely, just enough mince to do my speciality. And a red pepper. Now all we need is a tin of tomatoes.' He found one in the larder. 'Hey, our luck's in.'

'What on earth are you doing?'

'Braised meatballs in peppers and tomatos, senorita!'

'Yuk! Sounds disgusting.'

'Whena you eeta my meat balls, you eeta your words, senorita!' said Cane, putting on a plastic pinny with the motto 'DON'T FORGET TO HUG THE COOK' like a Latin dancer.

He felt a surge of exhilaration. It was like being a student when he used to do all the cooking for his flatmates, and once a month, host pasta night parties at their digs. Free dinner for any girl who brought a bottle of wine. Several of them gave the cook more than a hug. Cane kneaded the mince with bread crumbs, salt and pepper with his hands, rolled them into little balls, sprinkled some flour on top and threw them in a frying pan.

'Quite the artiste aren't we? You're a better cook than I am!' she laughed.

'There's some Coke in the fridge I think. And a couple of beers I think. Rip one open for me.'

'Cheers,' he said, raising his glass to hers.

'Cheers,' she replied.

'God, it's aeons since I did this,' he said pouring the tomatoes over the browned meat balls in a casserole dish.

'I must be the only Englishman who can only cook Italian food. Mum taught me.'

'My mum taught me too,' said Charlie. 'But there was no foreign food in our house, it was sausage, egg and chips or nothing. If I'd served dad meat balls he have chucked it on the floor and said, "If you's think I'm eatin' that foreign muck, you's got another think comin'. Gimme some proper fud!'

'How is your mum?' he said, picking the one or two remaining fresh-looking inner leaves of a limp lettuce.

'Don't remind me! I've not seen her for nearly two months. I phoned her last night and she seemed fine, but I keep putting off going home. I must go, I really must.'

'Yes, you must, just drop everything and go. I can do without you,' he said with a breezy disdain, before adding, 'for about forty-eight hours in a year! No, really, you must go. How is she these days?'

'Pretty good. I spoke to her last night and the doc is thrilled with her. You'll never believe it, she's on some health food diet and has taken up walking. Walking? She walks round the local park twice a day. Says she's lost a stone and has never felt fitter. It's about time I did the same.'

'You? You look great. And the boys?'

'Don't ask.'

'Why?'

'Billy's up to his tricks again.'

Two weeks before the referendum, he had been arrested for hitting a policeman outside a pub and was being held on remand. Charlie's mother didn't tell her because she was frightened it might get in the papers and cause a fuss in the run-up to the vote. But as soon as Charlie heard, she went back to Glasgow and got hold of a lawyer to get him out. It wasn't the only problem her mother faced. Charlie sent her £250 a month to add to her state pension and make up for the widow's pension the shipyard had denied her. She also borrowed £15,000 so her mother could pay for the damage when Billy wrote off an uninsured car. She told her mother not to tell him where the money came from because she knew he would rather go to prison than accept help from his sister. She hadn't told Cane, either.

'They worry you, don't they?'

'Families? We all have them, don't we?'

Cane scrutinised her. Despite working together almost seven days a week for nearly four years with only a few weeks' holiday a year apart, the two rarely discussed personal matters. She interfered in every part of Cane's political life but in no part of his family life. Her private life was a mystery to him. He knew she occasionally met up with girlfriends for a night out in London. But he was puzzled by the apparent absence of any man in her life. He had never heard her talk of a boyfriend, though like Lucy, he had heard rumours of a liaison in America. He was curious about her relationship with Greaves. Cane knew he was upset when she had returned from Washington to work at Number 10 and could sense that was not the only reason for the strained atmosphere whenever Greaves and Charlie were together. He wondered if they had had an affair, but had never asked either of them. He had seen stories in the gossip columns about her being seen at The Ivy restaurant with Innes, but she had business to do with Innes.

You didn't need to look at The Spectator cover cartoon of her on her office wall to be reminded of her sex appeal. Cane knew many men who found her attractive, but few with the courage to ask her out.

'You ever going to marry, have kids?'

'You must be kidding. What brought that on?'

'Just wondering, that's all. You know, good Catholic girl like you, big family, I wondered whether you might ... '

'Have five kids of my own, like mum did?' she spluttered. 'Not a bloody chance.'

'Not even one or two, come on, surely?'

'No thank you.'

'Never?'

Charlie swept back her hair. Cane could see a mark on her forehead.

'What's that mark? I've never noticed it before,' he said, leaning forward.

'You really want to know?'

She pulled back her hair further, revealing a sloping, inch long indentation beneath her hairline, like an 'e' acute French accent. She held Cane's finger and ran it along the mark.

'What is it?' he asked.

'It's what happens when your dad throws a whisky bottle at you.'

'Good God.'

Cane had never been so close to Charlie's face. He looked into her grey green eyes. He lightly traced the back of his index finger across the mark; it was the first time he had touched her face. Charlie felt his eyes on her forehead. He leapt backwards.

'What's up?'

'The meat balls!' he said, hurtling into the kitchen. 'The sauce'll be dried up!'

'Saved them – just!'

Five minutes later he came back with the casserole dish and the salad. He ladled the meat balls onto their plates and brought them to the table with a flourish. She was enjoying the role reversal. And so was he. Charlie detected the slightest shake as his long slim fingers held the bottle of Diet Coke and tilted it, filling her glass.

'Thank you maestro.'

'Cheers!' said Cane, swigging his beer. 'To a second term.'

'You bet,' said Charlie, her eyes narrowing as she chinked her Coke against his lager. 'A second term.'

No political crisis had brought them as close as this.

'You were saying ... ' said Cane, as they sat down ' ... why you'll never have kids. I hope it's not because of mine. I know they're a handful.'

'You think they're a handful?' she laughed, blowing cigarette smoke towards the ceiling. 'You must be joking. They're putty compared to some I know.'

'Who?'

'Who d'you think? Steven, the reason I don't want any is because I've already had them, that's why.'

'I don't follow.'

'Who d'you think helped mum when dad lost his job at the yard and spent the whole day in a wheelchair drinking and shouting? Me. Mum was at the laundry when we came home from school. There was no one to cook tea except me. Who had to sort it out when the boys were driven out by dad and got into fights? Me. I hated it. That's what drove me to get out – that and the snotty stuck-up bitches at my school.'

Charlie laughed. 'D'you know? A group of parents tried to get me expelled when I wrote a piece for the school magazine saying matron should be able to give us the pill – Jesus, it was only a joke. I nearly left in the fifth year and joined a squat, just to get out, but I thought no, get your exams and show them you're better than them and could do both; get out of Glasgow and get better results than them. And I did. I don't know what happened to them, and I couldn't care; probably married to accountants with two kids and a nice home in Edinburgh. But me? Kids? Raise a family? Forget it. I've done it, now I'm living for me.'

'I sometimes think I expect you to live for me, Charlie, that I ask too much. You've got to have someone to talk to at the end of the day. I've got Lucy, but ... '

He stopped.

'But what? You mean I haven't got anyone's shoulder to cry on. I don't need all that.'

She wasn't the only one who didn't have a shoulder to cry on. This time, he did look into her eyes.

'There's something I've been meaning to say.'

Charlie put down her drink.

'Yes, Steven, what is it,' she said slowly and quietly.

'I've been meaning to say to you. I'm really grateful for what you did for Lucy, getting her to that stylist.'

Charlie was shocked by the tinge of disappointment she felt, but hid it.

'I know she didn't like it but she looks better. I worry about Lucy, Charlie.'

'What do you mean?'

'You're not to talk about this to anyone else, not Lucy … '

'Are you sure you want to … ?'

' … tell you? Yes, of course I'm sure. Lucy's not well. I don't know what it is, but it's not just the comments about her clothes, there's something else. She's using the clothes thing to cover up whatever else is on her mind. I know her Charlie, I know there's something, but I don't know what it is.'

'What do you want me to do?'

'I'm not sure there's a lot you can. She and you aren't exactly bosom pals.'

'We're different, that's all,' she said, reaching for a cigarette.

'Leave it for the moment, but I must get to the bottom of it. I can't have it hanging over her in the election campaign.'

'I'll keep my ears open,' said Charlie.

Cane opened another beer. 'You're a brick Charlie Redpath, a real brick.'

She didn't feel like one. Two minutes ago she thought he was about to make a pass at her. Now he wanted her to save his marriage.

CHAPTER NINETEEN

The plastic pink pigs in front of him summed up everything Silverman hated about Blackpool.

Especially in the first weekend of October. It was so wet and windy that the few steps from the door of the Pembroke Hotel into a cab seemed like a ten mile trek across the North Pole. Pedestrians walked at a horizontal angle. Some of them were on holiday. Silverman had never been to Blackpool on holiday. The last time he was there was the year after the election when he was cornered by a group of trade union delegates in the Spanish Bar in the Winter Gardens. It was the last night of the conference and he was having a cup of tea while waiting to address a fringe meeting. The delegates had been drinking something stronger and had a competition to see who could find the most tasteless souvenir from the shops on the promenade. Silverman agreed to be the judge – it seemed innocent enough. When they called him over, the 'entries' were lined up on a table in the middle of the bar. Silverman inspected them one by one.

Just because he was born in Slough didn't mean he had no taste. If he'd known how crude the exhibits were, he wouldn't have agreed to be the judge, but he couldn't back out now. A crowd had gathered. He surveyed the souvenirs. The first one was a plastic nose with a strap and something rather unpleasant hanging from the right nostril. He resisted attempts to make him try it on. The second was a monstrously large-breasted doll whose clothes came off when you stroked her hand. He resisted that too. By now he was looking for a dignified exit.

He surveyed the other gruesome items and spotted a harmless-looking one: two plastic pigs. That would do.

As he held them up, beaming at Blackie Cole who had appeared from nowhere, the clockwork motion was set off and one plastic pig started rearing up and down on top of the other. The press corps who set him up roared with laughter. It was a toss-up which was the funnier aspect of the picture in the papers next day, the copulating pigs or the startled expression of the Cabinet Minister who was holding them at eye level.

Six months later when a member of the party's national executive proposed the party should stop going to Blackpool, Silverman's hand was the first to go up. Hardly surprising when he had been behind the move. In future he would make sure the party stayed closer to the new spiritual home he had relocated it to: Brighton, Bournemouth or perhaps Harrogate, places where people spent in plastic rather than bought it. But the rank and file members of the engineers union still liked Blackpool. And since its general secretary Ken Bird had played a large part in getting Silverman into the Commons, and could yet play a part in keeping him there, he accepted the invitation to go.

Silverman was due to address the conference the next day and had gone to Bird's room on the fourth floor of the Imperial Hotel, at the opposite end of the corridor to his own suite.

'Still stickin' to fookin' Virgins, Ronnie?' said Bird with a chuckle that threatened to bring up half the contents of his lungs. The Yorkshireman poured himself a treble Scotch and a tomato juice for Silverman.

Silverman managed a polite smile. Their physiques were as unlike as their drinking habits and concept of wit. When Bird was perched on the edge of the armchair in the room, little legs wide apart, his Toby Jug belly seemed to go right down to – and beyond – his groin, without any visible interruption. Wearing a black leather belt did more to define his stomach, like the equator round *The Globe*, rather than confine it.

'Gearing' up for election, Ronnie?' said Bird.

'Yes, it's all in hand, Ken.'

'I tek it you'll be wantin' a bit of an 'and from us, like.'

'Your moral and financial support at the last election was terrific, Ken, we couldn't have done without it. I'm really pleased you can help us this time. I know some of the unions aren't giving this time, but they're shooting themselves in the foot. Do they really think they'd be better off if the other side got back in?'

'God knows, Ronnie, but don't think I'm not taken' a fookin' risk given' you our money. Cos I'm telling' you, I fookin' am,' said Bird, who used the same number of decibels whether he was addressing 2,000 workers in a car park or alone in a hotel room with a Cabinet Minister. He had downed his Scotch in two gulps and got up to pour himself another one.

'I know that, Ken, that's why I've gone out of my way to help you in every way I can,' said Silverman, speaking even more quietly and deliberately than usual.

'It's not what it fookin' looks like to some of executive.'

'How do you mean?'

'These fookin' rumours about you dropping union rights bill from manifesto.'

'Ken, don't worry about it, we haven't made up our minds about what is going in the manifesto yet, it's just the press.'

'Ronnie, you've got to understand 'ow important this is. When you came to our conference last year, you gave a firm commitment to undo what t'other mob did, so we could restore union branches in firms where we'd been kicked out. There's some places, like Fleet Street, where unions are virtually fookin' banned, it's a fookin' disgrace!'

'It's still our intention to deal with it.'

'But Ronnie, you've got to understand, if it's not in manifesto, my members'll think you're gonna drop it. If that 'appens I'm in trouble, fookin' big trouble.'

'I know what you're saying Ken.'

'I 'ope you fookin' do Ronnie, 'cos it's been a fookin' difficult week for me. I'm one who told 'em "don't worry lads, access to union will definitely be in fookin' manifesto, Ronnie'll look after us." Then I turn round and read in paper it might not be. If it's nor in, I'll be fookin' out! Ronnie – simple as that! Those fookin' loony lefties on general council 'ave been after my fookin' job for years. 'They've been sayin' "Bird's been fookin'

196

shafted by fookin' Silverman." If they're right Ronnie, I'm fookin' finished! And where the fook does that leave you? I'll tell you – with fookin' loony fookin' lefties running biggest fookin' union in Britain. It's not exactly gonna look good for either on us, is it? I mean, it's your fookin' union as much as mine and you'll be fookin' blamed. And don't think it's just about me and thee. It's about fookin' election 'n all. You leave this law out of manifesto and 'ow much money d'you think fookin' executive'll give you for campaign? I'll tell you: fookin' sweet fanny adams. You're not t'only one who wants fookin' second fookin' term, I'm tellin' you. I want my second term too, but if we fookin' cock this up, neither on us'll get one. If you don't sort out manifesto, it'll play right into fookin' Bathurst's hands. They'll be fookin' all over you if Sullivan and 'is lot tek over. They'll say "'ere comes winter of discontent Mark Two" – you can fookin' 'ear 'em now. Then what the fook'll you do, eh lad?'

As Silverman watched Bird leap up yet again to refill his glass, the copulating pigs flashed back into his mind.

'You've put your case very ... very eloquently, Ken,' said Silverman, sipping the dregs of his tomato juice. He knew the glass was empty.

But burying his face in it was the only way he could avoid splitting his sides with laughter.

* * *

The heads of the two people in the car ahead had barely moved since they joined the A3 at Wandsworth twenty minutes ago, closely followed by two policemen in a patrol car.

As the evening light faded and they passed the junction with the M25, the head of the man in the driver's seat started turning towards the woman in the passenger seat for a second or two before facing the windscreen again. She didn't move, but kept facing ahead. After a minute or so she turned towards the driver, who looked at her for slightly longer intervals, revealing glimpses of the steering wheel as his shoulders turned. The car veered towards the nearside lane as he took his eye off the road before regaining control and steering it back into the centre of the fast lane. As it passed the signpost to Woking, the car slowed to 65 mph and weaved its way into the slow lane. The two officers in the police car were puzzled, but followed, keeping their distance. The woman's head in the car ahead moved more quickly, shaking from left to right. She seemed to wave something at the driver, then turned towards the window again, staring towards the dark fields. The driver was facing in the same direction as her now; his hands seemed to be hitting the steering wheel, but the woman did not turn round.

From the police car behind, the couple looked like the silhouettes of two crows pecking at each other. The police driver suddenly realised the couple were fast approaching a gravel lorry directly in front of them crawling up a slight hill at less than 50 mph. He rammed his foot on the accelerator of his Volvo 850, pulled alongside the car and beeped his horn, while the policeman in the passenger seat gesticulated to the driver of the car, pointing ahead to the truck. The driver of the car turned round and hit the brakes just in time to screech almost to a halt and avoid ploughing into the rear of the gravel lorry in front. He veered over onto the hard shoulder and stopped. The woman threw something at the man. He picked it up, examined it and slumped on the wheel. The policeman ran over to see if they were alright, but the driver waved them away. The policeman backed off.

* * *

It was hard for Cane and Lucy to have a row. When they were first married it was hard because they had nothing to row about; now he was Prime Minister, it was hard because they had nowhere to row. They soon discovered the more protection you have from the public, the less privacy you have from the officials, securitymen and others who are doing the protecting. They become as intrusive as the public they are shielding you from and could not know more about you if they were monitoring your life on closed circuit television. Which, a lot of the time, they were. But there was no CCTV inside their four wheel drive as Cane drove them to Guildford on Sunday night to meet Lucy's parents, where the children had stayed the weekend. They were alone. It was about the only place they could have a row. The dispute started shortly after they left the M25 behind them.

'Lucy,' said Cane, 'are you certain there's nothing on your mind? ... there's nothing worrying you you haven't told me, is there? If there is, we've got to talk it through and this is about the only place we can do it,' he said as he looked around the car.

'I've told you, there is nothing wrong with me. I'm a bit down, that's all. It's hardly surprising, is it?'

'I'm worried about you. I'm trying to be helpful, not difficult.'

'I've done everything you wanted. I've been to that fashion woman in the West End; what else do you want me to do?'

'Nothing, that's just it, I don't want you to do anything. Your clothes look fabulous, everyone's been saying so; you look great, but I'm worried there's something else.'

'There isn't, I've told you, there's nothing wrong. It's just the usual ... '

'What d'you mean? The usual?'

'The lack of a normal life! That's what I mean. I thought I'd get used to it once we were in Downing Street, but it doesn't get any easier.'

'But you said yourself ... what? – six months ago ... that you were beginning to enjoy it?'

'Well, I was wrong,' Lucy snapped, looking away again.

Cane wasn't sure what was wrong with her, but he knew there was something; and that something had got worse. He was sure there was more to it than criticism of her appearance and he was going to get to the bottom of it.

'It doesn't help our marriage having Charlie around the whole time,' she said.

Cane sighed. 'What's Charlie got to do with it?'

'What has Charlie got to do with it?' she bawled in disbelief. 'The same as any woman who comes between a man and a wife, that's what she has got to do with it!'

'Come on, that's not true, you know it isn't.'

'Oh isn't it? Then what is this, I'd like to know?'

Lucy rummaged in her handbag and pulled out a scrap of paper.

'What's that?'

'I'll tell you what it is, it's a note to you; shall I read it out? It says, "Thanks for last night, the best meat balls I've ever had." And at the bottom it is signed, "Charlie." Very cosy too,' she said waving the note in his face. 'Funny how you didn't mention to me that you had dinner together in our home when I dropped our children off with mummy and daddy last week, isn't it? Well?'

'Lucy, you can't be serious. Charlie and I were both working late. It was too late to go out, I cooked a quick meal, there was nothing to it. You know I cook for myself sometimes when you're not there. What was wrong in eating with Charlie? We got some work done.'

'Charlie, Charlie, Charlie, Charlie bloody Charlie, I'm sick to death of her name! She's around from dawn till dusk – and more – sometimes. When am I with you that long?'

'There is no one who could do that job like she does, you must know that?'

Lucy grunted with contempt but didn't answer. She stared through the passenger window at the dark fields.

'It'd be just the same if a man was doing her job, they'd have to be with us the same amount of time. If it's anyone's fault it's mine, not Charlie's.'

'Don't play the guilt game with me, Steven, just don't.'

'It's true. I couldn't do this job without Charlie. She's phenomenal. And she has done phenomenal things for you too. Look at the good press you've had since she took you to that fashion expert.'

'She got her money's worth out of that.'

'What's that supposed to mean?' said Cane, slapping the steering wheel in frustration.

'You should have seen her watching me being taken apart. You'd have thought she was the one on display ... the way she was dolled up – anything to make me feel worse.'

'That's unfair,' said Cane, taking his eyes off the road.

'Unfair? Look at you. You defend her but when do you ever defend me. When?'

He was suddenly aware of a car alongside him beeping its horn. He recognised one of his police bodyguards, his face contorted, his finger jabbing furiously in front of him. Cane looked ahead and saw the dark grey outline of the rear of a huge truck looming directly in front. He hit the break pedal, throwing both him and Lucy forward violently in their seats. Cane swerved onto the hard shoulder, just missing the mudguard of the lorry. The car slid to a halt and Cane looked anxiously at Lucy next to him. She was sitting with her head in her hands.

'My God. Are you alright?' he said, fearing she had smashed her head on the dashboard or windscreen.

Her head shot up. She hurled a piece of paper at him.

He unravelled it. It was Charlie's note. He fell on to the steering wheel.

* * *

Sunday was Charlie's day for 'slobbing out'. She wore a faded blue tracksuit and trainers; without a stitch of make-up. She spent most Saturday nights out with two girlfriends from Oxford who shared a flat in nearby Islington.

Like Charlie, they were unattached and the three of them would usually go to the cinema and have a meal at Charlie's favourite restaurant, Live Bait in The Cut near Waterloo station.

Occasionally they would go to one of the parties held by the Soho House crowd, though she didn't mix with Lomax. She'd had a brief fling with a TV producer she met there, but he went to work in Australia. But it was nothing like her Oxford days, when she came to London for the weekend and would be the first to get drunk and last to go to bed. Now she behaved in public with the restraint you would expect from someone frequently described as 'the second most powerful woman in Britain.'

Charlie heard the bell ring and went downstairs to open the door.

Silverman didn't normally socialise with Charlie at weekends; they saw enough of each other during the week, usually with Cane. But Cane's presence would not have been welcome on this occasion.

'What are we going to do about Lucy?' said Charlie. 'Apart from Gareth the bloody dinosaur, she's the biggest problem we've got.'

She hadn't told Silverman that is why she had called him to her flat, but he had guessed.

'It's been getting worse, and we can't just leave it,' said Charlie. 'What's going to happen in the election? At this rate, she'll crack up.'

'But I thought you sorted out the clothes issue; she looks much better – everyone says so.'

'I don't think it's got anything to do with clothes. I think she resents Steven being PM – she never wanted him to do it. She never liked it, but she's getting worse and worse. You should see some of the tantrums, Jesus. It's not just the election I'm worried about and how she'll react to three weeks on the campaign trail.'

'What's bothering you?'

'It's the effect she's having on Steven. It's starting to get to him. She's starting to affect his confidence. He's getting tetchy because she's getting tetchy with him. It makes me bloody annoyed.'

'We got her through the last election – just.'

'Don't throw that at me Ronnie.'

Nothing irked Charlie more than being reminded of how well everything had gone at the last election. It was before her time. She could claim no credit for winning the first term, they had won it without her; she had still to win her battle honours. It was why winning the second term was even more important to her than to them. She would not consider herself as their equal until she too had won an election, had inflicted some wounds on the Opposition and passed the ultimate political test, more satisfying to a fighter like Charlie than any other political achievement. Victory.

'Don't get mad at me,' said Silverman.

She slammed her Diet Coke on the table.

'I bloody well will get mad at you, Ronnie. We must win and we must stop Lucy getting in the way.'

'Hey, hey, hey, cool it. Let's think of the practical things we can do; practical ways to make the Lucy situation better.'

'Well don't look at me, Ronnie, whatever I do is like a red rag to a bull to Lucy. We come from different planets. You know what makes me so angry about her? She's had everything on a plate: fancy home, fancy parents, fancy education, the lot - not that she did much with it - Steven's working his socks off for people who've never had a scrap on their plate and his spoilt little wife sits at home complaining.'

'You'd better not share your thoughts with Steven, Charlie.'

'You know his problem, don't you? He's got a blind spot. He knows she's unhappy and blames himself for her unhappiness when it's nothing to do with him. God, you'd think she'd be the most proud woman in Britain, wouldn't you? D'you know, Ronnie, I sometimes think the only thing that could bring him down is that woman?'

'You forget, Charlie - Lucy's very different to you, but she's not to Steven. They're just as alike in their backgrounds as you and she are unalike. You resent her for being middle class - Steven doesn't, he's middle class too, he had things on a plate. It doesn't rile him the way it riles you.'

'He may have been born with a silver spoon but he threw it away. She was born with one in her mouth and it's still there. She hadn't got a clue about his politics when she married him - she'd've run a mile if she'd known and she's never got over the shock of finding out.'

'If only he'd married a genuine political wife, eh?' said Silverman.

'Yes ... exactly,' said Charlie, blindly.

'Such as a shipbuilder's daughter,' he added.

Charlie narrowed her eyes. 'Sod off!'

CHAPTER TWENTY

'Where do you see yourself in ten years?'

'Are we talking politics? Or are we talking personal?'

'Either or both,' laughed Sandy.

They were oblivious to the tiny click in an office five miles away triggered by their voices.

Greaves and Sandy had spent Sunday afternoon in her flat in Pimlico after walking to Tower Bridge and back on the Thames towpath in the morning. They had been together for nine months and were the subject of endless press speculation about whether they would marry. For years, Greaves had to do little more than be seen dining with a faintly attractive woman than to see his picture in the papers under a 'Wedding Bells For Greaves At Last?' headline.

While he was in his forties, getting married for the first time might seem unusual. Once he turned fifty, as he would next year, it would start to look desperate – as though he was only doing it to improve his chances of becoming Prime Minister one day. Greaves had always seemed much more desperate to become Prime Minister than to get married.

'Politics can change in a day,' he said, lying on a sofa with a mug of coffee on the floor. 'Who'd've thought Thatcher would have been brought down by her own party? Who'd've thought we'd wake up one day and find the Berlin Wall gone? Who'd have thought we'd be out of power for eighteen years? Who'd have thought we'd get it back in a landslide? Who'd've thought we'd lose the euro vote one day and win it the next?'

'You mean it's impossible to say?' said Sandy, who was sat on the floor, her back against the sofa, with her knees under her chin. He was stroking her long hair.

'Yes, and if you spend too much time thinking about where you want to be in ten years, you won't concentrate on doing the things now that you need to do to get to where you want to be. Does that make sense?'

'I think so. You mean if you want to succeed in your ambitions then get on with the job in hand now rather than dreaming about the future.'

'Spot on.' It took Greaves a long time before he started to talk to Sandy about his career – or himself. He didn't form close relationships easily with women – or men.

It was one of the reasons he seemed more distant and aloof than Cane. But he was closer to Sandy than he had been to any woman for a long time. They were away from the prying eyes and ears of Westminster. They were alone, well, nearly.

'Alright then,' said Sandy, 'what are your aims in the next few months - no - don't answer, I know that one: win the election.'

Greaves hesitated. 'Yes win the election, ... but there are one or two other things ... '

'What other things?'

'Well we've got to win it the right way this time.'

'How do you mean, the right way? You'll never win it by as much as last time.'

'No, I know that; I mean last time we were so terrified of the past, we over-reacted to criticism about what we used to be – we still do a bit. What I'd like us to do different this time is be a bit more faithful to our people, give them something to vote for, to cheer for.'

'You mean this hospitals thing, don't you?'

'Not just hospitals. I can't see the point of winning support from people if we don't use it to do what we always wanted to do. I sometimes think we copied our opponents' methods to win power on the basis that we had to, to get in, but now we've done it we're turning into what they were. What do we do for the poor? Nothing. The rich are richer under us than ever before.'

'But Steven doesn't want to put taxes up.'

'No and he won't spend it on those who need it, or not enough, anyway. What I've got to work out is how I deal with that. It's one thing for him to take that line, it's different for me. I'm not Steven Cane, I'm different and I have to be different ... otherwise ... '

'Otherwise what?'

' ... Nothing.'

'You mean otherwise you've no hope of succeeding him?'

Sandy had never before asked him directly if he wanted to be Prime Minister, though she read it in the press often enough. Greaves looked at her, wondering: was he close enough to her to speak his mind?

'Sandy, I've been in politics since I went leafleting with my dad in the general election when I was twelve years old – not all politicians take it up as a hobby you know. If I'd the chance to be Prime Minister, what d'you think I would do?'

'I see ...'

It wasn't only his feelings for Sandy that Greaves found hard to talk about. He had never discussed with her his feelings towards Cane, and she had never asked him. She had read about it, but she had never heard it from him. She seized the opportunity.

'What did happen between you and him?'

Greaves grimaced.

'It's simple really; a few months before the general election he took the Parliamentary seat I had nursed for five years while I was at the LSE, got into the House five years before me and the rest is history. There you are: a political biography in one sentence, or obituary maybe.'

He let out a resigned chuckle. But there was more pain than laughter within him.

And the pain went on.

Sandy caressed his hand.

'To think that I was the one who invited him to take part in the public meeting to save St Bernard's all those years ago. Me? I actually wrote the letter. I remember meeting him on a demo; he was wearing his doctor's white coat and I thought he'd be a good person to put the Health Secretary on the spot. I even suggested the question he should ask. I'd got hold of a document from a friendly civil servant which showed they had been planning to close Bernie's for years. I gave it to Steven because I was worried that if I did it, some people might know the official had given it to me. He made such good use of it that he got on TV. And after that he took over the whole campaign. It was all down to me, all me.' He shook his head in despair. She stroked his back to soothe him.

'And now?'

He looked at Sandy. 'And now, I have to watch him, the man I brought into politics, the man I created ... ! Ha! My creation! In Number 10! And doing what? Doing exactly what the last lot did, that's what. You'd have to go a long way to beat that for irony, wouldn't you? You know, a few months ago, I had a dream that he announced he was going to close St Bernard's and I stood up in the Commons and disowned him and he resigned and I became Prime Minister. How's that for a sad bastard? It was after he'd turned down my suggestion of a tax rise to sort out the NHS. A dream is all it's ever going to be.'

'You never know, Gareth, you never know, that's what you always say to me.'

'Yes, well ... '

Sandy struggled to offer some comfort.

'But you don't get on too badly, do you, you and Cane, I mean?'

'Get on is about it. I don't exactly have much choice, do I? I've got to be careful before I start stirring up trouble over tax – or anything else – but it doesn't mean I can't have my own views, or state them sometimes.'

'But if you push him on it before the election, won't that be ... ?

'Risky?'

'Yes, mightn't you end up having to resign?'

'It's possible. But would that be worse than not pushing for it, letting hospitals run down and people die in corridors?'

She slid her hand up his arm. 'You know, it's been really nice having you myself for the day, Gareth.'

'It's been great for me too.'

'I wish we could do it more often.'

'So do I,' said Gareth, putting his hand round her neck, as she sat on the floor against the settee where he was lying prone.

'What plans do you have for Gareth the human being as opposed to Gareth the politician?' she ventured, tossing her hair back playfully.

'Oh, marriage and eight children. We need to build up some supporters of the future!' he said.

'Eight? I hope you're joking!'

'Well maybe just the two then,' he said, lifting his head from the cushion to look at her as she sat below him with her long legs under her chin.

They had never talked about marriage or children before.

'Do you want children, Gareth?'

'Certainly ... yes, of course,' he said, sounding anything but. 'Do you?'

'No, I can't stand them.'

Greaves wore a confused frown; he wasn't good at this sort of thing.

'I'm only joking,' she laughed. 'Yes, I think I'd like children ... one day.'

'Would you? Really?' said Greaves excitedly. 'I'd thought maybe you'd like to carry on with your career, you know and, well, and maybe not bother with children.'

'I may look like a career girl but there is an earth mother bursting to get out from underneath – it's just that it's pretty well hidden under layers of mascara!'

Greaves looked at Sandy. She was intelligent, pretty, loving, funny, down to earth: all the qualities he had ever looked for in a woman. Very few of the girlfriends he had known had been prepared to accept the fact that his first love would always be politics. But Sandy? She seemed to understand, to accept. Would he ever have a better chance to marry and have a family? Would he ever have a better chance of eliminating the last difference between him and Cane? Would he ever have a better chance of preparing himself to make the final step up from deputy?

He pulled her towards him and kissed her, drawing her towards him till she climbed onto the sofa and lay on top of him. He kissed her cheeks, her lips, pulled down her T-shirt and kissed her shoulders and breasts. Sandy undid the buttons on his shirt and smoothed the thick down of fair hair on his chest. She slid her legs between his, pressed her face on his and they kissed passionately.

* * *

'You bastard, Greaves, you bloody bastard!'

Charlie had gone to a work an hour earlier than usual on Monday morning to listen to the tape recorder that had clicked into action the moment the bug in Sandy's living room started feeding a signal to the machine in her office in Number 10. She listened to the conversation between the two of them until the talking stopped. All she could hear was a muffled sound.

The sound of two people making love.

'Gareth ... oh darling ... oh, oh, oh ... ooh ... ooh.'

The chair went crashing over as Charlie kicked it with all her might. She switched off the tape machine, ripped the tape off, knocking the machine onto the floor by mistake.

'What goin' 'ere? De rehearsal for de next Brixton riot, or what?'

Dora was standing at the door. Charlie looked at her watch. Dora was fifteen minutes early; she hadn't even got a cup of coffee.

'What are you doing here Dora?' she snapped, fearful that she had seen her listening to the tape.

'I'm doin' you a favour Miss,' growled Dora. 'Your brother Billy phone you five minutes ago. I din' think you was in, but I thought I'd check. He wan' you urgent.'

Charlie grabbed the phone and dialled home in one frantic movement.

'What is it, Billy?'

'Mum's had another heart attack.'

'Oh my God!' said Charlie, 'how is she, how is she?'

'Unconscious.'

'What? How bad is it?'

'Worse than the last one.'

'Oh Christ no! How long's she been out, when did it happen?' Charlie gabbled.

'Three this morning, it's a bloody shambles.'

'How? What d'you mean?'

'We're in a corridor with her, that's what I mean! They've put her on a drip, but there's no bed. She's unconscious and they're talkin' 'bout movin' her. There's two wards been closed here because they haven't got the staff. It's bloody criminal. Can't you do something, Charlie? We're always reading how bleeding powerful you are, how one word from you and the whole world jumps. Well why don't you stop trying to save the country and start trying to save your mother and make some of these bloody doctors jump?'

'That's not fair.'

'Just get on the phone and do it!'

For all her sophistication, her education and her guile, she was never a match for her brother Billy, any more than she had been for her father Billy. Billy junior had only been to London once, for a football match when he was arrested for daubing anti-English graffiti on one of the lions in Trafalgar Square. But he had a crude but simple confidence in his prejudices that Charlie could never counter. And he had an even more powerful weapon in his armoury; one that Charlie had no answer to.

Guilt.

Guilt over leaving home, leaving Scotland for England, guilt that she, their wee sister, earned more than any of her proud brothers, guilt that it was only when she went to America that Billy turned away from school, and most crucial of all, guilt that she had left her mother. She had told her never to tell the boys how much money she sent her. They would resent that even more. Blood money. Jesus, how she wished she hadn't had a convent education.

Charlie hurriedly made a note of the details of the hospital, got through to someone in accident and emergency and bawled at them. The moment she had said she was calling from Downing Street, she knew it was a mistake.

'I'm sorry Miss, we're doing everything we can to treat your mother,' said a doctor at the end. 'But it's really no use your shouting at me. There are limits to what we can do, and if you'll permit me to say so, you're in a good position to know that and why.'

Charlie slammed the phone down, grabbed the bag with a change of clothes she always kept with her, and redialled the duty clerk at Number 10.

'Get me on the next shuttle to Glasgow.'

* * *

Cane always listened to the 'Today' programme between seven and eight straight after his half hour session on the bike machine and dumb-bells in the guest room at the flat.

'Dad, can't we have Radio One?' said Jessica, 'just for once dad, go on.'

'Jessica, dear, I want to listen to the headlines, they're on in a minute.'

'It's not fair, you're always listening to the news, we never get what we want.'

'You get plenty of things you want; now pipe down, Jessica, please, you can have it on in a moment, there's something I need to hear.'

She tutted loudly. Charlie had phoned him late on Sunday night to warn him a big health scandal was to be revealed by the Today programme. Health Secretary Hodgson was aware of the details and would respond on the programme.

'The BBC has learned that staff at a home for the handicapped in Norfolk have been suspended following allegations that they sexually abused people living at the home. Police have been called in to investigate claims that ten members of staff ran a paedophile ring based at the Oakwood Home in Norfolk. A former member of staff has told the authorities that he witnessed systematic abuse of handicapped people, mainly children and young adults, living at Oakwood over a period of fifteen years. He says that when he complained he was subjected to threats of violence and was told other staff would accuse him of taking part in the attacks. We will be speaking to the Health Secretary later in the programme to find out how the Government intends to respond to the allegations.'

Cane was shaking his head and looking at his own two children eating their cereal when Lucy arrived in the kitchen with their school shoes.

'What's wrong, Steven?'

'There's a sex scandal at a home for the handicapped, many of them are children. It's been going on for fifteen years, according to the radio. Fifteen years, can you imagine what it must be like to be in one of the homes and then be abused? My God, it doesn't bear thinking about. How can people do these things, how can they?'

Lucy turned away from the table where the children were sitting and leant on the blue and white tiled kitchen surface. Cane went across to her, pulled her towards him and hugged her to his chest.

'Go and clean your teeth, kids,' said Cane. 'Lucy, we're so lucky. Let's not get down about silly things, let's forget the row in the car. Look at those two,' he said, watching the children disappear to the bathroom. 'Look at them, they're lovely kids; look at us, look what we've got; our health, each other, let's be thankful Lucy, let's be happy, please.'

Her head was buried sideways in his chest.

She went limp and Cane hugged his wife harder to stop her falling.

* * *

The security man nodded through Silverman's car the moment he recognised the chauffeur-driven black Rover and the T registration number plate.

Silverman was no stranger to McLintock's office in docklands. He remembered his first visit before the election when McLintock took him on a tour of the building including a studio where a half-naked girl was being photographed for the next day's paper. McLintock asked Silverman if he wanted to pose with her. An appearance on Page Three in the election

212

campaign wouldn't do him any harm, said McLintock. It'd make him look more human. Silverman politely declined. There were several things he was not prepared to do for humanity.

McLintock's secretary met him at the main entrance and took him to the fourth floor through the swing doors underneath a large notice in red and white: 'YOU ARE ENTERING THE CENTRE OF *The Globe*.' It was like the large sign at the end of the players' tunnel at Liverpool Football Club, 'THIS IS ANFIELD'. It was the last thing visiting players saw before they walked onto the pitch. *The Globe*'s welcoming sign was intended to have the same effect on visitors.

Silverman walked past rows of people, mainly young men in white shirts, tapping away at computer terminals. There was very little noise. They could be accountants checking columns of statistics of no interest to anyone other than other accountants. In fact they were journalists writing columns of newsprint which would amuse millions, anger a few thousand and destroy one or two. If they didn't, then the journalists themselves would be destroyed – by McLintock. He had been known to stand behind a young journalist struggling to meet a deadline, peer at the screen, wait until he could see beads of sweat on the reporter's neck and say: 'You've lost it, pal, I'd try the French Foreign Legion if I were you.'

On the wall were silver engravings of some of *The Globe*'s most notorious front pages. CANE YOU BELIEVE IT! for the day of Cane's landslide was Silverman's favourite. McLintock saw him stop to admire it as he stood at his office door.

'Play your cards right Chancellor and you can have it!' shouted McLintock.

Silverman swung round on his heels and walked across to McLintock's office with its panoramic view of the Thames as it curled around docklands. But McLintock never gave anything away without extracting something in return.

'How's everything Ronnie? Isn't it about time you put us out of our misery and told us when the election's going to be?'

'Steady on, Warren, there's ages to go before we have to call the election. I'd have thought *The Globe*'s readers would be appreciating the rest from politics after the referendum.'

'Tell me about it. I aged twelve years waiting the twelve hours for that Mersey result to be reversed. It wasn't just your Government and the future of Britain at stake you know, there were really important things – like the credibility of *The Globe* as a serious paper!' McLintock chortled with laughter, Silverman smiled.

'Warren, I don't have to tell you what a great job you did.'

'Yes, I never thought I would team up with the Japanese Prime Minister to save a British government from ruin!' he said, chortling a little too loudly for Silverman's comfort. 'Still, as Maggie used to say to me, "it's a funny old world Mr McLintock." I'm not sure she would've been smiling when she heard we were backing the euro, but never mind, she never seemed to have much of a sense of humour. How you getting on with the BBC these days?'

He knew Charlie and Silverman worked hand in glove, and he had no doubt she had told him about her offer to let McLintock buy Radios One and Two and the World Service in return for him backing the euro.

'Fine,' said Silverman, taking a sip of tea to give him time to measure his words. 'We're looking at all that.'

'Looking at any decisions about it?' asked McLintock.

'Not yet. But we will be before long.'

'Before the election?'

McLintock had hit the nail on the head. He assumed Silverman had agreed to see him because he wanted to make sure *The Globe* would carry on supporting Cane through the election. He was right. Silverman and Charlie had discussed the World Service deal and decided the best way to guarantee McLintock's continued support for Cane through the election campaign was to delay the decision until after polling day. It would mean McLintock accepting less than what he had asked for – for the time being.

Silverman assumed McLintock had asked to see him to check he was going to be allowed to buy the World Service. He was only half right. McLintock was not a man used to settling for less than he wanted.

'I'm not worried about the Beeb deal. I trust you.'

'Good.'

'But there's something else I am worried about.'

'What's that, Warren?'

'These union laws.'

'What about them?'

'It worries me when I hear you might stick them in your manifesto after all. I mean, you told me not so long ago that you'd decided to leave them out of the manifesto, yet I've been hearing lately you might put them back in because that illiterate troglodyte, Bird, is threatening to cut your election funds if you ignore him.'

Silverman was flabbergasted. Not a single word had appeared in the press about his talks with Bird about reinstating the law in the party's manifesto. How could McLintock have got to hear about it? Silverman had only discussed it with Cane and one or two other ministers. But McLintock was famous for having spies in key unions – and the engineers were among those who were fighting to win back recognition at his production plant.

'You put that law back in and you might as well turn the clock back to 1979. You know that, don't you? The unions have been looking for a chance to get their foot back in the door ever since I screwed them fifteen years ago. Do you really think I'd throw *The Globe* behind you in the election so the unions could do that to me afterwards? I might as well give them the keys to the plant and say "here you are boys, it's all yours".'

Silverman did a double take. McLintock was mouthing precisely the exaggerated claims that Bird had predicted would be made by opponents of the measure. Yet McLintock and Bird were both allies of Silverman.

And he needed both of them.

CHAPTER TWENTY ONE

Father Adrian sat in the confessional box at the Sacred Heart Catholic Church, Highbury, waiting.

The unkempt red-brick church just behind a scruffy shopping arcade was not where he had envisaged ending his career when he took holy orders. He spent half of his time trying to keep going the appeal to repair the church roof that was launched ten years ago and was still only half way towards its £250,000 target, and the other half repairing windows broken most weekends by children from the local estate. Little had changed since he arrived fifteen years ago. Except the age of the hooligans. As he got older, they got younger. He kept reading that the Catholic Church was gaining new converts from the Church of England, but he hadn't seen much evidence of it at the Sacred Heart. The most remarkable thing was that so much of his faith and enthusiasm had survived. He was used to lapsed Catholics from the professional classes dotted around the more expensive parts of North London calling in to see his – when they were in trouble. They rarely returned, but he always had time for them.

'Father, I've not been to confession for some time.'

'That's quite alright, we don't keep a register, you know.'

'No, but I've not been in a very long time.'

'That could be two weeks or two years, a long time for one person is no time at all for another.'

'Father, it's twenty.'

'Well now, we could be some time, couldn't we? I'm trying to think of all the things I'd have to confess to over the last twenty years.'

'Father, I'm not sure why I have come here, I'm not sure I believe anymore.'

'We're here to listen to anyone, to help anyone; it's never to late to find belief. Find God and you will find yourself.'

'I don't know about that, but I have to talk to someone. And I couldn't think of anywhere else to go.'

'That's why God is there - for when you have nowhere else to go to.'

'I'm not sure if God will want to stay when I have told him why I am here.'

'When you go, he'll go with you - if you want him to, and if you come back, he'll still be here.'

'Father, I have done things I can never be forgiven for.'

'You can always be forgiven - if you repent.'

'For betraying a mother?'

'Why do you say you betrayed her?'

'I left her; she had no life while I ran away to get a life, a life that she never had, a life away from her.'

'All children must do that at some point. You can't stay tied to your mother's apron strings for ever.'

'I left her for five years, when I came back I promised I'd see her every two months, and I did, Father, I did ... at first. Then, oh, I don't know, I got caught up in work ... I was always too busy, I hadn't the time ... the time to care ... for my own mother. What sort of person does that make me, Father?'

'But you have come here, you've shown you do care, it is never too late, God will forgive you and, God willing, your mother will forgive you.'

'I don't think so, Father; my mother earned forgiveness, she believed, she went to confession every week. What did she have to ask forgiveness for? She spent her whole life giving. Why should she forgive me? Why should you, why should anyone?'

'If your mother believed in forgiveness, then she'll forgive you.'

'How can she?'

'I don't follow ... '

Charlie fell against the screen separating her from the priest.

'She's dead.'

'Oh my dear child, I'm so sorry, so very very sorry. When was it?'

'Last week.'

'I'm so very sorry. What happened?'

'She had a heart attack.'

'I am so sorry. You cannot blame yourself for that, it was not your fault.'

'But I didn't see her for a year, father, a whole year. She'd already had one heart attack. I should have gone home more often. I didn't even go home at Christmas, can you believe that? Not even Christmas.'

'I'm sure it wasn't because you were bad.'

'Oh, I could make a hundred excuses, but that's all they are – excuses. She's dead and I'll never see her again. I wasn't even there when she was on a trolley – on a trolley for heaven's sake, in a corridor! Dying! I was in London working, working, working, but what for?'

'That is not a crime, your mother would not want you judged for that.'

'Some members of my family do, my brothers, my aunts and uncles, they've judged me. And I don't blame them. I've judged myself.'

'When did you leave home?'

'When I was eighteen, to go to college.'

'And your father?'

'He died.'

'I'm sorry, when was that?'

'Fifteen years ago, but he died ten years before that, really.'

'In what way?'

'When I was twelve he was badly hurt at the shipyard, never worked again and became ... he became an alcoholic. He'd always had a temper but he was passionate, Father, he believed in things, he fought for people. God, he was in some fights. Not just ordinary fights, political fights, political struggles. Fights for his fellow man, Father, his fellow worker.'

Her father's passion came flooding back to her. Her passion. Worker. Struggle. It was odd even saying the words now. It was the language of another age, another place; her home, her upbringing.

'But he was a different man after the accident. He was violent, drunken, twisted. That's what they did to him.'

'They?'

'The shipyard, the bosses who sacked him and refused him a pension.'

'How did you cope?'

'I was the oldest; I helped mum with the boys and then, when I had the chance to get away, I grabbed it and never went back. Oh, I'd phone every week and sent her money, every week Father, I did, but she needed more than a cheque. She needed me and I didn't give her that, the one thing she wanted. Now I can't, it's too late. I've been so selfish.'

'It doesn't sound so selfish to me. If you had a child who'd had a childhood like that, would you resent it going to college, finding a career in London? I doubt it, my dear, I doubt it.'

Charlie slumped on the dark wooden desk in front of her and wept uncontrollably. People who knew her were always struck by the way she made her feelings known on any subject or individual. They didn't know her at all.

'You cannot blame yourself for what happened to your mother.'

'But that's just it Father, one of the reasons I didn't go home was because I was ashamed.'

'Ashamed of what?'

'Ashamed of what I'd done in London.'

'I don't understand.'

'Mother believed, Father, in a way that I've never believed.'

'She would not have disowned you for pursuing your belief in another way, not if she loved you, which I'm sure she did.'

'No Father, but she would have disowned me if she'd known what I'd done.'

'What do you mean?'

'When I first went to London, I met a man ... '

'Yes.'

'I wasn't sure if I loved this man ... '

' ... And?'

Charlie's sobbing intensified. She felt an almighty surge within her, as though she had been standing on an emotional precipice for years and was finally about to jump. She couldn't stop herself. She wanted to jump, to get it over with. She didn't care what happened when she hit the ground.

'We made love ... once. I'd had a lot to drink ... we both had ... and ...'

'That is not such a shameful thing, my child. You can be forgiven.'

'No, Father, it was shameful, it was ... '

'Why so?'

'I fell pregnant.'

'I see.'

'I didn't know what to do, ... I panicked.'

'What did you do?'

'I ... I had an abor ... a termination, Father.'

'What did your man friend think?'

Charlie went silent. Father Adrian could hear her trying to stifle her tears.

'I ... I ... I didn't tell him.'

'You didn't tell him you had a termination?'

She could hear the shock in his reaction. There couldn't be many times when Father Adrian was shocked. She momentarily checked, but it was too late. She had to finish, to get it out. If she didn't it would sink back within her and bury itself deeper than ever, eating her away like a cancer.

'I didn't tell him I was pregnant.'

'He never knew?'

'No.'

'How long ago was this, my dear?'

'Nearly ten years.'

'You have never married?'

'No.'

'Nor had children?'

'No.'

'And him?'

'No, he never married.'

'You lost contact?'

'For a while.'

'How?'

'I work with him ... in a way. I see him most days and sometimes I look at him and think ... I don't know what I think. I betrayed him as well, not just mother. I abandoned her and I abandoned him and I aban ...' She cried again. 'He's never forgiven me for leaving him, if he'd known – if she'd known what I'd done to ... what else I did, I don't know what they'd say. I'll never know what mother would say, but I don't need to, I know in my heart.'

She had hit the ground. She was shaking. Her face was a crumpled soaking mess.

* * *

Charlie was already waiting in the Prime Minister's study when Cane arrived first thing in the morning. She was busily reading a sheaf of papers, trying to look as unfussed as possible. Cane walked towards her, his arms extended. She looked up and looked down at her papers. He stood behind her and put both hands on her shoulders.

She stopped what she was doing and momentarily closed her eyes. Cane didn't see, but he felt her spontaneously relax and then tense, as she regained control of herself.

'How was it?'

'Grim.'

It was the first time he had seen her since her mother died the previous week. Charlie had managed to get her into a hospital bed three hours after her brother phoned her, but it was too late. She died at noon, an hour after Charlie had arrived straight from Glasgow airport. The doctors said it had made no difference; Charlie wasn't so sure – and she got no reassurance from her family.

'You should take some time off. I told you to stay with your family, not to come straight back,' said Cane.

'Four days was enough. The boys can look after themselves, they're not boys any more. You know I had six nieces and nephews there and I only recognised three.'

'Were all your relatives there?'

''fraid so.'

'How are they coping?'

'The same way they cope with everything else. Drink. That and by slagging off the Government – in other words me. I knew they'd make me suffer. They lost no chance to remind me I hadn't seen mum for months.'

When Charlie was a child, she had been brought up to hate the English. With her undiluted Celtic parentage, she had had little say in the matter. But she saw the Scots differently now she lived in England. And they saw her differently too. She was neither Anglo nor Scot. Billy would taunt her: 'You look English, you talk English, you are English, you're one of them.'

'You can imagine what they said about the cock-up over the hospital bed. It was all my fault; the health cuts; everything, my fault – Jesus! And you're not exactly Mr Popular with the Redpath clan, I can tell you. Billy's flipped since he joined the SWP. He frightens me. He'd do anything to hurt me. They wanted to put it all on someone else because they were down the pub when Mum collapsed. It wouldn't have happened if they'd got to her sooner. One of my cousins was there – she works as a singer on a cruise liner, a bloody cruise liner! And they kept going on about what a great success she had been, a cruise liner for Christ's sake! It was their way of rubbing it in. "Better than being a boring civil servant," I heard one of my uncles say. Billy chipped in "or a working class traitor." If I'd stayed any longer up there I'd have done something I'd have regretted. I had to get back. The last thing Billy said when I left was "don't come back, you don't belong here any more." And he meant it. You can't imagine what being back in that room was like; that room, where I used to try and do my homework while the boys were fighting. And Mum and Dad were worse. Dad'd be shouting at mum – that's if she wasn't at the laundry or out doing her cleaning job – complaining I hadn't made his tea, and I was trying to do some revision.

Charlie had stood in the doorway of her mother's kitchen. She kept looking at the seat at the kitchen table where Dad used to sit, hour after hour after hour. He used to cover his hair with Brylcreem and the mark it left on the kitchen wall where his head used to lean was still there; they hadn't even decorated over it. It gave her the creeps. Now the seat was occupied by another Billy. The thought of it scared her. Cane saw her tremble as though she was shaking off an evil spirit.

'What is it?'

'Nothing, now can we close the subject?'

It was what she usually did when anyone dug too deep. Close it down, move on, get back to business. She grabbed a packet of cigarettes and ripped off the polythene wrapping.

'But you must allow yourself ... '

'Steven, please! Drop it. Ronnie'll be here any second. Let's do what we were going to do, that'll be the best therapy for me.'

'OK, but ... '

'No buts, come on.'

Cane wanted to reach out to her, to hold her, comfort her. He could see how much she was holding back, but she had put a wall up. He knew better than to push beyond a certain point, and he had reached that point. She was right about Silverman; he walked in at two minutes past half past.

'Before you say a thing, I'm fine, Ronnie. I got your message about mum, we'll talk about it some other time. Can we please get on with the meeting?'

Silverman caught Cane's eye. He was shaking his head slowly, warning him off.

'Right then, it's November 1st, is it?' said Charlie, breezily, before they had a chance to persist.

'Tell us why it should be,' said Cane, letting her take control.

'From the top then: Bathurst is still all over the place after losing the referendum, we've re-established our lead in the polls over the summer – OK it's not as big as it was, but ten points is still comfortable – the euro's looking stable, there's still a chance of a downturn on the continent in autumn

and November 1st is the last day we can do it before we get right into winter – and they never make popular elections, people resent turning out in
the freezing cold. Also, we can announce it either during the last week of
September during our conference and send them home all fired up – or
the following week during their conference and steal their thunder. It's
either that or next spring – and by then we're getting close to our five year
deadline. Once that happens we'll start to look desperate and you'll find
yourself trapped.'

'It's hard to disagree,' said Silverman, 'but there's a few loose ends we
ought to clear up first.'

'Which are?' asked Cane.

'Armitage has been cutting up rough over my handling of civil servants,'
said Charlie. 'Has he mentioned it to you Steven?'

'Yes,' said Cane.

'We've got a bit of a problem over union laws,' said Silverman. 'Bird
wants them in the manifesto but McLintock wants them out. It won't be
easy to square those two.'

'Why not keep the commitment but water down the bits McLintock's
worried about?' said Cane.

Silverman knew how stubborn both men were, but knew of something
else that was even closer to their hearts than union recognition; recognition
of themselves.

'There's a third way out of this,' said Silverman.

'Which is?' said Cane.

'Honours.'

Split the difference between them on the legislation and throw in a
gong. The oldest solution in politics. Charlie had another thought. Patrick
Armitage might cause trouble; Sir Patrick Armitage would be as good as
gold.

But Cane knew there was another individual who had to be dealt with
before the election, and it was going to take much more than the power of
patronage to do it.

'The only other major problem I foresee is Saddam Hussein.'

Saddam had survived one full scale war by the NATO allies and in the last six months had inexplicably stepped up his murderous activities. He was believed to have been behind a series of terrorist attacks on Western targets, was accused of killing thousands of dissidents in Iraq and was on the brink of perfecting his own nuclear bomb.

'The Yanks are getting nervous and talking about a short sharp attack to stop him.'

'What does that mean exactly?' asked Charlie.

'I don't know, but whatever it is, they'll expect us to be in the front line with them. It could cause problems.'

That was only one aspect of the war. Charlie's mind was on the ratings war.

'Anything else?' said Cane.

'Saddam's not the only one who could do with a short sharp shock,' said Charlie.

'Meaning?' said Cane.

'President Greaves,' she said, stubbing her lipstick-stained cigarette into an ashtray.

'What about him?' said Silverman.

'He's out to cause more trouble,' said Charlie.

'How do you know? He's shown no sign,' said Cane.

'No, and the Mafia don't give you a month's written notice when they're about to blow your brains out,' she replied.

'How do you know?'

'I just do.'

'What over?'

'The usual – tax. Don't be surprised if he throws a spanner in the works soon. We've got to watch him like a hawk. It's another reason for going for November 1st; he won't have the nerve to cause a crisis in the run-up to an election. And afterwards? Well I know what I'd do.'

'What is that?' asked Cane.

'Sack him.'

CHAPTER TWENTY TWO

'You look absolutely fabulous.'

'Which one do I remind you of? Jennifer Saunders or Joanna Lumley?'

'I didn't mean that kind of absolutely fabulous and you know it, you really do look great.'

Lucy was wearing a powder blue Ronat Zilka suit chosen for her by Yolanda Hussey. It made her look slimmer, younger and, somehow, happier. Lucy and Cane were going to visit a hospital. But this was no ordinary hospital visit, it was at St Bernard's, where Cane had worked twenty years ago as a junior doctor. He had been invited to a party to celebrate St Bernard's 350th anniversary.

Charlie had not been slow to see its publicity potential. Cane hadn't announced it yet, but the election was only six weeks away and he hadn't received many hospital invitations recently. The NHS row had dented his popularity with his old profession and although his extra £400 million for hospital beds had been well received, the nurses had kept up their campaign. St Bernard's was one of the few hospitals where he could expect a warm welcome. There, he was known not as someone who closed hospitals, but as one who had saved them from closure. But that was before he was a politician.

It wasn't only an ideal opportunity for Cane to counter the NHS attacks on him, it was also an ideal opportunity to continue experimenting with Lucy's new image.

Her trip to Amberton had attracted a favourable response, but the beige suit was still on the conservative side, whereas the powder blue designer outfit she had on for the St Bernard's party was far more adventurous. Charlie sensed, that despite her initial hostility, Lucy was beginning to enjoy the benefits of getting a good press. It was just as easy to love them when they were nice about you as it was to hate them when they were nasty.

Charlie had arranged a photo call at St Bernard's after the party had finished. Cane was cheered loudly by the staff when he arrived at the canteen, where the party was taking place. He was due to make a brief speech and present a painting of St Bernard's to Staff Nurse Sister Melanie Smith, who started at the hospital in the same week as Cane, and was still there.

'It feels strange coming back here for the first time in twenty years,' said Cane. 'St Bernard's has a lot to answer for. If it hadn't been for this place, I would never have entered politics. I remember when we sat down for our first staff meeting to discuss how to stop the last Government closing it.'

Cane turned to Staff Nurse Smith alongside him. She had hardly changed since they first met. Her efficient and dedicated, if slightly humourless, approach to nursing was in the true Florence Nightingale mould. More gaunt than gamine, she had not married. She was trembling with nerves; the last man she had a crush on was standing next to her.

'D'you remember, Melanie, you said "if they close St Bernard's they close the whole health service next." Well, we stopped them closing St Bernard's didn't we? And we stopped them closing the health service. I know we've had our critics in the last year for not spending more on hospitals, but people forget what it was like only four years ago. Of course the health service needs more, and it will get more. But not if we lose power. There's another reason for keeping me in Number 10 – if we lose I may have to go back to medicine, then the health service really would be in trouble!'

The photographers took pictures of Cane presenting the painting to Staff Nurse Smith, and placing a kiss on her cheek, before he and Lucy prepared to return to their car waiting at the front entrance. As they were saying goodbye to the nurses at the canteen, Charlie was pulled to one side by one of the two Special Branch policemen who accompanied the Prime Minister everywhere. A small group of Socialist Workers Party demonstrators had arrived at the front door with placards. She hurriedly arranged for Cane's car to pick them up at the rear of the hospital.

Cane and Lucy must get to the back of the hospital quickly. Cane knew the way: it was the exit he had always used at lunchtimes when he worked at the hospital twenty years ago – directly opposite the Anne Boleyn pub.

When they got to the rear entrance the car wasn't there, and a man was striding towards them. He was tall, had salt and pepper hair, a weathered face, was in his fifties, wore a blue blazer and a trilby and had a pencil moustache. He looked like the doctors you saw in the old Ealing Comedies, the type who teased matron and had open-top MG sports cars. Charlie assumed he was a doctor; he didn't look like the sort of patient who lived anywhere near St Bernard's. He was a member of a profession, but not the medical profession.

'Andy Carmichael, Glasgow Herald, London editor, Prime Minister, delighted to meet you,' he said. Mr Pencil Moustache pulled out a pencil.

'The PM's not doing a doorstep here,' said Charlie dismissively. 'He made a few remarks inside, if you want them they're in a press release. You can get it from the press officer at the front.'

Charlie wasn't looking at Carmichael as she spoke, she was looking round the corner, trying to see if the PM's car was on its way. It was embarrassing for him and Lucy to be standing at the back of the hospital, waiting.

'Actually it was you I wanted to speak to Miss Redpath.'

'Really,' she said, disinterestedly, 'look Tony ... '

'It's Andy.'

'Sorry, look Andy, I'm not briefing here, do you mind getting out of the way?'

'I wanted to ask you about your mother.'

Charlie froze. She looked at Carmichael and saw him pull a tape recorder out and hold it towards her.

'You what?' she spat.

'Our paper is running a story today saying your mother died because she was kept waiting on a hospital trolley for three hours because of the effect on the health authority of government cuts. Would you care to comment?'

228

'How dare you ask me about my mother, you piece of scum, get out!'

Cane and Lucy were standing a forty yards away from Charlie, guarded by the two Special Branch officers, who were looking anxiously for the Canes' car.

'Miss Redpath, I apologise for approaching you like this, but we feel it is a legitimate question.'

'You have no right to make wild allegations about my family, now clear off!'

But Carmichael was not intimidated. 'They're not wild allegations, Miss Redpath, the allegations were made by a member of your family.'

'You're lying, get out, get out!'

Charlie's arm caught Carmichael on the chest.

'They were made by a member of your family, Mr Billy Redpath,' he repeated, after regaining his balance, 'who says government cuts were responsible for your mother's death.'

Before Charlie could react she saw Cane's black Jaguar coming round the corner. It was going much faster than the 15 mph speed limit on the hospital perimeter road. Three seconds later, she realised why. A group of demonstrators who had been waiting to ambush Cane at the front of the hospital were running behind the car. Charlie shoved Carmichael away as she ran to join Cane and Lucy who were shielded by the two policemen who were ready to bundle all three of them in when the car arrived.

Before it had even skidded to a halt, one of the Special Branch men pulled open the door. Cane jumped in on one side and Charlie on the other. But when Ronat Zilka designed Lucy's powder blue suit, she did not have speed and mobility in mind. She couldn't lift her knees in the tight skirt and tripped on the kerb as Cane gave her one last tug to help her get into the car.

As Cane was trying to lift her up and in, the demonstrators arrived. A spiky haired youth with a ring in his nose and ripped black jeans with chains dangling from them threw two eggs. One caught Lucy's shoulder; the other landed right in her handbag as Cane slammed the door shut and the car accelerated away. As he consoled his distraught wife and used his handkerchief to mop the egg off her suit and the black leather upholstery of the Jaguar, Charlie found one of the protestors' leaflets on her lap.

She picked it up. 'GREAVES IS RIGHT, SAVE OUR HOSPITALS.'

To hell with Billy; to hell with Greaves. To hell with the lot of them.

* * *

Charlie ripped the leaflet into a hundred pieces and hurled them in the direction of the waste paper bin by her desk and dialled the number of the editor of the Glasgow Herald about his front page story, 'CANE AIDE IN NHS STORM.' She angrily accused him of a breach of privacy and claimed a reporter had filled her brother with booze to get him to say what the paper wanted. She had made up the allegation, but she knew how much Billy drank – and how reporters operated.

She had one large stroke of luck. Not a single camera had caught the egg-throwing incident. If they had, it would have been front page news and led the TV news. Without pictures it would make two paragraphs, not that that would be enough to console Lucy. She told Cane the good news, but it did little to cheer him up.

'What's the matter?' asked Charlie, sat at her desk as he stood over her.

'It's Lucy,' he shook his head in despair. 'It's going to take a lot to get her confidence back after this.'

'There were no cameras there, it could've been worse.'

'Don't worry – it has got worse. Aunt Mimi's phoned. She's supposed to be a friend but that damned woman always makes Lucy feel worse. What was all that between you and that reporter?'

'Some ridiculous claims about my mother being kept waiting in a hospital corridor, it's total bullshit,' Charlie lied. 'Billy said something stupid to the papers.'

'Huh, families,' mused Cane.

'They're a bloody nuisance.'

'Come on,' he said briskly, 'neither of us feels like partying, but that,

Charlie Redpath, is exactly what the two of us are going to do. Right now.'

There was a reception in the dining room to present the prizes to the first graduates from supermarket boss Tom Innes's 'Cadets Of Industry Training College'.

As Charlie made towards the door, Cane stopped her and stretched out both arms to lift her to her feet. It was a supportive, sympathetic gesture, but that is not how it would have looked to anyone who had walked in on them. And when two seconds later, as Cane was still holding her, the door opened and Dora walked in holding a cup of coffee, that is not how it looked to her.

'Sorry,' said Dora, without a trace of embarrassment. 'I tort Miss Redpath here on 'er own, she ask for coffee,' she said. 'I didn't know you was in a ... in a meetin'.' She didn't bother to hide her sarcasm. Cane felt himself flush. He quickly withdrew his hands from Charlie's, causing her to fall back awkwardly in her chair. He briefly thought of trying to explain the situation before realising the preposterousness of it: justifying himself to the Downing Street messenger. Best to let it pass.

'That was twenty minutes ago,' said a flustered Charlie, who didn't bother to conceal her annoyance. 'Never mind, Dora,' she snapped. 'We're going to the party, forget the coffee.'

'Look like dem more than one party 'ere tonight,' she said, closing the door behind her, firmly.

Innes was talking to Silverman, when Charlie and Cane finally arrived at the reception. Silverman caught Charlie's eye and made a great show of pulling his cuff back to look at his watch, as if to say 'and where have you two been all this time?' Dora wasn't the only one who was watching them. Maybe he was jealous, not of Cane but of her, thought Charlie. It wasn't only women who found Cane's matinee idol looks attractive. Silverman might feel he could rebuke her, but he would never dare take such liberties with Cane.

'Ah, Prime Minister,' said Silverman, 'Lord Tom was telling me how he can keep one or two places at the college open for any ministers you think need a refresher course in trade and industry.'

'After today, I think I'd feel a good bit safer in a college than I would in a hospital,' said Cane.

'Yes, I heard you had a scrape,' said Innes. 'How's Lucy?'

'Not brilliant. And some nutcase was screaming abuse at Charlie.'

'I reckon Charlie's more than a match for any man – verbally or physically,' said Innes, winking at Charlie.

'We're here to celebrate the college, Tom,' she said, swiftly changing the subject. 'The Prime Minister thinks you've done a fantastic job.'

'Yeah, we've got some brilliant pupils. I hope one of them doesn't end up buying me out. Any news on the election, Prime Minister? Businessmen want it out of the way, you know, we hate uncertainty.'

'I always listen to business, Tom,' replied Cane, enigmatically.

'I've been telling Tom about how strongly we think any curbs on out-of-town shopping centres should take account of the job implications on the rural economy as well as the environmental impact,' said Silverman.

'Absolutely,' said Cane.

Innes wondered how much he knew about the party donations. Cane was supposed to know nothing, but he had always regarded blind trusts used before the party won power as a see-through device. A businessman didn't give money for nothing. Surely a politician couldn't expect to receive it for nothing.

'How about you and the family joining me and Liv at Cape Cod again this year, Steven?'

Cane, Lucy and the children had had a wonderful two week holiday at Innes's mansion in New England two summers earlier.

'We'd love to Tom, it was wonderful, just wonderful, we can never thank you enough. I can still taste those clams.'

'Anytime, Steven, any time.'

'And thanks for those Turnbull & Asser shirts. I'm so glad Rosebury's has moved into upmarket menswear!'

When they were on holiday with Innes in Cape Cod, Lucy had complained at how difficult it was for Cane to go shopping; he particularly liked to choose his own shirts and underwear. The day they arrived home, they found a package of fifty Turnbull & Asser shirts sent and fifty pairs of Yves St Laurent underwear and socks from Rosebury's with a note from Innes. 'There must be one or two here you like, Prime Minister. Hope they come in handy.'

'Tom's happy to do some cheerleading in the election,' Silverman chipped in. 'He says if you visit the Cadets College, he'll line up an open day.'

'It's already in the diary,' laughed Charlie as she turned to follow Cane who had gone to join some other guests.

'Seen any good tattoos lately, Charlie?' said Innes impishly, when Cane was out of earshot.

Charlie stopped dead in her tracks and looked daggers at him, before continuing after Cane.

'What was all that about?' said Silverman. 'I could have sworn you made her blush, not something she does too often.'

'No, I can imagine. It was nothing, a private joke,' said Innes, his face glinting as brightly as his gold earring.

First Innes, now Cane, thought Silverman. She'd better be careful.

'Anyway Tom,' he continued, 'I can't thank you enough for your donation to the special election fund. £100,000 was incredibly generous. I can assure you it was spent wisely.'

'I'm sure it was,' said Innes.

He cocked his head on one side and grinned at Silverman. 'You know, I never thought I'd ever say this, Ronnie.'

'Say what, Tom?'

'That you guys know more about the way business works than the last lot ever did.'

'I'll take that as a compliment.'

'It was meant as one.'

* * *

Charlie was wondering how to pass on to Cane the information she had just received.

She wasn't sure if he would be angry, shocked, upset or a combination of the three. There was no question which emotion was strongest in Charlie. Few things shocked her, and after the death of her mother, few things could upset her.

But she still got angry. And few things Greaves had ever done had made her as angry as she was now.

The day after the hospital fiasco, she had gone to her office to check the tape machine. She hadn't expected anything to be on it. She had had the bug fitted to Sandy's flat because it would have been too dangerous to put one in Greaves' flat or office. Greaves and Sandy rarely visited the flat. The recording of him threatening to revive his campaign over tax was an unexpected prize. But it was possible they had called in over the weekend. Charlie switched on the machine to check.

Most of the recording was taken up with trivia; what they were going to eat, what was on television. They reminisced about their first weekend away together when they stayed at The Mermaid in Rye and the creaky four poster bed and talked about going back. Charlie heard them discussing arrangements for a party, but she couldn't hear the details. She grew uninterested, she was only half listening, but her ears pricked up towards the end of the tape, when Sandy asked Greaves if he was still happy with his 'big decision'.

Charlie couldn't make out what the 'big decision' was.

It sounded more important as the conversation continued. It sounded serious, though there was the occasional snatch of laughter. Sandy kept asking Greaves if he was sure he wanted to go through with it. Greaves asked her and she replied 'Yes, oh yes darling, I'm sure it is right.' But Greaves wasn't saying much, his answers weren't clear; he must be facing away from the microphone or standing in the next room. Charlie leaned towards the tape, straining for a clue as to what they were talking about. But she exclaimed, 'Damn!' as the conversation fizzled out when one of them switched the television on.

'They're showing Notting Hill,' said Sandy. 'I missed it at the cinema, let's forget about politics and watch it together, Gareth.'

Over and over again she replayed the tape, straining to hear a snatch of conversation that would have explained the riddle. But it was impossible.

Big decision, big decision, big decision.

'Damn, damn, damn!' said Charlie. 'What decision? What's he up to?' Then she thrust her hand over her face. It couldn't be. Big decision. What was the big decision he had put off all his life? No, surely not. Marriage. He and Sandy marry? Charlie couldn't believe it. She was overwhelmed by a feeling of shock. But it wasn't only shock. It was deeper than that. She wanted to deny it, bury it, but she couldn't. She was jealous. 'Damn, damn, damn, damn you!' she shouted. No, she must be going mad. All she had heard were two words. It couldn't be. It must be something political, it must be. She willed it to be something political.

She drank her coffee and went to Cane's study at seven thirty for their usual morning meeting. As she walked down the corridor and across the Number 10 lobby, she was wondering what to tell him.

She had to tell him Greaves was up to something, but how could she? She couldn't tell him she had bugged Sandy's flat. There were some things she would never tell Cane, some things she had to protect him from. In any case, she couldn't tell him what Greaves was going to do, she didn't know herself. She simply knew he was on the brink of doing something dramatic – or it sounded that way. If he was about to announce he was getting married, it would hardly matter to Cane anyway. Unlike her, he didn't care whether Greaves got married or not, he probably hoped he did get married. Why shouldn't he? Either way, she didn't have a chance to attempt to explain any of it.

'We need to talk, it's urgent,' said Cane as she walked in.

The White House had contacted him to ask him if Britain was prepared to take part in a joint SAS–US Commandos operation against Saddam Hussein in person. Cane and Charlie weighed up the options. If the operation was a success, it would be a massive boost for Cane. Saddam had always been hated by the West. Now, new evidence of appalling atrocities against his own people had turned most of the Arab world against him too. Tens of thousands of dissidents had been killed. Inevitably, the killings that caused most outrage were the executions of two nuns; one Briton and one American, who were among seven nuns seized while in Baghdad on a humanitarian mission and accused of being spies. And Saddam's nuclear bomb plans moved ever closer to fruition. Being able to claim the credit for ridding the world of his menace would be a huge feather in Cane's cap.

It was natural that the Americans should come to him for support. He had backed every American military action; from Iraq to Bosnia and Serbia. Not bad for someone who asked his mother what a pacifist was when she took him, aged eight, on a section of the anti-nuclear Aldermaston march. When she had told him what it meant, young Master Cane told his mother, 'Mummy, I am going to be one.'

He never joined the Boy Scouts, or the Army Cadet Corps. You'd never think it to hear him make one of his trenchant addresses to the nation on television defending Britain's involvement in the latest US military expedition to a remote part of the world. Cane looked more like a youth leader than a war leader but he quickly adapted to the role, as he had with every other one he had played, from surgeon to statesman.

Charlie had been a far more enthusiastic pacifist. When she was at Oxford, she hitched the thirty miles to Newbury to join the Greenham Common protest against cruise missiles. She spent four weeks under canvas before returning when one of the protest leaders, a large woman with cropped hair who went by the name of Jennifer Juniper, tried to kiss her. Charlie had a lot of time for the sisterhood, but lesbianism had never appealed. Nor was she a pacifist by upbringing. Her father had only ever wanted sons and when Charlie was seven, he taught her to box. She used her fists more than most women – and a lot more than most pacifists.

'Steven, I don't see a problem with this,' said Charlie, glad for something to take her mind off Greaves and Sandy. 'Saddam has got few friends in the Arab world, and if this plan were to come off, it'd be fantastic. Imagine the effect on the polls: it's about time our side won a khaki election. Getting Saddam this side of polling day would be incredible. I say do it if the military are happy.'

'I'm due at the MoD for a briefing in five minutes,' said Cane. 'There's talk of a mission on October 11th, ten days tomorrow and only three weeks from polling day. It'd be risky to call an election without knowing if it was going to succeed. And we've got to announce the election by the end of this week if we're going for November 1st.'

'Who dares wins,' said Charlie.

'It'd be a very big decision,' he said as he left the office.

Big decision, big decision, big decision.

It hit her. Charlie hadn't told Cane about Greaves. How could she? She didn't know what Greaves' 'big decision' was – or what he had decided. Much better to find out before telling Cane. She didn't have long to wait. But Greaves told the world before he told Charlie or Cane.

CHAPTER TWENTY THREE

'If the operation is going to succeed, Prime Minister, it will have to be carried out on the 11th,' said General Nick Baxter. 'There's no moon and we can guarantee darkness to get over the border unseen.'

Any doubts Cane may have had about launching the attack on Saddam were removed when the Iraqi President seized seven nuns: five Britons and two Americans, who were on a humanitarian mission to Iraq. One British and one American nun were executed and the other five had been imprisoned and tortured.

Baxter's rugged complexion, muscular build and businesslike manner told you he was no armchair general. He was well acquainted with the risks of any operation involving the SAS, having been its former head and taken part in the attack on the Iranian Embassy in London. Nor was he a stranger to American military operations. He was on secondment to the Pentagon when US Special Forces attacked Panama when they seized General Noriega.

Whenever he was with Baxter, Cane felt like a junior subaltern. In fact Baxter was only three years older, and the smallness of the age and cultural gap between them only struck him when he heard a voice shout 'Steven' and turned to see Baxter in the crowd at a Rolling Stones concert. But this modern military man observed traditional formalities when dealing with Cane as the Chief of Defence Staff. It was Baxter who called Cane, 'sir.' Baxter was the most senior member of the armed forces, but there was one person above the CDS, the Prime Minister.

It had been a long road from Aldermaston.

It wasn't the first time the Americans had considered targeting Saddam personally. But for it to succeed, his precise whereabouts had to be known and he constantly moved between his various residences spread around Iraq, all fitted with bombproof bunkers. Some were built by British firms when he came to power in the Eighties and convinced the West he would be a bulwark against more militant elements in the Middle East. Now, those militants had moderated while Saddam had become ever more extreme. While he was in his western-built bunkers, it was impossible for western forces to get at him. But he was about to give them a chance.

'American intelligence has learned that he intends to travel to his southern capital on the 11th for a meeting with regional officials,' said Baxter.

'He wants to appear there in a show of defiance to local dissidents in the area. The Americans are pretty sure they know when he will be leaving Baghdad. He plans to fly to a small military airfield 250 miles south and then drive twenty four miles to the government residence. There is only one road to it and he will have to go across a bridge near the isolated village of Ulqita. It's an ideal opportunity to get him. The People's Resistance Army has grown considerably since it was formed nine months ago, and as you know, sir, it has already made one unsuccessful attempt to kill him. As you also know, sir, we and the Americans have been working on a joint operation and like you, sir, understand the importance of involving the PRA.'

'I think it will make it much more acceptable to world opinion if the assault was led by them with assistance from us rather than us doing it alone. It will make it much easier for our allies in the Middle East to accept it.'

'I appreciate that, sir. I must say I did have some reservations about the PRA's abilities, but with our assistance they have developed a hard core of very good soldiers.'

'What is your estimate of the chances of success?' Cane asked.

'Ninety five per cent, sir.'

'And the risk of casualties?'

'Five per cent, sir.'

'Civilian casualties.'

'Virtually nil, sir, there are no houses nearby.'

'You're sure?'

'As I can be, sir.'

'Tell the Americans, I agree to the proposal.'

'Thank you, sir,' said Baxter.

* * *

Wearside Miners Social Club was a scruffy building. The only previous occasion it had been visited by the national media was when Arthur Scargill came to address the local branch of the NUM during the miners strike.

It was not a Scargillite stronghold and he got a taste of his own medicine when he was picketed by a group of pitmen opposed to the strike. Among them was a 63-year-old retired miner who got involved in a stand-up row with him. He jabbed the miner's leader in the chest and shouted, 'You've betrayed the miners not defended them, Mr Scargill. If you did this in your beloved Soviet Union they'd send you down the salt mines.'

The man was cheered by his colleagues and Scargill's attempt to strengthen the strike in the North East backfired spectacularly. The retired miner's name was George Greaves. It was from his father that Gareth Greaves got his compassion, socialist values and an abhorrence of injustice.

'There's no point in toeing the line if the line's being pulled in the wrong direction,' was one of George Greaves' favourite sayings until he died in 1989. His son had been loyally towing the line ever since Cane had become party leader. For the most part Greaves had been happy to do so. He would always bitterly regret not standing against Cane for the leadership, but the combination of Cane's appeal to Middle England and Greaves' appeal to Northern England had been a winning formula. In the early days, Greaves had fully supported Cane's mission to redefine socialism, but they had grown apart now it was clear – to Greaves at least – that Cane's real mission was to bury it. Greaves had swallowed a lot of pride to give up his promise to introduce a wealth tax in the party's manifesto after

Cane pleaded with him, 'We've got to do it Gareth – to show them we have changed.'

But when the problems in funding hospitals, schools and welfare mounted, Cane still refused to put up income tax. Even on the rich.

Greaves got a rough ride from his local constituency association at a meeting called to discuss the decision to scrap plans to slash the repairs budget for Wearside's two main comprehensive schools, both of which had leaking roofs and 'temporary' classrooms made of little more than cardboard and which were more than a decade old. He went through the motions of defending the Government until an ex-miner friend of his father stood up and said, 'Your father had a saying, Gareth, "there's no point toeing the line if it's being pulled in the wrong direction".' He got the biggest cheer of the evening.

Greaves could think of nothing else for days. It was after that meeting that he returned to London and talked it all over with Sandy at her flat. Charlie had heard the conversation, but not the end of it. She hadn't been able to bug their car when they finished it the morning as Sandy drove him to Downing Street.

Greaves had deliberately kept plans of his announcement a secret. He contacted Number 10 at the last minute but was unaware that Cane was in an important meeting with defence chiefs. Charlie got the message minutes before Greaves stood up to address the press conference at Wearside Miners Social Club. She tried to contact him, but he had anticipated her and turned his mobile phone and pager off. She switched the television in her office to Sky News to watch the press conference live.

'I have called this press conference today to make an important announcement about my position. I have been concerned for some time about the direction this Government has been taking on a number of issues. When we were elected we committed ourselves to maintaining a sound economy and said we would not make the mistakes we made in power in the past, when our social objectives were thwarted because we lacked the discipline to put them into practice in a prudent, practical way. This Government has many fine achievements to its name and I have been proud to serve in it, ... '

'I don't believe it, I don't bloody believe it!'

She knew what was coming next and she remembered.

Big decision, big decision, big decision.

She thumped the palm of her hand against the side of her temple, reeling back in her chair. Why hadn't she realised? How could she have been so dumb? To think she had imagined he was going to get married. She was embarrassed; appalled at how she had allowed her personal involvement to blind her. It was stark staring obvious. If only it had dawned on her she could have prepared for it.

She wouldn't have bothered trying to talk him out of it. No, she would have leaked something to Sharpe; that Cane was losing patience with Greaves' rebelliousness; feared he was losing his grip; or maybe that the rest of the Cabinet had lost confidence in the whingeing DPM. Anything to get her retaliation in first. As it was, Greaves was about to knife Cane, the Government and her all in one go. She could guess which of the three would give him most pleasure.

' ... but I feel I can no longer continue to be a member of the Government and have therefore tendered my resignation this morning. I sincerely believe we can do more for our hospitals and our schools, schools like Wearside Comprehensive round the corner from here. I would like to thank the Prime Minister for the opportunity of serving in his Government and would like to make it clear that I remain one hundred per cent loyal to the party we both belong to.'

It was the most spectacular resignation since Michael Heseltine walked out of the Cabinet over a helicopter company no one had ever heard of called Westland. Now Greaves had resigned over a school no one had ever heard of. But Wearside Comprehensive wasn't the battleground, any more than Westland was the trigger. The issues weren't policies and principles; they were power and pride.

Charlie decided against paging Cane in the middle of his briefing from Baxter to tell him about Greaves' resignation. Instead she walked the 200 yards from Number 10 to the MoD directly opposite the Downing Street gates, to make sure she met him on his way back before the press got to him. This was no time to repeat the ambush she sprung on him the last time he emerged blinking into the sunlight – at the High Wycombe Odeon.

Cane could see from Charlie's face that something was wrong, badly wrong.

'Steven, we must talk – alone, now,' she said.

'What is it? It's not Lucy, is it?'

'No, no, no. There's only one way to say this, Steven.' She gulped, 'Gareth has resigned.'

She watched as the horror of what she had said sank in. It was like watching in slow motion as someone came to terms with the instant that their life had been changed for ever. The expression on his face altered second by second from shock to bewilderment, resolve and fear. Hers had gone through the same cycle thirty minutes earlier, but it ended on fury, not fear. Cane grasped for words. His mouth opened, but none came.

'We can't talk about it here, we'll have to get back to Number 10,' said Charlie.

Since the press had no idea about the Saddam briefing there was little chance of them being outside the MoD to meet him. Cane had planned to walk back to Downing Street, but Charlie couldn't take the chance. She sent his car to the front door of the MoD to drive him across Whitehall into Downing Street. It was as well she did had. A posse of reporters had gathered at the gates of Downing Street. Cane's car cut a swathe through them.

He was temporarily blinded by the flash of a camera thrust at the window inches from his face as they drove past, like the photographers who leapt up at police vans trying to get a photo of the condemned man as he was taken off to prison.

Cane was grateful to get back to Number 10 to try and plot a political escape route. He may be under siege, but it was home, it really was. Everyone in the building from the doorman to the secretaries, the officials, even Dora in her perverse way, treated him as though they could only ever be loyal to him. Never mind that they made his predecessor feel like that – and would do the same to his successor.

It was a sign of fealty not fickleness. Cane could see the anxious looks on the faces of his staff as he and Charlie reached his study.

'He says it's over hospitals and schools; he must have flipped his lid, he's finished,' said Charlie, sitting in her office.

'He's finished if we win the election, yes,' said Cane, who kept his cool as easily as Charlie lost hers, 'but if we lose it, he's made, isn't he?'

Cane didn't look like an ordinary politician. He looked like a good looking young doctor with a wife and two kids who had found himself running the country. Which is what he was. Yet his political brain could work as fast as Machiavelli. Somewhere in the middle was the real Steven Cane.

'The election will have to wait till spring,' he said 'Banking on the Saddam operation being a success is one thing – going into an election on the back of a Cabinet crisis is another. It'll have to be put off. We've no choice.'

'I wouldn't be surprised if that's why he did it now,' said Charlie.

'What do you mean?' said Cane.

'He must have guessed – or found out – we were going for an October election and calculated his best chance of wrecking it was for him to resign. Think about it: he would know that after all the trouble between him and you, there was a chance you would dismiss him after the election. If he wants to succeed you, the only way he can do it is to resign on a so-called point of principle, then he hopes that you lose or cling on by such a small margin that it looks like defeat – that the party dumps you and he takes over. He doesn't care if he is Prime Minister or Leader of the Opposition; getting you out is more important to him than keeping Bathurst out. Don't you see?'

She intentionally fuelled his anger. It would help him cope and help him respond. She was puzzled when he let out a nervous laugh.

'What's funny?'

'I've just agreed to finish off one politician and I find that in my absence, a member of my own Government has been trying to finish me off.'

'There's a slight difference. Gareth has just finished himself off. He must be out of his mind. How could he betray us after everything we've done? Forgive me for not seeing the funny side, Steven,' she said sarcastically. 'We've put up with his moods and tantrums for four years – now he does this in return. He makes me so fucking angry!' She prowled up and down the room liked a caged tiger, flicking the ash from her cigarette indiscriminately.

'Hey, calm down, calm down,' said Cane. 'It's me he's getting at, not you.'

He had just been addressed as 'sir' by the commander of the armed forces. He was not beyond pulling rank with Charlie, even when she was as warlike as this. He looked at her raging expression. She was fired up ready for battle, with Saddam, with Greaves, with anyone who opposed her, anyone who opposed him. He pictured her standing on Boadicea's speeding chariot, the knives on the wheels slashing her enemies to pieces. God, she was magnificent. How lucky he was to have her. Her blood was up; now his blood was up. He imagined going to war with her.

And going to bed with her.

Cane had suspected Charlie and Greaves had been lovers when they worked together before she left abruptly for the USA. Charlie was a junior official then and Cane hardly knew her. He knew Greaves better, but Greaves never gave much away about anything, his politics or his private life, certainly not to Cane. He had known him for nearly fifteen years but they had never once discussed anything intimate. He was too understanding, too honest to deny Greaves the right to feel bitter at the way he had left him in the permanent position of runner-up. It was hardly any wonder that Greaves was unwilling to share his innermost thoughts with Cane. Nor had he raised the matter with Charlie, though he found himself becoming more and more curious about it. Did they have an affair? If so, was that the reason they hated each other so much now. Had one done something terrible to the other? Did Greaves still hanker after her? He had asked Silverman once, but it was a mystery to him too. Silverman was convinced there was some dark secret that divided them, but he had no idea what it was and had never asked.

'We have got to keep our personal feelings out of this,' said Cane as Charlie stood at her window, looking out onto Downing Street.

'I'm sorry, Steven,' she said, calming herself, 'but that man is despicable.'

'First things first,' said Cane, 'we've got to find a replacement for Greaves, we don't want any ... '

' ... drift and indecision,' she completed the sentence for him.

'At least that shouldn't take long,' he said, 'Where's Ronnie?'

'On his way over.'

Cane's surprise showed. He and Charlie had often discussed who might succeed Greaves, and had agreed Silverman was the obvious choice. But for her to assume that was his decision – and to tell Silverman – that was stretching her role to the limit. Charlie realised it.

'Well, I er ... assumed you'd want to see him for one thing or another,' she said, as if in mitigation. 'He phoned here when he heard Greaves had resigned and I said why didn't he come over. And, no, Steven, I did not tell him he was succeeding Greaves, I would never do that.'

Cane could have challenged her explanation, but he chose not to. He could do without any more confrontations. Silverman entered. Cane asked him to be Deputy Prime Minister as well as Chancellor.

He accepted and Cane stepped forward to embrace Silverman, taking him by surprise. In more than ten years of being friends and colleagues, they had never embraced. It was the first sign of vulnerability in Cane that Silverman had ever seen. It was also the kind of hug he wanted to give Charlie, but daren't. As Silverman patted Cane on the back, his head facing Charlie, his new deputy smiled broadly.

'It won't be easy, Ronnie,' said Cane, releasing himself. 'Gareth'll give you a tough time from the back benches.'

'Joe will arm me with every statistic ever recorded,' laughed Silverman.

'And I'll have a few tricks up my sleeve,' laughed Charlie. 'You've no idea the difference it will make having a DPM we can trust. Someone we can invite to meetings without worrying whether it is going to be leaked so that he gets the credit.'

'When do I start, boss?' asked Silverman.

'Five minutes ago,' said Cane.

After Silverman left, Cane realised that in the panic caused by the resignation, he hadn't told Charlie of the details of his meeting with the army chiefs over the Iraq plan.

'Brilliant!' she said. 'That'll put Greaves on the spot; let's see if he's got the guts to disown it. If the Saddam operation succeeds, Greaves' resignation will soon be forgotten. Leave him to his childish stunts in Wearside Miners Social Club, you'll be feted on the steps of the White House. By Christ, he'll look a fool.

'You know, Steven, Gareth has spent all this time gritting his teeth under you, convincing himself he is more in tune with people than you are. He hasn't got the slightest idea of the real world and he's going to find out pretty soon that while he's got a dedicated band of supporters prepared to tell him he's Mr Wonderful, other people don't give a damn about him.'

Cane looked at Charlie, full of fire, from her flame lipstick to her flammable personality. She had blowtorched his opponents and would do the same to his former deputy. Charlie saw Cane looking at her. She had seen him look at her before, but not the way he looked at her now. Cane thought of Lucy, forty five miles away in Guildford with her parents. Charlie thought of Greaves, 250 miles away in Wearside with Sandy. Cane put his hand on her head. She moved towards him quickly and pressed her lips against his.

It was a long time since he had been kissed like that. And he responded.

CHAPTER TWENTY FOUR

'Polly, they'll be here in eight minutes,' said Major Richard 'Rich' Russell. 'Ready?'

'Ready, sir' said Warrant Officer Mick 'Polly' Mahoney.

Russell and Mahoney were part of a sixteen-strong SAS team on a joint mission with sixteen guerrillas from the PRA. If Operation Dune went to plan, within four hours, they would end the reign of terror of the world's most murderous dictator. Two wars against Saddam by America and NATO and year after year of economic and diplomatic sanctions had failed to dislodge him, as had the bungled assassination attempts by the PRA. It was the task of thirty four year old Rich Russell of the SAS to ensure that this attempt was successful.

It wasn't the first time Saddam's fate depended on the West; he had had a heart attack last year and would have died, but a leading French heart surgeon was secretly flown to his palace and saved his life for a fee of one million dollars. No one knew how many people Saddam had killed. The Red Cross claimed he had slaughtered more than 15,000 Kurds in the north and another 5,000 dissidents in the south after stepping up his reign of terror to try and stamp out mounting opposition.

Russell left Sandhurst with honours, going on to become a Captain in the Devon and Dorset Infantry Battalion before joining the SAS. It seemed a natural progression for him to join the Army the minute he left Sherborne School in Dorset. After all, his father had been awarded the Military Medal for singlehandedly catching two IRA gunmen after a firefight. He went to Sherborne too.

It was easy to imagine neat and angular Russell as a pinstriped suited stockbroker commuting on the seven nineteen from Royal Tunbridge Wells to Charing Cross each morning; which is what he would do when he left the army with a pension in three years.

But for the moment, he was in the killing business, not the money making one. He had learned Arabic when he spent a year assigned to the Foreign Office Middle East department and together with his experience as a troop leader with the SAS in the Gulf war this meant he was ideal for the mission. He could converse with all sixteen Arab guerrillas, not just the PRA's charismatic leader, Mohammed Assan, who spoke English with a broad American accent.

'Sarry Rich, blame CNN! That's where we learn English these days – not the World Service – old boy,' he teased Russell, imitating the Major's plummy baritone.

The allies had been waiting for years for the chance to deal with Saddam. Now they had it. A member of the PRA who had infiltrated his personal guard had given them details of his trip to his southern base.

The PRA had been trained and supplied by the West, but they were still amateurs by modern military – and modern terrorist – standards. Cane had a long discussion with the Americans as to whether Saddam should be assassinated, or merely kidnapped and put on trial for human rights abuses and war crimes.

But Cane argued in favour of killing him on the grounds that the West had paid a heavy price in the past for waging war on brutal regimes but failing to remove the dictators who ran them and that attempts to use more conventional methods such as bringing them before War Crimes tribunals had proved largely fruitless. The extreme nature of Saddam's crimes, from genocide, to developing an A-bomb and seizing the nuns, justified extreme measures.

The best way to counter claims that Britain and America had no right to kill the head of state of another country was to make sure that the PRA were seen to lead the operation, even if their presence was largely for public relations reasons. Letting the SAS and US Commandos team up with the PRA would give the assassination a legitimacy that a lone Anglo-

American assault would lack. But two weeks before the operation, the Commandos were pulled out.

The American President called Cane to say they were needed to deal with a siege at the US embassy in Bolivia by South American drugs gangsters. The risk of two anti-terrorist operations at once was too great. The Americans would still provide air cover for the attack and Apache helicopters to get the hit squad out, but not troops. Cane met Baxter again to ask if the mission was too dangerous without the Americans.

'I'd rather not be quoted on it sir, but I'd say it would be less risky without them,' the general replied. 'We've already got to hold the hands of our friends from the PRA, and I fully appreciate the reasons for that, sir, but frankly, not having the Yanks will be one less thing to worry about. Remember what happened when Carter tried to get the hostages out of Iran?'

The SAS contingent was doubled from eight to sixteen. Baxter wasn't the only one who was pleased. Russell had already expressed private doubts to him about Cane's insistence on involving the PRA in the operation. None of them would qualify for the SAS on merit. But Russell knew enough about politics, especially modern politics, to understand why they had to be on board. It didn't mean he had to like it. Maybe the 'PR' in PRA stood for public relations, he mused, though not out loud.

The American withdrawal gave Russell the excuse he wanted to call up Warrant Officer Polly Mahoney as one of the replacements. He had wanted him on the mission from the outset. The pair had worked together behind enemy lines in the war with Serbia when they rescued two British pilots shot down near Belgrade. They were dropped by helicopter near where the men's Tornado had come down, found them before the Serbs, hijacked a car and drove more than 100 miles to the Albanian border with the pilots in the boot.

Mahoney's family left Northern Ireland to escape the troubles when he was two. From the age of twelve, he wanted to be a policeman. He spent most of his teenage years worrying he wouldn't get in. By the time he was nineteen, it was obvious he was never going to be taller than five feet seven inches. He pleaded with the Metropolitan Police to make an exception. His former headmaster wrote to the Chief Constable to tell them the former head boy of his comprehensive school had the potential to be a superb policeman. But the Met refused to budge and wrote to Mahoney saying 'The minimum height requirement is essential so that policemen can see over the heads of crowds.'

Mahoney told the story to Russell at his interview for the SAS posting when he candidly asked Russell if his lack of height was considered a handicap. 'Don't worry Polly, the SAS don't make a habit of operating in crowds.' It didn't prove a handicap in the SAS training squad when he came top of his group on joining from the Paras.

His large crook nose was responsible for his nickname, Polly, as in Polly the Parrot. His nose wasn't his only large facial feature. Everything on it was outsized, nose, chin, wingnut ears and the half moon smile permanently stretched from one lobe to the other. This mission was far more important and far more dangerous than the rescue of the pilots in Serbia. The Americans would send eight helicopters: four Apaches and four Black Hawks, to get the squad out when the operation had been completed.

But first a smokescreen had to be created to get them in.

A US F1-15 aircraft on a routine patrol deliberately strayed out of the no fly zone in southern Iraq, provoking an attack by one of Saddam's SAM missile bases. The aircraft had no difficulty in avoiding the missiles.

The Americans falsely denied they were to blame and used the missile attack to launch their own counter attack on the missile base. While the Iraqi army was distracted, four Land Rovers drove unnoticed over the border with Kuwait at night in a desert region 212 miles from the attack location, Ulqita.

Russell, Mahoney and fourteen SAS comrades were inside. Seven hours later they rendezvoused with the PRA half way to their target, where they exchanged their combat gear for Arab dress. The thirty two strong team spent the next three nights trekking across the desert on camels which carried their arsenal of weapons: twenty Heckler Koch machine guns, thirty two nine-millimetre pistols, twenty pounds of plastic explosives, four

51-millimetre high explosive mortars, four hand-held anti-tank missiles systems and forty hand grenades. They spent the days sleeping and resting in PRA hideouts.

As planned, they arrived at Ulqita thirty six hours before the attack. The PRA had prepared a base, hidden in the rocks in the foothills of mountains two and a half miles from the bridge.

They separated into four groups. The observation team would hide near the road, six miles from the bridge, to tell Russell of the convoy's approach. One 'close' team would rig the bridge with explosive charges at key stress points. The aim was to make the entire bridge collapse into the river bed below in one piece.

The 'cover' team, led by Russell, would hide 300 yards from the bridge directing operations. They would also provide cover for the 'close' team nearer the bridge. The second 'close' team would fire mortars and anti-tank missiles at the convoy as soon as the bridge was blown. Simultaneously, the second 'close' team led by Mahoney would go in for the final kill. Their job was to make sure Saddam was dead. And that meant making sure everyone was dead.

Russell would use his satellite communications link to tell the US army base over the border that the mission had been accomplished. Forty minutes after that, the helicopters would arrive to rescue them, hopefully before any of Saddam's forces had been scrambled. That was the plan.

Russell put down his binoculars. He would soon press the button on his radio transmitter that would blow Saddam Hussein and his seven-car convoy sky high.

All four teams were in place. The night before the attack, the explosive team placed the charges on the arched steel bridge. And at eleven thirty five am, a PRA spy at the military airfield called Russell on his mobile phone, as arranged, to confirm that the dictator's plane had touched down on time.

At four minutes past twelve, he called again to say the convoy had left the airfield. At twenty eight minutes past twelve, the observation team radioed Russell from their point six miles away to say the seven-car convoy had passed them travelling at 45 mph. Russell radioed Mahoney, 'Polly, they'll be here soon. Ready?'

'Ready, sir' said Mahoney.

'Keep an eye on those PRA guys.'

'Don't worry sir, they'll do the job.'

'Good luck, Polly.'

'Thanks sir, I don't expect to need any.'

At twenty four minutes to one, Mahoney saw the convoy emerge from the liquid horizon through his binoculars. Saddam's seven limousines looked like a black necklace being drawn across the sand.

It was another four minutes until the cars reached the approach to the old metal bridge. Mahoney waited ... waited ... waited until the first three were on it, then depressed his right index finger on the remote control device on his lap. He held his ears in anticipation of the deafening noise that, two seconds later, shook the air and then the ground as the bridge exploded in a cloud of dust, bricks and metal. Russell saw several black lumps fly through the air, cars or bits of them. He didn't expect to see any bodies: they would be in bits too small to see.

As soon as the last pieces of debris had hit the ground, Russell gave the order to one of the close teams to fire mortars and anti-tank missiles into the remains of the cars and their passengers.

It was hard to imagine any of the nineteen people in the convoy could have survived. Mahoney's job was to guarantee it. He ran towards the bridge followed by Assan and the rest of the Anglo-Arab 'close' team. They stopped forty yards short of the bridge and hurled grenades into the wreckage. Bits of bumper, doors, rubber from the tyres flew into the air.

Mahoney and Assan ran towards the cars firing their machine guns into them. They kept firing for sixty seconds, then stopped.

There were bodies, limbs, heads everywhere. Mahoney's men stood still in the silence, watching for the slightest sign of movement. There was none. Assan moved from car to car trying to find Saddam.

He was lying face down, underneath the shredded remains of a red leather car seat. Both his legs had been blown off. Assan turned Saddam's head to one side. He ran his finger down the left side of his cheek alongside his moustache and smiled. It was the line of a small scar caused when shrapnel from the earlier assassination attempt led by Assan a year earlier had narrowly failed.

Assan gave the thumbs-up sign to the rest of the team. The three other Arabs punched the air in jubilation. Mahoney was angry. The job wasn't over yet. He pulled out a miniature camera and took three photos of Saddam. It wasn't a souvenir snapshot of his trophy, but proof to the whole world that Operation Dune had been a success. Mahoney radioed Russell, 'Mission accomplished, sir – over.'

'Well done Polly, bloody well done. Any injuries to our boys?'

As Russell waited for Mahoney's reply, he heard a single shot. Mahoney was below the bridge, out of sight from Russell, 500 yards away.

'What the fuck was that, Polly?'

There was no reply but Russell heard a volley of machine gun rounds follow the single shot. As the three Arabs had rushed over to join Assan by Saddam's bloodied corpse, it left only the three SAS watching for survivors.

And they weren't looking in the trees, which is where one of the dictator's motorcycle outriders ended up when he was hurled forty feet into the air by the bomb blast. He had been parted from his machine, but not his machine gun. When Russell asked Mahoney on his radio to confirm that Saddam was dead, he couldn't reply: Mahoney was dead, shot in the back of the head by a single bullet. A split second later, the man was riddled with machine gun fire as all other seven men in Mahoney's 'close team' reacted simultaneously.

'Polly! What the fuck's happened!?' shouted the voice at the other end.

There was silence.

'Polly, I said what the fuck's happened?!'

'Hello?'

It was an Arab accent. he sounded panicky, frightened.

'Who the fucking hell's that!?'

'Rich, it's Assan.'

'Where the fuck's Polly? Put him on!'

'Rich, I ... '

'What the fuck's happening, Assan?'

'Rich, Polly's dead.'

'What!?'

'I'm sorry Rich,' jabbered Assan. 'There was one we didn't see, we've slotted him now.'

'You fucking arseholes!' shouted Russell.

He threw the radio receiver down.

'Rich? Are you there? Rich. Rich?'

Russell picked it up.

'Yes, I'm fucking here. What about Saddam?'

'Dead. Polly got ... we've got a photo.'

'Any more of ours dead or wounded?'

'No.'

'Bring the photo with you. We're getting the fuck out. The choppers are on their way. And keep Polly with you. We're not leaving him. If he doesn't get on with us, I'll fucking throw you out, you Arab arsehole! D'you hear me?'

Russell dropped the radio and rammed his boot into the desert, sending a cloud of sand into the air.

'Fucking PRA! Fucking politics! Fucking Cane!'

* * *

Mahoney's death was not reported in that afternoon's West End final edition of the Evening Standard that dropped onto Charlie's desk at ten past three London time, eight hours after the attack. The front page headline was 'SAS KILL SADDAM.'

'I can't believe it Steven, it's worked, it's bloody well worked,' she said excitedly to Cane, holding up the front page as he walked in.

He could hardly believe it either. He knew the consequences if the SAS raid had gone wrong. But it hadn't. Word of Mahoney's death had not reached him yet. But that was a tragedy for Mahoney and for Russell, not for Cane.

The mission had been a success.

'Jesus, I wish we'd gone ahead with the election. We'd win one tomorrow by a landslide.'

'If you think I'm going out there dressed in army fatigues to announce a snap election, you're wrong, Charlie Redpath,' he smiled. 'There are some things I won't do – even for you.' It sent a tingle down her spine. He saw it in her eye. 'Anyway, we haven't told the Queen.'

'Bollocks to the Queen!'

'You can still be sent to the Tower for that.'

'Only if you told her I said it – and you haven't got the balls. We don't need a snap election Steven, the afterglow from this will last us right through winter.'

'It'll damned well have to since we can't hold an election until spring.'

'It'll be more than enough to put a certain former deputy in the shade,' said Charlie.

'D'you think so?'

'I bloody know so. You've put your beloved bloody Maggie Thatcher in the shade. Even she wouldn't have had the guts to do what you just did, Steven.'

They decided against making a statement on the outcome of the attack. Prime Ministers never spoke in public about the activities of the SAS. Officially, the attack had been carried out by the PRA, who, as agreed, had claimed responsibility for it. There was no need for Cane to boast about the SAS involvement. It soon became known. Charlie saw to that. When asked on the 'Today' programme the following morning about whether the SAS had taken part, Cane said,

'I can confirm that the PRA asked for and received our support but I never comment on the activities of British special forces. If you are asking me do I think the world is a safer and more humane place after Saddam Hussein's death, then my answer is yes, it is. He killed thousands upon thousands of his own people, would shortly have had his finger on a nuclear button, and seized seven nuns and killed two of them, including a Briton.

We failed to stop that happening but I hope we have succeeded in stopping it happen again.

'I want to make it clear that we have no quarrel with the people of Iraq. We hope to bring relief to the suffering they have endured under Saddam. Lastly, I would like to praise the courage and skill of the PRA team who carried out the operation. I hope that before long, Iraq can choose a democratically elected government and that this action today will mean freedom and stability can return to Iraq. Just as the defeat of Hitler saved millions from tyranny in Europe, I hope the defeat of Saddam will save millions from tyranny in the Middle East.'

When he got back to Number 10, somebody was waiting to speak to him on the phone.

'Steven?' drawled the US President.

'Hi,' said Cane.

'I wanna tell you I'm real real proud of what you guys did. Fantastic, just fantastic! What would we do without you Brits? I'm sorry you lost one of your guys, but I wanna tell you, those SAS guys are real amazing. If you ever wanna trade 'em, Steven, just name your price.'

'Thanks but they're not for sale,' said Cane. 'As we agreed, I'm not saying anything about their involvement, but it's in the papers already.'

'Listen, Steven – the whole goddam world is callin' you a saviour. All this time we've been trying to deal with that evil son of a bitch and he's made monkeys of us every time. Now we've – sorry Steven – you've done him, you've done him for good. I'm just sorry we weren't there with you, but it looks like you didn't need us anyhows.'

'Thanks.'

'And Steven?'

'Yeah?'

'Doesn't this just show when the chips are down it's the Yanks and the Brits who do the business?'

'Yeah, I suppose so.'

'No s'posin' about it. It's true. And I'll tell ya somethin' else.'

'What?'

'We won't forget it the next time they say your seat on the UN Security Council should go to the EU – d'you think the Frogs or the Krauts would ever do what you just did?'

'Maybe not.'

'No way maybe. I'm tellin' you they'd run a mile. Hey, and Steven, there's one other thing I wanna ask ya.'

'What's that?'

'How's that press secretary of yours?'

'Oh, Charlie. She's ... she's fine thanks.'

'Give her my regards, won't ya?'

Part Three

CHAPTER TWENTY FIVE

It was the first time in twenty years it had snowed at Chequers at Christmas. Sam and Jessica were having a snowball fight in the garden together with two of Sam's friends who had come for the day.

'Don't throw them so hard, you're doing it to hurt, it's not fair!' said Jessica as she was hit on the nose by a giant snowball thrown by her brother.

'Oh stop moaning, you always want to play games with us, then you moan when you do.'

Jessica left them and came back inside.

'What's up, Jess?' said Lucy, when Jessica appeared in the sitting room.

'Oh nothing, it's Sam and his mates, they're such a pain. Where's dad?'

'I'm afraid he's with his mates too.'

The remark was over Jessica's head – or so Lucy thought.

'Charlie and Ronnie have come to see him. They're in the study.'

'Dad's as bad as Sam isn't he, mum?'

Lucy checked herself. 'Not really, darling, there's an election coming up, he's got to start planning it.'

'M-u-m?' said Lucy, stretching the word to three undulating syllables in the way that always rings alarm bells with parents. It usually means they want a favour or are about to ask a question the parent would prefer not to answer.

'Yes, darling.'

'Do you want dad to win the election?'

Lucy blinked and put her hand on Jessica's shoulder. 'Of course I do, darling. Why do you ask?'

'Oh ... nothing.'

Lucy could either drop it – or pursue it. 'Why do you say that, darling?'

'It's just that ... is it bad to say I wish he didn't have to spend so long at work, that he could be a ... you know ... a normal dad?'

'Darling, he is a normal dad. Not every daddy makes the breakfast at least twice the week and helps his daughter with her maths homework on a Sunday.'

'I know, but I mean a normal dad, you know, one who has a normal job and isn't flying off all the time.'

'Darling, we would never be able to have a lovely house like this if he wasn't Prime Minister and you should be proud of him, he is doing a very important job ... '

' ... I know, I know, I know all that, mum. But if we lived in a normal house, I'd have some of my mates to play with. You try being the Prime Minister's daughter at school.'

Lucy put her arm round Jessica. She could never tell her the truth – that she agreed with her about the election, the loneliness and the claustrophobic abnormality of their life. And that she yearned for a normal husband as much as Jessica yearned for a normal dad.

Two rooms away, Cane and his 'mates' felt as comfortable and fulfilled doing what they were doing as Lucy and Jessica felt uncomfortable and unfulfilled.

The three of them had sat in the same room on the same day nearly a year ago and discussed the same subject they were discussing today: when to call the election. Election speculation now dominated the newspapers on a daily basis. Cane's options were closing in on him like the snow clouds that hung low above Chequers.

His five year term was running out. He had to call the election by the end of May at the latest. Once Greaves' resignation had put paid to an November poll, they had decided against rushing into a winter election.

Tradition - and the weather – were against it. But it was no use delaying too long. Leaving it until May, the last possible moment, would look desperate – and leave no escape route if something went badly wrong.

That left March and April. It would provide Cane with just enough of a gap before the May deadline to enable him, if not too convincingly, to claim that he was taking the initiative, rather than being hemmed into a corner.

Either way, he was faced with the prospect of a non-stop election campaign lasting anything up to four months. He was confident the longer he was in the spotlight against Bathurst, the more he stood to gain. She had performed creditably well and had drafted in new young talent to the Shadow Cabinet that had given weaker members of the Government front bench a run for their money.

But Bathurst suffered from what one pundit called 'the Kinnock Factor'. She was a worthy leader and had carried out worthy reforms but would never bridge the two swords' lengths between her place at the despatch box to the left of The Speaker's chair, and the one occupied by the Prime Minister to the right of The Speaker's chair. Or to quote *The Globe*'s more pithy version, 'Mad Bat's got as much chance of winning the election as she has of winning Miss World.'

If modern elections were beauty contests, there was no bigger mismatch than Cane versus Bathurst. It hadn't stopped the Government's lead being reduced from twenty five points, when he, Silverman and Charlie met a year ago at Chequers, to fifteen points now.

But it hardly amounted to a serious threat. And it had more to do with Cane's difficulties with his own party than anything Bathurst had done. Greaves' resignation had caused a Cabinet crisis. Within ten days, the Government's lead in the polls dropped to two per cent, the lowest since Cane came to power. But once the Saddam ambush went successfully, it bounced back.

It dropped again after Britain faced a backlash from some Middle East countries. UK Aerospace lost a £10 billion order to supply tanks to Jordan, with the loss of 10,000 jobs and a group of terrorists claiming to support

Saddam, called the 'October 11' group after the day he was killed, vowed revenge.

Silverman was forced to announce an aid package to help the sacked workers, but the attack had raised Cane to the status of international superstar. As predicted by Charlie, he was invited to the White House where the American President teased him, saying if he'd known what a success it was going to be he would not have diverted his Commandos to Central America and missed a share of the glory. Cane and Charlie were confident Greaves could cause them few problems between now and the election.

'So we make a final decision in February on which date to go on in March or April? said Cane. 'Agreed?'

There was no dissent. Silverman could use the March budget to cut the basic rate of tax and beat the Opposition at the game they had used to keep his party out of office for two decades. Bribery.

'I'll plan some more foreign trips to follow up next week's EU summit in Florence,' said Charlie. 'The more you're seen abroad with world leaders the more Bathurst looks like a Little England nonentity.'

Britain was due to take over the Presidency of the EU in the New Year and Florence would be a perfect opportunity for Cane to show off as the unofficial leader of Europe, which he had become since Britain voted to join the euro. The coins were due to come into circulation in two days on January 1st, and the whole continent was in a state of excitement. Cane was already the longest serving leader of all the main countries, yet also the youngest. Some European leaders had criticised the killing of Saddam, but most secretly envied him for having the guts to do it.

'We're going to face a very long campaign. I only hope we've all got the stamina,' said Cane.

'We'll kill the bastards and then ... ' Charlie stopped when she saw Cane and Silverman look towards the door. She swung round.

'Sorry to interrupt, daddy.' It was Jessica in her nightdress.

'Jess ... hi ... we're just finishing,' said Cane. He looked at his watch; it was half nine.

'Mummy said could you come and say goodnight to us,' said Jessica.

'Have you decided when the election is going to be?'

'Well it's a secret, but sort of,' said Cane. 'How many do you think we will win by?'

'I hope you lose.'

Cane was stunned. Charlie and Silverman were speechless.

'Pardon, Jess?' said Cane.

'I hope you lose, then you can kiss me goodnight every night.'

The three adults laughed nervously.

But Jessica wasn't laughing.

Cane silently walked over to his daughter, gathered her in his arms, smothered her in kisses and took her upstairs to bed, leaving Charlie and Silverman alone.

A few seconds later, they saw Lucy walk past the doorway, briefly glancing in the room, before following her husband and child.

'I might have known,' said Charlie.

* * *

Cane was still shaking as he boarded Flight BA093 to Florence.

Lucy hadn't said much as they were driven to Heathrow. But when she came out of the ladies at the VIP lounge he could see she had been crying. They were surrounded by nine officials from Number 10 who were accompanying him on the trip, plus his three bodyguards and the military police in charge of the VIP suite.

'What ever is it darling, what's the matter?'

He could see two tiny pools of water on her pupils as she sat staring straight ahead, her bottom lip white where she was biting into it hard.

'Let's go over here, Come with me,' he said tenderly, holding her hand and leading her into a room off the main suite. The moment he closed the door, she released the flood of tears she had been holding back.

'I can't ... go on ... I can't ... go on,' she stuttered.

'Why ever not? What is wrong? You must tell me.'

'I can't go on, I just can't ... I've tried but I can't.'

'But what is it, Lucy, what is it?' he implored.

'I can't face them.'

'Who? Who can't you face?'

'All of them, the pushy wives, the press, the banquets ... none of it,' she cried, sobbing still louder.

'But ... ?' Cane didn't know what to say. The disastrous visit to St Bernard's, where egg was splattered over her dress, had been followed by two or three much more successful photo calls. She had lost more than a stone in weight and had received flattering reviews in the press for the way she looked. 'Hello' magazine had even asked her to do a fashion photo shoot with the proceeds going to her favourite charity, the NSPCC. They would see a different picture if they looked under the surface. But they hadn't looked and Cane couldn't see.

He was worried about her, but he was also exasperated. He had done so much to make sure they continued to live as normal a family life as possible in Number 10. He had even sent her to a health farm for a week in the summer while he took a week off to look after the children. What was that if not being a caring, sensitive, modern dad? It wasn't the sort of gesture any other occupant of Number 10 had ever made to his wife. For most of the last five years, Lucy had suffered bouts of depression which she was never fully able to explain. It was true that sections of the press had been cruel to her at times, but they had been just as exaggerated in their praise for her new, slimmer, smarter look in recent months.

For a while it seemed to cheer her up, but it never lasted. A few weeks later she would sink down again. Confiding in Aunt Mimi, who Lucy had been close to since she was a child, obviously hadn't helped.

Lucy said her aunt understood because she had her own problems. But it annoyed him. He phoned Mimi in a rage on one occasion, without telling Lucy and told her she had no right to burden his wife with her own problems, whatever they were. She should stop calling her. Aunt Mimi didn't argue with him and stopped phoning, or at least, she no longer called while he was around. Whether she had told Lucy of her conversation with Cane was unclear, but Lucy never raised it.

Cane was alarmed by his wife's condition, but he was also frustrated that he, a doctor, couldn't diagnose it, let alone cure it; and that what should have been a hectic but golden period in their lives was tarnished with unhappiness. It wasn't the only frustration he felt. Their sex life was non-existent. As he pleaded with her unsuccessfully in the VIP suite to explain why she was so upset, he knew what it was building up to.

'I can't go to Florence. I'm sorry, I know how much it means to you, I just can't, I can't.'

Cane struggled to keep his temper. He knew it was wrong to get cross when his wife was clearly unwell, but he couldn't help himself.

'Lucy, please, this summit is so important, you can't pull out now. What ... '

' ... go on, finish the sentence, "What will the press say, what will it look like" – that's what you were going to say, isn't it?' She pulled away violently and it was all he could do to stop her running out.

It was as well he hadn't told her that the party had spent £55,000 flying David Puttnam and a team of assistants to Florence to make a film of Cane and Lucy with other European leaders for an election broadcast.

'That's not true, please listen. It's just that it's the last big foreign trip before the election. If we were to lose, this would be the last trip I ever did.'

Lucy didn't respond. Cane guessed why.

'I hope you lose.'

It was what Jessica had said. Her mother knew better than to say it, thought Cane, but that is how she felt too.

'There's nothing I can do, is there?' he said, resigned.

'I'm sorry, Steven, I'm sorry,' said Lucy. Her saucer-like eyes turned her entire face into a watery, blotchy and bloodshot mess when she cried.

'It may sound glib to you, but we will have to explain to the press why you're not there.' His embarrassment and concern had turned to despair. He was tired of her constantly letting him down, of having to spend as much time worrying about her as doing his job. Everyone thought he could cope so easily, didn't feel the pressure, could smile through every crisis. They were also the ones who thought he was happily married. They didn't know anything.

'I'm sure your press secretary will come up with something convincing – she usually does.'

Cane ignored the jibe. Lucy convulsed. 'I'd better go before I cause an embarrassing scene.'

No matter how great his anger, he still wanted to embrace her. But she turned away as he moved towards her, saying, 'Please, Steven, don't. Not here. Just arrange for someone to take me to Guildford so I can meet up with the children.'

The children. How many times would she use that weapon against him?

As Lucy got in the car, she didn't even look at him as he waved good-bye. But another pair of eyes were fixed on him with laser-like intensity as he walked up the steps of the Boeing 727.

Charlie had gone ahead to check the position of the film crews waiting on the tarmac to film Cane's departure and was unaware of what had gone on with Lucy. She realised something was wrong when Cane came out of the VIP suite late and alone, and walked straight past a TV reporter she had allowed to ask him one or two questions.

'What's happened? Where's Lucy?' said Charlie, the moment they were sitting together at the front of the plane.

Cane explained, quietly, so that the other officials on board could not hear.

Charlie closed her eyes for a few seconds, then opened them and put a reassuring hand on his right forearm, before exclaiming, 'Puttnam's film crew!'

'I know, I don't suppose he's used to the female lead not turning up on the set,' said Cane, without a trace of humour.

'Never mind, we'll still be able to get lots of great shots of you. It won't all be wasted.'

'Thanks, Charlie,' said Cane.

'For what?'

'For looking on the bright side. I'm glad someone can.'

'It's in the breeding,' said Charlie. 'Whenever there was a disaster at home, which was most days, my Mum would always say "worse troubles at sea." She would've said it if she'd been on the Titanic when it was sinking!'

Charlie laughed and Cane laughed too. He took a deep breath and looked at her. She returned the look. Her eyes stared right inside him.

'There's going to be a bit of a gap at all the banquets unless ... ' he said.

' ... unless what?' said Charlie.

'Unless,' Cane paused, 'unless you fill in for her.'

'Are you sure that's wise, Steven.'

'I'm quite sure it's what I would like to do.'

'Well I am quite sure that it would be most unwise.'

'You're right,' he said. 'The German Chancellor's just got divorced again so he'll be on his own too.'

'Don't bank on it!' said Charlie.

'It's the only summit the Italians don't bring their mistresses to!'

'Remember when the Greek Prime Minister turned up at that reception in Dublin with that woman who looked like a prostitute?'

'She was a prostitute!' said Cane.

They laughed again.

My, it was good to laugh with Charlie, he thought. Almost as good as it had been to kiss her.

They hadn't kissed since. There had been few opportunities. But there was a familiarity, an intimacy between them that was growing and that both were aware of. It could only be a matter of time before others suspected something.

The shots of Cane standing in the middle of the other fifteen EU leaders in Florence's Pitti Palace, where the meeting took place, were duly recorded by Puttnam. Walking with fellow EU leaders in the palace's Boboli Gardens with a backdrop of fountains and statues of Gods, admiring the amphitheatre, where the Medicis had held extravagant fetes and balls. It was the photo opportunity of a lifetime; surrounded by a powerful setting and powerful people.

They'd have to find another opportunity to take some pictures of Lucy. Nothing much of substance took place, but then nothing much of substance was on the agenda. The main purpose was to congratulate themselves on the successful introduction of Europe's first ever common coinage. Charlie told the reporters Lucy had pulled out owing to a 'family illness.'

The journalists seemed to believe her. Except one.

When Blackie Cole heard Charlie's explanation, he couldn't help remembering another time fifteen months ago when Lucy had left Cane in the lurch.

Blackie could still see the rear of the Range Rover disappearing towards the Downing Street gates and the shirtsleeved Cane left standing on the steps. The images appeared in his mind with the red viewfinder of his Nikon F5 in the middle, the way he saw most of the important events of his life. How he regretted surrendering that film.

There was nothing else to suggest anything was wrong with the Canes' marriage until a strange remark made some time later by another woman in Downing Street.

Blackie had known Dora Benjamin for years. They both came from Tooting, though Blackie had moved to Chiselhurst, twelve miles south in the commuter belt, soon after getting a job in Fleet Street.

He occasionally saw Dora on her midmorning bacon sarnie run to Churchill's. Blackie often called in about that time for a mug of coffee and two or three sausage rolls if he had a job in the Westminster area. He often called in about that time if he didn't. Blackie knew better than to pump Dora for gossip. She would never deliberately reveal anything she had seen at Number 10. But some contacts were worth nurturing if you thought they might give you just one nugget in a lifetime. Even if only by accident.

The week before Christmas he had seen her at Churchill's and swapped Christmas greetings. Dora sat at his table as she waited for her order of eight bacon rolls and eight coffees and Blackie commented on how much trimmer Lucy had been looking.

'She lookin' pretty on the outside, Blackie, but she ain't the pretty li'l thing the boss lookin' at these days,' said Dora.

The moment she said it, she glanced up at Blackie with a look that showed she knew she shouldn't have. Blackie was too professional to let any response show. But he knew. It was a nugget.

'She ain't the pretty li'l thing the boss lookin' at,' pondered Blackie, as he sat with the press corps at the rear of the plane to Florence, when Charlie wandered down the aisle to explain Lucy's absence. What did Dora mean?

He had no firm evidence that the Canes' marriage was on the rocks, but after the way she had blackmailed him, he had concrete evidence that Charlie was a cheat.

Chancing on Lucy storming out of Downing Street was the best picture he had ever taken of a politician – until Charlie took it from him. Chancing on her rowing with Greaves at the nurses' rally was the second best. It won him the Nikon award for the top news photograph of the year and extended his flagging career. Even Charlie couldn't take that away from him. But he wouldn't take any chances this time. He would follow his hunch and follow the two of them everywhere.

Attending Euro summits was a surreal experience for a journalist. On the one hand, you were much closer to the politicians than you usually got, spending two or three days in the same conference building with them. On the other hand, you spent most of the time watching them on the television monitor – even when they were only a few feet away in the next room and the rest of the press entourage were booked into the same hotel as the PM's team, the £350 a night Hotel Cesari which looked out on to the Duomo cathedral. Not that they were likely to catch more than a glimpse of them. The British delegation had booked the entire fifth floor and the press were not allowed anywhere near. Cane even had his own lift.

Blackie smiled when he found out which room the PM was staying in: room 525, the honeymoon suite. He didn't bother going to the opening ceremony, where Cane was available to be photographed in a series of 'grip and grin' shots, shaking hands with other leaders.

He spent the afternoon looking for a more interesting vantage point and found it at the Hotel Rialto. It was just outside the security cordon thrown around the conference. There was little likelihood of any of the leaders – or the press – staying there. No photographer would be seen dead in a £40 a night hotel – not in Florence on expenses. But Blackie wasn't there for comfort. He wanted the view from the top floor on the east side. A £100 bung to the deputy manager ensured he was given the room he wanted – on the fifth floor. It looked directly towards the Hotel Cesari and directly towards the balcony of Room 525. When he swivelled his hand on the camera focus control, it told him how far away it was: 200 metres. Well within range.

Blackie took up his position and waited.

He knew from the official programme that Cane was due back at his hotel at 5 pm. There were no official engagements after that. The banquet was tomorrow night.

At 5.05 pm, he recognised one of Cane's bodyguards peering over the edge of the balcony. Blackie trained his camera through the curtain and onto the balcony. A telephoto lens picture of Cane sitting on the balcony reading his documents, or perhaps having a glass of wine, would be ten times better than one of him shaking hands with yet another fellow EU leader in the Boboli Gardens. And who knows? He might get something a thousands times better. Or a million.

The white-uniformed waiter was serving drinks. Blackie could see Cane, Charlie, and two men he didn't recognise. Foreign diplomats probably or aides. They all had a glass of wine in their hand, except Charlie who had her left hand on her hip and her right elbow tucked into her ribs with a cigarette burning between the forefinger and middle finger of her out-stretched right hand.

One by one, they left, until Charlie and Cane were alone. Blackie saw them lean over the balcony looking towards the Duomo. They were close, but not close enough.

'She ain't the pretty li'l thing the boss lookin' at.' It couldn't be true. It just couldn't.

Blackie's adrenalin was pumping. One more move by either of them and he would have a picture that could destroy a government; even better, destroy Charlie.

They were facing each other some ten feet apart. It still wasn't incriminating. He was willing them with all his might to move closer. He got several shots in the bag, but they weren't the ones he really wanted. He was too far away to be able to hear what they were saying, but from the relaxed position of their bodies bent slightly towards each other, both leaning on the balcony, they weren't talking about monetary union.

Blackie held fire like an assassin. He waited, waited and waited. After fifteen minutes Cane stepped back and inside the room. Charlie followed him.

'Bugger!' cursed Blackie. 'Bugger, bugger, bugger.'

Charlie closed the balcony slide doors and drew the curtains behind her. And in doing so, she drew the curtains on Blackie's chances of glory and revenge.

* * *

When she turned round to face Cane, he was pouring himself another glass of wine, his fourth of the evening. Charlie had never seen him drunk; he rarely drank more than two glasses in one night. The day he won the election he didn't have a single glass of champagne. He and Lucy had a quiet dinner at Number 10 the following day when Cane opened a bottle of their favourite French white wine Pouilly Fumè, that had been served at their wedding. They didn't finish it.

Cane's indifference to alcohol was a big help to Charlie. It was one of the reasons she could not imagine working for Greaves. Like Cane, he usually sipped the occasional glass of wine, but unlike Cane, from time to time he would be gripped by the black dog of despair. And when that happened, Greaves drank to get drunk. When she first worked for him, he downed three bottles of red wine the night he missed out on his first chance to be promoted from the backbenches. Then there was that night they lost the election. She could still see the purple stain on his lips as he lay asleep in his bed when she closed the door and left him. She had drunk herself to oblivion with him. If she stayed with him she had little doubt it wouldn't have been the last time. They were too alike.

'Another Diet Coke?' said Cane as Charlie walked towards him from the balcony.

'No thanks, I've had my daily caffeine quotient.'

Cane had had more than his daily alcohol quotient.

'Well Charlie,' he said, raising his glass, 'it's back to reality tomorrow morning.'

'Back to London, you mean.'

'Yes,' he said, without looking at her.

'Steven, you're going back to win an election. Remember?'

'I'm going back to a lot of things.'

She knew what he meant. And he wasn't thinking about politics. He slumped on the edge of the bed, loosened his tie and took a large swig from his glass.

She moved towards him, stopping a couple of feet short. Charlie was used to motivating and encouraging him when he was down. It gave her pleasure to do it. In the four years Charlie had worked for him she had noticed Lucy's behaviour become more unpredictable. It had worn down Charlie; now it was beginning to wear down Cane.

She knew little of the Canes' physical relationship, but she found it hard to imagine it could have been unaffected by the cooling in their affections for each other in public.

There was nothing cool in the way Cane had kissed Charlie in his office the day Greaves resigned. It was the kiss of a man who was desperate; desperate to be loved. The more Lucy had withdrawn from Cane, the more he was drawn to Charlie. Never more so than now, in Florence, without the wife who had left him standing on the tarmac.

And why? He kept thinking. Because she was more concerned about an aunt's problems than her husband's problems, a husband who happened to be Prime Minister. Who the hell did Aunt Mimi think she was? And what the hell did Lucy think she was doing giving more attention to her than to her husband?

Cane resolved to tackle it once and for all when he got home to Lucy tomorrow. But he wasn't at home, he was in Florence with Charlie. He looked up and held out his hand to her. She clasped it. She waited for him to pull her towards him. This time, he could take the initiative.

As he pulled her down with his right hand, he put his left hand around her waist and guided her on to his lap. He reached his left hand up to the back of her head and pulled it gently towards his.

As he gazed at her, mesmerised by her lips he applied just enough pressure to the back of her head to bring them against his.

Her kiss was so much fuller than Lucy's. Everything about Charlie was fuller than Lucy. Her lips, her breasts, her enthusiasm, her personality – and her passion. As Cane fell back on to the bed with her on top of him, his foot kicked over the remains of his glass of wine on the floor. He caressed her neck, pressing her harder against him; before drawing his index finger between her shoulder blades from the nape of her neck right down to the small of her back. She purred. And smelled differently. It was not the odour of her perfume, 'Obsession' by Calvin Klein, but something far more powerful.

He pulled her blouse from under her skirt so he could feel the skin on her body. His first touch of her flesh aroused him further. He wanted her. This woman who had devoted every waking moment of five years of her life to him, who was more responsible for his success than the rest of the Government; this woman who wanted him. He had known that for a long time but ignored it. He wouldn't ignore it any longer. He couldn't.

Why should he? When he had lived under such unbearable pressure and had no way of releasing it.

He was so used to the contours of Lucy's body, that it was strange to caress Charlie. He moved on top of her, undid her blouse and bra and kissed the top of her breasts. He stood up and took off his shirt and trousers, watching Charlie's voluptuous body on the bed.

She slapped her hand across her face to stifle her giggles.

'What have I done?' he said, laughing at her laughing.

She pointed at his groin.

'Underpants by Yves St Laurent? Rosebury's by any chance? Come prepared haven't we, lover boy?'

She didn't tell him she'd seen a similar pair before. Worn by the man who owned the store.

Cane threw himself on top of her, thrilled by the touch of his bare chest against hers. As his mouth passed over her left nipple he was vaguely aware of a blueish shadow on her breast. He pulled back, expecting to see a birthmark. But as he lifted his head and his eyes were able to focus on her, he saw it wasn't a birthmark. It was a tiny tattoo, a circle with an upturned Y inside, the CND symbol.

He burst out laughing.

'Oh Jesus, you've seen it,' she said with a feigned look of innocence.

'When the hell did you get that done?' he said, doubled up in stitches.

'Drink, students union, Ronald Reagan, cruise missiles. Need I say more?' Her grin was defiant, proud.

'All those times you and I sat in with defence chiefs telling them they needn't worry, we weren't going to scrap their nuclear weapons, you were sitting alongside me with a ban the bomb tattoo on your boob!' Cane guffawed so much he fell off the bed.

'Oh Charlie,' he said when he picked himself up and leaned over her. 'Charlie, you are utterly, gorgeously, amazingly, sensationally, wonderfully, uniquely beautiful.'

'Am I?'

'Yes,' he said, giggling, 'and it's time I got tough on defence.'

'Now Steven,' she said, licking her lips, 'you're not going to nuke me, are you?'

He plunged his head on to her breast and sucked and sucked at the CND sign.

'Steven! You'll give me a love bite.' She grabbed a tuft of his black hair and pulled his head back inches from her face.

'As someone once said, frankly my dear, I don't give a damn, not a single goddamn damn.' He laughed, then the smile fell from his face. He stared into her eyes. He had never looked at her like that. 'My God Charlie, I want to make love to you ... '

'You can, Steven, you can, you can,' she said, with an expression that dared him not to.

'You're sure, quite sure?' said Cane.

'I'm sure, quite sure you can, my darling,' she said with a smouldering smile. 'And I'm quite quite sure you're going to.'

CHAPTER TWENTY SIX

The look on Charlie's face when he opened the door to her at a quarter to eight the following morning was very different.

'What's up?' said Cane, who for a moment thought someone must have discovered them.

'A group of MPs have been taken hostage in Egypt by the "October 11" group; you know, those fanatics who said they'd avenge Saddam's murder.'

'What in heaven's name were they doing in the Middle East?'

'Looking at Egypt's attempt to rebuild the tourist industry after terrorist attacks on holidaymakers.'

'Brilliant, so they go there as holidaymakers and get seized by terrorists themselves!'

There had been a lively discussion in the Commons Trade and Industry Select Committee when it was invited to visit Egypt. It had already used up its annual budget for foreign fact-finding visits, but the problem was solved when the Egyptian Tourist Ministry offered to pay for the trip, including a stay at the Old Cataract Hotel at Aswan, where Agatha Christie wrote Death On The Nile.

The nine MPs were returning to their hotel late at night when the terrorists leapt out from three four-wheel drive cars, grabbed two MPs who were trailing behind the rest of the group and drove off.

Nothing had been heard of them in the six hours since the attack happened.

Cane was about to leave the airport to return to London. Luckily the British press who had followed him to Florence had already left on an earlier scheduled flight so there would be no need for him to appear in public until he got back to Heathrow. That would give him time to find out more information and make a considered response.

'You'll never guess one of the MPs they have seized,' said Charlie.

'Who is it?' said Cane.

'Poynter.'

Quentin Poynter was one of the few people Cane hated. He was the one thrown out of the Commons for calling Cane a traitor over the Mary Fallon affair. Now the scourge of terrorists had been seized by terrorists.

The other MP was Matthew Lewis, at twenty six, the youngest MP, whose startled look the night he won his seat at the election had come to embody the innocence of the new regime. Charlie and Cane spent the two hour return flight to London discussing how to respond to the crisis when he got to Heathrow. He had agreed to give a brief TV interview as soon as he landed.

From the moment Charlie had arrived at Cane's hotel door at seven forty five that morning with his bodyguard, to the moment the plane touched down at Heathrow at noon, the two did not have a single moment alone. Nor did they have a chance to discuss what had happened between midnight and one thirty, when Charlie had dressed, left the Cesari's honeymoon suite and returned to her own room at the end of the corridor.

No words were exchanged but as Cane ran his finger along the words of the statement she had prepared for him, her hand twice touched his. If Cane noticed, he didn't react. As he stood at the top of the steps of the British Airways Boeing jet on the tarmac at Heathrow, he recognised the craggy face of Adam Boulton, Sky TV's political editor, standing on the tarmac.

One of the disadvantages of using a scheduled flight instead of the specially fitted RAF VC10s the Prime Minister often used for trips, was the lack of communications facilities. If anything happened while you were in mid-air, you didn't know about it until you landed. Something had happened mid air. It was only five seconds after putting his foot back on British soil, that Cane knew about it. A Foreign Office aide phoned Charlie on her mobile while the plane was taxiing. But Cane was already walking down the steps.

'Prime Minister, what is your reaction to the reports that the two MPs, Quentin Poynter and Matthew Lewis, have been killed trying to escape from their attackers in Egypt?' asked Boulton.

'Pardon?'

'Quentin Poynter and Matthew Lewis, Prime Minister, your reaction to their deaths?'

'I, I er ... I'm appalled to hear that,' said Cane, his eyes darting to his left in search of Charlie. She was scrambling to get alongside him.

'Is this the first you've heard of it?'

'Yes, Adam, I've been mid-air for the last two hours. I am deeply shocked by what you say.'

'The terrorist group who carried out the attack said they did it in response to Britain's role in the assassination of Saddam Hussein. Does today's tragic development together with the decision by some Middle East countries to cancel valuable contracts with UK firms lead you to wonder whether it was wise for your Government to take the lead role in assassinating him?'

'Really Adam,' said Cane, adopting his familiar tactic of trying to embarrass the interviewer whenever he felt vulnerable. 'I'm surprised you can ask such a question. Saddam Hussein is responsible for killing hundreds of thousands of people and the action we took was fully justified. If it is true that people acting in his name have killed two MPs, it merely underlines the evil of the man and all those who support him and the necessity of combating the evil methods he espoused.'

Moving herself opposite Cane, to the side of Boulton, Charlie held her finger horizontally against her throat. Cane ended the interview.

He swept across the tarmac to the VIP terminal where he could recover from the shock of what Boulton had just told him and start working out its implications.

As Cane walked away, Boulton addressed the camera. 'Well, as you could see then from the Prime Minister's reaction, he was clearly very shocked to hear of the reported deaths of the two MPs Quentin Poynter and Matthew Lewis. It does of course mean that there could be by-elections in both their constituencies before the general election next year, though that is not certain since the general election is getting close. If the by-elections are held, Bathurst and co shouldn't have any difficulty in holding Poynter's Mid-Shropshire seat, and they could gain Lewis's Thames Valley East, which they had lost for the first time ever at the last election.'

Cane had more immediate concerns.

In four hours he had to face Prime Minister's Questions – now it would be dominated by the killing of the MPs. He would have to lead the tributes to both, starting off by praising Poynter, who had spent the previous four years goading and insulting him. The tribute to Lewis would be even harder. He had only stood in Thames Valley East for the experience and was more startled than anybody when he won it. The Opposition rarely got a sniff of Cane's blood; now they would be baying for it like starved hyenas. And his own side would be in a state of shock that Lewis, one of the most blameless politicians ever to sit in Parliament, had become its unlikeliest victim of war, Cane's war.

The tributes duly delivered, he sat opposite Bathurst, steeling himself for the inevitable.

She blamed him for the MPs' deaths, claiming Cane's warmongering had made Britain a target for every group of fanatics in the world. Cane countered by revealing the MPs had defied a specific warning to them by the Foreign Office not to go to Aswan because the 'October 11' terrorist group was known to be active in the region.

Three times Bathurst tried to pin the blame on Cane; three times he threw her accusations back at her. She sat back on the green leather bench, her short legs bouncing up and down.

No one saw her as a future Prime Minister; she was holding the fort until her party returned as a serious force with a serious leader. Everyone knew that, including Bathurst herself. The fact that she had become leader at all reflected the depths to which they had plumbed rather than a realistic attempt to pull themselves out of it.

She always did her best, but this time Bathurst shook her head at Madam Speaker, indicating she would not make a fourth attempt, when she was entitled to six. Cane had weathered the storm; he sighed with relief and willed his muscles to relax.

But they seized with terror when he heard Madam Speaker's next three words.

Madam Speaker had perfected a hundred ways of introducing an MP. The way in which she annunciated an Honourable Member's name was the best guide to his or her status at Westminster. If it was someone she respected she would declaim their name solemnly; if she liked them she would say it in a warm, friendly way; if she disliked them she would bark it; if it was an irritating upstart she would deliberately get the name wrong. She had different voices for different occasions too. The tone she chose for this occasion was more than grave, it had the ring of history.

'Mr – Ga-reth – G-reaves!' she boomed slowly and portentously, as though she was introducing the executioner at a public hanging.

The raucous jeering and cheering that had gone on throughout Cane's exchanges with Bathurst was replaced by a stunned hush as Greaves rose. He was sitting in the second seat below the aisle in the third row back from the gangway, the precise spot from where Sir Geoffrey Howe, another embittered former deputy, was transformed from Margaret Thatcher's dead sheep into the wolf who savaged her.

Cane felt the rope tighten. No, wait, Greaves had taken Lewis under his wing. Perhaps he simply wanted to add his own tribute. Cane prayed that was all it was.

MPs murmured 'ssshhh.' They wanted to savour each and every one of Greaves' words.

Often when he was being attacked by an opponent in the Commons, Cane would ostentatiously talk to the Minister next to him, pretending he was oblivious. He didn't attempt to ignore this. Instead he sat bolt upright looking straight ahead as Greaves stood addressing his back from behind him to the right.

'First of all, I would like to add my tributes to both the late Honourable Member for Mid-Shropshire and my Honourable Friend, the late member for Thames Valley East. I hope Honourable Members opposite will understand if I say that while I never agreed with the Honourable Member for Mid-Shropshire's politics, he was an individualistic, courageous and colourful Parliamentarian.'

Poynter's former colleagues responded with an appreciative rumble of 'hear, hears.'

Greaves went on, 'And I hope Honourable Members opposite will also understand if I say that the death of my Honourable Friend, the Member for Thames Valley East, has caused me particular sorrow. He had become a dear friend who represented everything that was fresh, young, vibrant and good about this party and this Parliament and will be missed by all who knew him.'

More 'hear, hears.' The rope relaxed. Cane waited for Greaves to sit down. But he didn't.

'Now I would like to address a more serious matter.'

His tone changed from solemn to urgent, businesslike. Cane felt the rope tighten again. Even worse, Greaves was behind him; he couldn't even see the man who might be about to kick the chair away and leave him dangling. He dare not look round. He was too scared.

'Is the Prime Minister aware,' started Greaves, 'that according to a memo from the intelligence service that has been sent to me concerning the killing of Saddam Hussein ... '

He was interrupted by gasps of amazement.

' ... according to an MI6 memo sent to me concerning information at the Pentagon relating to the killing of Saddam Hussein, the reason the United States Government withdrew from the operation was not, as was claimed publicly, because they had other pressing military commitments in Bolivia ... '

An MI6 memo? Secret information from the Pentagon? This was the stuff that destroyed governments; it was out of a Le Carré novel.

' ... the real reason they withdrew, according to the MI6 memo, was because the National Security Adviser to the President of the United States told the President that the likelihood of, and I quote, "commercial and terrorist retaliation against the US" was too great.'

Greaves delayed for a moment to allow the explosive impact of his remarks to sink in, like a depth charge. It was as though Cane's stomach had been removed.

'Was the Prime Minister aware of the MI6 memo and could he say what he thinks it says of this country's relations with the United States that they apparently let us carry out the assassination of Saddam Hussein knowing that it was likely to lead to this country suffering the damaging commercial consequences we have seen and the tragic terrorist consequences which have cost the lives of two Honourable Members of this House?'

Greaves sat down. MPs were struggling to take it all in. This was no time for the usual baying and catcalling – even the most stupid realised that. Cane was so shaken that his legs were trembling and he could only get to his feet using the despatch box top to steady himself. He had no idea what Greaves was talking about, but he had to reply.

'As my Right Honourable Friend ... ' he broke off, long enough to imply doubt in Greaves' right to be considered honourable or a friend, ' ... knows, I never comment on security matters and I am surprised that my Right Honourable Friend, a member of the Privy Council, should raise them in such a way. However, I will of course look into the substance of his remarks later.'

Cane wasn't sure which treachery was most shocking; America's – assuming the allegation was true – or Greaves'.

He would have known the devastating effect his words would have – it could only be a deliberate attempt to sabotage Cane. The fact that he was well ahead in the polls and that according to one recent opinion poll, only four per cent of the electorate regarded Madeleine Bathurst as a 'potential Prime Minister' was no excuse.

But his anger paled alongside the anger of the woman sitting a few feet away immediately next to the chamber. It was just as well the Speaker had not heard the stream of expletives she delivered under her breath during Greaves' attack. And it was just as well that her seat was directly beneath the press gallery, hidden from view from the lobby correspondents.

One of Charlie's civil service colleagues had to restrain her from leaping to her feet. Watching Cane seated on the front bench, physically shrunk after his pummelling, she felt every blow as though it had hit her too. She was boiling with rage not just with what Greaves had said, but the way he had said it, the way they had all listened reverentially as though he was some kind of Messiah. The MPs around him leant back and upwards at him as though scared of being electrified by the aura around him. Opposition MPs were cowed into silence in a way that Cane rarely achieved. What was it about this man, Greaves? At times he seemed to be in a semi-permanent sulk; and yet he could dominate the Commons without raising his voice or so much as a theatrical finger. Moving from the front to the backbenches had changed him; freed him from Cane's shackles. He seemed physically bigger. And from his new vantage point on the raised terraces, he towered over Cane like a dark, menacing shadow. His presence was as much animal as intellectual and no one was more aware of its power than Charlie. She wanted to march over and punch him. How dare he betray his own party? All because he was jealous. Jealous of Cane's success. Jealous of her too, probably. How dare he humiliate him? How dare he risk throwing the election away because he hated to see a better man than him leading the party? How dare he?

She threw off the official who had pulled her back to her seat and shook her fist at Greaves. Even though they were separated by countless rows of bobbing heads of MPs, she could see him sitting in his seat. And she knew he would look across to her. And when he did, he did not need to be a lip reader to know what she was saying. Her glowering contorted face and her clenched fist said it all. She hated him. Now she had attracted the attention of Madam Speaker. The official pulled Charlie back into her seat quickly. She looked at Cane and wanted to rush across and embrace him, protect him, comfort him.

And love him.

* * *

'BY-ELECTION SENSATION'

For once the use of the word 'sensation' in a newspaper was justified. From the moment Lewis and Poynter had been killed, the papers were full of by-election speculation. There are no hard and fast rules concerning how soon a by-election should be called once a seat becomes vacant. But by precedent, it is normally held within three months to ensure the voters are not left unrepresented for too long. However, if a general election is due within six months, the by-election can be avoided to save the trouble, expense and inconvenience of making constituents vote twice in a short time.

Poynter and Lewis's deaths posed a delicate problem for both Cane and Bathurst. Since they occurred in January, and the general election had to be held by next May at the latest, they were within the six month period. And unusually, both sides had good reason for wanting to put them off.

The party that previously held the seat has the right to move the writ in Parliament for the by-election, which put Bathurst in the driving seat for Mid-Shropshire and Cane for Thames Valley East. But neither was keen to turn the ignition. The long slim shadow of Simon Darius hung over Bathurst's short tubby frame and she knew that if she called a by-election, Darius was likely to stand, especially since he had been a close friend of Poynter. The moment he walked in through the door of the Commons, her job as leader would be under threat. There was plenty of time for her colleagues to sack their leader in favour of someone they thought would have a better chance of winning. Bathurst had seen them do it to one woman; they would not think twice about doing it to her.

For his part, Cane was anxious to avoid a by-election in Mid-Shropshire for the same reason. Bathurst's weak leadership was one of his greatest assets. The last thing he wanted was to go into an election facing a resurgent Opposition led by a vibrant, charismatic leader. Cane knew the power of that combination. It's what had got him into Downing Street.

And a by-election in Thames Valley East, the timing of which he could dictate, would be just as counter productive. Everyone knew it would revert to Bathurst's party at the next election, and the last thing Cane wanted to do was to hand them a publicity coup and reduce his Commons majority.

With mounting rumours that the general election would be held in spring, only three or four months away, most people seemed happy to let the matter rest. There were rumours that several unnamed MP admirers of Darius planned to put pressure on Bathurst to call a by-election in Mid-Shropshire. But they were too scared to go public; they knew they'd be sacked for disloyalty.

But Lady Hermione Poynter was not like most people.

Daughter of an aristocrat, and a former debutante who went on to become a bestselling author of racy novels about bed hopping among the upper classes, she had been a perfect match for Quentin Poynter, who, when she met him, seemed destined to become Prime Minister. It was not to be. By the end of his career it was hard to believe it ever could have been. Poynter eventually became junior Education Minister in his mid fifties when the previous incumbent was caught with his hand in the till. Poynter lasted only eight months. He was caught with his hand on the bottom of a pretty French assistante when he visited a comprehensive school after one too many long lunches.

He went back to the backbenches, took up a handful of part time directorships in the City, and became an elder statesman even though he had never been a statesman in the first place. Lady Hermione had been praised for her dignity when her husband was shot in Egypt, notably for flying to Cairo the next day to hold a press conference to condemn the killers, challenging them to meet her face to face to justify their 'heinous and cowardly violation of humanity.'

Her appearance was as dramatic and elegant as her language. At 62, she was as photogenic as she had been at 22. Her powerful oration at her husband's memorial service in Westminster Abbey, attended by Cane and Bathurst, where, her aquiline face half concealed by a black veil, she said he would far rather have been assassinated by terrorists than appease them, turned her into a national heroine.

The terrorists who killed Poynter ignored Lady Hermione. But that option was not open to Cane and Bathurst when, after a New Year memorial service for her husband, she said the delay in calling a by-election was a 'contumacious defiance of democracy.' They had no choice but to consult their dictionaries – and submit.

A week later, the by-election writs for Mid-Shropshire and Thames Valley East were moved in the Commons and the date set for Thursday, February 14th, St Valentine's Day.

A day after that, Bathurst discovered that her party's local chairman in Mid-Shropshire had issued a statement that he would be honoured if Simon Darius would agree to be their candidate.

A day later, he did so.

And on the third day, Lady Hermione said her husband had regarded Darius as the most brilliant and courageous politician since Churchill. His warning after the Big Wheel bomb that Cane was a 'dangerous young whipper snapper who is playing with dark forces of which he has little or no knowledge' now seemed like a premonition and made people revise their view of Poynter from that of an elegant alcoholic buffoon to soothsayer. The most unlikely candidate for martyrdom ever to emerge from the plush green pastures of Shropshire or the Commons backbenches.

There was nothing Bathurst could do about it. The party rules had changed greatly in recent years, but one remained the same: local associations had almost complete freedom to choose who they wanted to stand as their Parliamentary candidates.

The question of how to respond to Darius's comeback had made Charlie forget about the other by-election in Thames Valley East. But she was woken with a jolt by a report in the Telegraph on the day both constituencies were due to make their final choice.

'NEW BY-ELECTION SHOCK.'

The report by Drew Sharpe said,

Next month's twin Parliamentary by-elections took a sensational turn last night when it emerged that former Cabinet Minister Mike Turnbull is expected to stand in Thames Valley East.

He is to resign as a European Commissioner to enable him to put

his name forward as Opposition candidate at tonight's selection meet-
ing. The move paves the way for a double leadership challenge to party
leader Madeleine Bathurst before the general election which must be
held by the end of May.

Ever since it became clear that Simon Darius is set to be chosen as
the party's candidate for Mid-Shropshire, Westminster has been
buzzing with rumours that he could attempt to oust Mrs Bathurst.

But the disclosure that Mr Turnbull is set to contest Thames Valley
East has fuelled speculation that the two men could fight it out to
replace her. Mr Turnbull, 59, is the standard bearer of his party's lib-
eral pro-European wing, with Mr Darius, 46, the champion of the right.
Mrs Bathurst will not be alone in being concerned about the surprise
development. It will worry Downing Street too.

Previous surveys have indicated that if either Mr Darius or Mr
Turnbull leads Mrs Bathurst's party, they could gain up to ten points in
the polls.

Outspoken Mr Turnbull lost his seat at the last election. Until now
it seemed he had turned his back on British politics. But colleagues say
he is ready to stand in the by-election because he does not want his
long-time political enemy Mr Darius to take over the party and thinks
that under his own leadership, they would have an outside chance of
beating Mr Cane.

* * *

Charlie put the paper down and rang Cane's mobile. He had gone to
Chequers for the weekend with his family.

The atmosphere at Number 10 had been tense since their return from
Florence. Charlie had never had much contact with Lucy; they had hardly
spoken in the last six months and this week Charlie had avoided her completely.

She assumed Lucy would think it was because of the scene at the airport. It wasn't the only strained relationship in Number 10. Charlie and Cane had barely had a moment alone together since Florence. Charlie looked for signs as to his feelings for her after their love-making, but there were few. He sometimes seemed in a daze. The election was approaching like an onrushing train; the controversy over the Saddam raid still raged; he lived in fear of another ambush by Greaves; and on top of all that, his private life was in turmoil. She had read of Prime Ministers falling victim to paranoia and paralysis in office. Surely it wasn't happening to Cane, the most level headed, unegotistical and sane person ever to stride across the threshold of Number 10.

She had looked just as closely for signs as to his feelings for Lucy. She had noticed that each morning when Lucy went to work, she didn't bother to turn and wave to Cane at the last minute as she usually did. Nor did he call her in the flat from his office at tea time, as he usually did.

Charlie waited for Cane to press the answer button on his mobile phone and say, 'Hi,' in his cheery voice. But the voice that answered from Chequers was screaming and unhinged.

'It's you, isn't it? Go away, go away! I hate you, I hate you. Leave us alone, just leave us ... !'

It was a demented Lucy.

Charlie could hear a male voice shout, followed by a bang, a scream and the sound of the phone falling on to the floor followed by a crash in the background.

Then it went dead.

CHAPTER TWENTY SEVEN

Neither of them said a word as they drove the thirty seven miles from Number 10 to Chequers. The children were in the back, miles away listening to their Walkman's.

When they arrived, Cane and Lucy went through the motions of polite conversation when the four of them sat down to supper. Cane asked the children what they had done at school. Sam described how he had scored his first goal for the Under 14 soccer team and Jessica proudly showed Cane her certificate for passing her first flute exam.

Afterwards, the children watched television before going to bed just after nine, leaving Cane and Lucy alone in the sitting room. He had never endured such anguish. His marriage had always been the most important thing in his life. Not only had he never had an affair before, he had never considered sleeping with another woman – until Charlie. He knew Lucy had never slept with another man, that she never would. She was loyal by instinct as well as inclination; like him – or like he used to be.

Adultery.

The very word sounded ugly and sordid, never mind the act. And he had committed it with a woman his wife knew – and loathed. How could he have done it? He was not religious: his mother was an atheist. But Lucy was strict C of E, at least in the social sense, and she liked them to go to the family service once a month.

Cane did not need a clergyman to tell him he had sinned. He started to wonder whether he had done it. He had always loved Lucy, even when the first signs of disaffection turned into something more serious after he became Prime Minister. He put it down to the stress of being in the public eye. But the more she failed to respond to his attempts to sympathise with her, the less sympathetic he became.

As the gap grew wider and wider, he became closer and closer to Charlie.

Initially there was little sexual attraction on his part. He had always gone for softer, more demure, more giving women. Women like Lucy. It amused him that Charlie was every other man's pin-up. Lucy was jealous from the start, though she had nothing to be jealous of. But the more estranged he became from Lucy, the stronger became the pull of Charlie's animal appeal. The more irritated he became by Lucy's passivity, the more attracted he became to Charlie's fervour. Nor was Lucy the only person pushing him towards Charlie. An attack by Greaves was not just an attack on Cane; it was an attack on her. They were like frightened comrades cowering together in a trench.

The only thing that surprised him was that until Florence, Cane had not realised the strength of his longing for Charlie – or hers for him. Telling Lucy was unthinkable. Yet not telling her was unthinkable. He was no coward, neither physically nor morally. He had been brought up not to cheat to himself – or to cheat others. But he had cheated. He had cheated the one person he sworn at the altar never to cheat. And unlike some people, he had meant every word. He was genuinely puzzled by friends who divorced when they had children. He knew what it had done to him and to his mother. Now he was going down the same path himself. He was ashamed. He had to put it right somehow. It wouldn't be easy, there were huge risks. It might be better to stay quiet, say nothing, to protect her from what he had done. But he couldn't do it.

He would rather confess his betrayal and face the consequences than lie to Lucy – and himself. He couldn't deny he still lusted after Charlie, but it was nothing against his longing and love for his family; his children and the mother of his children. He could live with his deceit no longer.

From her cold, frigid demeanour since Florence, Cane suspected Lucy already suspected him. Every day he expected her to confront him with his infidelity. He would rather volunteer a confession than suffer the added shame of having one forced out of him. But it was Lucy, not Cane who broke the silence.

'Steven,' she said calmly, 'I have something to tell you.'

They were sitting opposite each other on the two gold sofas in the White Parlour. It had always been their favourite room at Chequers. They both loved its stunning view of the rose garden and of the magnificent Victory Drive that led to the entrance. Lucy adored the whitewashed pannelled walls which were so much less masculine than some of the other darker rooms. Cane liked to work at the French writing desk. And the children played games on the gold patterned carpet or watched TV. It was smaller than some of the grander suites and more intimate. Small enough for two people to talk to each other, alone.

Cane went to interrupt her, but she stopped him. 'Please!' she said. 'Let me finish!'

'I have something to tell you.' It should be him, not her, uttering those words.

But it was too late.

'There's something I've been keeping from you,' she said, looking at the floor. 'Something truly awful.'

He wanted to shout, 'Stop, stop! Whatever it is, it can't be as bad as what I have done.'

He tried hopelessly to utter something, but the words wouldn't form. And Lucy raised her right palm to stop him. 'No, Steven, no, I want to say this, you'll never know how long or how much I've wanted to say it. And nothing will stop me now.'

She sounded hypnotised, as though putting herself in a trance was the only way she could say what she had to say. Cane looked at her. The outline of her prettiness was still there, but her delicacy had turned to frailty. He recalled when they bought their first house in Blackheath, and she told off a burly string-vested builder repairing their roof for making a mess. 'She's like a little pixie, isn't she?' the builder shouted to Cane, amused at being rebuked by a prim-looking waif.

She still was pixie-like, though not quite so little. Nor so young. When, as now, she was tired, her face looked all her forty two years – and a few more. Her eyes looked hollow and haunted. Inexplicably, Cane heard himself speak.

'Aunt Mimi,' he mumbled. He didn't know why he had suddenly thought of her.

'What? What did you say?' replied Lucy distractedly.

'Aunt Mimi,' said Cane a little louder, catching up with his unconscious. 'This doesn't have anything to do with her, does it?'

'Wel l... no, yes ... no ... not really,' replied Lucy.

'What do you mean?' asked Cane. 'Does it or doesn't it?'

'Steven, leave me, let me explain it in my way. Please!'

And she told him the story of a young mother who was out walking her baby in its pram one sunny Sunday afternoon in September down a pretty country lane near her village. The child was gurgling and the mother was looking forward to the child's christening the following week. The mother stopped by a bend to pick some blackberries and left the pram on the gently sloping grass verge. After a while she went into the field and worked her way along the other side of the tall bush to get more berries, leaving the pram on the other side. She heard the sound of a car coming from the direction of the village. She couldn't see the pram, but it should be safe enough. She had left the brake on. Or hadn't she? My God, she wasn't sure. The pram was only ten feet away on the other side of the hedge, but to get to it she would have to run twenty five yards to the end of the field and then round the other side. As long as the driver was looking ahead, it shouldn't matter too much.

Before the young mother got to the end of the field, she heard a bang. She looked back and saw a brief glimpse of white chrome, the colour of the second-hand carriage pram her mother had bought her, amid the branches of the bush. By the time she got to the road side, she could see the pram lying upside down on the verge, the large silver handle bent double. The baby was crying and covered in blood. The mother ran the half mile to the village to get help. The baby was rushed to hospital with serious injuries.

'I don't understand the story, what does it mean?' said Cane.

292

Lucy looked at him, the dark blue circles under her eyes moist with tears. She was haggard, beaten.

'I was the driver,' she said with expression.

Cane sat motionless. 'You ...?'

'I was the driver,' she repeated in the same lifeless monotone.

Cane was so shocked, he found it hard to get to his feet. But he did, walked across the room and put his hands round her shoulders.

'My darling, I'm so sorry. I don't know what to ... why haven't you told me this before?' he said hugging her as tears welled up in his eyes.

'Because I never told anyone.'

'I don't understand.'

'I didn't stop.'

'What?' he said, disbelieving.

'I didn't stop.'

'But why, why Lucy?'

'Because I panicked. I hadn't got a driving licence. I was going to take my test in three weeks. Daddy had taught me to drive and he and Mummy had gone away for the weekend. I was at home on my own with a school-friend, Phoebe Howard. She was always more daring than me and dared me to take Mummy's Ford Escort out for a drive. Stupidly, I did it. I was trying to put the radio on when we ... when we ... '

Lucy threw herself into Cane's lap. Both of them sobbed.

She pulled back, wiping her eyes, determined to finish. ' ... when we ... hit the pram. Phoebe screamed at me, "Drive on! Drive On! Don't stop, you fool!" ... and ... and I did drive on. I drove all the way home and put the car back in the garage. Phoebe said it was only slightly damaged, that no one would notice and that the baby was probably ... probably OK.

'We were too scared to put the radio on in case it was on the news. I said we should tell the police but Phoebe said it was too late, we would be arrested for a hit and run. Then Mummy and Daddy got back the next day. I didn't tell them but I saw in the paper the next day a baby had been badly hurt in a hit and run. It said the mother hadn't seen the car because she was in a field collecting blackberries, otherwise I don't think we would have got away with it. I don't know how I kept it from Mummy and Daddy. Mummy hardly ever used the car so she didn't see the dent on the bumper. But Daddy did two weeks later, when he was washing it. He confronted me and I told him everything.'

She told Cane how her parents had decided to keep quiet. They feared Lucy, who was seventeen and had just started her second 'A' level year at school, could be jailed.

They also feared the scandal would end her father's ambition to become chairman of the British Medical Council, which he duly did six months later.

'Aren't you going to ask me what happened to the baby?'

'What did happen to it?'

'It was a baby girl ... she was hurt, very badly hurt. Her back was broken and when she came out they said she was brain damaged too. It was horrible, Steven. We knew who they were, they only lived five miles from us. I saw the mother in the high street six months later and fainted. She and her husband – they were only twenty one – tried to cope with the baby, but they gave up after a year or so.'

'What happened to her?'

'She went into a home.'

'And then?'

'She's ... she's still there,' said Lucy, shaking with tears.

'How do you know?'

'Because I keep in touch with her.'

'You what?' said Cane, his jaw wide open.

'Not me, but a ... a friend ... a friend does it for me.'

And then it dawned on him. The dank dark fog that had clung to the horizon for years was lifted. He was overcome by a rush of astonishment, relief and horror.

'It's Aunt Mimi, isn't it? Aunt Mimi, it's been Aunt Mimi,' he mumbled incoherently.

Lucy nodded, waiting for him to complete the riddle for himself.

'It's Aunt Mimi who keeps in touch with the child, isn't it?' he said, pulling Lucy round so he could see her face.

'Yes ... yes ... yes. I wanted to know how Kelly ... '

' ... Kelly?'

'Kelly Hetherington, that's her name. I wanted to know how she was getting on. She was abandoned by her parents. I couldn't go, but Mimi goes for me, takes her presents, makes sure she has everything she needs, she is just a visitor.'

'And this is what's been making you ill, isn't it? All these years when you've been going to see Mimi and coming back in a terrible state?'

'Yes, but I still haven't told you where she lives.'

'Does it make a difference where she lives?' he said, puzzled.

'If you've lived at Oakwood House it does make a difference,' said Lucy, watching his face closely.

Oakwood.

Cane closed his eyes in horror. The name conjured up the same chilling image of children suffering as Aberfan or Dunblane. Kelly had not been killed, but she had lived to suffer every bit as much. And her suffering was endless.

He remembered hearing of the Oakwood child abuse scandal for the first time on the radio as Sam and Jessica ate their breakfast in the Number 10 flat. He remembered announcing an inquiry into the affair on the day he visited Lucy's own Amberton special needs school.

Special needs? She worked with handicapped children when she had...had made a child handicapped. Cane looked at Lucy.

'Lucy, when you became a special needs teacher ... ? Was it ... ? Was it ... ?'

He didn't know how to say it.

'Was it because of what I had done?' she said for him. 'Is that what you were going to say? Yes, Steven, that is why I failed my exams, why I became a special needs teacher. I wanted to make amends. It is, will always be, my penance.'

He felt ashamed. Ashamed that he had been married to her for seventeen years without ever realising the unbearably cruel burden she had carried alone all those years and without ever realising her courageous, truly heroic attempt to atone for her moment of teenage madness. Ashamed of the fact she couldn't bring herself to trust him with her secret for all those years. And shame was not a sufficient word to describe his disgust at the way he had betrayed her with Charlie.

He held her, stroked her head and said, 'It's over, it's over.'

'But it's not, Steven, it's not.'

'You mean the little girl, her suffering's not over?'

'No, we'll never know what happened to her, she can't speak. No, Kelly's in a new home now. Mimi says it's lovely.'

'What isn't over, then?'

And she explained how last week, Aunt Mimi had been visited by a journalist investigating the Oakwood scandal. He wanted to know why Aunt Mimi had taken such a long and close interest in Kelly Hetherington when she had no obvious connection with her.

Mimi was Lucy's childhood nickname for her mother's sister. Her real name was Ursula Jennings. Whenever her aunt visited and read Lucy and her brother Mark a story, both children would shout 'Me, me! Me first!' She would always reply, 'My name is not "Aunt me, me," it's Aunt Ursula.' But it made no difference; from then on she was Aunt Mimi.

The reporter was leaving Aunt Mimi's house, when he saw a picture hanging in the hallway of her standing with Lucy and Cane when she visited them at Downing Street.

'You know them do you, Mrs Jennings?' said the reporter, who until now, had been satisfied by her explanation that she had no special reason to drive all the way to Oakwood once a month to visit Kelly other than a desire to help a child in need.

'Yes, they, er ... Lucy is my er ... niece,' stammered Aunt Mimi, seeing no option other than to tell the truth.

The stammer did not go unnoticed. And three days later Mimi had a call from an official dealing with the Oakwood inquiry to tell her a reporter had phoned to ask if they knew of her link to Lucy. It set alarm bells ringing with Aunt Mimi who called Lucy to warn her of the risk of her being contacted by a reporter.

'I got the message from her when we were at Heathrow, about to go to Florence,' said Lucy, her gabbled words pouring out in a flood of tears and hysteria. 'I thought it was to be all over the papers, that's why I couldn't go. You understand now, you do understand now, don't you, Steven?' she bawled, looking up at him, tugging desperately at his arm, her face red and swollen.

Cane felt as though his head was about to implode. The conflicting emotions, pain, guilt, sympathy, anger, love, self loathing, were too much. It was like a brush with death; his whole life, marriage, past, present and future, his career as Prime Minister, his affair with Charlie, rushed past as though he was falling through the sky.

He held Lucy tighter than he had ever held her. She buried her head in his chest, unable to see his eyes, see what he was seeing.

He was walking away from the private room in the VIP suite at Heathrow, getting on to the plane, next to Charlie, in his hotel room, on the balcony and ... in the bed, the bed he would have shared with Lucy, him, kissing Charlie's neck, licking the CND tattoo on her breast, pulling Charlie's clothes from her, digging his hands into her trim buttocks and making love. To Charlie.

Cane squeezed his eyes to try and expunge the image. It came back again and again. Each time he strengthened his grip around Lucy to try and strangle it. The last time he had held anyone so tight, his arms were clasping Charlie's naked flesh, his hands stroking her, exploring her. Lucy was so much smaller, like a crushed bird. He had no right to touch her.

No man had ever betrayed a woman the way he had betrayed her. As Lucy's sobbing slowly subsided, a sharp pain jabbed in the recess of his soul and he knew it would never go. Like Lucy's crying, it would subside, he would learn to live with it like an amputated limb; he would forget it, but it would return. Always.

He had been so close to telling her of his adultery, to plead her forgiveness. He could never tell her now. How could he expect her to forgive him when he had left her at the airport cursing about what the press might say about her absence? What would people say if they ever found out about him and Charlie? His wife had spent more than twenty years fighting to control a personal nightmare. What he did in ninety minutes in bed with Charlie was far worse. His wife's action was a tragic mistake; his was deliberate.

Just as Lucy had kept her secret from him, now he would have to do the same. Not for his own protection, but to protect her. If he told her what he had done it could kill her. Or she might kill him. She was so weak and unstable. Perhaps it was just as well he hadn't blurted out his secret. As he released his grip, she looked at him. Her large round eyes had never looked so vulnerable and frightened. And trusting.

'Lucy, I love you, you'll never know how truly, truly sorry I am. For my unforgivable, selfish, cruel thoughtlessness towards you. If only I'd known ... I could have helped. You should have told me, darling. Didn't you think you could trust me?'

'How could I tell you?' she said. 'Once I'd driven past and Mummy and Daddy told me not to tell the police, it was too late. They were frightened for me – and themselves.'

'But ... ?'

' ... but what?' raged Lucy. 'What was I supposed to do? Call in at a police station a year later or ten years later and say, "Hello, I didn't mention it at the time but I left a baby brain damaged in a hit and run accident ten years ago, so I thought I'd own up?" It's not on, is it? Imagine the press coverage you'd get for that. Even Charlie Redpath would have trouble spinning that one, wouldn't she? Maybe we should put it to the test. Of course, I could go to a police station and do it today!' She pointed at the door, as if she really meant to go.

Cane took her in his arms and held her tight. In the last six months they had hardly touched each other.

'Steven, I do still love you, I do, I really do.'

She was looking up into his face. Her stiff resistance to him was gone, she was willing him to protect her and love her. He kissed her lips. She threw her hand round his neck and pulled his face onto hers, kissing him with desperation.

She fell back on the sofa, pulling him on top of her. 'Love me, Steven, love me, love me. Please love me.'

He hesitated.

'You do still love me, don't you, Steven, you still find me, attractive don't you?'

'Yes, my darling, I do still love you, but ... '

'But what?'

'But here? What if the children ... ?'

'They're in the pool, they won't be back for three quarters of an hour. Please, Steven, love me, like you used to.'

He leaned over her and kissed her long and passionately. She sucked his neck and throat and remembered what it was like to feel his weight crushing her, touching her, pulling her skirt up, stroking her leg, pulling at her knickers.

'Love me, now Steven, now, now.'

He pulled his trousers down and entered her, his feet still on the ground to support him.

'Yes, Steven, love me, love me, make love to me.'

And he did.

Afterwards as they sat on the sofa, she lying on his lap, recovering, saying nothing, the silence was shattered by the twitter of Cane's mobile phone.

It lay on the writing table just beyond Lucy's reach.

'Oh, who the heavens can that be?' she said, rising to pick it up and press the receive button. 'It's probably the Archbishop of Canterbury phoning to ask why the Prime Minister hasn't been to church on Sunday.' Cane couldn't remember the last time she had been so lighthearted.

'Yes, PM here,' she said, playfully imitating Cane's voice.

'Hello? ... Hello?' said the voice at the other end. 'Steven? Are you there?

Lucy held the phone away from her face. The calm, satisfied, happy expression that had radiated across her after their lovemaking was replaced by a manic look of anger and hatred.

'It's you, isn't it? Go away, go away! I hate you, I hate you. Leave us alone, just leave us ... !' she screamed.

Cane rushed across and grabbed the phone from her. There was a struggle; Lucy fell backwards, dropping the phone on the floor, and grabbed hold of Cane, as they fell on the writing table which collapsed with a crash beneath them.

Cane picked up the phone. The line was dead.

CHAPTER TWENTY EIGHT

He had read the letter a thousand times. But he had never worked out exactly what it meant.

Dear Gareth,

> *This is a very hard thing for me to do. When I left your flat the week before last I needed to get away from London. I know I should have written before now but I couldn't do it. I didn't know what I wanted. I'm not sure I do now, but I think I'm beginning to get my thoughts clear.*

> *I know none of us could come to terms with what had happened. I know you had more reason than I did to feel devastated. It meant more to you than almost anyone, though I wanted it with all my heart too. I need to get back to see Mum. She hasn't been well. And Billy's in trouble again.*

> *But that's not the main reason I am not coming back. Please don't be shocked when I say that. I just can't face returning to it all. We've spent years changing everything but nothing's changed. We lost.*

> *I so admire what you have tried to do. From the first time you hauled me out of that poll tax demo, took me to the pub and told me swinging a punch at a policeman was 'not the way to change society in the latter half of the twentieth century' – remember saying that? It still makes me laugh.*

> *You're so brave for resisting the attempts by all the other new wave types who want to get rid of everything we have stood*

for, people like Cane. They make me sick the way they act as though all we have to do to win power is to copy our opponents. If people like Cane had their way we'd nick their manifesto, put our name on it and say vote for us.

The sad fact is they are going to win the argument. You could see it in the election meetings. You spent most of the time in the North East, but I saw them in London, all these yuppie types, pollsters and media experts. You should have heard what they were saying about our   policies.

They're embarrassed by them. And I can tell you this, Gareth, they are going to be running the party. You're fighting a losing battle. People like you have grown up hating our class enemies, but there's not many of us left. God I'd love to get those bastards out, I'll never stop hating them.

But the way things are going by the time we get them out, we'll be the same as they are. What can I say about what happened after the election between you and me?

I don't regret it, but it's not what I want. I don't know what I want. I don't know whether you remember what you said. But the word 'love' came into it an awful lot. Perhaps it was the emotion of the night, or the drink, but I'm just not ready for it. I don't know if I'm in love with you, Gareth. I think I probably said it that night, but I didn't mean it. You probably don't even remember! But I do.

I don't know what I'm going to do, but I'll probably travel a bit, maybe America; there's a speech writing job for a US Senator on offer there. I hope this letter makes a bit more sense when it arrives than when it leaves here. There are other things I can't even come to terms with myself, let alone explain to you.

Good luck Gareth. Love and devotion for ever.

It was signed 'Charlie'.

Greaves put the letter back in the drawer when he heard the front door bell ring.

'Hello, Charlie.'

'Hello, Gareth.'

Her phone call had come out of the blue.

She rang him the day after his Commons attack on Cane over the Saddam raid, when he produced the leaked memo from MI6 revealing the CIA's secret advance warning to the American President about the danger of a backlash.

'I'm not sure whether your visit here is going to achieve anything,' he said.

'I hope so, Gareth, or I wouldn't have asked to see you.'

She looked around the flat. It was much more tidy than she remembered. Sandy's influence.

There were few other signs of her. One picture of them together on top of the television cabinet. And that was it. Perhaps there were more in his bedroom. But that was one room she would not be seeing on this visit to Greaves' flat. She didn't choose to meet him there. She wanted to meet him on neutral territory, a pub or a restaurant, but Greaves had refused. He said it would be 'inappropriate' for them to meet in public, but she could always come to his flat ...

Charlie wasn't sure whether he wanted to see her or not. She half suspected it was an attempt to intimidate her; that he thought she wouldn't accept it.

'Still looks the same,' she said nonchalantly, as she walked past him into the front room.

It saved her having to say, 'Look Gareth, we both know when I was last here and what happened, now let's get down to business, shall we?'

He gestured to her to sit down on the settee.

'I assume Steven knows you're here.'

'Does it matter?'

'Well, you'd better say why you've come.'

'You know that, Gareth, but I'll tell you in my own words anyway.'

'The floor's yours,' he said sarcastically.

'What the hell did you think you were doing going for Steven over the Iraq raid and the MI6 memo?'

'So nice of you to come to the point straight away.'

'I should have thought any MP who sits on the Government benches has a duty to explain it when he acts in a way which is deliberately calculated to damage the party in the run-up to a general election.'

'Come off it, Charlie, there's not a chance in a million you're going to lose the election ... even after the Saddam affair.'

' ... You're?' she exclaimed, 'what do mean you're? That just about sums it up, doesn't it? Even if we don't lose, comments like yours could cost us seats. How d'you think MPs fighting to hold their seats feel about you making it more likely they'll lose them?'

'Actually, I've had a very supportive response from backbenchers to my remarks,' said Greaves. 'You'd be surprised how many agreed with me. Quite a few wrote saying how glad they were that at last someone had the courage to speak out against the leadership. I'd show you their letters, but I don't think they'd want me to, do you? You might still have time to get them deselected.'

'This is bloody ridiculous, Gareth. Do you really think you can spend the election campaign touring the country slagging off your own party leader? You must have taken leave of your senses.'

'I haven't taken leave of anything, Charlie, except the Cabinet of course.' He seemed more relaxed than she could ever remember him. More relaxed even than when she had worked for him when he was a novice backbencher. He had always seemed tense, driven almost. But not now. Something had been lifted from his shoulders, his eyes danced where they had frowned. He seemed ten years younger than when he left the Government. He'd lost weight and the jowls that had made him look prematurely middle aged were gone. She could see the young Gareth, the witty Gareth who had inspired her as a raw graduate. He drove home his advantage.

'I still have the same sense of what's right and wrong that I had when you worked for me Charlie. It's not me who has taken leave of my senses.'

'What are you talking about?'

'There was a time when you agreed with me on these things. What was it you said now? Oh yes, "I'm sick of these new wave backbenchers who want to get rid of everything we have stood for, people who want to nick their opponents' manifesto and put our name on it, people like ... " now what were the names? Yes that's it "people like Cane".'

He spoke the last three words with a slow, drawn out snarl. Charlie felt as though she had been given an electric shock. She remembered sitting in the kitchen of her mother's flat writing the words Greaves was quoting back at her. Good God, he'd kept the letter. He was quoting from it verbatim.

'"I saw all those yuppies and pollsters, I tell you this, Gareth, they're going to be running the party. By the time we get into government we won't stand for anything." Prophetic words Charlie, and all yours, every-single-one-of-them.'

He had a game, set and match expression on his face. Charlie shuddered at the thought of the havoc he could wreak if he ever leaked the letter. He wouldn't dare. She consoled herself that it was highly unlikely. For one thing, he would have to admit to Sandy that he had had an affair with Charlie and she doubted he had done so. Secondly he had written even more emotional letters to Charlie and if he leaked her letter, she could leak his. He couldn't do it, wouldn't do it. Or would he? There was something desperate in his eyes, something she had seen before. It was the same calm, controlled, trance-like expression he had in the Commons that day when he brought Cane to his knees by leaking the Pentagon memo. It was clear to her. He wanted revenge. On her, on Cane, for everything they had denied him.

It was as as though he was possessed. She was frightened, but dared not show it. She would not give him that. She defended herself in the only way she knew: attack, attack, attack.

She advanced towards him, her index finger raised to his face. 'The trouble with you Gareth is you have become eaten away by jealousy. Yes, I did admire you – once – but that was when I didn't know you. You've got a nerve throwing back that letter at me. How old was I when I wrote it?

Twenty five? What did I know about politics? I'm not sorry for what I said. But I've got the sense to realise I – and you – were wrong. Steven was right. Even you can't argue with his record. It's sad what has happened to you. Deep down you know what he has done is right, but you can't come to terms with it because you're jealous.'

Greaves scoffed with contempt, but Charlie rode roughshod over it.

'You've been jealous of him from the moment you asked him to join the campaign to save St Bernard's and he ended up taking it over and then taking the West Ham seat from under your nose. For a while you settled for being his number two, thinking he might make you his heir, but when you could see that wasn't going to happen you chucked it in and now you think your best hope is to undermine him from the backbenches. Every night you go to bed you lie there thinking, "If I hadn't got him involved in the St Bernard's campaign, he wouldn't have gone into politics and I would've become Prime Minister." You're a bitter and twisted wreck.'

Greaves stood his ground, waiting for her to finish and smiled enigmatically, as if to say 'have you finished?'

'I can assure you, Charlie, I'm a very happy man indeed when I lie in my bed these days,' he said, making sure she saw him look at the framed Country Life picture of the girl with long flowing chestnut hair on the wall.

She tossed her head back and gave a manic laugh. 'Ha! Do you really think I'd be jealous of her? You don't love her. You're just pretending. You know Gareth, I feel sorry for Sandy. What a nice middle-class girl is doing with a bloke like you I can't imagine. I can just picture your discussions about all your grand political dreams. What's her contribution? "How will it affect the showjumping world?" I hope to God she knows what you're playing at. You're not going to marry her, it's all a sham, isn't it? Isn't it? Come on, admit it!'

If he had been trying to make her lose her temper, he had succeeded. Usually, Charlie was never more in control than when she lost her temper. Not today.

Greaves never raised his voice; it was one of the things that irked her most about him.

'I'll ignore what you said about Sandy, since your remarks are beneath contempt. They reveal far more about you than they do about her. You're quite right to say that one of us is motivated by bitterness, but it isn't me, you know,' he continued. 'But you know, Charlie, I worry about what has happened to you. You started out bitter with what happened to your father, bitter at the way you were treated at school, bitter at the life your mother had, bitter at the life your brothers had. You wanted to change it all for something better.' Greaves chuckled. 'D'you know, when you worked for me and I used to get a bit down, I'd look at you and think "now there's someone who understands what we're in this for, there's someone who understands what political values really are." But what do you stand for now? I don't think you know yourself. You were so passionate ...

He stopped dead, sensing he was beginning to show more than he meant to, and resumed at a softer tone.

' ... but somewhere along the line you gave up wanting to change it, now you just want to keep the others out – and yourself in. And you'll do anything, anything to achieve it, won't you? That's all it's about now, isn't it? Don't you ever look in the mirror and ask yourself what you're doing it all for? You must be desperate to be prepared to walk through that door and tell me to shut up and stop wrecking our chances. You needn't have troubled yourself. It's not me that's wrecking this party, Charlie, it's you.'

They had fought themselves to a standstill.

'There was something missing in that letter you sent me, Charlie. You said something about "other things I can't even come to terms with myself." What were they?'

The saliva evaporated from her mouth.

He was leaning forward, willing her to explain. His anger had gone.

That letter. He almost knew it by heart. Nearly ten years after she had written it, he could recite every line like a poem learned by rote at school.

He was more familiar with it than she was herself.

'I ... I er, can't remember,' she replied, trying to conceal the flush that swept over her. 'It's too long ago, it was nothing.'

Charlie avoided his eyes. How would he react if she told him the truth?

That she had written the letter after discovering she was pregnant by him; that she panicked; that she was frightened of having her own children; that she didn't think she loved him enough to have his child, wasn't sure if he loved her; that she was sick of politics and could see no future in it for either of them. Every man she had loved had betrayed her, ended up hating her. Her father had turned on her; her brother Billy had turned on her; Stuart Donovan had turned on her. She'd had to get away. America was the perfect way to escape Britain, failure, her party, her family, motherhood and ... him. She had never stopped to think of the effect it had had on Greaves. It was just a one-night stand, wasn't it? They were drunk and needed to escape from the defeat, to find some other emotional outlet.

Five years in America changed her view of everything, of herself, of life, of politics and of politicians. Before she left, she had thought Greaves was the answer. She came back because she knew it was Cane. It was more than enough to make Greaves hate her, and he had not disappointed her.

His feelings were as impenetrable as a dark, dense forest. She had never understood him when she worked for him; she understood him less now. He was deep, complex and shy; but brooding too. It was much easier to understand and warm to straightforward, confident, outgoing Cane.

Charlie had nothing more to say to Greaves. She had said too much already. She just wanted to get out, get away from him. Just like before.

She was determined to show nothing he had said had affected her. And she needed to deliver a warning.

'Frankly, Gareth, I'm tired of hearing this old refrain about Steven and me and how we've betrayed the party et cetera, et cetera. It's all bullshit and I'm afraid I've got better things to do. But I hope you meant what you said about not causing more trouble. You're not the only one who's kept a few letters you know.'

'The same old Charlie, eh?'

'Pardon.'

'Always did like to have the last word, didn't you?'

As she walked away, she glanced at the picture on the wall. She wondered if he had written the sort of love letters to Sandy that he had written to her.

CHAPTER TWENTY NINE

William MacLeish was the type of person who reminded Charlie why she had gone into politics. He had been the Queen's Private Secretary for six years, but had a long way to go to beat the record of his father Sir Edward, who had done it for twenty three.

MacLeish had ruddy cheeks, the kind that went with drinking and hunting, thinning blond hair, and a firm but stocky build. To those he served he was clever and charming; to those he expected to serve him he was supercilious and arrogant. It was in the breeding: he was one of a disappearing species; the cadre of genteel functionaries who were dwindling in direct proportion to the Royal Family. A member of a Scottish aristocratic family who tried to help Charles I escape before the Parliamentarians chopped his head off in Whitehall, a couple of hundred yards from Charlie's office, he had the right CV for the job.

He grew up in his parents' grace and favour apartments in Hampton Court; went to school at Gordonstoun; and eight members of the Royal Family, including the Queen, attended his wedding to a daughter of one of the Queen's Ladies in Waiting. Prince Charles was godfather to one of their three daughters.

MacLeish spent ten years as an officer in the Scots Guards and a spell as a director of the Queen's bank, Coutts, before joining the Palace staff. He was brought in when the Palace came under heavy pressure to reform the monarchy. MacLeish was ideal; steeped in Royal tradition, but at the same time, at forty three, young enough to present the young face needed for the post of Private Secretary to the Queen at the start of a new century. The appointment was seen as preparing for Prince Charles' eventual succession to the throne. The two were good friends and the Prince had often used MacLeish's uncle's castle near Perth for trysts with Camilla Parker-Bowles.

Charlie and MacLeish got off to a bad start after claims that the Queen was angry with Cane for upstaging her at his first State Opening of Parliament when he went on a royal-style walkabout. A Sunday newspaper report said the Queen regarded Cane as 'an upstart' – Charlie knew it was genuine but it wasn't the Queen who had said it. She had heard MacLeish mutter it to a colleague at a Palace reception earlier that week and made sure it received the wider audience she felt it deserved.

Not that their relationship ever had much chance of succeeding. It was doomed from the moment Charlie found out who MacLeish's uncle was. Lord Archie MacLeish was the former chairman of Dawes' Shipbuilders on the Clyde, the shipyard owner who refused to pay her father a penny in compensation when he broke his back falling from scaffolding.

Charlie had often thought of mentioning it to MacLeish, but decided against. He was the type who regarded anyone from the working class who had been successful to be 'chippy'. She didn't want to give him the satisfaction of knowing she had another reason to resent him.

'Good afternoon Prime Minister; Miss Redpath,' said MacLeish, as he ushered them into the ante room, where Prime Ministers traditionally waited a few moments for the Queen's arrival.

'Hi, William,' said Cane.

MacLeish did not grate with Cane, the way he did with Charlie. Cane got on as well with MacLeish as he got on with everyone else. Cane was as 'unchippy' as a man could be. He knew how to deal with the MacLeishes of the world; his own school had been full of them.

In the first few months of his premiership, the Queen was frightened by signs of growing hostility to the Royals. But she had been charmed – too easily charmed in the eyes of MacLeish – by the way Cane persuaded her she had nothing to fear and everything to gain by reforming the monarchy. And the Prime Minister was charmed – too easily in the eyes of Charlie – by the monarch's warmth, wit and wisdom. It was the only thing MacLeish and Charlie had in common; jealousy driven by a fear their master and mistress got on so well together that their two subordinates were redundant.

'Good afternoon, Your Majesty,' said Cane.

'Hello Prime Minister,' said the Queen, removing her half-moon glasses. 'I trust you had an enjoyable Christmas with your family.'

'Yes, thank you ma'am, the children loved the snow. I trust you had a good Christmas.'

'Splendid. Mr MacLeish persuaded me to go for a ride at Windsor in the snow. I hadn't done that for years, it was marvellous. The corgis hated it though, they got stuck in a drift; Philip had to prod the snow to find them, the grandchildren loved it. And what pressing affairs of state are occupying you, Prime Minister?'

The two by-elections caused by the deaths of Poynter and Lewis had been held the previous day. As expected, Darius won Mid-Shropshire and Turnbull won Thames Valley East.

Cane, Charlie and Silverman had agonised over the timing of the general election. They had less than four months left. There was no denying an Opposition revival was under way. As yet it was no real threat to Cane, but it could be. A leadership contest was almost a certainty now that Darius and Turnbull had been elected. Their party would see its chance of an enormous pre-election boost by getting rid of their biggest handicap, their leader.

But it gave Cane an opportunity.

Battling Bathurst would not go without a fight. One in five of her MPs had to sign a motion calling for a contest, a big hurdle. It would all take time or it might never happen. But one thing was certain: the party would be plunged into chaos for weeks as the various factions fought it out.

Charlie and Silverman had convinced Cane he must seize the initiative by calling a general election the moment the by-elections were over. It meant the Opposition would either be stuck with Bathurst for the general election or they would spend the entire campaign fighting among themselves.

'Actually ma'am, I have decided I would like to hold the election on

March 14th, four weeks from yesterday, and I would like your permission to announce, later this afternoon, the dissolution of Parliament.'

'Oh,' said the Queen. She wasn't the only one who was taken by surprise. It was the first time for years that the press had not known in advance of a Prime Minister's visit to the Palace that he was about to call an election.

'How unusual, Mr Cane, to call a general election straight after two by-elections.'

'Yes, ma'am, but I believe it is the only way to end all the speculation; it has reached absurd proportions and I think it is time to, well, time to get it over with, don't you?'

The Queen appreciated his unstuffy way of dealing with the formalities of state. It was only a year or so ago that the Queen had been given the vote. She had no plans to use it. But if she had, and she had lived not in Buckingham Palace but in the Parliamentary constituency of West Ham, she would be very tempted to mark her cross next to the name of Steven Romano Cane.

'Good luck Mr Cane,' said the Queen. She meant it.

* * *

'Joe? Bathurst has called a sudden press conference on TV. We don't know what it's about. Charlie and I need to watch it, I'll call you when it's over.'

'OK, Ronnie,' said Lomax.

Silverman quickly put his mobile phone back in his pocket before striding down the corridor into Charlie's office. She glanced briefly at him. 'It's about to start,' she said.

The victories of Darius and Turnbull were no surprise. What the whole of Westminster wanted to know was how Bathurst would deal with the two new arrivals. Both were far more popular with their party and voters than Bathurst. But, stubborn as ever, she had made it clear she had no intention of standing down just before the election she had spent years preparing to fight.

As Cane was on his way back from the Palace after getting the Queen's permission to dissolve Parliament, a friend at the BBC had phoned Charlie to tell her that Bathurst was holding a press conference in Central Office at Smith Square in an hour. Turnbull and Darius would be there with her. There were no details as to what it was for, but Charlie had little doubt; it would be what she would have done in the same circumstances: get the other two to take an oath of allegiance in public to snuff out all talk of a leadership challenge.

She smiled as she watched Bathurst shuffle on to the mauve platform, Mad Bat's new colour for her party. Pity no one had told her it didn't go with her ice lolly orange blouse. Charlie couldn't help but have a sneaking admiration for the funny little woman who sat behind the microphone, dwarfed on either side by burly Turnbull and preening Darius. Their frames were twice as big as Bathurst's; their egos twice as big again.

Charlie was fascinated by how Bathurst would handle the situation. She looked like a tiny headmistress who had summoned two large school bullies to bang their heads together in front of the rest of the class. Good for you, thought Charlie. What right had they to turn up at the last minute and say to her, 'Move aside, this is a job for a man.' It was great theatre, or at least an amusing sideshow, all the Opposition was good for these days.

'Ladies and Gentlemen, I think you know these two individuals on my ... ahem, left and right ... '

The press corps burst out laughing, as did Turnbull, appropriately placed on Bathurst's left and Darius, equally appropriately on her right. They didn't have the air of men about to be put in their place. Surely she must have told them what she was going to say, thought Charlie.

She had.

'First of all I would like congratulate Mike and Simon on yesterday's Valentine's Day massacre of the Government. Their magnificent success in crushing Cane's puppets in Thames Valley East and Mid-Shropshire will be seen as a watershed in our country's history.'

There was something about her relaxed, sardonic tone that reminded Charlie of Margaret Thatcher's last performance in the Commons, the day after she had resigned, when she seemed to cast aside all her inhibitions, at one point grandly declaring, 'I'm enjoying this.'

Bathurst was enjoying herself. But why?

'What the devil is she playing at, Ronnie?' said Charlie.

'It can't be ... ' he mumbled.

'What? What do you mean?'

'No, it can't be ... I don't know, listen,' said Silverman.

'I expect you're wondering why I have brought you all together today,' said a preening Bathurst. And turning first to Turnbull and then to Darius, 'I expect you two are wondering too,' she grinned wickedly.

'That's a fib actually,' she added, 'of course they know'

More laughter.

'Get on with it, Maddie,' shouted a Cockney voice crouched behind a wide angle lens eight feet in front of Bathurst.

'Thank you, Blackie, you're quite right; I will get on with it.

'Now I know a lot of you have been saying that as soon as these two gentlemen returned to their rightful places in the House of Commons, it'd be curtains for me. And none of you have believed me when I kept saying that it'd be no problem at all. This morning I hope to demonstrate why I'm right and you have all been wrong. Throughout my life I have prided myself on being a realist. The reality of the situation facing the party that I love is this: the general election is only a couple of months or so away and the campaign is about to begin in earnest.

'Unlike some, I refuse to believe we cannot win. The present Government is one of the most dishonest and cynical governments of all time. Oh yes, they're very clever at manipulating the media and the public; they know how to spin, how to deceive and how to mislead. But I sincerely believe that we will be able to show that many of their so-called solid achievements are as solid as a limp blancmange.

'Reality also tells me we are behind in the polls. I don't know by how much, but let's say we have some ground to make up. Now, ladies and gentlemen, to the crux of the matter. When I took on this job, it was the proudest day of my life. I can't say I spent my formative years imagining I would one day lead my party. To be frank, I didn't think I was good enough. But I have never shirked a challenge and when my party asked me to stand, I stood. When I won, well I must say no one was more surprised than I was!'

More laughter from the audience. But Charlie wasn't laughing.

'I have done the job to the best of my ability,' said Bathurst. 'But I'm not vain enough to think that there's no one in the world who could do it better. And I'm not selfish enough to prevent someone better than me doing the job if I thought they could do it better and would have a better chance of winning in the election. Well, it is not true to say there is one person who I think could do a better job. No, ladies and gentlemen, not one.'

By now, the press corps were completely baffled. But Turnbull and Darius were still smiling.

'No, there is not one such person, there are two!' she said triumphantly, holding her stubby little arms behind Turnbull and Darius like a midget impresario introducing a new double act.

'And, as a result, I have decided that it would be in the best interests of my party if I stand down immediately to allow the party to choose a new leader in time for the election!'

A shocked cry went round the room. Several reporters rushed out of the room immediately to file the sensational news:

BATHURST QUITS.

When the hubbub died down, she continued, 'I'd be guilty of a terminological inexactitude if I pretended my initial reaction to them coming back was positive; it wasn't. I'm human. I could see some people might think they would do a better job as leader, and yes, I felt threatened, I wanted to stay leader. But when Lady Hermione intervened and ensured the by-elections took place, I don't mind admitting, I felt degraded, degraded that I had tried to stop them; and guilty that I was putting myself, my vanity, before the interest of the party. I did some very serious soul searching.

'Oh yes, I'm sure I could do a pretty reasonable job as leader in this election but a pretty reasonable job is not good enough. We need someone who will do a brilliant job, ladies and gentlemen. And I submit to you that either one of these two gentlemen,' she held out her stubby arms to the shoulders of each man, 'could do not a reasonable job, but a brilliant one. When the three of us discussed this earlier, both very gallantly said they would like me to be deputy to whichever of them wins and I will do whatever my party wishes me to do.

'Ladies and gentlemen of the press: both these fine chaps have a distinguished record in Government; and since they reflect the two main streams of thinking in the party, I am today calling on our party to ensure this contest is a straight fight involving no other candidates. That will enable us to forego the usual preliminary rounds and settle the matter in one week instead of two or three, thus allowing time to take up the real fight – against this regime of phonies and cronies!'

Two or three of the hardened hacks present were so taken aback by the sheer breathtaking bravado, wit, originality and sheer selfless honesty of her performance that they burst into applause.

Five seconds after Bathurst stopped speaking, Charlie called Cane. He was back from the Palace. The Queen had agreed to dissolve Parliament. There could be no going back. He couldn't return to the Palace and say, 'Actually, maam, could you keep it going for a few more weeks? I've changed my mind.'

'Charlie, we need to work out ... ' he gabbled.

' ... who we want to win, Darius or Turnbull, and how we do it' she interrupted. 'Don't worry Steven, Ronnie and I are doing it now. Come and join us.'

'Well, the Mad Bat's not as mad as we thought,' Charlie said to Silverman when she came off the phone. 'We've got to announce the general election date and work out our response to Bathurst – fast.'

They agreed the result of the leadership contest would be close. Right-wing Darius was more popular among MPs. He was thirteen years younger and better looking, but was still living down the days when he walked out of the last Government complaining it wasn't radical enough. He had mellowed since then, though he was still prone to the occasional rash outburst such as accusing the Germans of using the euro as a 'peacetime Panzer division to create a fourth Reich.'

Turnbull was getting on a bit to be a new leader, but was acknowledged to have been a good Foreign Secretary. The only outbursts he had were if he was kept waiting for the bottle of red wine he had every lunchtime in his favourite French restaurant near his EU office in Brussels before resigning to fight the by-election. He was one of those people who had florid cheeks, were two stone overweight and yet still looked the picture of health, a man of substance. And he appealed to grassroots supporters who now had far more say over the choice of leader.

Darius was taller, with narrow shoulders and a square jaw that made him look like a tailor's dummy. But in the past his physical attractiveness had not been sufficient to compensate for the unattractiveness of some of his political views.

He had the bravery to enter controversies where other less principled souls feared to tread. But sometimes he got it wrong, badly wrong. It had earned him a reputation for being wild, even though many of his controversial views of yesterday had become the conventions of today.

Voters knew what Darius stood for, which was a lot, and were mildly alarmed. They didn't know what Turnbull stood for, apart from Europe and red wine, and they were charmed. Charlie and Silverman agreed there was no reason to alter their view that Turnbull would be a bigger threat electorally, because of his all-round appeal and greater experience. But something else was on Silverman's mind.

'What is it Ronnie?'

'This is not for repetition to anyone; agreed?' he said. Charlie knew that meant Cane too.

'If it's about Darius being gay, forget it Ronnie, it's hardly a big deal,' she said.

'There's rather more to it than that.'

Charlie knew Silverman and Darius were friends at college. She suspected they had had an affair at college, but had never asked.

317

Now, Silverman told her about it, including how he had advised Darius against going through a sham marriage to wife Olivia.

Charlie wasn't sure where the conversation was leading. Everyone at Westminster assumed Darius was gay; thinly veiled references to the fact often appeared in diary columns. But because he was discreet, his wife was loyal – and because homosexuality, to a large extent, had been destigmatised, it wasn't an issue.

When Silverman heard from a gay friend two or three years ago that Darius was still active as an homosexual, he was curious, but not overly surprised. It was risky for a married politician, much more so an ambitious one. But certain gay politicians had a remarkably good track record of finding wives, and keeping them, without ever being caught out.

'I don't understand the relevance of all this,' said Charlie, 'everyone knows Darius is gay, but it's not going to feature in the campaign. No doubt his wife has already flown back to pose as the dutiful Mrs Darius, and since we have three openly gay Cabinet Ministers – including you Ronnie – I can hardly see us attacking him over it.'

'Yes, yes, yes, I know all that, Charlie,' said Silverman, irritated. 'But in all the years I have known Darius, one thing has never changed about him. He is flawed. He's always likely to say – or do – something foolish.'

'You mean he has, don't you?' said Charlie. 'What has he done?'

Silverman told her how he had met a gay stockbroker friend at a Cane fund raising bash six months ago who told him he had had a brief affair with a tall, beautiful young man he met at a gay bar, The Parasol, in Soho.

The stockbroker was shocked to discover that the 'man' was a Portuguese rent boy called Paolo Ramirez who wanted money. He was more shocked when he found out he was sixteen years old and he was even more shocked when he saw a picture of Ramirez with his arm around a man on the bedside cabinet of Ramirez' room. He said it was a picture of a friend called 'Leendsay', but didn't appear to know his true identity.

The stockbroker knew immediately; it was Simon Lindsay Darius.

Ramirez told the stockbroker he had had sex with him just over a year ago, when a drunken Lindsay had picked him up outside The Parasol.

Ramirez was fifteen years of age at the time and Lindsay paid him £500, four times the going rate. 'Simon must have been out of his mind to do it,' said Silverman.

'Ronnie,' interjected Charlie, 'are you sure this is true and if so, can we be clear about why you are telling me this and what you propose to do about it – if anything?'

'Why am I telling you? Because I have had a long time to consider whether I would ever attempt to use this information. And I concluded the answer is yes – but only if Simon ever posed a direct threat to Steven.

'There is no doubt whatsoever that it would completely destroy him,' said Silverman. 'Being gay doesn't come into it. Having sex with a fifteen year old member of either sex is not just wrong, it is illegal. And it is punishable by a prison sentence. And there's another factor. When we reduced the age of consent from eighteen to sixteen, he wrote an article attacking it. It was crass hypocrisy.'

The door opened.

It was Dora. 'Sorry to be bodderin' you Miss, but Mr Silverman office been on. Dey say they need to talk to him urgently but his mobile phone engaged all the time.'

'I haven't been using it,' said Silverman.

'I only tellin' you what I been told,' said Dora, walking out without waiting for a reply.

Silverman reached into his top pocket. There was an echo when he put his ear to the ear piece which disappeared when he pressed the 'off' button.

He phoned his office and told them curtly he would be back in five minutes. It was only next door, after all.

' ... anyway, as I was saying, the point is, Charlie, while Darius deserves to be exposed, we have to decide whether it is in our interest to do so.'

'And the answer to that is?' said Charlie.

'No, or rather, not yet. There's no point in doing it straightaway because if we did it would simply bring about the result we don't want – it would knock Darius out of the leadership contest and hand it to Turnbull on a plate. And that is the last thing we want. But if, on the other hand, Darius were to win ... '

' ... we can use it against him much more effectively,' said Charlie.

'Exactly,' said Silverman, 'we can knock out not just Darius but knock the entire Opposition out of the election.'

'Brilliant, brilliant,' said Charlie.

'But under no circumstances do we do it before we know if Darius or Turnbull has won,' said Silverman.

'Absolutely none.'

'And under no circumstances do we tell anyone else about this conversation.'

'Absolutely none.'

It was too late. Someone else had already heard it.

CHAPTER THIRTY

'I don't care how long it takes, but I'm gonna get you. I don't care how long it fuckin' takes, I'm gonna fuckin' get you for what you and yer mate did to me and my Sheila, you treacherous fucker. I'll fuckin' walk to London if I 'ave to, but I'm gonna get you. Got it?'

Lomax couldn't understand what Quinlan was talking about when he answered the phone.

'But it's all sorted, Tony, you got your money, we all got our money, what's the problem?'

The 'problem', as Quinlan explained mainly in four letter words of one syllable, was that he hadn't got his money. Or not all of it. Lomax had given Williams the £66,000 that Silverman had obtained via Cane's blind trust from Innes's £100,000 donation. Williams was to keep £33,000 and give £33,000 to Quinlan to buy their silence over the euro referendum scam. And that should have been that.

Except Williams had not given Quinlan his money. Lomax had been aware that Williams had not been around at Soho House lately. Quinlan's phone call explained why: Williams had given Quinlan £10,000 in dribs and drabs and said the rest would come in instalments. But he had kept him hanging on and eventually Quinlan realised there weren't going to be any instalments, there wasn't any more money. Williams had spent it. Lomax tracked down his friend who told him he had blown the lot on a City shares spread bet that had gone wrong. The bailiffs threw the Quinlans out of their house and Sheila had left him. Not because they were bankrupt, but because he had told her what he had done. 'I can live with no money, Tony, but I can't live with someone who lied to me.'

Quinlan had no one to take it out on except himself – and Lomax. There was only one way Lomax could rid himself of Quinlan's bloodcurdling menace. And now he had the chance to kill two birds with one stone.

It took him three days to find Ramirez. Lomax knew The Parasol. Lomax had been there several times with gay friends, though not Ronnie. Silverman never went to gay clubs. Lomax went to the club on Friday night, twelve hours after Bathurst announced she was stepping aside as leader. He recognised the barman, Sean, and asked if he knew anyone called Ramirez.

'You mean Paolo,' said the barman. 'He goes to Amsterdam once a month, he'll be back on Tuesday.'

Tuesday nights were Aussie night at The Parasol and it wasn't hard to spot a swarthy Portuguese seventeen year old among a room full of Aussie blonds. Lomax could see how Darius had come to take such a risk.

Ramirez was five foot eleven, with a triangular frame that narrowed to a tiny waist. His glossy jet black hair, tied in a pony tail, was the same colour as his leather jeans and his canary yellow Hawaiian shirt showed off his dark skin and dark eyes. He looked more Cuban than Portuguese and sat at the far end of the bar drinking beer from a bottle, chatting to a man in a suit when Lomax walked in. The barman pointed Lomax in the direction of the canary shirt, adding, 'I'd wait till the other fella's gone if I were you.'

Lomax got tired of waiting, so approached Ramirez.

'Paolo?' said Lomax.

'Oo's asking?' answered Ramirez.

'My name's Joe,' said Lomax, 'we have a mutual friend.'

'Oh yeah, 'oo is it?'

'Look, I'd rather talk about it privately, over a drink maybe,' said Lomax, looking at the man in the suit, who seemed nervous.

'I'm beesy,' said Ramirez.

'It'd be very worth your while,' said Lomax.

He could see Ramirez quickly put something in his pocket.

'Look, I can come back in a minute if you like,' said Lomax.

He had bought enough cocaine himself to know what was going on.

It was a good sign. A man with a drug habit needed money, lots of it.

Lomax knew.

'What you wan'?' said Ramirez, as the man in the suit left.

'I want to know if you know this man?' said Lomax, holding a photo of Darius.

Ramirez studied it. 'Why?' he said, looking at Lomax suspiciously.

'Because it's important.'

'Oo are you?'

'I'm a regular here, ask Sean, he knows me. I'm surprised we haven't met here before.'

Ramirez went over to Sean. Lomax saw him nod in assent.

''E says 'e don' know you well, but you OK,' said Ramirez. 'Oo are you and what do you wan' from me?'

'Paolo, if you know this man I think you would be able to earn a very big sum of money. That is, if you are interested.'

''Ow beeg?' retorted Ramirez.

'Very big,' repeated Lomax.

Ramirez scrutinised the picture more closely.

'Yes, I know 'im. 'Ee came 'ere last year, maybe before, I theenk. 'ee was drunk, very drunk. 'Ee called Leendsay and wear sunglasses – even in the club. We go to my place. 'E pay me very well, very well,' said Ramirez, raising his eyebrows in memory of the fee. 'But 'e get very angry when my friend come home and take a peecture of us. 'E said 'e must 'ave the film but when 'e go 'ome, 'e so drunk, 'e forget!' Ramirez tossed his head back and laughed.

'I keep the picture for fun, my angry eenglishman. You know 'im.'

'Paolo, are you interested in earning some money from this?'

'I am always interested in earning money, Mr Joe,' said Ramirez, 'but it depends 'ow much.'

'I know someone who would pay a lot of money for that picture.'

''Ow much is a lot?'

'More than you have earned in your entire life.'

Ramirez' hand froze a few inches from his mouth, wrapped around the beer bottle he was about to take another swig from.

'Oo is this man? 'Ee famous?'

'Never mind, I'll tell you later, but first, if you really want the money Paolo, you must trust me.'

'OK, OK, I trust you.'

'And you must not say a word to anybody, unless I say.'

It was obvious from Ramirez' reaction that he had no idea of his English friend 'Leendsay's' true identity.

It was also obvious he was most definitely interested in earning a lot of money without asking too many questions. Lomax knew that at some point he would have to tell Ramirez who Lindsay really was. He might take fright when he was told what he would have to do. But Lomax doubted it. They agreed to meet at noon the next day by the Eros statue in Piccadilly Circus. Ramirez was wearing a red silk shirt with the same black leather trousers when Lomax met him there. They walked half a mile to a side street off Piccadilly until they reached an office with a brass plaque marked: Clive Ford Enterprises.

Clive Ford was a most unlikely supporter of Steven Cane. Cane was so horrified when he heard Ford had endorsed him he wanted to disown him publicly. Charlie told him it was not worth the fuss. What she meant was that it was not worth making an enemy of him. Ford had played a part in the destruction of half a dozen ministers in the previous government. If he turned against Cane, he could do the same to this one. Ford's long cavalier moustache, open face and tall upright bearing gave him the air of a Shakespearean actor. He could equally have been a spiv; his accent was half way between Eton and Essex.

He had ruined more people from Eton than from Essex.

When he had phoned Ford the previous day, Lomax said he would do business with him as long as his name was kept out of it. Lomax knew enough about Ford to know he would keep his word.

It was one of the contradictions of Ford's operations that while he traded in human misery, he had his own code of rules and was known to stick to them. Ford knew enough about Darius to know this could be his most spectacular coup of all time. An hour spent talking to Ramirez in his office, and seeing the photo of him and Darius, removed all doubt from his mind.

When Ramirez learned how much money he was being offered, he immediately signed the contract Ford put in front of him. Lomax was too shrewd to sign a contract, and Ford was too shrewd to ask him. Ramirez was whisked away to a country house in Wiltshire to carry out his side of the contract.

Lomax had already carried out his side. He was relieved, jubilant and bursting to tell Silverman, but daren't do so over the phone and he wasn't due back in London from an election trip to his constituency in Cheshire until Thursday night.

'Champagne, eh?' said Silverman, when he walked into the door of his house and saw Lomax standing in the hallway wrestling with the top of an unopened bottle of Dom Perignon.

'A bit premature Joe, it's not polling day for another three weeks and remember what I keep drumming into everyone: anything can go wrong in elections and usually does.'

'I think you'll agree I've got some pretty damn special news,' said a beaming Lomax, when the cork flew out. 'Woah. You're going to be extremely excited with me when you hear what I've done,' he added, gyrating his groin, and thrusting a glass into Silverman's hand.

'For God's sake Joe, behave yourself. What is it?' said Silverman, letting himself flop on to the sofa, taking a sip of the bubbly Lomax had given him. 'I'm tired, it's been a long day and I've got to be up at six.'

'What would you say Ronnie if I ... if I told you ... '

'Told me what, get on with it,' said Silverman, flicking through that night's edition of the Evening Standard.

' ... if I told you that Simon Darius ... '

Silverman dropped the paper.

'What about Simon Darius?' he asked urgently.

' ... that Simon Darius is history,' sang Lomax, thrusting his glass into the air.

Silverman's tired frame went rigid.

'What?' he said, leaping to his feet. 'What the hell are you talking about?'

'Simon Darius is history ... or will be by Sunday.'

'What the bloody hell are you talking about?'

Lomax was non-plussed by Silverman's response. He must know something, surely.

'His under-age Portuguese boyfriend ... it's going to be in the paper on Sunday, they know all about it.'

'What?'

'He's told them his story, the whole lot.'

Silverman grabbed him by the lapels.

'What the fucking hell's been going on, Joe, what have you done?'

Lomax was frightened, confused.

'I found the rent boy, a bloke called Ramirez ... '

Lomax could see Silverman's eyeballs bursting in their sockets, inches from his own; his lips felt the breath pumping out through Silverman's nose.

Silverman shook him, signalling him to carry on.

' ... I took him to ... '

'You took him to who?' shouted Silverman.'

'I don't know why you're angry with ... '

'Never mind that!' screamed Silverman. 'Finish the story, who did you take him to?'

'To Clive Ford – he's on our side Ronnie,' said Lomax. 'Ford has given the story to the News On Sunday,' said Lomax. 'I thought you'd be pleased,' he begged. 'Darius'll be ruined. I thought ... that's what we want ... what you want, isn't it?'

'How the hell did you know?' shouted Silverman, shaking Lomax.

'Ronnie, you're hurting me, stop it.'

Silverman ignored his pleas.

'How-did-you-know? Tell me!'

'I heard you telling Charlie about it ... you left your mobile on after you'd been talking to me. I went to call you again a few minutes later and I could hear you ... telling her about Darius and his rent boy ... '

Silverman let go and threw him on the sofa.

'How dare you?! How dare you listen to my private conversations? You idiot, you fucking idiot. And who gave you the right to go blabbing the whole lot to that piece of filth Ford?'

Lomax was cowering on the sofa.

'No one did, Ronnie ... I thought you wanted it to come out so Darius couldn't be leader.'

'No, you brainless fucking fool! I said that was the last thing we wanted because we don't want Turnbull to be leader. I said we'd only use it as a last resort – if Darius became leader and became a threat to Steven!'

'I ... I ... I did ... n't ... hear ... that bit,' faltered Lomax.

'Why didn't you tell me what you were going to do?'

'I ... thought it ... I didn't want to involve you ... I wanted to protect you. I'm sorry Ronnie, I'm sorry! I always ... let you down'

Silverman ignored him and snatched the phone. He walked into the hall.

'Charlie, we need to meet tomorrow. It's very important. Seven thirty after the election press conference, Downing Street. OK?

Silverman slammed the receiver down.

He turned to Lomax's prostrate body, face down on the sofa. He could hear his muffled sobbing and see his shoulders jerk.

'Turn over, Joe,' said Silverman, coldly. 'Turn over!'

Lomax turned his face towards Silverman.

'How much, Joe?'

'What?'

'You heard! How much? How much did Ford pay you?' He crouched down and grabbed Lomax's face.

'How much did he pay you!?'

'£50,000.'

Silverman squeezed Lomax's cheek bones so hard his lips were forced into an oval with a kink in the middle. The boy thought they would break. They were the same cheek bones Silverman had caressed so often, the same lips he had kissed. How had he come to place such trust in someone so weak, so venal, so corrupt? As he held Lomax's contorted features in his hand, he knew the answer.

He loved the boy. It was irresponsible, irrational, mad, but it didn't matter. He fell in love with him the instant he watched him nimbly weave his way between the tables at The Berkeley the first time they met, his beautifully layered blond hair rising and falling gracefully back into place like a swan's feathers. He adored his face, his young body, his vibrancy, his wit, his mischievousness, his vulnerability, his unpredictability. They were qualities that excited him; qualities he had never had. Lomax had told Silverman he loved him, but Silverman didn't believe it. He may be besotted, but he wasn't stupid. Lomax wasn't the first special adviser to use the casting couch to get to the backbenches. That didn't bother Silverman. But it had come as a shock to learn that what Lomax really wanted him for was money. It made him feel sick. Charlie had warned him about Lomax's devilishness; that he would go too far. And now he had. Silverman knew he should have got rid of him after the referendum affair, but he couldn't bring himself to do it. Now he had no choice. He'd gone too far, much too far. There was only one other thing Silverman cared for: himself and his career. Lomax was going to destroy him. So he had to destroy Lomax.

He let go of his face, fearful of what he might do if he exerted more pressure.

'I had to have it, Ronnie,' spluttered Lomax. 'Quinlan's on my back again ... he's threatening me. He says he wants more money. Marc didn't give him the cash you got from Innes. I couldn't come to you again for it, could I? I thought you wanted Darius brought down, I really did. I thought I was helping – both of us.'

'Get out,' said Silverman, quietly.

'What?'

'I said, get out,' Silverman repeated, his back to Lomax.

'I can't, it's late.'

'I don't care. You're fired. Get out.'

Lomax didn't move.

'What?' he said feebly.

'I said you're fired.'

Silverman turned round, his face whiter than ever.

'If you don't get out, Joe,' he said, hands raised and voice raised in fury as he strode across the carpet. 'If you don't get out, I'll ... I'll ... just get out, get out!'

Lomax rolled off the sofa to avoid his lunge. He got up and ran to the door. Silverman came after him. Lomax thought he was going to hit him. He turned to protect himself. Silverman opened the door and pushed him onto the landing where he fell over. He threw Lomax's jacket on top of him and slammed the door.

* * *

When Silverman met Charlie at Number 10 the following day there were thirty six hours to go before the story was printed in the second edition of the News on Sunday which would roll off the presses at half past ten on Saturday night. Really big scoops, such as this, were kept out of the first edition to stop rivals picking up the story in time for their own late editions on the same day.

'It's my own stupid damned fault,' said Silverman. 'I accidentally left my mobile on before I told you about Darius last week. Joe went to phone me and heard our entire conversation. Remember when Dora came in and said my office couldn't get through it was because my phone was on? I checked and switched it off. Joe had been listening in, but it was only after that that you and I discussed why it was vital to do nothing yet. He didn't hear that bit.'

'And he went off, found Ramirez, took him to Ford and sold the story?' said an incredulous Charlie.

'Yes.'

'The fool, the stupid fool.'

'Why don't you say it? I'm the fool for employing him,' said Silverman.

'Because there's no time for blaming anyone, Ronnie. If only we could stop the story or get it delayed. The leadership contest result is due on Wednesday, and according to the press, Darius is in the lead. If this story appears on Sunday, he will have to resign immediately and Turnbull will get it and Steven will have a real fight on his hands. If only we could get the story held back, they could use it the week before the election and give them no chance to recover.'

'Are you going to make the call or am I?'

Charlie hadn't spoken to Warren McLintock for several weeks, which was unusual for an election campaign. There had been no need. McLintock's papers, *The Globe* and its sister paper, the News on Sunday, had stayed loyal. They hadn't shown the fervour they had at the last election, when Cane was a novelty. *The Globe*'s readers got bored quickly and they had become bored with Cane. As had McLintock. But his only interest was where the power lay. He knew it lay with Cane and would continue to do so after polling day on March 14th. So there was no danger of McLintock, or his papers, straying too far 'off message'. Charlie arranged to meet him on Friday evening at his Knightsbridge apartment. She could not risk being spotted at his office.

Ford had been true to his word. He did not tell the News On Sunday how he had obtained the story. Ramirez didn't know Lomax's surname, and had been warned he would not be paid a penny of his £100,000 fee if he did anything without Ford's approval. Charlie knew she would have to approach the issue carefully. McLintock poured her a Diet Coke and himself a martini. He sat in his penthouse, with his back to a panoramic view of Hyde Park. He was as interested in how she came to know about Ramirez as in what she wanted him to do about it.

Only four people at the paper knew about the story. McLintock, the editor, the chief reporter who interviewed Ramirez and the chief photographer. They would not dare to leak it.

And McLintock knew Ford would never do such a thing.

McLintock's wolf-like eyes searched her for a clue. She lit a cigarette and looked straight back.

'Exactly what is it that you want?'

'Hold the Darius story.'

'Hold it? Why should you care? He's your enemy, he'll be dead in the water, we're doing your dirty work for you,' said McLintock before adding, 'not for the first time.'

'I don't think it will benefit anyone.'

'What exactly does that mean?'

'There's been very little dirt in this election and I think we'll all lose out if this story runs.'

McLintock snorted.

'We'd get along so much better Charlie if you treated me like a grown up, you know.'

'I don't follow.'

'I think you do. You don't want Darius knocked out because you want him to win. You know Turnbull'd be a far more dangerous opponent. He'd give Cane a run for his money.'

Charlie said nothing.

'You know as well as I do that if I don't run this story, Ford'll sell it to one of my rivals, so what's the game, Charlie?'

Charlie looked at him.

'You haven't got the guts to say it, have you? Why don't I say it for you?'

McLintock got up and walked towards Charlie.

'You want me to hold the story this week, let Darius become leader and then use it next week or the week after, just before election day so you can finish them off properly. That way, you won't just win the election, you'll get another landslide.'

By the time he had finished, McLintock was standing over Charlie.

'Am I right?'

She looked up at him, but said nothing.

'Well, well, well.'

He strolled back to his seat by the window. It was more than thirty feet away from her seat. McLintock looked across the park. After half a minute he swivelled round.

'The answer is no, Charlie, that's N-O.'

He saw her take a deep breath. He waited another fifteen seconds, turning up the heat.

She remained silent.

'So it's the fifth amendment is it, Charlie? It doesn't suit you. I don't care how long you sit there dumb, the answer is still N-O. Let me tell you why. You want me to drop one of the best stories we've had in years to help you. Well, it wouldn't be the first time we've done that for a friend, and you have been a friend – though not as friendly as I'd like. And if I did drop it, I'd have to have a very good reason or I'd be risking it appearing in another paper. Once I say no to Ford this week, he can do what he likes.'

Charlie couldn't hold back any longer. 'You wouldn't have to do that, you only need wait a week.'

'Ah ha!' said McLintock triumphantly. 'At last! It speaks! Now we have it from the horse's mouth, don't we? So much for all that stuff about not wanting this sort of mud in an election. You don't want any mud this week, but a nice big bucketload next week would suit you fine, eh? I'll have to try that one out on the Press Complaints Commission some time.'

McLintock circled her like a snake wrapping its coil around a victim.

'Darius isn't even one of yours,' he continued. 'You're asking me to do this to help you get the Opposition leader you want. Forgive me but don't you think all this power you exert is going to your head a little? Not satisfied with manipulating everything that moves in the Government, the civil service and the media, you want to manipulate the Opposition too.'

'Come off it, Warren. You've had a bloody good deal out of this Government. You got a peerage, you more or less wrote the union laws and you've had the sort of access most businessmen would pay millions for and a whole lot ... '

' ... of excuses for not giving me the BBC World Service,' said McLintock, cutting her dead.

It was true: Cane had broken his promise to let McLintock buy the BBC. Charlie floated the idea with a friendly journalist but it had caused a massive backlash led by Melvyn Bragg, David Attenborough and all the other luvvies. They had organised a massive march from Broadcasting House to McLintock's office to protest. More than 200,000 people turned out. It was like the Countryside March against the ban on fox hunting – and had the same result: Cane gave in to Middle England's Militant Tendency.

Cane had promised to compensate him by offering some other deal but McLintock had not forgiven him.

'Warren, I give you my word. After the election, the luvvies can go to hell. Steven can't stand their whining and moaning. We won't have to worry about them. I told him he'd regret putting them all in the House of Lords. Believe me, after the election we won't give a damn about them, we won't have to. You'll get the World Service, I guarantee it.'

A devilish grin spread across his face.

'I may have a solution,' he declared.

'Good, I knew we could sort it out,' she said, brightly.

'Since you are offering me a guarantee, why don't you write it down on a piece of paper?'

'Pardon?'

'I told you: you said you could guarantee I will get the World Service, right?'

' ... Yes,' she replied hesitantly.

'And this whole mess arose because I thought you guaranteed it last time, right?' Charlie didn't answer. 'Right?' McLintock said again.

She knew she was being drawn into a dangerous game. ' ... Ye-es.'

'So this time, you write it down on a piece of paper and sign it.' McLintock walked over to a desk and pulled out a blank piece of paper, removed the cap from his fountain pen and started scribbling. He blotted it, got up and handed it to her.

'It's nothing legal ... just a written agreement between friends.'

She read it.

'I, Charlotte Redpath, guarantee that Steven Cane, if re-elected Prime Minister, will let Warren McLintock buy the BBC World Service.'

She thrust it back at him.

'I can't sign that and you know it,' she said in a flat expressionless voice.

'Why not? After all there is a precedent, isn't there? It's exactly what Cane did when Greaves was worried he wouldn't be made deputy. You told me the story yourself, remember. You said Cane was so fed up with Greaves' paranoia that he would not be Deputy Prime Minister that Cane wrote it down on a piece of paper when they were together on a train one day, "Gareth Greaves will be my deputy" – just like that – and gave it to him. It was a bit of fun, but it showed he meant it. That's all I'm asking you to do. If you mean it, really mean it, you'd sign too, because you'd know I'd only use it against you if you ratted on it.'

Charlie got up and walked towards the door.

McLintock got there first.

'You've got until six o'clock tomorrow night to get the note to me. You know where I am.'

CHAPTER THIRTY ONE

'Madam Speaker, I wish to make a personal statement.'

It was possibly the only sentence guaranteed instantly to pack the House of Commons.

Attendance at the Commons on a Monday was always sparse; many MPs left Westminster on Thursday night and didn't return until Tuesday morning when the committees started. Unlike the chamber, attendance at these was compulsory. It meant they could have a four day weekend, which for the conscientious, comprised four days of opening fetes, visiting factories and schools, a cheese and wine party for local activists and dealing with constituents' problems. For the unconscientious it comprised four days off.

Attendance in the chamber this Monday was even lower than usual. The first Monday of the month always began with agriculture questions. Suckler pig supplements, hill farmers' subsidies and reforming the Common Agricultural Policy are not Parliamentary crowd pullers. Normally, attendance in the press gallery above the Speaker's chair was just as thin. A reporter from Hansard, one or two agricultural correspondents and maybe a lobby journalist trying to catch up on some sleep or sober up.

In any case, most MPs had already gone back to their constituencies to start preparing for the election campaign. It would start officially on Thursday when Parliament was dissolved. Drew Sharpe had not once attended agriculture questions in fifteen years at the Commons. But today he was in his position on the extreme right of the press gallery, directly above the government benches looking directly at the Opposition side. Sharpe wasn't the only reporter making a rare visit: the entire press gallery was packed.

The handful of MPs who specialised in agriculture and were used to conducting their debates in a deserted chamber with no audience, looked up in bewilderment as the audience grew towards the end of their one hour session. After agriculture questions finished at three thirty, a debate on the report stage of the Education Bill was due to begin. It was one of the last pieces of legislation still to be completed before the election.

At three twenty four, a murmur went round the press gallery. A tall, elegant man in a dark blue suit with a taut expressionless face, entered the chamber, stopped at the bar of the House, next to where the Serjeant-at-Arms sat, and nodded in the direction of the Speaker's chair. He walked to the gangway half way along the Opposition benches and climbed the low carpeted steps to the first seat on the left in the third row. It was the position he had chosen when he took his new seat the previous Tuesday.

On that day, he was cheered to the rafters by his own MPs who treated him as a conquering hero. On this day, they looked up at the rafters too embarrassed to speak to him. They knew what he had come to do. Only one thing travels faster along the hundreds of miles of corridors in the Palace of Westminster than the smell of blood. And that is MPs running towards the chamber when they sense some is about to be spilled in it. By the time Madam Speaker rose to her feet at 3.30 pm, the trickle of MPs wandering into the chamber had turned into a flood. They sat in their seats with grave expressions, as though it was their Parliamentary duty to be present, when what had drawn them was the same instinct that attracted the tricoteuses to the guillotine.

'Mr Simon Darius,' announced Madam Speaker.

'Madam Speaker, I wish to make a personal statement.'

It was not done for Cabinet Ministers to take their front bench seats for such spectacles, but they could stand discreetly at the 'bar' of the House, the line on the carpet between the double doors at the end of the chamber and the debating chamber itself. It was a kind of no man's land, which was not officially part of the chamber.

Standing anonymously in the middle of the fifteen or so MPs at the 'bar' of the House, the Chancellor of the Exchequer could not see Darius's right hand which was holding the prepared statement he intended to read out. It was shaking so much that it was blurred; he wished he had printed the text in a bigger type.

'As Honourable Members will be aware, certain aspects of my private life were reported in the newspapers at the weekend. They concerned my relationship with a young man, Paolo Ramirez, I met some time ago. I met him just over a year ago in a night club. As some Honourable members will know, I am gay ... '

An audible gasp went round the chamber.

' ... I am sorry if this statement is shocking or offensive to some people, but I have decided that in the light of what has happened, I have no choice but to be candid with the House and my constituents. I am gay and have been since first discovering my sexual leaning at university.'

Silverman saw Darius survey the government front bench, as though he was looking for him. Silverman couldn't breathe.

'With hindsight, perhaps I should have been honest when I first entered public life and stated openly that I was gay instead of allowing people to think I was heterosexual. It is easy to say that now, but twenty years ago, when I first stood for Parliament, attitudes were very different. It would have been impossible for me to have become a Parliamentary candidate, certainly in my party. That is no excuse for my lack of candour, however, and I am glad to say that times have changed. There are three gay members of the Cabinet, and I hope it won't damage their careers if I say that they include some of the most talented politicians of our day ... '

Silverman mopped his brow.

' ... and I look forward to the day when there are openly gay members of a Cabinet formed by my party. But I digress. I would like to explain in full, the events that led to what happened between myself and Mr Ramirez. To do so, it is necessary for me to go back some time.

'When my wife Olivia and I married, we were genuinely close and we both thought there was every chance the marriage would succeed. The prospect of not having children did not greatly concern her since her main priority was to make a success of her career in banking, as mine was to be successful in politics. The marriage was successful for eighteen years, but over a period of time things changed. To put it bluntly she wanted a divorce. I am not proud to admit that the main reason I was opposed was that I feared it would have a damaging effect on my political career. I feared it would lead to my homosexuality becoming public and that that in turn would prevent me from ever becoming leader of my party. The night that I met Mr Ramirez, I had had a bitter disagreement with my wife. Until then she had been prepared to remain married as long as we led separate lives, me in London and her in Australia with her bank. But she returned eighteen months ago to tell me she had formed a close relationship with another man in Australia and wanted to marry him. Rashly, I accused her of betraying me and ruining my career. She left saying she was returning to Australia where she would file for divorce. I went home and got drunk. I phoned a friend and he said he would take me out to cheer me up. We ended up at The Parasol, a gay meeting place in Earls Court. My friend left but I got talking to Mr Ramirez.

'And ... ' Darius inhaled deeply, ' ... I paid him to sleep with me. To be frank I cannot remember a great deal of what happened because I was drunk. Until I saw the papers on Sunday I couldn't even remember the young man's name. I hope Honourable Members will believe me when I say I had no idea he was fifteen years old at the time. He seemed a grown man to me. Had I known his age I would like to think I would have desisted from what was not just totally irresponsible but also illegal behaviour. But, given my condition at the time, I cannot say with any certainty that that would have been the case. I would like to make it absolutely clear to the House and to my constituents that I hold myself entirely responsible for what has happened to me. I can blame society for my predicament but not my behaviour. I would like publicly to apologise to my wife ... ' Darius faltered. He put his right hand on the back of the row of benches in front to support himself, before straightening. ' ... to my wife who has acted with such dignity and honesty throughout our marriage, to such an extent that she ended her relationship and did not file for divorce because she did not want to harm me. All I can say is ... I do not and have never deserved her.'

338

He halted again. 'And nor do I deserve my party. I am today withdrawing from the contest to succeed the Right Honourable Lady, the member for Kent Downs, as leader of my party and am also withdrawing as Parliamentary candidate for Mid-Shropshire in the general election. Thank you Madam Speaker for allowing me to make this personal statement.'

As Darius sat down, a quiet chorus of respectful 'hear hears' and sympathetic moans emerged from the backbenches, washed over him and was gone.

The cruelty of the Commons didn't stop it being humane, especially when the victims of its blood sport embraced their fate with such dignity, nobility and courage.

And Darius's exit was as dignified, courageous and noble as its cause had been squalid. The man standing in the centre at the 'bar' of the House had never felt more ignoble – or scared.

As Darius resumed his seat, Silverman led the surge of MPs who left the chamber. He had to get out. Most rushed out to put a fresh lump of ice in their gins and tonics left on the bar and to discuss Darius's performance. He dodged a group of reporters waiting in the grey stone-floored Members' Lobby, turned left towards the library, with the Thames visible through its arched window, turned left again as he passed the stairs in front of the tea room, and walked along the ministerial corridor that ran parallel with the chamber and was lined from floor to ceiling with glass bookcases full of red and green leatherbound copies of Hansard debates going back centuries. He reached the Speaker's Office at the end and turned left again, bringing him directly behind the Speaker's chair, where he hoped to get to his room before anyone else could reach him.

Darius was also keen to avoid the scrum he knew would be waiting to ambush him in the Members' Lobby. He left the chamber at the other end, next to the Speaker's chair. As he emerged into the corridor, he saw Silverman walking straight towards him. Darius saw the look of horror on Silverman's face.

'Good God, Ronnie,' said Darius cheerily, 'you look like I ought to feel.'

Silverman stammered, ' ... I ... '

'Don't worry, don't worry, I know what you want to say – you don't have to.'

'Simon, you were so ... '

'Ronnie, you're going to embarrass me. When I said it was all my fault, I meant it. In an odd way I feel a huge sense of relief. It's all out now – I'm out!' he burst out laughing.

Silverman didn't join in.

'Come on Ronnie,' Darius chided. 'I'm damned if I'm going to cheer you up. It's not your fault, for goodness sake. I'm not feeling sorry for myself so you needn't either. I'm sorry about that line about me finding out I was gay at college. I knew you'd be dreading what might be coming next – I looked over to your place on the front bench, but you weren't there. Is that why you're shaken up?'

'No, no ...' said Silverman as other MPs came over to commiserate with Darius.

Silverman composed himself. 'Simon, if there's anything, anything I can do, please don't hesitate to ask – anything.'

'Yes, you can pay for our next bistro dinner in Cambridge,' he laughed. 'Seriously, there's nothing,' he added as Silverman walked away.

'Well I'm blowed,' said a short stout right-wing MP who heard the end of the conversation. 'Always thought Silverman was a nasty bit of work, might have to change my mind about him.'

'Yes,' said Darius, watching Silverman as he disappeared round the corner, 'I've always considered him a loyal and true friend, whatever our differences.'

Silverman walked up the spiral stairs to the narrow corridor, at the end of which was his office. He closed the door, went to the drinks cabinet without turning the light on and poured himself a tomato juice with half a tumbler of vodka.

A very Bloody Mary.

He sat in the semi-dark, drank it, poured a second, walked across to sit in the chair behind his desk, took a deep breath and went to close his eyes, to shut himself off, to think. He couldn't think. He struggled to breathe. As he put the glass on the mahogany table, he saw the red light of the Ansaphone flashing. The throbbing red light was all his eyes could see. He could see two – and both were a blur. He jabbed his forefinger erratically to turn it off, but missed and hit the 'play' button by mistake.

'You have two messages,' said a Dalek-like voice. Silverman stabbed the phone again, but again missed the off button. After the beeps, there was a long silence. 'Fucking phone, go away.' He was about to hit it a third time when he heard a clatter on the recording machine.

He leaned over it and listened. There was a clanking noise. It sounded as though someone had dropped the receiver. Silverman pressed his ear to the speaker. He could hear the sound of choking.

'Ronnie ... '

It was fuzzy and slurred, but Silverman knew who it was. 'Ronnie ... it's me ... ' There was another clatter; the phone went dead.

'You have a second message,' said the Dalek.

Another long beep. 'Come on, come on,' said Silverman, shaking the phone.

'Ronnie, ... I'm sorry.' Silverman could hear the sound of crying.

'Ronnie ... I didn't know ... please ... I want my job back ... please.'

The phone went dead again. Silverman replayed the messages, his hands shaking. He put his elbows on his desk and wept.

He had destroyed the only two men he had ever loved.

CHAPTER THIRTY TWO

It was a piece of television and political history.

The first face to face confrontation between a Prime Minister and the Leader of the Opposition to be broadcast live on air.

Charlie had persuaded Cane to promise to take part in a live election debate on television when Madeleine Bathurst was Opposition leader. No one was more surprised than Bathurst when Cane accepted one of her repeated challenges to do so. Conventional wisdom was that the only person who could gain from such a high risk contest was the underdog; and Bathurst was the underdog's underdog.

But convent girl Charlie never placed much reliance on conventions. The television camera was even more unkind to Bathurst's lopsided features than nature had been in the first place, while Cane sometimes looked more like a TV star playing the role of Prime Minister rather than the other way round.

He glowed under the studio lights; Bathurst fried. It seemed like a good idea at the time. But that was before Bathurst resigned; before Darius quit last week. And before the weekend poll showing the Opposition was making a late surge after Mike Turnbull became leader.

With two weeks to go before the election, amid a growing restlessness among voters since Greaves' resignation and the backlash to the Saddam killing, something strange was happening in British politics; Her Majesty's Opposition was on a roll. No one thought they could win. But a MORI poll showed they had nearly halved the gap from an average fifteen point deficit in the last three months to eight.

It was too late to reverse the decision; in twelve hours Cane had to go on television to face the Opposition leader. If only it was the Mad Bat who would be sitting in the matching black leather chair. There was nothing mad about Mike Turnbull. He was as normal as you could get. The sort of politician who went to football matches because he liked soccer; went to fish and chip shops even when there were no TV cameras there and had given up a cushy £150,000 job in Brussels for the unrewarding task of leading his party because he wanted to give Cane a bloody nose.

Which he had done frequently when the up and coming Cane had his first Shadow Cabinet post as his party's employment spokesman when Turnbull was Employment Secretary. Cane was good, but not good enough to outdebate former barrister Turnbull's engaging mixture of brains and bluster.

He was the one person with the charm and guile to match Cane blow by televisually synchronised blow. If Turnbull had any doubts about Cane's fear of him, they were removed when he offered him the EU post after he lost his Commons seat. While most Opposition MPs were obsessed with the dated right-wing idealism of Darius, Cane, Charlie and Silverman realised Turnbull was, even at 59, potentially, a far more dangerous adversary.

Charlie constantly warned Cane that if Turnbull got back into the Commons through a by-election and replaced Bathurst as leader, it was the only thing that could prevent him winning a second term. It was her nagging that prompted him to give him a one way ticket on the Brussels gravy train. Turnbull would think twice before returning to the derailed wreck his party had become.

So he would have done – until Bathurst phoned him and told him if he and Darius won their seats, she would stand down immediately and let one of them take over. Turnbull was far from confident he could defeat Darius, but even the remote prospect of returning to London and pitching straight into a general election battle with his old sparring partner Cane was too much for the gambler in him to resist. And the thought of handing over his party to the romantic lunacy of Darius without a fight clinched it.

He knew he would be too old to become leader after polling day; they were hardly likely to choose a man who would be in his sixties by the time of the next election. What had he got to lose by going for it now?

When Darius resigned, the first half of Turnbull's gamble had come off. He immediately pulled off a second coup by persuading Darius to change his decision to withdraw as a Parliamentary candidate. His act may have been technically criminal, said Turnbull, but only a handful of people had ever been prosecuted for having gay sex with a fifteen year old – unless there was evidence of coercion.

And since Ramirez was a self-confessed cocaine addict and gay prostitute who admitted the barman at The Parasol had spiked Darius's drinks to coerce him to part with his money, their behaviour was arguably more immoral and illegal than Darius's.

If the electors of Mid-Shropshire forgave him by re-electing him in the general election, then he would have every right to remain in public life – and hold high office. It was the combination of old fashioned common sense and liberal compassion that made Turnbull so popular.

His refusal to employ a spin doctor had its disadvantages; his scruffy suits and lanky hair earned him the nickname 'le vagabond anglais' – the English tramp – from the Brussels press corps. But it was in affection, not in contempt – and 'vagabond' sounded positively dashing in English. But it had its advantages; no one had ever accused him of being obsessed with his image. If he was, he would have cut down on the fish and chips to help conceal the tum that was occasionally glimpsed between his bottom two shirt buttons.

He had something that no image maker could create; a good reputation. A reputation as a good family man – he had four children aged from ten to twenty five (he jovially admitted the last one was a mistake); a good husband – he and his wife Maureen had been happily married for twenty nine years; a good sport - he had an England rugby trial but refused to play against the South African Springboks because his best friend at Oxford was a black exile from apartheid; and a good politician – he was one of the few Cabinet Ministers to emerge from the last Government with credit.

'Don't be intimidated by him,' said Charlie, as she dabbed Cane's forehead with face powder to stop it shining under the studio lights.

She had taken over the job of applying his make-up after a recent interview where he was hurriedly prepared by a BBC girl who made him look like a painted doll. Charlie dabbed his eyebrows, brushing from one side of his head to the other.

She leaned over him, her eyes focusing on his forehead, but she knew he was looking at her. Her bosom, emphasised by her close-fitting black cotton jumper, was inches from his face. He would only have to tilt his head a fraction forward to kiss the small firm white patch of skin that separated her breasts. He was used to having the scent of 'Obsession' about him. But when she was this close she had a different scent, one which Calvin Klein had not yet bottled. It reminded him of Florence.

As Charlie's fingers brushed away the last traces of powder on his forehead, they moved to the side of his temple and rotated in a massaging motion. She lowered her eyes to his. The night at the Hotel Cesari a few weeks ago seemed like years. They had not kissed since; they had barely touched; they had not discussed what happened. She had noted a reserve in his behaviour towards her and wondered if his feelings had changed.

'OK, so what are the three main objectives?' she said, checking her watch. Cane's mind needed to be on Turnbull, not on the honeymoon suite at the Cesari. But Charlie only saw one side of the cauldron of emotions swirling around his head. His thoughts were everywhere except on the most important interview of all the thousands he had done in his career – and which was about to begin in five minutes.

'The economy is in good shape and we need a second term to finish the job we have started,' he repeated in a drone-like mantra.

'Steven, that is not good enough,' she reproached him. 'You're on TV in front of millions, not addressing the annual general meeting of your local party.'

'OK, OK, OK, I know,' he said.

She went to adjust his tie.

'It's OK, I've done it, I've checked in the mirror.'

She backed off.

Arranging the terms of the interview was only slightly less complex than negotiating peace terms in the Balkans. Eventually it was decided to allow the three top interviewers from each network, John Humphrys of the BBC, ITN's John Sergeant and Adam Boulton, collectively interview Cane and Turnbull. Having three political giants of the box join forces sounded like more than any politician could handle; in fact it played right into their hands. Which is why Charlie insisted it was done that way.

Traditional heavyweight political interviews were like boxing matches. Anything from three rounds on Breakfast With Frost to fifteen with Humphrys On The Record – and may the best man win. Knock-outs were rare, but they were always possible if the interviewer got the politician on the ropes and pressed home his advantage. The way to ensure they never landed a blow was to handcuff the television Tysons to each other. Instead of being allowed to throw as many punches as they wanted, they could ask no more than two questions at a time, in turn. It was as exciting as the Eton Wall game.

The format had produced a series of non events in American Presidential elections which, after being hailed as proof that American democracy was the most rigorous in the world, only served to prove it was the most rigged. Charlie knew that; she had rigged one when she was in Washington.

Charlie's US Senator boss came out ahead, though it had nothing to do with his answers. Charlie knew one of the lighting engineers and persuaded him to alter the lights to exaggerate the size of her opponent's large nose and slight double chin, both of which he was self conscious about.

The closely monitored audience reactions showed each candidate fared the same in his answers, but Charlie's man won by a much bigger than expected margin in the 'which candidate do you like the look of best' category. Their opponent couldn't understand how he had ended up looking like a cross between a walrus and a parrot.

By such means was the leadership of the most powerful country in the world decided. Now Charlie had helped bring them to Britain.

There was no blue corner and red corner, but Cane and Turnbull entered from separate sides of the studio. Cane noticed something different about Turnbull's hair. It was a while before he worked out what it was. Then he realised: he had never seen it combed before.

'Prime Minister,' said Humphrys, 'if I may start with you, could you tell us why you think the British people should re-elect you?'

He followed up with the same question to Turnbull: why should the British people elect him instead? The questions that followed weren't quite so straightforward.

'Prime Minister, why do you think your lead in the opinion polls has nearly halved in the last five weeks?' asked Humphrys.

'Well, John,' said Cane, smiling, 'I think you'd find most governments in the western world would happily change places with us. I don't actually pay too much attention to opinion polls, there's only one poll that matters and that is on March 14th, but I think it is clear we have commanded the support of the public right from the start of our term in office to the present day. Very few governments have been able to do that. I can only conclude we must have been doing something right.'

Not too cocky, thought Charlie. Just as well foxy Humphrys didn't have a third bite at the cherry. She could see him champing at the bit.

'May I take up that point, Prime Minister?' said Boulton.

Charlie was surprised. In the American election interviews, the pundits usually deliberately avoided the subjects raised by their rivals in an attempt to show off. Cane glanced at her.

'Notwithstanding your consistent lead in the polls,' said Boulton, 'why do you think it has reduced so sharply in recent weeks?'

Charlie went to strike a cigarette, but the studio manager wagged her finger and pointed to the overhead sign: No Smoking.

'Well, Adam, being in government means making tough decisions. You can't make every decision on the basis that it will win you a point or two in the next opinion poll. You have to govern in the long term interest and that sometimes means taking decisions that may take some time to take effect.'

'Do you not think it is partly owing to the deaths of the two MPs following Britain's role in the assassination of Saddam Hussein?'

Unable to smoke, Charlie rubbed her thumb hard over the flint of her lighter.

'Let me say this to you,' said Cane confidentially but firmly. Charlie anticipated a change in his expression. It followed as Cane tensed his forehead muscles.

'The killing of the two MPs was an appalling act of terrorism. I deeply regret the pain and suffering caused to their loved ones. But I also know of the pain and suffering of the thousands, possibly tens of thousands of people that will be avoided because we played a part in bringing the savage reign of Saddam to an end. I say here and now, I am proud that we did that though of course it can never compensate the families of the two MPs who died.'

It was Sergeant's turn. Phew, thought Charlie, a change of tack.

'But in the light of the disclosure that the Americans pulled out of the attack on Saddam because they were warned of a terrorist backlash, do you not feel you were let down by our biggest ally?'

Shit! She closed her eyes and threw her head back. The three of them were acting as one, each developing his predecessor's line of questioning, making it the equivalent of a tough one-to-one confrontation instead of a shambolic free for all. They'd stitched Cane up.

His furrow deepened.

'As you know the United States Government is holding an inquiry into those allegations, so I cannot comment on them, John. But I think it is worth remembering that while it is possible for broadcasters to play fantasy politics; to imagine what might have been and pretend they have the power of hindsight; I'm afraid Prime Ministers do not have that luxury. When you are Prime Minister you have to decide what to do in the best interests of your country and your people, and sometimes those decisions have to be taken quite quickly. I do not claim to be perfect, but I am prepared to be judged on the decisions I have taken by the people of this country on March 14th.'

Charlie eased her grip on her lighter; he had kept his cool – just.

'Mr Turnbull,' said Humphrys, 'do you think it is reasonable to ask people to elect you as Prime Minister when you have only led your party for two weeks?'

'I think it's eminently reasonable, after all, it's not as if I'm a new boy,' said Turnbull, with the disarming schoolboy cheek that made him seem more like 29 than 59.

Clever, thought Charlie; he has confronted his biggest weakness – his age – head on and made light of it.

'People know my record,' said Turnbull. 'I hope they remember me for making a pretty decent fist of Foreign Secretary in the last Government and for helping to steer the EU through difficult times in the last year or so.'

'But you didn't even write your own manifesto, it was written by your predecessor, Madeleine Bathurst. Can you assure us you have actually read it?'

Turnbull burst out laughing.

'Yes, Mr Humphrys.' No senior politician was less stuffy than Turnbull, but he never referred to interviewers by their Christian name.

'I have read it, though I can't promise I can tell what it says on page twenty four, paragraph five, subsection three. The point is everybody knows instinctively what our party, sorry my party – forgive me, it still sounds strange – stands for: individuals, competition, liberty, choice, freedom,' he said, placing his palm on the arm of the chair to emphasise each point. 'Every manifesto we have ever published stands for the same values.'

He pointed across the studio. 'Unlike Mr Cane over there, whose party's policies and values have changed more often than the traffic lights in Parliament Square.' Turnbull let out one of his cheery chuckles.

Charlie had never felt like laughing less.

'But you only became leader because your chief rival for the job was forced to stand down for personal reasons, didn't you?' said Boulton. 'Your own party preferred him to you, so why should the public make you first choice if you were only the second choice of your party?'

'I don't accept for one moment I would have lost to Simon Darius. And since the contest never took place you can't possibly know either. In any case Mr Cane had already been kind enough to make me his own first choice when he appointed me to the Commission. I keep reading in the papers that he did it because he was frightened of me becoming leader of my party.'

Now the studio audience was laughing. With Turnbull and at Cane.

'I don't want to seem ungrateful,' said Turnbull, 'I was flattered by his decision to send me to Brussels. I only hope I haven't frightened him too much by coming home.'

It got the best laugh of the night.

At the end of the hour-long interview Cane walked off and made straight for his car, waiting outside. He didn't bother to go to the 'green room' – the celebrity suite where guests normally go for a drink with the hosts to relax after a show.

Charlie got in beside him. Cane's eyes remained fixed straight ahead.

'Well done, Steven,' she said briskly, turning towards him and putting her hand on his thigh, first making sure it was out of view of the chauffeur's mirror.

'He came up with the sort of cheap wisecracks we expected,' she said. 'It looked smug; you were much more statesmanlike, much more. If that's the best Turnbull can do, we haven't got too much to worry about. I thought he'd take it much more seriously than ... '

' ... Don't,' said Cane, removing her hand from his leg without looking.

'Don't what?' said Charlie turning face on to him.

'He won.'

'Don't be ridiculous, he may have shaded it here and ... '

'Don't lie to me!' he shouted, his face contorted with fury.

'Steven?' said Charlie, recoiling. She had seen him cross with others, though even then he never lost control. He didn't have a temper. His anger was like the rest of him, moderate in its nature. He had never even raised his voice with her, until now. This was not the Steven she knew, the Steven she had loved. He could see the effect his outburst had had on her. He didn't apologise, but repeated himself, though this time calmly.

'I said, don't lie to me, Charlie, he made mincemeat of me. We're in trouble.'

The quietness with which he spoke was, if anything, even more chilling than his rant a few moments earlier. She had never seen him like this.

They left the studio in silence.

CHAPTER THIRTY THREE

The Queen had given up taking her favourite horse, Misty, out for a gallop some time ago. It was MacLeish who persuaded her she should ride more often and that a gentle gallop round Windsor Great Park or Sandringham would be good for her. One of the princes had joked to MacLeish that if the Queen had to choose between giving up her crown or giving up her stable, it was a two to one on bet that the crown would go first.

He was not a natural rider. He had had two bad falls as a child which put him off, but he forced himself to overcome his fear. Not all senior Palace officials rode. But those who did found it much easier to get on with the Royals; and MacLeish was keener than most to get on. He had joined Prince Charles's Beaufort Hunt, but only hunted with them when the Prince did. He occasionally rode with Camilla to keep her company when the Prince was abroad.

It was a chance to talk to her alone about how to improve her public image, her future with Charles and how to deal with the young princes as well as her own children. But MacLeish's success in getting the Queen to ride more regularly gave him even more satisfaction.

'THE ROYAL HORSE WHISPERER,' was how *The Globe* headlined its exclusive report. It was accompanied by a picture of them galloping past the Copper Horse, the giant statue at the end of the Long Walk in Windsor Great Park. The Queen was surprised and angry that it had been published. The only person who had taken a close up was someone who appeared to be a tourist. MacLeish was less surprised – and even less angry.

It was he who had arranged for a photographer from *The Globe* to be tipped off, dressed as a tourist.

They were back at the Copper Horse today, looking in a straight line down the wide gravel driveway of the Long Walk to Windsor Castle, clearly visible two and a half miles away at the other end. Their only company was a young armed policeman who had just joined the Royal Protection squad, who was riding 100 yards behind them. Other police in Land Rovers remained further back, hidden. As they began to descend the slope at the start of the Long Walk, MacLeish said, 'What do you say we try a trot, ma'am?'

'Why not, William? Just a little way perhaps,' she said.

'You first, ma'am.'

The Queen waited until the slope evened out, dug her heels gently into Misty's ribs and relaxed the reins. The six year old chestnut mare broke into a sedate trot. MacLeish had been unable to ride his own horse, Scarlet, which had strained a leg muscle. He had borrowed another horse from the castle stable, Hatty, one of Prince Charles's favourites.

Scarlet had learned to adopt the same position as MacLeish, slightly behind whichever particular member of the Royal circle they were with that day. But bringing up the rear was a new experience for Hatty, who was used to leading from the front under the firm hand of Prince Charles.

She didn't like it at all and had no intention of deferring to Misty – or a monarch. MacLeish pulled the reins in as hard as he could against Hatty's bit. She shook her head furiously as he battled to hold her back. It was too much. No sooner had the Queen started a slow trot, than Hatty was bursting to break into a gallop. MacLeish fought to control her.

'Oh, please, control the horse, I can't cope,' cried the Queen.

'Don't worry, ma'am, I'll stop her.'

But he couldn't. Hatty veered into Misty and one of its rear legs kicked Misty in the ribs as Hatty finally broke free with MacLeish powerless to stop her. His mount set off towards the castle like a race horse entering the final furlong.

MacLeish tried frantically to stop her, but it was no use. He looked round to make sure Misty hadn't given chase. He thought he saw the horse buck when Hatty kicked it, but he wasn't sure; he was too busy hanging on for his own dear life.

He cursed himself for taking out Charles's fastest horse. The Prince had warned him it was headstrong; far too strong for MacLeish. Hatty was galloping pell mell towards the busy Old Windsor road, which crossed the Long Walk half a mile from the castle, and MacLeish was powerless to do anything about it.

He was terrified of falling off; terrified the horse would not stop at the road which was always full of tourist coaches; terrified it would charge straight across. But he had a far bigger fear: that the Queen's horse had bolted too.

He tried to look behind again but nearly fell off. With luck the Queen had stopped her horse safely and dismounted. At least the policeman riding behind them would have come to her help. MacLeish could see a tourist coach stopped on the road ahead. It had slowed to a halt so the passengers could catch a glimpse of the castle at one end and the Copper Horse at the other.

The blurred printed letters of the coach company on the side of the vehicle doubled in size every few seconds as he hurtled towards it like a human zoom lens.

If Hatty didn't slow down now he would smash into the coach or the horse would swerve and charge straight across the busy road. MacLeish was too scared to jump off; in any case his left foot had gone right through the stirrup and his ankle was trapped. Whatever he did he could be killed.

He was about to shut his eyes when his body was thrown forward on to the back of Hatty's head. She was pulling up as violently and uncontrollably as she had set off. The horse stopped twenty yards in front of the coaches and stood, snorting, as though it had all been a practical joke. MacLeish, dripping with sweat, plunged to the ground with his left ankle still stuck in the stirrup and twisted 180 degrees. He shrieked in agony as he extracted it; it must be broken, but he was relieved to be alive.

He looked back up the driveway. He could see two horses standing in the middle, some 600 yards away. Both were riderless. He saw the dark blue figure of the policeman crouching. Underneath him was a body.

354

It was motionless.

Behind them on the horizon was the mocking and sedate figure of the Copper Horse, a picture of equine elegance.

* * *

'I suppose this is what they call a wobble,' said Charlie.

Silverman had come to her office at half past seven that evening to review the second week of the three week election campaign. Cane had joined his family for supper.

Margaret Thatcher's government wobbled in her third election when, a week before polling day, she was convinced she was going to lose to Neil Kinnock. She didn't. The same happened in reverse next time round, when, four days before the vote, Kinnock, this time firm favourite to win, suddenly thought he might lose.

He did.

'We're eight days away from polling day and they are six points behind us,' said Charlie, removing the coffee cup so she could use the saucer as a second ashtray. The first was overflowing with lipstick-stained stubs. 'It was sixteen two months ago, sixteen! I don't like it, I don't like it. They're bloody well catching up.'

'They may be catching up, but they're still nowhere near – they'd need another month to get anything like close. And they've got a week, one week.'

She got up from her seat and grabbed a Diet Coke from the fridge.

'You're tired – we're both tired and we both need to calm down,' said Silverman, 'it's been a difficult two weeks.'

They were still shaken by the resignation of Darius. Silverman had told Charlie how Lomax had come to help Ramirez sell the story, and how he planned to give Lomax his job back to keep him quiet, but not until after the election. They didn't tell any of it to Cane.

To rub salt into their wounds, Turnbull's arrival as leader had exactly the effect they feared. His ratings rose again after the television confrontation.

'We just have to keep calm,' said Silverman, swivelling in a chair by Charlie's desk as she paced the room. 'A six point lead going into the last week is more than any governing party has a right to expect. All we have to do is to play it straight, not take risks, not make mistakes.'

Charlie didn't reply. She wasn't looking at Silverman. She wasn't thinking about the threat from Turnbull. She was thinking about the threat from Greaves. Ever since Cane had become leader his personal popularity had run miles ahead of that of his party's. Now it had slipped behind. For the first time the party was more popular than the leader.

And one private poll showed that a majority of party supporters thought it might do better under a new leader. It led to a front page story in the Telegraph alleging a group of thirty three MPs were secretly preparing to start a campaign demanding Cane's resignation if he lost the election. The name of the person they wanted to succeed him? Gareth Greaves.

Greaves had taken little part in the election campaign since attacking Cane over the Saddam killing. Committing treachery against a leader may help get rid of them, but it didn't help you succeed them. Michael Heseltine learned that the hard way.

Losing the election to Turnbull was unthinkable; losing the leadership to Greaves would be unbearable.

'It would help if you stopped concentrating on what Greaves might do next,' Silverman snapped, correctly second guessing her thoughts. 'We aren't going to lose the election and Greaves isn't going to take over, will you get that into your head, Charlie? It really is time you gave up this obsession with the man.'

'I don't know what you're talking about. I can assure you my only obsession with Greaves is to make sure he doesn't ruin Steven's premiership. If that's an obsession, then I plead guilty.'

Silverman got up and walked across to Charlie, who was looking out of the window onto Downing Street. He put his arm on her shoulder.

'Come on,' he said quietly, 'we're doing exactly what you shouldn't do in a wobble; argue among ourselves. There's no need. Steven's got two pages in *The Globe* tomorrow and McLintock promised to put it on the front to make up for doing over Darius and landing us with Turnbull.'

Charlie turned round. 'You're right.'

As she sat down at her desk, her mobile phone went off.

She answered it.

'Jesus! When? ... What happened? ... That's all you know? ... Thanks.'

Silverman was straining to listen across the desk. Charlie put the phone down and stared blankly at him.

'You can forget about those two pages in *The Globe* tomorrow, Ronnie. He'll be lucky to make two paragraphs. That was the Palace. The Queen's had a riding accident. It's bad, she's in intensive care.'

She underestimated *The Globe*. There were four paragraphs about Cane; there were twenty pages on the Queen.

'QUEEN FIGHTS FOR LIFE,' was the front page headline, surrounded by a black border.

Even the sniffy Guardian devoted eight pages to it. Its front page report said:

'The Queen was unconscious in intensive care in hospital last night after a riding accident in Windsor Great Park.

Campaigning in the general election ceased as a mark of respect, following the incident in which the Queen fell from her horse when it is believed to have bucked as she was returning to Windsor Castle yesterday afternoon.

She is thought to be suffering from serious neck and head injuries. A statement by a spokesman for the St Margaret's private hospital, Windsor, half a mile from the scene of the accident, said she was in a "critical condition."

The Queen went riding yesterday with William MacLeish, her private secretary. Mr MacLeish's horse bolted at the same time, causing him to fall off several hundred yards away from where the Queen was hurt. He suffered cuts and bruises.

An armed policeman, who was following the pair, was first on the scene.

He radioed for an ambulance which took the Queen to the nearby St Margaret's hospital. Her condition is thought to be too serious to move her to a bigger hospital.

Prince Philip and the Queen's four children, Prince Charles, Princess Anne and Princes Andrew and Edward, were at her bedside last night. Prime Minister Steven Cane led a flood of messages from well-wishers all over the world.

Announcing an indefinite suspension of the election campaign, Mr Cane said, "We wish our beloved Majesty a swift and speedy recovery. Our thoughts and prayers are with her and her family".'

The ashtray had been emptied by the time Charlie was back in her office at five to six the following morning. There was a scribbled note on the desk.

'Do not stub cigarets in sorcers, or we only give you paper cups.' Charlie didn't need to look at the signature. The Queen was at death's door; the Prime Minister was in danger of losing his job in six days; and Dora's only concern was that Charlie had used a saucer as an ashtray. She struck her lighter, held it to the paper, held it while it burned and dropped the ashes into the saucer. Five minutes later, when Cane and Silverman arrived together, Charlie was putting the phone down.

'MacLeish has been on. She's stable but unconscious and still critical,' she said as they sat down. 'She's broken her neck and is on life support. It could be some time before they know if she's going to live.'

'How long?' asked Silverman.

'They don't know,' replied Charlie.

Cane didn't have much time either. Polling day was only six days away and within hours of the accident, radio phone-in programmes were flooded with calls demanding the election be postponed out of respect until the Queen's fate was known.

Charlie was convinced that after the shock of the accident, the next day's big story would be whether or not the election should go ahead. The usual daily election press conferences had been cancelled today; as had Cane's plan to fly to Norwich for a whistle-stop tour of East Anglia. But should the campaign resume? If so, when?

Cane had consulted the Attorney General the previous night. Under Section 20 of the Representation of the People Act 1985, an election must be postponed for two weeks if the monarch dies during the campaign, but there were no rules if the monarch was ill.

'We have got to play it by the book,' said Cane.

'Turnbull will jump on the bandwagon and say the election should be put off because he knows he's gaining,' said Charlie.

'Any delay will help them and they're ruthless enough to use anything to win.'

She was beginning to regret not having shown Cane some of the more depressing private party polls showing that Turnbull was even closer to them than the published polls suggested. She had done it to protect him. It didn't seem such a good idea now.

'I hear what you're saying Charlie. I still say we have to play it by the book. Let's talk to the Palace. See what they think.'

* * *

'ELECTION CHAOS' screamed the *The Globe* the next morning, claiming there was mass confusion over whether the election would go ahead or not. Inside were articles stating the case for and against and others trying to work out how the accident had happened.

Charlie looked up from the paper in the back seat of her chauffeur driven Mondeo as it curled round a steep road alongside a massive wall, took a sharp left turn off and passed a forbidding black statue of Queen Victoria. Two guardsmen wearing bearskin hats stood between a crowd of people and the gates of 900 year old Windsor Castle. Charlie felt she had waited almost as long for this opportunity.

MacLeish took her to the temporary office he set up after the accident, where they sat alone. Beneath his desk, she could see his left leg was in plaster.

'How is she?' said Charlie.

'Her Majesty is still unconscious,' he said, glaring, noting her deliberately offhand tone and failure even to acknowledge his injury. 'But she is off the danger list, thank the Lord,' said MacLeish. 'We're very grateful for the way the Prime Minister acted so quickly in suspending the campaign.'

'We believe in doing things properly.'

'Yeees,' mused MacLeish. 'We've er ... been thinking about what should happen next Thursday, election day,' he said awkwardly.

It was something Charlie had observed him do before when making a remark that was anything but casual. She was tempted to ask who this 'royal we' was. Not the Queen; she was unconscious. The Duke of Edinburgh? Prince Charles? The entire Royal Family? Or was 'we' MacLeish? As the Queen's most senior personal adviser they would rely heavily on him, especially since they knew she had such a high regard for his judgement.

'What do you think?' said Charlie, determined to make him play his hand first.

'It is not so much what we want to do, but rather our keenness to take heed of what the people want us to do.'

Charlie stifled a derisive laugh.

'They do seem to think,' said MacLeish, ignoring her reaction, 'that the election should be deferred – and I have to say we are in accordance with that view. We are deeply conscious of what has happened in the past when we did not pay sufficient attention to the wishes of the people and we have no desire to make that mistake again. In short we do feel that the election should be postponed for two weeks. We consider that that is what Her Majesty would want. Indeed I think I'm right in saying there is a law along those lines.'

'That law relates to the death of a monarch, not an injury to one,' said Charlie without emotion. 'And I must say you seem to be very sure all of a sudden of what the people think.'

'It is you who taught us the importance of doing so, for which we are grateful,' said MacLeish. 'And I must say I regard your insolent tone as an insult to Her Majesty, Miss Redpath. You have made it quite clear from the start that you abominate both me, her and the entire institution of the monarchy, but I should have thought that even you would have had the common decency to show some respect at this particular moment, that is if you know the meaning of the words.'

'Do you really, Mr MacLeish?'

'Yes I do,' he harrumphed.

'And tell me Mr MacLeish, do you think the people have an equal right to know how the accident happened?'

Charlie saw him swallow hard.

'Perhaps you'd care to elaborate.'

'I think you heard. I said: do you think the people have a right to know what happened?'

'I'm sorry ... '

'Oh puh-lease, Mr MacLeish, puh-lease.'

'I don't ... er ... follow.'

'Let me explain then. Do you think the people have a right to know the reason the Queen fell off her horse was because you were stupid enough to encourage her to race back to the castle even though you were riding a horse you couldn't handle that kicked hers and threw her off?'

MacLeish was trying – and failing – to conceal the terror in his eyes. Charlie hadn't wasted the eighteen hours that had elapsed between his phone call yesterday and their meeting today. She had made some interesting discoveries.

By the time MacLeish had got his ankle out of the stirrup, checked it wasn't broken and limped back to where the Queen had fallen off her horse, she was being carried into an ambulance, surrounded by paramedics.

He thought she was dead.

He wandered off in a daze and collapsed under the trees on the grass verge, sobbing, 'It was my fault, I told her to trot and Hatty bolted. I've killed the Queen! I've killed the Queen!'

He didn't hear the young policeman who had been following them approach him from behind to console him. But the policeman had heard MacLeish; MacLeish could see from his stunned look. It was the look on a child's face when they heard something terrible they knew they shouldn't have heard, that they wished they hadn't heard.

When MacLeish came to his senses later that night he knew what to do. Formally interviewed by police later in the day, he denied making the remarks, claiming the inexperienced young policeman must have been confused. MacLeish told them he now thought he could remember a loud noise which had frightened the horses, a gun perhaps.

The young officer who had found him stuck to his version of events, but after being told the consequences for his career of accusing the Queen's Private Secretary of lying, he soon backed down.

MacLeish's 'confession' was scotched from the official record. But the official record was not the one Charlie got when she used her own contact in the law enforcement agencies.

'Where did you hear these lies?' said MacLeish confidently, his well honed instinct for self preservation kicking in hard.

'There is only one person who's been lying and it's you, Mr MacLeish. And if the original report filed by the young policeman you browbeat into changing his account should ever fall into the wrong hands, you'd have to flee the country – especially if the Queen dies.'

Charlie let the last four words 'if the Queen dies' – sink in slowly, until they reached the pit of MacLeish's stomach. She could see him squirming in his seat.

'As I ... as I ... said, Miss Redpath, I think you have been misinformed,' he said unconvincingly.

Charlie moved in for the kill.

'I don't think so, Mr MacLeish. Now. Shall I tell you how I see it? The way I see it,' she said, swinging round in her seat while he sat rigid, 'is that there are great dangers in deferring the election. Of course if you ask us to do it, we could, but now that the Queen is off the danger list, I think there is a danger it might be seen as an ... an over-reaction, shall we say? For example, it would be particularly unfortunate if people thought certain royal courtiers were making mischief out of this because of their support of the Opposition and were trying to delay the election in the hope that they might have a better chance of winning in a month or so.'

'What are you talking about?'

'I'm talking about the senior royal courtier who gave £150,000 of the personal fortune he inherited from his shipping father millionaire to the Opposition's election fund six months ago. I know you're rich, Mr MacLeish, but surely even you remember writing a cheque out for that amount?'

The law enforcement agencies were not the only special sources Charlie had access to. Charlie pictured what was going through MacLeish's petrified mind: the destruction of his reputation, the sack from the Queen's service, banished by his family, his name dragged through the papers. It would mean exile; prison even, for trying to pervert the course of justice. He started to shake.

'Don't expect any sympathy from me, you creep.' She stood directly in front of him. 'Pull yourself together. Now then, here's what I think we should do. I suggest you start listening. D'you hear me, MacLeish?'

How good it sounded to call him that. MacLeish. Like a common criminal. He nodded meekly. She stood up and strutted round his office, glorying in her domination of him.

'What I think we should do is for you to persuade your people that the dangers of the unelected royal family doing anything to interfere in the democratic process are too great to ask for the election to be deferred. If you do decide to do that, I should have thought you might just as well make a virtue of it and make it known publicly that far from wanting the election to be deferred, the people's monarchy would very much like it to go ahead. Why not see it as a decent and respectful statement of how the monarchy has changed to be in tune with the new millennium? Of course there'd be no need for you actually to make an announcement, we could handle all that for you at Number 10. All you need do, MacLeish, is to indicate your approval. Why don't you call me tonight to let me know your reply?'

She picked up her bag nonchalantly, and strode to the door. 'I'll let myself out.'

Her car was waiting for her in the courtyard. Charlie walked directly towards it without once looking at the castle courtyard all around her. She got in.

'Downing Street, ma'am?'

'Yes.'

Through his rear view mirror, the driver saw her reach into her handbag for a handkerchief and dab her eyes. He was barely out of Windsor town centre when he saw her keel over onto the seat.

He pulled over and stopped. They were on the Old Windsor Road, next to the Long Walk. The driver jumped out, opened the rear door and leaned towards her.

'Miss Redpath, Miss Redpath, are you alright?'

She was wailing. He pulled her up by the shoulders. She was holding something to her breast. She released it just enough for him to see it. It was a small, creased, black and white picture of a man, a tall proud man in a cloth cap, standing on a platform, his hand aloft in leadership, addressing a huge mass of men on a dockside with row upon row of derricks in the background; an enormous ship, clad with scaffolding; and in the foreground, to one side, a banner which read: 'PAY UP MACLEISH.'

Charlie was muttering the same sentence over and again. 'That was for daddy, that was for you daddy, that was for you daddy; I did it daddy, I did it daddy, I did it daddy. I got them, I got them, I got them for you.'

She let the driver hold her. 'Alright, ma'am, alright ma'am, calm down now, calm down now.'

* * *

'And now follows a special broadcast by the Prime Minister, which is being shown simultaneously on ITV,' said the announcer.

'Three days ago, this country was shocked by the Queen's tragic riding accident in Windsor Great Park. Like millions of other people, I and my family were devastated by the news. Like millions of others we have prayed that she makes a full recovery.

'Indeed, all our hearts were lifted today by the confirmation that Her Majesty is no longer on the danger list.

'As you will know, the election campaign was suspended as a mark of respect for her. There are now four days to go before polling day and we have to decide whether to continue with the election or whether to defer it to a later date.

'Strong opinions have been aired for and against. My initial view was that we should defer it. There are still three months remaining in the five year Parliamentary cycle and it would be possible to delay the election for several weeks. But before making a decision as Prime Minister, I felt it was appropriate to consult the Royal Family to consider their views.

'It was their strongly expressed opinion that Her Majesty would not want the democratic process interrupted. They said that under no circumstances would she want the election deferred on her behalf and that, to the contrary, she would not want her injury to disrupt the everyday life of the country or affairs of state.

'Their view was clear: we should go ahead and hold the election on Thursday as planned. I have thus decided that the Royal Family's wishes should be respected and the election will go ahead. The Royal Family also said the suspension in campaigning should end immediately so that the last few days of the election could proceed normally.

'I would like to take this opportunity of expressing my genuine and humble personal thanks to them for the love and support they have shown to the Queen, the dignity they have shown in grief and for the courage and leadership they have shown to us, their loyal subjects.'

The broadcast ended with the National Anthem.

CHAPTER THIRTY FOUR

'Good evening, this is Trevor McDonald with Election News. The polling stations have just closed in the general election and according to an ITN exit poll, Prime Minister Steven Cane is heading for victory. Our survey indicates that he could have a Parliamentary majority of 39 seats.

'If the findings are accurate, Mr Cane's majority is a considerable reduction in his margin of victory at the last election. But it still provides him with a clear mandate to rule for the next five years. Likewise, Mr Turnbull's performance is a huge improvement in his party's poor showing last time, but it shows his party still has some way to go before voters feel it can be returned to power.

'The election was dominated by the Queen's riding accident which led to campaigning being suspended for three days. After consulting the Royal Family however, it was decided not to defer polling day. The latest statement by Buckingham Palace on the Queen's recovery says she has now regained consciousness. Surgeons are not sure whether she will make a full recovery from the broken neck she sustained in the accident, but say she has responded remarkably well to treatment.'

* * *

Cane was at West Ham town hall on polling day, waiting for the last few boxes of ballot papers to be sorted when the first results came through from Sunderland just after eleven o'clock and Torbay one minute later.

Victory in Sunderland and narrow defeat in Torbay, but both followed the same voting trend predicted by the ITN poll; the opposition gaining votes, but not nearly enough to win the election.

He was in his car on his way to a victory party at London's Festival Hall, when Turnbull conceded defeat at two thirty am on Friday morning as Cane notched up the magic number of 326 seats needed to command an overall Commons majority. Charlie was with him; Lucy had stayed at Number 10 with the children.

'You've done it, Steven, you've got your second term!' she said ecstatically. 'You've won your second term and I've won my first!' she said. 'We've done it, we've done it!'

Perhaps that was why she was more ecstatic than he was. It was her first victory, her first taste of defeating the Opposition. He had been down this road before, the route from his constituency to the Festival Hall for the celebrations. The same media outriders followed him that time. The second time could never be as good as the first. The only difference was that last time he was sitting next to Lucy. This time he was to meet her at the Festival Hall. Charlie turned to Cane on the back seat and reached out her arms. What could be more natural than a victory hug?

Charlie embraced him and pressed her body against his. It was the closest physical contact they had had since Florence. He placed his hands on her shoulders, but it was she who clasped him. Charlie noted the lightness of his touch but dismissed the doubts from her mind.

The driver might not be suspicious, but if Blackie Cole came alongside at a junction, held his flash camera up to the window and the picture appeared in *The Globe*, ten million of their readers would be. So might Lucy. But Charlie wasn't the only one thinking of Florence as they drove through the City of London.

This could be their only moment alone together for the mad 48 hours that followed an election victory. The radio was on loud, reporting the latest election results, so the driver wouldn't hear them. She was half frightened, half excited. She kept thinking of the TV interview with Turnbull when he had shouted at her.

There was a flash at the window. Two television camera crews who had pulled level at the lights by Southwark Bridge and were filming Cane's progress back to the Festival Hall.

There was no time to talk now.

As they drove along the Embankment at one twenty, dogged all the way by the four-wheel-drive monsters of the television companies with lenses almost against the side windows, they could see a golden aura from the other side of the river, drawing them closer. They could hear the thump, thump, thump base rhythm of Cane's disco-rap style election theme tune, 'The Best Is Yet To Come' wafting across the water from the Festival Hall. Cane's victory party was in full swing.

All that was missing was the victor.

But as they passed by Cleopatra's Needle, they didn't see the scruffy man with a hangdog face, bloodstained coat and a trilby, who emerged from the slime covered steps that led down to the river. He was one of the thousands of party members who had made the journey to London. It had been a harder road for him than any of them. But he was the only one who hadn't come to celebrate. If Cane and Charlie had seen him they would have assumed he was a tramp. No 'tramp' had ever come so close to changing the course of European History. The 'tramp' shielded his eyes as the headlights of the outriders flashed by and he recognised Cane's motorcade.

'Bollocks to the lot of yer,' growled Tony Quinlan before looking furtively in both directions and dissappearing into the night.

When the car pulled up at the main entrance, security guards ushered Charlie and Cane into the foyer where Lucy ran to his arms. He held her tight. Lucy's parents were there; so was Cane's mother, Carla; Sam and Jessica were there. Charlie had never seen the entire family together.

'Charlie!' shouted a raucous, well educated voice, coming to her rescue. It was Innes, wearing white trousers and a white shirt with the top three buttons undone, standing at the bar with Silverman.

'Come and join us, I want to give you a big kiss.'

I bet you do, she thought. She was bursting with pride, exhilaration and adrenalin. Yet something was wrong. Something about Cane's behaviour in

368

the car had been wrong. He had got the second term he craved, a full second term, that they both craved, that she had sacrificed so much to win for the party, but most of all for him – yet he seemed half hearted.

There was nothing half hearted about the way Innes grabbed her. He kissed her on the lips and he squeezed her hard, his hands closer to her bottom than her back, his groin against hers. She wondered if Cane would ever grab her again like that.

The embrace with Silverman was more like one with a soul mate. They knew what each other had had to do to survive, and would never forget. He clung to her for half a minute.

'I told you you'd do it, I told you!' said Silverman.

'I couldn't have without you,' she replied, using his shoulder to absorb her tears.

'I'd do anything for you Charlie.'

'And I for you, Ronnie.'

'Would you? Would you?' he said.

It was the first trace of brittleness she had ever heard in his voice. By the time they followed Innes to the bar, he had poured three more glasses of champagne.

'Come on Charlie, this is no time for Diet Coke,' said the beaming businessman, rocking back on his heels with a glass of bubbly in one outstretched hand and a bottle in the other. To hell with restraint. She grabbed the glass and downed it in one. As she replaced it on the bar, she saw his face at the opposite end, surrounded by a group of supporters. Union pals. They were drinking beer. Charlie nudged Silverman and pointed.

'He's got a nerve, hasn't he?' she said.

'More front than Selfridges.'

'I don't see Sandy anywhere.'

'You won't,' said Silverman.

'Why?'

'They've split up.'

Charlie spun round.

'What?'

'They've split up, I assumed you knew.'

'No I didn't know,' she said. 'When? Why didn't you tell me?'

'Gareth Greaves' love life has hardly been uppermost in my mind in the last three weeks,' said Silverman.

Charlie checked herself. 'Quite ... no,' she said. She saw Silverman glance at her.

'Apparently they fell out over something a while ago,' he said, 'nobody knows what. Gareth didn't want to make the break formal until after the election – you can understand why. Now it doesn't matter so much.'

'No, of course,' said Charlie, looking at her watch.

'Goodness, I'd better move, Steven should be making his speech soon, I'd better find him. It'll take us twenty minutes to get through the crowd to the balcony. See you.'

Charlie saw Cane and Lucy among a group of party workers. She looked genuinely thrilled. Charlie had noticed a marked improvement in her demeanour in the last few weeks. At first, she had assumed it was another of the brief bursts of cheerfulness that lifted her up for a while before she sank back into her normal churlish self. But this bubble hadn't burst. Nor had Charlie ever known Lucy spend so much time at Cane's side.

As the deafening echo of the party's election song, 'The Best Is Yet To Come' bounced off the buildings on the other side of the river, Cane climbed onto the rostrum and surveyed the sea of faces around him: supporters, friends, family, cameramen, photographers and reporters.

Charlie saw only one.

As she took her place at the bottom of the rostrum, she looked across the front of the balcony. Right on the margin, she saw Greaves, standing alone and looking in her direction. Their eyes met in the middle as Cane started his address.

'WELL WE DID IT, DIDN'T WE?' he said with a 'who's a clever boy, then?' grin.

The crowd cheered. Cane was too civilised; too reasonable; too nice to be a rabble rouser. But he knew how to arouse.

'OH YES, WE DID IT ALRIGHT, WE GOT WHAT WE

WANTED, DIDN'T WE?'

'YES!' screamed the crowd.

'AND WHAT DID WE WANT MORE THAN ANYTHING ELSE?' he said, holding his hands out wide, palms open, inviting them to provide the answer.

'A SECOND TERM!'

'I DIDN'T HEAR YOU!'

'A SECOND TERM!'

'LOUDER!'

'A SECOND TERM!'

He waited until the cheers died down; until there was complete silence.

'And I make this commitment to everyone here and to the British people who have given us this second term,' he said solemnly.

'That from this day on we will work every single day to earn the right to serve a third term, just as we worked every single day to earn the right to serve a first term and now a second. We will never take the British people for granted, we waited too long for the chance to serve them and we know what they expect of us. They expect the best. And we will give them the best. Because if we don't we will not deserve to be standing here again in another five years.'

A group of supporters started chanting the chorus from 'The Best Is Yet To Come, Yes It Is, Yes It Is.'

Cane smiled as he raised his hand to quieten them. 'Please. I've heard that song so often in the last three weeks, Lucy says I've been singing it in my sleep!'

Charlie winced.

'Talking of sleep,' said Cane, 'I think Lucy and I have got some catching up to do, as we all have.'

Charlie winced again.

'We're going home now – I'm glad to say we haven't got to move house!'

'HOORAY!'

Charlie winced a third time.

'Enjoy the party, but remember: five years more hard work starts tomorrow.'

The crowd erupted into a chant of, 'Five more years! Five more years!' as Cane stepped down from the rostrum, reached out for Lucy's hand and led her through the hundreds of arms slapping them on the shoulder and hands reaching out to touch them. Charlie's eyes were focused on their hands before she got separated from them and felt an arm grasp her shoulder.

It was a man in a plain dark suit in his thirties; he looked serious.

'Miss Redpath?'

'Yes.'

'Could I have a word, please, miss? It's urgent.'

Charlie threaded her way to the side of the foyer, where the inspector was waiting.

'Detective Inspector Moore, Metropolitan Police, miss.'

'It had better be urgent, inspector, I'm supposed to be following the Prime Minister to Number 10.'

'I believe you can tell me where Mr Silverman is, miss..'

'Yes, why?'

'I need to speak to him – urgently.'

'What for?'

'I'd prefer to tell Mr Silverman, thank you.'

'He's on the balcony. Wait here, I'll take you to him.'

Charlie told a party official to get a message to Cane explaining she had been delayed; she would meet him at Number 10 in five minutes. Silverman was standing near the rostrum where Cane had made his speech, looking across the river. Charlie saw his face tense as he turned to see her and the policeman approaching.

'Mr Silverman.'

'Yes.'

'DI Moore, Metropolitan Police. I need to speak to you, sir. I think it had better be alone.'

'It's alright inspector, we're friends,' said Silverman, still clutching a half empty glass of champagne.

'Alright sir, I believe you are an acquaintance of Joe Lomax.'

'Yes,' said Silverman calmly.

'I'm afraid he has been involved in a serious incident.'

'What incident, what are you talking about?'

'I'm afraid we found his jacket on the steps by the river wall at Cleopatra's Needle.'

'What about it?'

'We believe he fell in, sir.'

'What?' said Silverman, reaching out to Charlie.

'I'm afraid we believe he is dead, sir.'

'How do you know, how can you be sure?'

'The details may be distressing, if er ... Mr Silverman was er ... close to Mr Lomax.'

'Yes, yes, just get on with it, man,' snapped Silverman.

'He left a note in his jacket, sir. It was addressed to you, sir. Naturally we have read it.'

'Where is it, where is it, man?'

He gave it to Silverman.

'Dear Ronnie, I can't go on, I've done so many wrong things. I can't cope. I've had more horrible phone calls. I haven't got time to say any more. I've got to meet someone. I may go away for a while, a long while. Love, Joe.'

'I'm afraid a body has been washed up on the shore down the river at Blackfriars, sir, the body of a young man. We think it is Mr Lomax.'

Silverman put down his glass of champagne on the rostrum and sat on the edge, elbows on his knees, head down, staring at the concrete balcony floor.

'Could you tell me when was the last time you saw Mr Lomax, sir?'

'Six or seven days ago,' muttered Silverman.

'I thought you were er ... partners, sir? Was there any reason why ... ?'

' ... What the bloody hell has that got to do with it!' Charlie butted in angrily. 'He was a mixed up kid, he's killed himself, you don't have to be

Sherlock Holmes to see that, do you? Jesus, inspector! You're talking to the Chancellor of the Exchequer!'

'I'm sorry miss, I have to ask these questions.'

'Even when it's obvious what's happened?' protested Charlie.

'I'm sorry miss, it is not clear it is suicide at the moment; we have not yet ruled out suspicious circumstances.'

Charlie looked at Silverman. He shut his eyes.

CHAPTER THIRTY FIVE

The heavens opened as Charlie's car swung past the handful of people who were still standing at the Downing Street gates at five minutes to two in the morning. She leapt out of the car and ran the short distance to the Number 10 door. The door opened as though by remote control, the custodian could see from a TV monitor who was outside.

Charlie gave him her dripping coat and went to Cane's study where she expected him to be waiting for her. As she approached, she could hear loud voices inside. Charlie looked around. There was no one in the corridor.

She recognised Cane's voice.

'It's not that easy, I know I said I'd do it, but you don't understand, you don't understand, it's more complicated than you think,' she heard him plead.

'But you promised me, Steven, you promised. You said you'd do it the moment the election was over. Now you're going back on it!'

Charlie recognised the second voice. Lucy's bubble of cheerfulness had burst. A year ago, Charlie would have shaken her head in despair. Not now. A year ago Cane would have expected her to help him sort it out. Not now. He could start sorting out his own problems.

He knew the solution. Charlie leaned towards the door; she was racking her brain trying to work out what they were arguing about.

'Hello, Miss Charlie.'

Charlie jumped.

'Dora ... why ... er ... hello, what are you doing here at this time of night?' said Charlie, briskly, willing her cheeks not to colour.

'Why don't you's go in?' she said with a deadpan expression.

'You know very well why,' barked Charlie, too tired to play games, 'because they're having a row!'

She turned round and marched towards her office.

'Don' get so angry. You's acting like you married to de man,' said Dora.

Charlie stopped in her tracks and turned. 'Don't you ever speak to me like that again.'

She didn't wait for Dora to apologise; she would have looked an even bigger fool.

'I see de victory party over then,' grunted the tea lady, as she strolled off, unconcerned.

When Charlie reached her office she phoned Cane.

'Charlie, hi, I ... er, no stay there, I'll come to your office. I'll be there in a minute.'

She plucked a cigarette from a half empty packet and waited. She got up, sat down, got up, paced the room, sat down, lit another cigarette. Was it possible? Really possible? That he and Lucy were splitting up? That he had kept it all under control while the election was on, controlled his feelings, because he knew he could only deal with it after polling day? She had almost given up hope of anything happening between them, that his feelings had cooled. Jesus! After all her doubts, was he now going to come and tell her he was leaving Lucy. She daren't even think it.

Lucy is probably crying her eyes out by now, she thought. Thirty minutes passed; it was twenty five past two. She dialled his office again; the line was engaged. Ten to three. Still engaged. Charlie reached for another packet of Marlboro's. Damn it. She had run out. She couldn't phone Dora for a coffee. And she daren't stand outside Cane's office and eavesdrop; Dora would probably lollop round the corner holding a cup of tea the moment she arrived. She phoned 'Switch'. They said Cane had taken an urgent outside call forty minutes ago, but the girl who took it had gone off duty; they didn't know who it was from and hadn't got time to check the log.

'It's not that easy, I know I said I'd do it, but it's more complicated than you think.'

'You promised me, you said you'd do it the moment the election was over.'

376

The words were ringing round her head when the door opened. Cane walked in; she had never seen him look so haggard. Lucy must have done something dreadful, really dreadful. Charlie's heart was thumping, half with with horror, half with excitement, in anticipation. Cane was bedraggled, terrified. Jacketless, tie hanging half way down his shirt, he looked like a man who had just killed someone.

The horror was in his staring eyes. The Mediterranean warmth in his eyes had turned to a haunted emptiness. He stood still in the doorway, looking straight at her, hand on hips. She'd seen him stand like that once before. When was it? She racked her brain. Yes, it was the one he adopted when he was about to read the riot act ...

'You said you'd do it the moment the election was over.'

... or fire someone.

'I ... don't ... believe ... it,' she mouthed. 'I don't ... bloody ... well believe it,' her voice rising as she slowly stood up.

Cane was shaking his head very slowly from side to side. 'Charlie, we've got to talk ...'

She put down her cigarette, narrowed her eyes and advanced towards him. He was struggling to summon the courage to say it. A tidal wave of rage surged through her.

'Don't try to outwit me, you ... you ... !' she lunged at him. 'You bastard, you treacherous bastard.'

Cane put his hands in front of his face to hold her off.

'Charlie! Get off me, get off, what the hell do you think you're doing?' he shouted, pushing her away.

She slipped and fell back onto the floor, losing one of her black high heel shoes, her head narrowly missing the corner of her desk. Cane went to help her then retreated. She pulled herself up, one hand on the desk, and tried to put her shoe back on as she rose. Her head was spinning. She'd had four glasses of champagne and the man she thought was in love with her was about to sack her.

'You're pathetic, you're weak, I hate you, I despise you,' she screamed. She walked straight towards him slightly lopsided still with only one shoe on. He stepped back until he was against the wall. She kept coming until they were eyeball to eyeball.

'You're so weak you think you can fire me because Lucy wants me out of the way. You must be mad! I heard the two of you.'

She mimicked Cane's quaking voice, 'I know I said I'd do it, but it's complicated.'

And Lucy's hysterical squeak, 'You promised Steven, you said you'd do it the moment the election was over.'

'Too damned right it's complicated, mate,' she spat. 'If you think you can toss me aside like a piece of filth, you've got one hell of a think coming. You don't realise how complicated it is, not by a half, but then you never did, you left it all to me, didn't you?'

'I have not come to sack you, Charlie!' he bawled in her face. She could feel the flecks of his saliva on her face.

She backed off. 'I don't believe you.'

'I know, Charlie,' he said more softly, now he had finally got her attention. 'I know about the Palace ... and the election.'

It was the first statement devoid of emotion either of them had made since Cane walked in.

Charlie blinked. 'What did you say?'

'I know the Palace asked for the election to be deferred and you refused claiming I was against.'

She prided herself on her ability to react, but she couldn't react to this.

And Cane knew by the look on her face – she knew.

'I don't know how you knew Lucy had asked me to sack you, but you're right, she did, and yes, I said I would, but it doesn't matter now. And it's got nothing to do with why I'm here. After Lucy went to bed, McLintock phoned me – that's why I was so late. He's got hold of a tape recording of the Duke of Edinburgh talking to a friend on a mobile two days ago saying – God knows where they got it from.' Cane pulled out a scrap of paper with some scribbled notes and read it out,

'We asked Cane to delay it for HM's sake but the bugger wouldn't. He talked us out of it with a combination of threats and bullshit and then had the cheek to go on television and say it what was we wanted. He's a bloody liar. I'll never forgive the cheating swine.'

'McLintock played the tape down the phone to me Charlie,' said Cane. 'He read out the statement from the Palace confirming it is genuine. They are running the thing in the last of edition of *The Globe,* which is being printed right now! I begged him not to run it, and you know what he said? He said we should be grateful they hadn't run it earlier and lost the election for us – the Palace refused to confirm it until the outcome was known because they didn't want to be accused of affecting the result. It was you, wasn't it Charlie, it's what you said to MacLeish, isn't it? Isn't it?'

Now it was he who advanced on her, holding the piece of paper.

'What was it you said? "Don't worry about MacLeish, leave him to me." Now I understand. Say something woman! *The Globe*'ll be on the streets in three hours! Why Charlie? Why? Why, why, why?'

She forced her face against his. 'Because I loved you and I wanted you to win, that's why! The polls showed they were catching up; our private polls showed they were catching up even faster. We kept them from you to stop you worrying. If we'd put it off, Steven, you wouldn't have got your second term, you'd have lost!'

'But why didn't you tell me?'

'Tell you?' she bawled, her voice breaking. 'Because I wanted to protect you! D'you think I'd tell you every sordid little detail of every sordid little deal it took me and Ronnie to keep the Steven Cane show on the road for the last five years? All the times I've had to lie and threaten people to save your fucking neck, to make you look strong, tough, fair, loving, clever, funny, noble – you name it, I've done it, all for Steven fucking Cane. Jesus! I even ran down the street after your pathetic little wife when she drove off with the kids leaving you on the front door step looking like the biggest fucking idiot in the world. I've sat there dabbing your make-up on because you got upset when some TV twat made it look as though you had lipstick on. And where's my life been this past five years? Where's my life been? I haven't had a life! My own mother – dead – with me nowhere to help because I was too bloody busy trying to run around after you 24 hours a day. And you, Mr Steven "isn't he a wonderful loving family man underneath it all" Cane? You haven't got the faintest idea what I did. Did for you! And you don't give a fucking damn!'

She walked to the window, shaken by her own outburst. She nodded to herself. 'And I was stupid enough to think you loved me, to think it might ... Jesus, what a fool.' She let out a manic laugh.

Cane stood, watching.

'I'm resigning, Charlie, we're both finished. We have no choice. I'm sorry if I've let you down. But it doesn't matter. What you did was wrong, it was corrupt. Nothing is worth that sort of dishonesty, not even winning an election. Lying to the Royal Family when the Queen was on the brink of death. You made me lie on television, telling people they had asked us to go ahead with the election when they asked us to do the exact opposite. You must be mad, absolutely mad. How the hell did you think you could get away with it. Presumably you had something on MacLeish, like you've got something on everyone, and you used it. All the manoeuvring and manipulating. It went too far, you went too far, you were too good for Christ's sake. I should have stopped you, but I didn't. I can't believe some of the things I have done, some of the things we've done. It started out with such hope; passion; beliefs; ideals. Everything we did was for a purpose. But it got twisted along the way and I ... I didn't even know it was happening. First it was what we were doing here. Then ... and then ... '

' ... and then you slept with me and got found out,' she hissed.

'Yes, I slept with you. I'm disgusted by what I did.'

She ran at him, lashing out at his face with her fingernails. One of them caught his eye, drawing blood. He struggled to restrain her, squeezing her as hard as possible to stop her hitting him.

'Bastard, bastard, bastard!' she screamed, trying to break free.

'Disgust? You didn't seem too disgusted by me in Florence did you, eh lover boy? Remember Florence?'

She was nearly as strong as Cane and forced him to let go. 'You get me to do your dirty work for five years, five bloody years, seven days a week, twenty four hours a bloody day, heart and bloody soul and you treat me like a piece of shit the moment it goes wrong! If you had any balls you'd deny it, but you haven't, have you? It's only the bloody Royal Family - who the fuck are they? You've got more in common with them than your own bloody supporters. Those middle-class wankers who voted for you because you convinced them you were one of them. It was supposed to be a means to an end, for fuck's sake, to give us the chance to do something for our people. But it wasn't an act, was it? The joke was on me all the time, wasn't it? You really are one of them, aren't you? Aren't you? I must have been mad to have loved you, mad not to have seen through you. You're nothing! Nothing!' she yelled.

'You're wrong. I did believe in what I was doing. I still do. It wasn't an act. You're the one who fooled yourself into thinking we were something else. You're the one who has changed, Charlie, not me. Who was the one who hated – I mean really hated Greaves? You Charlie. It was you, not me. Now you're starting to talk like him.'

'And as for Florence,' Cane continued after a pause, 'it was a terrible, terrible mistake. I should never have done it.'

The words fell softly, like the last leaf that glides down after the tree is felled. He was no longer frightened of Charlie. There was nothing else she could do to him.

'It was my fault,' said Cane. 'I wanted you, but I shouldn't have done it. I was running away from Lucy, I didn't know what she had been going through ... '

'What? What is this bollocks?'

'You don't know what hell Lucy has been going through for years and years, you'll never know, Charlie.'

'Spare me the self-righteous bullshit, please!'

'It wasn't her fault. I could never leave her, never.'

'You make me sick.'

Charlie's mind was whirring. Back to her schooldays. She was at a party. She saw a youth walk up to her. It was the smooth, suave, dark, elegant Stuart Donovan. He was with prim and proper Rosemary Wilson. Donovan was laughing at her. It had happened again. This time it wasn't

Donovan who was mocking her, rejecting her.

It was Cane.

Outside Number 10, Cane's supporters were still celebrating his famous victory, the first person to win a second term they expected to last a full five years. They didn't realise the size of the hangover that was in store for them. Cane could barely believe what he was saying and the calmness with which he was saying it.

'My mind is made up, Charlie. I intend to issue a statement at eight am.' He looked at his watch. 'Christ, that's only four hours.' The enormity of what he was doing hit him, but he quelled his feelings. 'I'll say that I am resigning, I'll take full responsibility, but of course I'll have to make some reference to your role and obviously, you will have to resign too. Frankly, I can't think any further ahead than that.'

'I will not be resigning,' she said.

'Sorry.'

'You heard. I said I will not be resigning.'

'But ... '

'Nor will you be making any reference to my role.'

'You can't be serious, Charlie,' said Cane, throwing his arms up in despair. 'There are some things you can't lie and cheat your way out of, can't you see that? You need help if you don't.'

'I'll be needing help alright,' she said. 'You're certainly right there.'

'Are you crazy?' Cane seized her arms, shaking her violently. 'For God's sake pull yourself together! It's over! Everything's over! Don't you see what you've done?'

Charlie made no attempt to resist him this time.

'Careful, Steven, you shouldn't do that to a pregnant woman.'

His hands slowly released their grip on her forearms. She stood her ground, making him take a step backwards.

'What did you say?'

'You heard.'

'You're lying,' he said, fixing her with his stare for one blink that would tell him it was untrue.

'I'm afraid not. Do you want to see the pregnancy test result?'

'You can't be, you can't.'

'Withdrawing at the last minute is not a reliable form of contraception. You're a doctor and I'm a Catholic, we both know that.'

'I don't believe you. You're playing games,' he said, hoping against hope that she was.

'You could always come to family planning with me and find out for yourself,' she said.

Cane was numb.

'Shall I tell you the statement you will be making in two hours, Prime Minister?' she sneered. 'You will take full responsibility for what happened and you will make no reference to me. Because if you do, I will be making a statement of my own and I shall deliver it not to the nation but to your wife. And when she discovers that the Prime Minister made me pregnant in the honeymoon suite of the Hotel Cesari in Florence when he was at a European summit and his wife was supposedly in agony at home, you will lose not only your precious job but also your precious wife and your precious children! You'll be lucky if you're not strung up from a lamp post.'

Charlie opened her top drawer, grabbed an armful of papers, stuffed them into her bag, brushed past Cane, walked out and slammed the door. Twenty seconds later, he saw her walk past the window of the office on her way out of Downing Street.

The rain was still lashing down.

CHAPTER THIRTY SIX

Her right finger hovered over the door buzzer.

Twenty five minutes earlier, when she scurried out of her office, she told her driver to take her home.

'Anything wrong, miss?' he asked, after she dived in to the back, slammed the car door shut and scrabbled around in her bag for a cigarette.

'No, no, just take me home, now!'

He drove along Whitehall, round Trafalgar Square, along the route he always took to her flat. The dawn cleaning crews were arriving at the cinemas in Charing Cross Road; a minicab driver trawled the streets for stragglers from the night before's revels; a van driver threw batches of tightly bound newspapers on the door step of a newsagent's. Newspapers! Among them would be *The Globe*. It would be the last edition; the one that was circulated in central London. She wondered what the front page would say.

CANE IN ELECTION FIDDLE? No. Really sensational stories, as opposed to the ordinary ones *The Globe* presented as sensational most days, don't need long headlines, McLintock had told her once.

CHEAT? Better.

She asked the driver to stop so she could take one. But before she got out, she realised she didn't have the knife needed to cut through the plastic straps that the bundles were bound in. In any case, she was scared.

'D'you want me to drive on, miss?'

'Wait a minute,' she said. The panic in her voice had vanished. The driver checked his rear view mirror.

Her eyes narrowed. After sitting outside the paper shop for half a minute, she said, 'Don't move round till I say.'

She reached into her handbag for her make-up. She wiped the moisture from her eyes, dabbed on some mascara, retouched her lipstick, tried to brush the dampness from her hair.

'OK, back down Whitehall.'

It was a quarter past four. The car passed Trafalgar Square and took the Whitehall turning. It passed the bearskin-hatted guard outside Horse Guards Parade. He spent most of the time posing for tourists; but his job was to protect the monarch.

If he'd known how the passenger in the blue Daimler had abused the monarch, he would have had every right to use the ceremonial sword hanging from his waist and run it through her. A hundred yards from the Cenotaph, the driver indicated right, ready to turn into Downing Street.

'No, no, no, we're not going to Number 10, drive on, drive on. Go round Parliament Square and take the first left pass the Abbey.'

Three minutes later, they arrived. Charlie's finger hovered over the buzzer.

It wasn't too late to walk away. No one had seen her. And although she had told her driver to leave, she could easily phone him and get him to come back and pick her up, or hail a cab to get home to her flat. But then it would be too late.

It was now or never.

She stood in the rain, pressing her finger down on the white plastic button. There was no response. She pressed the buzzer again; longer and harder this time. Still no response. She was terrified someone might answer, but even more terrified when no one did. Her last hope was gone. She walked away, her shoulders sagging in despair. All she could do now was to wait; wait for the dam to burst. Wait to be torn limb from limb.

She was twenty yards from the door when she thought she heard a faint noise behind her. No, she'd imagined it. But she stopped, straining for any sound. There it was again. She turned quickly. She ran through the puddles and pressed the button again and put her ear to the plastic speaker.

There was nothing. She hit it with the palm of her hand.

'Hello?' said a bleary and confused voice at the other end. 'Hello, who is it?'

She swallowed and breathed in hard before saying, 'It's Charlie.'

'Who?'

'It's Charlie.'

'Is this a joke? It's four thirty in the morning.'

'No, it is not a joke, can I er ... can we talk?'

'Go away, just go away.'

The intercom went dead. Charlie hit it frantically. No reply. She kept stabbing the plastic button.

It crackled into life again.

'For God's sake, Charlie, what do you want? It's nearly five am. What the hell are you doing?'

'I just need to talk ... please, if it's um ... convenient,' she said as contritely as she could.'

'Wait,' said the voice, wearily. Her heart leapt. 'Push the door.'

She heard the bleep which activated the door lock, pushed and entered. The door to the apartment was open when she got to the top of the stairs.

'Hi,' Charlie said nervously. She was dizzy; she'd had five glasses of champagne at the Festival Hall.

It was how she felt the first time she was in this flat, with this man. She had been drinking that night too; cheap Bulgarian red wine.

'Hi,' said Greaves, looking at her dishevelled appearance and rain-smeared make up. He was wearing the same green towel dressing gown she had seen hanging on his bedroom door when she left him that morning, when he was still asleep, when she had left him. Judging by his ruffled state and the bags under his eyes, he had got through a lot more drink since she saw him around midnight at the Festival Hall a few hours earlier. She doubted whether it had all been champagne.

'Are you drunk?'

'No Gareth, I am not drunk.' It wasn't completely true.

'I'm warning you, Charlie, if you've woken me up at this ungodly hour to gloat then I'll throw you out of the bloody window, d'you hear me?'

'I haven't come to gloat.'

'Then what have you come for?'

Charlie tilted her head to one side and looked behind Greaves, towards the sitting room, trying to make him aware she was still standing in the doorway.

'Alright, come in.'

She followed him through the corridor to the sitting room.

Her eyes scanned the television cabinet. There was only one photograph there. Greaves with his mother and father. Greaves lifted a stack of newspapers off the only single sofa in the room and sat down, pulling the bottom of his dressing gown over his knee. Charlie sat on the settee opposite him.

'What is all this about?'

'I've had a row with Steven,' said Charlie timidly, her face pointing slightly downwards, her eyes peering up at him from beneath her eyelids.

'You've woken me at five in the morning to tell me that?' said Greaves, shaking his head in disbelief and getting up to walk away in disgust.

'There's more to it than that, Gareth,' she pleaded, 'a lot more, please, please listen.' He slowly sat down again. 'I don't know how to say it all, where to begin.'

'What's happened?'

Charlie lifted her head and looked at him.

'I know you hate me Gareth, but can I ask you a question?'

He shrugged his shoulders as though he didn't care.

'Have you and Sandy split up?'

'Yes.' His voice was clipped, embarrassed. He looked away from her, towards the television where Sandy's picture had been.

Then he suddenly shouted, 'It's none of your damned bloody business! Who d'you think you are, charging in and out of my home as you please?'

He leapt to his feet and walked to the wall, facing away from her. Charlie stood up, but was too nervous to move across to him.

'I'm sorry ... I'm sorry, I didn't mean ... '

She saw his head drop; tiny movements in his shoulders; she heard him sniff. Charlie slowly approached from behind and circled him until she could see his face, the welling up in his eyes.

'I'm sorry Gareth, I'm so sorry, I had no idea you were so upset; you're right, I had no right ... ' She backed away and picked up her bag. She got to the doorway.

'Don't go.'

Charlie turned, still holding her bag.

'Pardon?'

'I said, don't go.'

She slowly walked to back to him and sat down beside him. 'What happened, Gareth, what happened with you and Sandy?'

He went across to the drawer of his desk, pulled out an envelope, took out two sheets of notepaper and held them up.

'It was this that did it,' he said.

It was the letter Charlie had written to Greaves ten years ago.

'I don't follow. How?' she said softly.

Greaves put the letter on the coffee table and thrust his jaw into his hand, as though it was the only way he could stop his face convulsing. He was looking at the letter in front of him, not at Charlie.

'She let herself in one evening last week; the radio was on and I didn't hear her. I was lying on the bed and she walked right in ... '

'And ... ?' said Charlie

'I was reading it.'

'Reading what?'

'That, I was reading that!' he said manically, pointing to the letter as though it was cursed.

'She saw my reaction when she walked in and asked me what it was. I couldn't speak. What could I say? She took it from me and read it. I just lay there while she read it. I'll never forget the look on her face. She stood over me and said ... and said ... '

'What did she say, Gareth?' said Charlie.

'She said ... "you still ... love her don't you, you still love her".'

Charlie reached across and touched his forearm.

'I did love her you know, I did love Sandy, but not ... '

'Not what?'

'Not the way I love you.'

He raised his head. His eyes were bloodshot and swollen, his cheeks drained and hollow. But he was calm. He looked like a man who had exorcised a demon. But his expression changed, as though he had suddenly come to and regretted baring his soul.

'You still haven't said what you're doing here.'

'Why d'you think I've been the way with you that I have?'

Greaves shook his head.

'Why, Gareth? Think. Think!'

'I don't know!' he shouted. 'Stop playing games. Stop it!'

Charlie stood up and began to pace the room.

'When I left Britain, I loved you. I went to America, because ... because I had to. I was too young, I was confused, by the defeat, by my own feelings, by lots of things. I didn't want to be in love, I didn't want to get married, ... I didn't want what went with it; every man I'd ever loved hurt me. I didn't want you to hurt me, Gareth. I wanted to get away, from my family, from this party, this country, and yes, from you. It all seemed a waste of time. America changed me. It changed the way I saw politics and the way I saw myself. And I admit it, it changed the way I saw you. You seemed, well ... out of touch. It seemed to me there was only one way to do things and that was ... '

'Cane's way,' Greaves butted in.

'Yes, Gareth. The old way didn't work, did it? Look what happened to us in that first campaign. We really thought we'd cracked it, but we hadn't. America showed me we'd got it all wrong. Cane learned that even before I came back, but you hadn't. You were stuck in the old way. I knew you'd hate me for going to work with him – I did write to you, but you never got the letter – remember? And then, I don't know, we just seemed to lose sight of what it was all about. It all went so well, Steven was doing so well, I was doing well. It had to be right, didn't it? When you have that kind of success it completely takes over. You know, all the stuff about means justifying ends. I was on such a high. I was virtually running the country! Me! The loud-mouthed scruff from Glasgow, the woman you pulled off the barricades! Everything took second place to keeping it going; protecting Steven; doing anything, anything at all, to protect him. You lose sight of what you're doing it for. Every time a housewife farts in a focus group in Watford, you throw out another policy – and another. They're a tyranny, those bloody things. And so it goes on until there's nothing left – and you stand for nothing and your own family turn on you. Once you step inside that black door, it's you against the rest of the world. Jesus, some days we spent more time worrying about which tie he was wearing and whether there was time for him to have a haircut before PM's questions than on whatever policy it was we were supposed to be announcing. It seems mad now, but it didn't at the time. And you, Gareth, you were the enemy, just like everyone else on the other side of the door. You were worse than most of them, because you wanted Steven's job and, even worse, you kept telling the world that he was a class traitor. Oh no, you didn't come out and say it, but everyone knew. Then there was Sandy. I admit it, I was jealous. I hated you when I saw you and she were happy. I know I had no right to feel that way, not after the way I left you and then came back to work for Steven. I betrayed you, not once but twice. As soon as that sort of hatred gets a grip it's hard to let go, isn't it? It just feeds on itself. It was the same for both us, wasn't it? You forget everything else. Then something happens to make you wake up.'

'What do you mean?' said Greaves.

'Something happens to make you realise the truth.'

'I don't understand.'

'When Ronnie said to me at the party tonight – last night – that you and Sandy had split up, I can't describe what went through my mind. Everything hit me at once. How I had lied to myself over my feelings for you, how I had lied to myself over my feelings for ... '

'For Cane?'

'Yes ... oh this must sound crazy ... but yes, I did think I was falling for Steven, I did, I admit it. Me and thirty million others! But it wasn't real. I knew that the moment Ronnie said you and Sandy had split up. It was all to spite you. Every time you attacked him it just made me more determined to be loyal to Steven. I'm not saying you were right all the time, oh no, you weren't. You were wrong about a lot of things, but you were right about a lot too; I see that now, just like I saw it when I first met you. But every time you accused me of selling out, I convinced myself it was because you were jealous of Steven; it drove me further away from you and closer to him.'

She sucked her top lip. 'But you weren't the only one who was living a lie, Gareth. Some of the things that were done to win this election were awful. That's why I had a terrible row with Steven. The moment I heard about you and Sandy at the party, it was as though I had been woken from a dream.'

She stopped, grabbed her handbag and rummaged round in it. Eventually she found what she was looking for. She pulled out her hand and lay open her palm. On it was a shiny lump of coal.

'So that's where it went,' said Greaves. 'You took it! You mean you've had this with you all this time?'

'Yes.'

She had taken it the morning she left him after they had lost the election, all those years ago. It seemed to say so much about Greaves. Dark, granite-like, unchanging, anchored to the party's roots. She nearly threw it away when they fell out, but could never quite bring herself to do it and buried it in a drawer. She forgot about it and came across it by chance a few weeks earlier and put it back in her bag on impulse.

She stood before him, stroking it gently and handed it back. 'I suddenly realised where it had all gone wrong, where I had gone wrong. There, it's back where it belongs now,'

'And so are you, Charlie, so are you.'

He put down the lump of coal and reached out to her. She looked into his eyes. As he stood up, he took hold of her other hand, pulling her up with him. He released her hands, cupped his around her chin and kissed her.

Charlie surrendered as his hands moved around her back. Their tongues wove around each other. She pulled his dressing gown aside and ran her lips along his shoulder blade. When she looked up, his face was pointed to the ceiling, his eyes closed in ecstasy. He lowered them as she took his left hand and led him to the bedroom. He picked up a framed photograph that was standing alone on his bedside cabinet.

It showed a young girl, red hair flowing over a white T-shirt down towards figure-hugging Levis, who was struggling to keep up with a lank-haired man with a serious expression, striding along the pavement, a college scarf trailing from his neck and handing out leaflets. Both were wearing huge red rosettes.

'You see, you were here already,' he said, carefully replacing the photograph and beckoning her to join him.

Still fully dressed, she released the cord on his dressing gown, exposing his naked flesh. He tore her blouse off and released the catch on her bra. He buried his head in her breasts as she put her arms behind her head, giving herself to him.

'Darling, Gareth, my dearest darling, Gareth. I'm yours.'

They made love with a violent passion Greaves had not experienced for a decade.

CHAPTER THIRTY SEVEN

Greaves had only been asleep for an hour when his pager went off. He had taken the phone off the hook when he and Charlie collapsed with exhaustion. She had turned her mobile phone off the moment Greaves had invited her in. It was a message from his secretary. 'Cane making emergency TV statement 8 am, have you seen Globe? Is your phone broken?'

Greaves looked at his watch; it was three minutes to eight. He gently rocked Charlie's shoulder. She screwed her eyes up, moaned and rolled over, away from him.

He rocked her again. 'Charlie, wake up, Cane's going on TV.'

She groaned and pulled the sheet over her head.

Greaves got out of bed, put his trousers on and turned the television on. What was it Charlie had said the previous night?

'Some of things done to win this election were awful, that's why I had a terrible row with Steven.'

If he was on television, Charlie should be with him. Why was she here, with him? As he waited for the picture to appear, Greaves went to the front door, picked up the daily papers on the mat outside and quickly scanned the front pages.

'CANE AGAIN,' said the Mail. 'TRIUMPH NUMBER TWO FOR CANE,' said the Times.

It was the same story in all the others Greaves flicked through. Pictures of a beaming Cane and Lucy from the previous night's party were on all of them. All paid tribute to the emergence of a great modern leader: there was no hint of any emergency. He couldn't flick through *The Globe*; it was the only paper he didn't take. He had cancelled it eight years ago when they 'outed' a councillor friend of Greaves' who was married with two children. The man killed himself as a result of the paper's exposure.

Greaves returned to the bedroom. Charlie was still asleep. He left her and went to the sitting room to see the second hand approaching the twelve on the screen clock.

'The eight o'clock news will follow in five minutes after this live broadcast from 10 Downing Street by the Prime Minister, the Right Honourable Steven Cane.'

Greaves gasped the moment he saw Cane's face. It was hard to believe it was the same man whose vibrant face lay on the front pages lying on the sofa. It looked as if he had been in a fight. There were beads of sweat on his brow – and he hadn't even started. His mouth, normally stretched wide in a confident smile, was turned down at the edges and twitching.

Even his hair was untidy.

'It is with great sadness and humility that I make this statement to you today. Yesterday my government was returned to power with a clear majority in the general election. Today, I had hoped to form a new government to carry out the pledges made in our election manifesto.'

'Had hoped?' said Greaves aloud to himself. 'What on earth are you talking about, man?'

'As you will recall, the campaign was suspended for four days when Her Majesty the Queen was involved in a riding accident. It was resumed after consultations between my office and Buckingham Palace. I said that the Royal Family had requested that the election should go ahead. Many of you will by now be aware of reports today that the Royal Family disputes this account and contend that I misled people by suggesting otherwise. It is my duty to inform you that their assertion is correct.'

'CHRIST!' said Greaves, throwing his hands up in the air in shock. 'CHARLIE! QUICK CHARLIE!'

'While there has been an element of misunderstanding, it is none the less true that I said I felt it would be best if the election went ahead and said that this was their view too. It was not. I can only say that I apologise both to the Queen and to the nation for this act of unforgivable deceit. There is no hard and fast rule which dictates what should happen in the event of a monarch being seriously injured during an election campaign. Public opinion was divided; the Royal Family wanted it deferred and I wanted it to go ahead. And yes, I admit part of my reasoning was that my support in the opinion polls was slipping, and that I may have fared less well in an election deferred, say, for a month or so. By way of explaining my actions, all I can say is that the pressures of office affect people in different ways.'

Greaves didn't hear Charlie enter the room. She stood at the door behind him, wearing his green dressing gown, watching.

'When I was first elected Prime Minister I promised I would carry out my duties faithfully. I have tried my very best to do so, until this incident when I readily acknowledge I let my country, my Queen, my party, my family and myself down badly. I have therefore informed the Queen that I am resigning from office today. But please believe me when I say this: this act of deceit was my responsibility and mine alone. Thank you.'

'CHARLIE!' yelled Greaves, leaping to his feet, thinking she was still asleep. He only just had time to avoid knocking her over as he ran towards the bedroom.

'Charlie, he's resigned, he's bloody well resigned!' he said, grabbing her. 'He says he lied to the Queen! The bloody Queen! I don't believe it!' His eyes were bulging in amazement; he danced around as though standing on hot coals.

She anticipated his next question.

'Did you know? Charlie, did you know all this? That he was going to resign. You must've done, you must.'

'Gareth, calm down, calm down. It's why I walked out on him,' she said, drawing on every fibre of every nerve she had.

She felt his eyes drilling through her.

'I told him he couldn't do it, but he wouldn't listen; he thought if he delayed the election he'd lose. I told him it was too dangerous. He wouldn't listen to me Gareth, he wouldn't listen. You must believe me, you must.'

He was silent. He was still searching her for any trace of uncertainty, the tiniest grain of self doubt. She steeled herself again.

'It was the last straw, Gareth. I kept going right through the election, even though I had stopped believing in what I was doing. I didn't know anything about this until last night – after the party. I'd just seen you, Ronnie told me you and Sandy were finished and then when I met up with Steven back at Number 10 he told me ... '

'Told you what?'

' ... that *The Globe* had a tape of Prince Philip saying Steven had lied about the Palace not wanting the election deferred. Yes I knew what Steven had done but I wasn't involved, I swear by Almighty God. Steven wasn't thinking straight. He had terrible problems with Lucy, you wouldn't believe what went on between them. I think he was cracking up. When I left him last night, I had no idea he was going to resign; he could have denied it, blamed someone else, I just wanted out. I knew I wanted something else, Gareth: I wanted you.'

The flame that had been held to her face was slowly, very slowly being withdrawn.

'You know what it means, don't you?' he said.

She had anticipated this too.

'Yes,' said Charlie. 'A leadership contest.'

Greaves' eyes left her for the first time in five minutes. He looked towards the window, outside.

'You could do it, Gareth, you really could.'

He didn't answer. He couldn't take it all in and leaned on the window for support.

'I don't believe I'm hearing this, I don't believe it's happening.'

'It is, my darling, it is,' she said, holding his arm. 'I've learned a lot of things in the last twelve hours. But the most important thing I've learned is this: I love you,' she said, reaching out both arms with upturned palms. 'I'd do anything for you.'

'Anything?'

'Yes, anything.'

'What do you mean: anything?'

'What I said.'

'Do you really mean: anything.'

'Yes, if anything means marriage, yes, if it means children, yes, if it means help you become leader, yes, if it means help this government achieve things for real people, people like us, like our families. Does that make things clearer to you?'

The years of losing her, hating her, wanting her, aching for power, losing it, seeing her help his rival, fearing she had fallen in love with him were written across his face. His mouth was wide open in a silent cry; his eyes stared half in horror, half in wonder. She stroked his forehead and eased his head onto her bosom. He still didn't know whether to believe what was happening.

'Charlie, do you mean all this, I mean really, really mean it? It feels like a dream.'

'Yes, Gareth, I really, really mean it,' she said, with a mesmeric glow.

'The leadership.' He said the words slowly, as though in awe of them. Something he had not dared think of, let alone say, for years. The angst was replaced by animation; the trepidation by excitement as his mind raced through the practicalities, implications and permutations.

'Who else will stand? When will it be? He said he was resigning immediately, didn't he? What about Silverman?'

Charlie laughed joyously and squeezed him.

'What is it?'

'Oh come here into my arms, my darling Gareth.'

He obeyed.

'I'm laughing because I never thought I – we – would ever be like this.'

He kissed her again, but withdrew suddenly.

'What are people going to say about us?' he said. 'They're going to think it bizarre that you leave him and come and work for me, and be my, my ... '

' ... your what? Your lover, adviser, wife?'

' ... well yes, any of them, all of them, I don't know. Come on, that's your job, what does the spindoctor prescribe?' he said, lifting her off her feet.

'One at a time, please,' she joked. 'Steven has said he will take full responsibility – and believe me, he has no choice,' she said, using a fraction more emphasis than she intended.

She'd already thought out the next stage. They wouldn't announce themselves as an item immediately. Nor would she work for him formally. She could do so just as well behind the scenes, biding her time until the dust had settled from Cane's resignation. As for leadership rivals. Silverman was unlikely to stand: he knew his limitations. And after Lomax's disappearance, he would hardly wish to subject his private life to the forensic scrutiny that attempting to become Prime Minister involved. He would happily settle for remaining Chancellor and Deputy PM: it was all he had left.

'Ronnie's said to me that it's taken several hundred years for this country to accept a gay Deputy Prime Minister and that it'll be a few hundred more before it's ready for a gay Prime Minister. He'll serve you just as he served Steven, I promise you. Anyway, he's got one or two things to sort out. I was just thinking of what McLintock said to me about you not long ago,' she said, still trying to control her laughter.

'Go on; what?'

'He said, "Charlie, I could warm to Greaves, you know, but I'd have to see him with a wife and couple of kids on his lap to convince me he's not a poof!"'

'Damned cheek.'

'Let's prove him wrong then,' said Charlie flirtatiously.

'Pardon?'

'You heard.'

'Aren't we rushing things a bit?'

'Come off it Greaves. I'm thirty seven and you're pushing fifty – I've got over my horror of kids, I want some of my own – our own. And if we leave it any longer, I'll be pushing you in a pram as well as the baby. Let's do it.'

'You mean – now?' he said.

'Yes.'

'Right this minute?'

'Yes Mr Prime Minister-to-be.'

She was already undoing the green dressing gown cord around her naked body.